PROMISES TO THE
DAMNED

PROMISES TO THE DAMNED

TYLER JAMES

TYPEWRITER PRESS

ISBN: 978-1-951996-02-4 (e-book)

ISBN: 978-1-951996-03-1 (paperback)

Book Cover designed by MiblArt

Second edition 2023

Typewriter Press

Visit the author's website at: www.tylerjamesbooks.com

CONTENTS

1. Doorway to the Mountains   1

2. A Drink of Madness   11

3. The Warden   19

4. Prison Arrival   25

5. New Cellmate   39

6. First Day of Prison   49

7. Complications   59

8. Truth Uncovered   71

9. A Proposal   81

10. Crystal Caverns   91

11. Mining Away   101

12. Dangers of Spirits   111

13. Secrets   117

14. The Bridgeway   129

15. A New Opportunity   141

16. One Last Gamble   151

17. Dazh Con-Tsuran   161

18.	Hidden Ways	171
19.	The Warden's Room	181
20.	Pain of Failure	189
21.	Their One Friend	197
22.	Shadow Striker	207
23.	The Lightless	217
24.	Vengeance	227
25.	Run	235
26.	The Pits	251
27.	When the Soul Cries Out	261
28.	A Final Offer	267
29.	The Promise	275
30.	Onward, Forward	285
31.	Path of Destruction	295
32.	The Warden and the Shadow	307
33.	The Forming	321
A Word from the Author		331
A Study of Worlds		332
About Author		345

Promises to the Damned

1

DOORWAY TO THE MOUNTAINS

T heir eradication will come by their own arrogance. I watch their moves, the pieces they set, the games they play. It amuses me how prepared they see themselves, but they do not see that I have moved as well. My pieces are in place. The Fire is Coming, again. And when the fires end, when the last song is sung, only then will a better world come.

-The Last Bridgemaker

Nasna sat as one shadow among many. These shadows crowded the corners of the room, draping over the chained prisoners like personal hoods. No one spoke, no one moved, for they all knew they were dead. And the dead should not be disturbed.

The only light came from a few smaller lightstones embedded in the ceiling. The room, a mere holding cell for today, had no windows or doors. Nasna knew there would be small holes in the walls to let breathable air in, but otherwise the guards sealed the room. Only a Builder could escape. Nasna had been in rooms like this before, and they never appealed to her.

Criminals convicted of crimes ranging from the pettiest of thefts to the most heinous of murders stood inside this wooden container of a room, all waiting for their dread to become reality. They stood among many, yet still much alone. And they waited for the Abyssal to claim them.

Nasna looked at those around her, at those sent away for the safety of Rajalend. She, however, was not a prisoner. Rajalend had convicted her of no crime, nor sentenced her to any prison. Of everyone here, she was the only one who wanted to be in this room.

The room was quiet, but Nasna could not meditate or drift off into dreams of bright and swift days. No, today's task weighed too heavy to abandon all sense right now. Her fingers itched to retrieve her looped string from her bindings, itched to create and form, but she kept her hands still, prepared to end and deform.

She wished time would speed up and let her get it over with.

Nasna sat as unmoving as the rest, though her scrutinizing gaze was busy taking in every detail of what and who she could see. No one bothered her. Prisoners took a single look at her wrappings and tried giving her as wide a berth as possible.

Nasna had wanted to choose a gray color for the wrappings, to help meld in with the awful prison garb, but her ruse required white cloth. When someone looked at her, all they could see were strands of white bandages wrapped around every inch of skin, including her entire head and neck. At a glance and even with a close inspection, no one would notice the crimson red skin of an ordîn hiding underneath. They would only conclude what she wanted them to: that she was nothing more than a disease-ridden human on her way to die a criminal's death.

Yet, she was here for so much more.

Nasna glanced over at her target once again, taking in as many details as she could through the slits in her head wrapping.

Female human. Age: mid-thirties. Hardened expression and broken nose showed a thug-like occupation. Hair remained full with a healthy sheen, showing she'd had access to nectar. No affiliation tattoos, so came from a low-rung gang in lower Al'Rajak, since it was the only nectar tree in all of Rajalend.

This woman, Sitora Whitestone, was the only human woman of the prisoners. There were a handful of human men, but most of the prisoners were tatzons. And while masquerading as a human was degrading, Nasna had to admit that physically speaking, she'd never be able to impersonate a tatzon.

The wrappings would have disguised the fact that she didn't have gray skin or those tattoo-like markings every tatzon had. But most of the tatzons here had three arms and no amount of cloth could mimic another arm growing from her side. Even a two-armed tatzon wouldn't do for her, since the first arm, the only arm tatzons were born with, was the priarm, which was always longer and larger than other arms.

All of this combined to mean that the human, Whitestone, was Nasna's only viable option. Failing to make the switch would delay her mission.

A crack of wood sounded through the room, and everyone looked up. At the far wall, a split appeared in the wood, rising from floor to ceiling. The wood of the opening then rolled back on itself like a scroll, revealing a hallway and the guards beyond it. The wood stopped and two Builders materialized in front of the hall, unpossessing the tree. These four-armed Builders grinned at the tatzon prisoners, many of whom reached for the iron collars strapped around their necks which prevented them from possessing.

Half a dozen guards, dressed in finer uniforms of Rajal green and brown, lined the hall, some with spears, most with sharp axes. The Builders only had their arms, grown from their sides like a spider, but the power these arms granted them made them more dangerous than a hundred spears. A pair of guards stepped forward, both with grins.

"Your transport is arriving soon," one said. "So, it's time for you all to get moving."

The prisoners filed out of the room, never letting go of the tatzon next to them. An intimately relational species, these tatzons clung tight to each other, though it was doubtful anyone knew each other. It was customary to separate friends and Partners from each other and send them to different prisons. Nasna watched the pairs, watched their linked arms, as they left.

She looked to her side, where no one sat. Where no one had sat for too many years.

3

Most of the guards watched the prisoners, but the two Builders caught Nasna's eye. She gave them nothing more than a nod. She had already given them their instructions. They just needed to follow them. And they would. Even out here, the name of the Shadow Strikers carried weight and fear.

Nasna did not rise from her bench, but waited until the guards ushered out all but Whitestone. The rest of the guards followed the convicts, but the Builders stopped the woman.

"You're to wait here."

Whitestone frowned even more than before, but the Builders glanced at Nasna and then vanished from sight as they possessed the surrounding wood. The opening curled back together and sealed, as though no one ever opened it.

"Hey! What's going on?" Whitestone cried. She scratched her head and stepped back from the wall, only then noticing Nasna. The woman looked between her and the opening, but said nothing more. She moved back to a corner, monitoring the wall and Nasna.

Everything had gone according to plan. Everything was set. Yet Nasna did not budge from her seat. For a moment, she wondered if there was any other way for her to do this, but something stirred inside her and a voice spoke from beyond.

It is time. You know what you must do.

She nodded and tried to push her doubts, and the rising bile, down. Her Path had spoken, all she could do was follow.

Nasna rose from the bench and strode to Whitestone. The woman turned to her, hands rising.

"Who're you?" Whitestone asked. "This your doing?"

Nasna approached.

"Hey, back off." With a practiced movement, Whitestone jabbed at Nasna. But with an even more practiced movement, Nasna glided between the strikes and placed a hand on Whitestone.

With a single touch, Nasna felt all the energy within the woman. This coursing energy of life and power filled Whitestone just like it did with every other person. For whatever reason, energy always had the distinct feeling of a river, but Nasna couldn't explain why she thought that.

Whitestone attempted to strike again, but Nasna sent a paralyzing pulse through the woman's energy, stilling the river within. She froze solid, her fist halted inches from Nasna's temple.

Nasna, however, hesitated. And as she did, something inside her strained.

The voice from beyond, the voice of her Path, rose in her again. *Kill.*

"I'm sorry," Nasna whispered as she grabbed hold of a single droplet of energy within Whitestone's heart, grabbed onto the raw force of life, and released it. She could almost hear the tiny eruption that killed Whitestone, though that could have been her imagination.

Whitestone collapsed to the ground, and the bile rose higher in Nasna's throat, but she kept it down. After all, as far as deaths went, this was quick and painless. Especially compared to what had awaited Whitestone in the mountains. What Nasna had done was merciful. A kindness.

As the lie swirled through her mind, nausea hit. Nasna tore at her head wrapping, pulling the cloth away from her mouth to let the vomit spill onto the floor and not the wrap. Even when it stopped, her body shook, and she had to sit down and take in a few deep breaths.

She shut her eyes tight and tried to think of happier things, tried to take herself from what she'd done. But images of a child with sky blue skin and hair as white as clouds flashed across her mind, which only made her heart race faster and her grip to tighten around the bench legs.

Focus. Walk the Path.

Nasna gasped out all her breath as her Path took the memory back, keeping her safe from it. It did not hurt. In fact, everything hurt less now. She readjusted her wrappings and rose to her feet. This was no time to wallow. She had a contract to fulfill.

She headed for the opening, but paused and forced herself to glance at Whitestone. The woman was as she left her, crumpled next to Nasna's breakfast. Her heart twinged and she dragged Whitestone away from the vomit and positioned her in a more respectful way, legs straight, arms crossed, eyes closed.

"I'm not sure if you worshiped," Nasna said, kneeling. "But I wish a swift journey through whatever vortex you find yourself in." It wasn't much of a prayer, but she doubted this woman would have cared. Soon, Nasna wouldn't either.

Soon, her Path reassured her. *It will be over soon.*

Nasna nodded. Yes, it would. Soon Clear Sky could rest. Soon Nasna would be free of weakness.

She knocked on the opening, waited a moment, and watched the split form again as the wood rolled back. The two Builders reappeared, glancing between Whitestone and Nasna.

"Make sure she's disposed of well," she said. "As long as no one finds her or hears anything about this, you can expect to live a long life without ever seeing another Striker."

One cleared his throat, but avoided her gaze. "We won't say nothing, of course. I, er, the transport's here and they... well, they need—"

"Just close up this room and continue your duties. Take care of her later."

And be respectful with the body, she thought. Her Path forbade her to utter the thought out loud.

The Builders nodded, closed off the room, and led Nasna away from another kill.

The tree they were in was a white-flecked oak, tall but not thick, perhaps only a few hundred feet across. This meant that while there were many floors, there were only a couple of rooms on each. The holding room was a few floors up, so the Builders led Nasna down the stairs to meet with the rest of her now-fellow prisoners. A few glanced at her, but if any of them wondered about Whitestone, they didn't say.

They emptied from the final stair to the main loading area in the tree. It was a wide open space with a rectangular hole in the floor, flat along the edges and extending down to the earth, some fifty feet below. There were another dozen guards here, including another pair of Builders, all armed and watching the prisoners.

By some unspoken signal, this second pair of Builders walked toward the wall next to the hole and vanished, possessing the wood of this still-living tree. A large split formed down the center of the wall, similar to what happened in the holding room but on a grander scale. The wood of the tree, its very bark, curled back and away, opening to the outside world. A sharp wind cut its way in, sending a shiver through Nasna. Through the tree opening, she saw the rocky tundra of the surrounding land. Few trees grew here at the base of the Iron Mountains, so her vision was unimpeded for many miles northward. Save for the massive beast entering through the gap.

The opening spread all the way to the ground, so the goat could enter the hole, its head level to the floor Nasna stood on, making this a Large beast. It had thick and rounded horns curling over its head and long, sharp tusks curving down from its upper jaw. On its back, it carried a large wooden construction, which was long and rectangular. Straps of thick leather held the transport to the beast, while wooden beams stretched over the shoulders and down the sides to keep it upright. In front, right behind the goat's neck, was a separate construction that had opened windows. Inside she saw three tatzons, all with three arms, which would have been the Wranglers, beast possessors, who drove this transport. The fourth Wrangler possessed the goat right now, the only reason it was staying so still and compliant. Transports like these were common in Rajalend, though Nasna had never seen one with such poor construction as this one. A prisoner's comfort wasn't anyone's primary goal, it seemed.

The wood near the transport rippled and some prisoners made a step back, though they weren't near it. As if growing a new branch, a wooden footbridge grew from the tree out over the hole and connected with the doors of the transport. The Builders who'd done this materialized close to the bridge, unpossessing the tree.

Every tatzon, including the guards and possessors, stilled as the door of the transport clicked open. The door slid to the side and three newcomers strode out. They each wore crisp blue uniforms, thick and warm, yet sleek and elegant. Even their leather boots were dyed a dark blue. This made quite the contrast with their bright white hair, light gray eyes, and varied-colored skin. The one in front had orange skin, while the two behind him had blue and violet hues. Their features were like a tatzon's or human's, except far more angular and lacking the misshapen imperfections common to the other races. They stood shorter than most tatzons, yet the large leathery wings, kept tight against their backs, made their figures more impressive. The wings matched their skin color and added a few feet to their height, and Nasna knew from personal experience how much larger they were unfolded.

Nasna glanced the leader over. Male ordîn. Age: orange in cyan cycle. Keeps a thin dagger hidden under the left flap of his coat, a high likelihood of it being made with ivory or crystal. Eyes stay focused on his target, keeps his hands at the ready. First estimation: Exorcist.

She looked the other two over. Given how their eyes darted to each possessor, and they wielded spears, they both would be Sensors.

The Exorcist ordîn stood at the end of the bridge, looked the prisoners over with little effort to hide his disdain, and gestured to the female Sensor behind him. She carried a large satchel from which she pulled a file of papers. Without a single announcement or introduction, he read from the papers, reading off names. The tatzon guards broke from the stillness and grabbed prisoners and brought them forward. One by one, the ordîns read a name, and the guards brought each individual forward. This was why Nasna had to infiltrate these prisoners now. The tatzons could be disciplined if they wanted, but once out here, it was easier for them to overlook things. Ordîns, however, had no such variations. They took their orders seriously.

She was no exception.

"Sitora Whitestone."

The two Builders from before, those she'd given her instructions to, came up beside her and led her to the ordîn. As she walked toward them, she couldn't help but stare at their wings, a primary marker of an ordîn. And the significant difference between her and the rest of her kind.

When she reached the bridge, he looked up from his papers and furrowed his brow. "Stop. Builders, has this one contracted the hans?"

The Builder on Nasna's right cleared her throat.

"Yes, she did."

"This was not in any of the reports we've received concerning the prisoners."

"Yes, sir. It occurred before we could send the new updates, sir."

"I assume you have the update with you, then?"

The second Builder stepped up, handing over the papers Nasna had brought with her. The Exorcist read over the papers. These papers were forged, of course, but by the Shadow Strikers. Nasna needed to trust the skill of her associates. Though, she was glad the head wrapping veiled her expression right now. She was never great at hiding her emotions.

After several minutes, the Exorcist rolled the forged papers and handed them to the ordîn behind him.

"We bringing her, sir?"

The Exorcist did not take his gray eyes off of her. "We let the Warden decide what to do with her. It's our job to escort prisoners. It's his to decide their fate."

They nodded and the Exorcist continued to read off the names of prisoners. Nasna followed the ordîns up into the transport, taking a seat in the far corner where they chained her feet to the floor. But she'd made it through the easiest part of this job. Nothing onward would be as straightforward.

But after twenty years, she would soon know peace.

This thought did not make her smile.

2

A DRINK OF MADNESS

Your mistakes are unforgivable and quite reprehensible, General. I will hear none of your excuses concerning the power of our enemies, you have failed us. These foul, blasphemous tatzons must not overcome Oushwala, and thus, we of the Luminars have removed you from your office. Swiftrider shall take your place from this day forth. He has already accepted despite the birth of his daughter for he understands the sacrifices we must make. For that is what we are. We are of the Luminous. We are ordîn. We are Sacrifice.
- Luminar Stargazer, in the 2844th Lunar Cycle

Far beyond these mountains, beyond these unending visions of gray and white, laid lands of verdant fields that morphed into towering trees that held the sky aloft. In those trees was a call to freedom, a call to the endless hunt and the ever growing adventure. Dangerous, blood-thumping adventure. The kind that proved one was alive.

But Tsuran was not in those fields, he did not run without care through those forests. Instead, he stood atop the world, covered head to toe in thick, white furs, shivering. Where as the trees of his youth kept the sky from falling, it seemed as if these mountains stood atop of the sky itself. Glancing over the cliff's edge, far far below, Tsuran saw the unmoving swathe of gray emptiness that was the gathering of clouds around these mountains which stretched in all directions, never seeming to end.

"The team's ready to head in."

Tsuran breathed out, frost forming in his beard, as he turned toward Leof, a bulky Rajal tatzon, with dark brown markings that resembled lines of rectangles. And, for the last year, had been Tsuran's cell-mate.

"Great, the sooner these idiots kill themselves, the sooner we're out of this Abyss." Tsuran adjusted his cloak, ensuring his three arms stayed wrapped and warm, and looked over his fellow prisoners. They stood atop a flat plateau at the mouth of a mighty cave, perhaps eighty feet tall, shivering in the stiff wind.

This team, made up only of tatzons, provided most of the food for the Iron Mountain Prison by hunting beasts that lived in these forsaken heights. Tsuran had a hard time thinking that there were creatures that chose to live here, but after months of hunting he learned there was just as much life here as in any forest of Rajalend or on any island in the Dragon's Maw.

Leof shuddered beside him, though the look in his eyes showed it wasn't because of the cold. "You sure this will work? It's suicide if you're wrong."

"The prison is suicide itself. It's only a little slower. Just keep to the plan and we'll be fine."

"Plan? What plan? All you said was to follow your lead."

"It's my go-to plan. It never fails me, except when things go horribly wrong."

Tsuran waited for a chuckle, a snort, or even the hint of a groan and eye-roll. Leof gave him nothing. Tsuran shrugged. Leof was his cell-mate, and soon travel companion, but not a friend. The last friend Tsuran ever had charged him with desertion and banished him to this grave.

Tsuran cracked his neck. "Ready?"

"This is madness," Leof said. "You realize that, right?"

"Madness is the drink of life, brewed for folks like us. I like mine with a squeeze of citrus, you?"

"How is it no one's killed you yet?"

Tsuran smirked. "Many have tried, most failed."

The two joined the rest just inside the lip of the cave, where the team leader was going over the hunt's plan once more. By Tsuran's count, that was the fourth time just today he'd blathered on and on about tactics and strategies that the idiot couldn't comprehend himself.

Tsuran ignored him and the laid out plan. He and Leof had different aims today. They weren't going after a beast or a kill. Today they were escaping. Deep within this cave was a crystal deposit that could make anyone rich. But more than that, Tsuran heard rumors of secret passages beyond that lead out of the mountains. That was the aim. They'd grab some crystal on their way if they could, but those passages were the true treasure.

He regretted having to leave behind his personal statue, the one the Warden kept hidden away, but freedom was worth it. It had to be.

He glanced at all of the other hunters and then to the weapons they used: stone statues.

"Everyone got it?" the leader asked. The others nodded, though, to Tsuran's surprise, no one yawned. Everyone seemed a bit on edge. And given the size of this cave, he understood why. Beasts of this size were not something to laugh about.

"Last thing," the leader said and pointed at Tsuran. "Deserter, you're taking point."

"Or, and hear me out, I don't do that."

While everyone was half paying attention to what was going on, no one missed the opportunity to shoot hateful glares at Tsuran.

"Just do your job, deserter," another hunter said.

"Not sure, why I need to go first," Tsuran said.

The leader smiled. "If something goes wrong, better you die first than us."

"Ah, of course! How silly of me to forget such crucial details." Tsuran smiled and met the gazes of each hunter, enjoying how his unflinching confidence made them squirm inside. It wasn't their hatred of him that pleased him. It was that despite how much they wanted to kill him, they couldn't. Despite what they told themselves, they needed him to go first, needed him on their team. Not as bait, but as their unspoken savior.

Nine others moved away from the pack and picked their statues, roughly carved pieces of stone their own height, though everything about the statue was a vague approximation of a real tatzon. They equipped each statue with a long spear tipped with iron. The hunters, all Guardians, vanished from sight, as though snuffed from existence, and the statues animated to life.

Tsuran winked at Leof, who frowned back, and, with nothing more to it, body-possessed the remaining statue.

His body, clothes included, became immaterial and swift like the wind as he flew toward the statue and plunged deep into it. This body of stone became his body, its eyes his eyes, its imperfections his own. It wasn't cold anymore as his rocky physique was impervious to the mountain's touch. But much of the world was duller now, too. The eyes of this statue had not been carved well, so he could not see as much as normal, and the ears were nothing more than slits, so most sound had a slight whistle to it. As he took possession of the statue, he took in a deep, unnecessary breath. As a statue, he didn't need to breathe, but it was one of those habits of life.

The ten in the statues, the active hunters, led the way into the massive cave, Tsuran in the front. The other ten, the inactive hunters, followed at a safe distance behind. The inactive would be ready to take over a statue when an active had reached their limit. In the real world, this was always done with a person's Partner, the one they shared life and soul with. But that relationship was too important for a criminal to have. No one could have their Partner in the same prison, so instead, everyone was forced to treat their cell-mate as a pseudo-Partner.

"Stay in your group of five," Tsuran said to the actives. "Spread out, half eyes forward, rest up and behind."

Although he wasn't the leader, Tsuran couldn't help fall back into old habits.

"See those lightstone veins up top? Something's scratched against the rock and broken the stone away. Yeah, I know that's too high for a Common, shut up. We're following those veins. It'll lead us to our target. Stay low, stay quiet. We don't know how good of hearing the thing has, and Abyssal's tail this place is huge. Didn't think it'd wind around this much either. What? No, I said you stay quiet. Keeping my voice quiet would be crime against the world."

They entered a cavern that dwarfed every room they'd passed through. No more twisting passages, no more pillars of stone, no more multitude of rocky walls. A city could have sat inside this cavern with no issue. Further out was a massive hole in the cavern's ceiling, opening to the outside which allowed bright light to illuminate the space, though the cavern continued on beyond what the light could touch. From this hole poured a waterfall which emptied into the lake that made up most of what Tsuran could see.

Before he could contemplate the water's origin or just how freezing that water had to be, a single sight took his gaze captive, unwilling to let it go. In the center of the lake, a fair distance from the shore, stood a red-crystal deposit.

The crystal, twice as tall as it was wide, stretched to the ceiling, resembling a dancing flame that froze solid. The crystal had a pure red glow throughout, a small mountain of scarlet worth an incomprehensible amount. Fistfuls of red-crystal cost more than what most merchants made in a year. This... this had to be worth half the wealth of the nation of Rajalend. Perhaps more. Tsuran had never seen this amount of red-crystal before, hadn't even heard of such a deposit in legends.

And beyond this lake, somewhere in that blackness, was his path to freedom.

A tremble pulsed through the ground. Large bubbles rose and burst from the lake as the water churned. Tsuran stopped himself from crying out orders as a massive clawed paw broke out of the water and crashed down near the shore. Another followed as the water parted and a beast pulled itself from its watery slumber.

The monster stood over a hundred feet tall at its haunches, making it a Colossal. It stood on six trunk-like legs, its body surrounded by a thick black shell which seemed out of place in these frosty mountains. It had a long, fur covered neck, and two long ivory tusks with black marbling protruded from its lower jaw. Tsuran had heard that some turtles enjoyed the frigid weather, but with a joke he'd dismissed it as the ravings of a mad woman. Facing a beast twenty times taller than him, he realized he had one more thing to apologize to Idida for.

The thought of her was why Tsuran didn't react fast enough.

The Colossal attacked, charging forward and swiping with its claw. Most of the hunters dodged out of the way. One didn't. The claw struck, the sound of cracking rock accompanying it, and flung the hunter into the air.

Tsuran shook the creeping memories from his mind and rushed forward as he empowered his possession.

Warmth flooded the statue as he used two of the three empowerments a Guardian could use. He reshaped his statue, thinning his body and narrowing it while giving his feet some claws to aid in traction. Then he increased his speed, twice over. With the combined empowerments, he shot through the cavern toward the Colossal as though a bolt from a ballista.

This was why no one did anything more than glare at him. They hated him for many reasons, but he liked to think that top of the list was jealousy. Everyone here could body-possess a statue, bring their entire being inside to animate and control it. But only he could empower it.

He would need to hurry though. Everyone had a limit. Some had fewer than others, but most had a definite time limit of one hour for safe possession. After that, they needed an hour rest, or else risk Remnancy, where the body became hollow and the soul a monster. Tsuran had a greater capacity than most, but even he had limits. It was important he never went beyond them. No one here was worth becoming a Remnant.

Although outmatched, the other hunters tried to coordinate an attack, but the Colossal didn't give them much chance to do anything more than annoy it. Tsuran noted that a few hunters left their statues after a direct hit. It seemed the strikes were too jarring for these unhardened convicts.

But he wasn't here for this giant beast, nor was he here for the crystal. He sped around the chaos of hunters who were half-heartedly trying to attack their fears manifested. Tsuran found Leof, himself rushing from his hiding place with the other inactives.

"There's a statue there," Tsuran said pointing to the first abandoned statue. "Grab it before someone else does."

"I know what I'm doing."

Leof vanished and the statue moved, pushing up from the ground. Leof nodded.

"Let's go."

They ran, Tsuran no longer empowering his speed. The hunt, the battle, continued beside them, hunters rushing, attacking, fleeing all as one disordered unit.

Tsuran and Leof ran for the water's edge, looking for the shallow areas to head across. The cavern shook and quaked with the unrelenting power of the beast, but Tsuran tried to stay focused and not think of how quickly that thing could kill him.

"How do we find the path?" Leof asked.

"Walk in, search around."

"I can't swim."

"We're stone statues, neither of us can swim."

"This water's too deep, you sure this is the right area?"

"Shut up and move before I decide to leave you here!"

They splashed through more of the water, closer to the cavern wall. "Here," Tsuran said. "The water is shallower here, we'll cross this way."

"Con-None...."

Tsuran looked back and halted. The cavern's chaos had died down, the ruckus gone. There weren't any other hunters in sight, though he counted three bodies. However, the Colossal remained. And it stared the two down.

Tsuran gripped his spear tight. "Abyssal take me. Run!"

The Colossal launched at them, slamming a clawed foot into the wall in front of them, cutting off their path forward. They rushed back, away from the lake, but the Colossal was fast.

One paw struck Leof, sending him flying into a wall, statue cracking and splitting.

Another sped toward Tsuran. Years of training kicked in and Tsuran used his third type of empowerment. He hardened the stone, increasing its strength and durability.

The Colossal hit him with enough strength to topple trees and for a brief second, Tsuran flew, until he slammed into the ground multiple times. Even with hardening the statue, the stone was shattered. If he moved, it could fall apart, which would kill him.

He unpossessed the statue and embraced the still coldness of the cavern.

"Con-None, help!"

Leof crawled from the wreckage of his statue, leg broken. The Colossal growled, attention focused toward Leof, and Tsuran took a step forward, toward the cell-mate who needed him. He had to do something. He was a Guardian of the Sea.

But the darkened forest took over his vision and a voice more familiar to him than his own echoed around him.

"Just do what you do best. Run."

Tsuran stopped. He stepped back. He stepped again.

"Run. Just run."

Tsuran's feet took him away from the place, rushing after the rest of the hunters. He didn't notice the turns he took, nor the intense cold he breathed in as he ran. He didn't notice the resounding crash of Leof's death, and he ignored the blaring light as he left the cave. The cave shook with the Colossal's roars and a haunting numbness gripped his fingertips. He could not stop here, he had to get back to the team. The beast could come for him, yes, but something worse waited for him if he didn't find anyone soon.

Rocks fell around him, ledges gave way beneath him, snow slid into him. But he wouldn't stop running. He needed to be fast. Needed to find the team. He couldn't let Solitude settle in. Not out here.

And it was coming. Like a nightmarish mist, it was coming.

Even when he caught up to the team, even when he was safe from Solitude, in his mind, there was only that forest and that beloved and most vile voice.

"Run."

3

THE WARDEN

*Y*ou do not understand the severity of this drought, Stargazer. Our crops are withering away while our wells dry up. Even the beasts are turning from the land. You know as well as I that it must be connected to that child of Death, however if we are not to rid ourselves of that curse, then we must convince General Swiftrider and the other Luminars to make a grander push beyond the Barrier. Families already try to fly over to get even a sip of water. Mark my warning, without water or rain, we shall lose this war.

- Luminar Soilshifter, in the 2867th Lunar Cycle

Tsuran and the other hunters stood in front of a single iron door embedded in the stony face of the mountain, a door that led to punishment. The rest only looked at it, a few whispering amongst each other, likely making their last debates about whether to face the mountain or the Warden.

Tsuran rolled his eyes and pushed past the group and pounded on the door. He hated waiting for the inevitable. Better to face it and move on.

A minute passed before the doors opened and several guards, all ordîn, marched out. They wore their usual blue uniforms which either matched their skin color or contrasted with it. There was a green skinned guard, though most had some shade of cyan or violet. The guards ushered the team inside the winding hall.

They entered the loading bay which had a gaping hole in the mountain's side, acting as an entrance to the prison for transports and was perhaps eighty to ninety feet tall and half as wide. Opposite to the massive opening, without pomp or decoration or ostentatious addition, stood two enormous iron doors. Twenty feet tall, ten wide, three thick, the doors to the Iron Mountain prison did not stand as the first defense from outsiders, but as the ultimate barrier to insiders. Two large cranks on either side connected to the gears that opened, closed, and locked these doors, requiring two individuals per crank to use. And they could only be opened from this side.

However, Tsuran's gaze drifted above them to the small, unassuming balcony. It had the perfect view of the entire cavern and of anyone entering or exiting the mountain. Nothing went unnoticed by the watchful eye on the balcony. Today, Tsuran did not see the Warden, who typically watched them reenter his domain. Tsuran wasn't sure if the Warden's absence was a good sign or not.

Tsuran scoffed to himself. Of course it was a bad sign.

A loud thud echoed through the cavern as the prison doors unlocked. Gears clicked and strained against one another as four ordîn guards worked the cranks, and the door opened with a low groan. Ancient iron ground against even older stone, following tracks and grooves made from centuries of use and Tsuran shielded his eyes as an intense white light burst out through the first crack of the doors.

The prison entrance was not as dark as other places, since the opening let in plenty of natural light. However, it was a soft, almost muted light. That which poured from the other side of the doors was anything but muted. It was like standing amid the whitest snow without a single cloud to cover the intensity of the sun. The guards covered their eyes with tinted goggles, but Tsuran and the others had to squint or close their eyes.

The hallway beyond the doors was rectangular. Smooth floors, smooth ceilings, even smoother walls. And it was made with lightstone.

Of all the crystals, white-crystal gave off the brightest glow and was one of the most commonly found. A perfect light source since it never waned and the light never ended. Most Rajal homes had at least some lightstone, but vast quantities remained for the rich and well-off. However, no where in all of Rajalend, even in the homes of the Oligarchs themselves, would anyone have been able to imagine a hallway made from it. A hallway where not a single shadow could exist.

He followed his escorts through a bustling room and marched up the stairs in the back with the rest of the team. Most prisoners never ascended these stairs. The next floor was reserved for the ordîns only. Only the hunting team ever came up, and only those dropping off the statues. It was odd for the entire team to follow up, not a single one with their statue.

They entered the statue store room, which was small and darkened. A single figure stood inside, wearing the shadows like a cloak, his gaze resting on the empty spaces where the statues went. The ordîn had short-cropped hair, a distinct style considering the long braids of the other guards, and a blue skin that matched his uniform. He kept both wings pressed tight against his back and did not face the team as they entered.

He let them wait in silence for a minute or two before he spoke, his voice as even as a windless sea and as dangerous as the Dragon's Breath.

"Con-Alkaios, why are the statues not with you?" the Warden asked. The guards holding the leader stepped forward, pulling him along.

"We had no choice"—the tatzon's voice was smaller than when he commanded the team around—"we went to the cave just like you had us but we couldn't do anything because there was this beast there and—"

"Is that not why I sent you in the first place? To kill a beast?" The Warden turned his face toward the leader. It was expressionless, as always, and yet the power behind his precise words and unblinking eyes caused every prisoner to avert their gazes and try to become small, unnoticeable. Only Tsuran stood upright. But even he didn't look the Warden in the eyes for long.

"But not a Colossal. We weren't—"

"Con-None," the Warden said, cutting the leader off. Tsuran brought his full attention to the Warden. "This Colossal, it guards the crystal? You confirm you found it?"

Tsuran nodded. "Massive deposit of red-crystal. Almost as big as the Colossal itself."

"And was there any way you could have killed this beast?"

"With only ten teams and with the statues we had... no. We couldn't have done it."

The Warden paused, though his expression remained a constant unreadable slate the entire time. "You, Con-None, I know have killed Colossal beasts before. What would it take to kill this one?"

Tsuran fought the urge to roll his eyes. Sometimes talking with the Warden was like reporting to a ship's captain, and doubtless the Warden wanted to command navies instead of overseeing a prison.

"If you want the beast killed, you'll need two things," Tsuran said. "First, get better statues made of a better stone. What we had was fine against Commons and even some Larges but not a Colossal. If you could get any kind of crystal or ivory embedded in them, all the better. Second, you need a larger hunting party, no less than fifteen teams. Otherwise, the beast goes nowhere."

A moment of silence echoed between them. The leader glared at Tsuran. He shrugged. Wasn't his fault the Warden preferred his opinion over the rest. The Warden, not changing tone or expression, said, "You are all stripped from the hunting team."

Tsuran's stomach turned. He stood his ground, trying to not flinch. It was something he'd expected. But it still delayed his escape.

"From this point forward not one of you will return to it. All of you will return to the mines and there you shall remain. Each of you must make penance and shall relinquish your meals for the next three days. Last, I shall relinquish all benefits until you have made payments to replace the statues you have lost."

A few ex-hunters looked ready to throw a fist, but no one drew up enough courage to try. "You are all dismissed," the Warden said. "May you dwell on the mistakes you have made and the grace you have lost."

The guards escorted the other hunters out, but Tsuran resisted and caught the Warden's eye.

"Con-None?"

"Just needing to know what cell I'm in."

"I am unaware of anything changing regarding your cell."

"You had to have noticed that my cell-mate isn't here."

The Warden stared unblinking.

"Right, well, I don't have a cell-mate now. So... I'll need a new cell."

"Your assigned room is not changing, Con-None."

Before he could stop himself, Tsuran reached for the Warden. The guards moved, but the Warden reacted faster. Without glancing his way, the Warden caught Tsuran's wrist and held it firm. Those unflinching eyes turned toward him.

"Sorry, sorry," Tsuran said. "But, I'm a tatzon. I need a cell-mate. I can't be alone."

The Warden did not release him. "I am aware of your kind, Con-None. And I am aware of you and your crimes. I have no reason to accommodate you."

If Tsuran's stomach lurched or his heart pattered, he did not know, because emptiness filled him. An emptiness that caused a tremor to strike his legs, making them weak.

"I could die!"

"When you deserted the Rajal fleet, you had already chosen the death of a coward."

He let go of Tsuran who pushed away from the guards trying to grab him. "Warden you can't do this. I'm your best hunter! You need me."

The guards gripped Tsuran and dragged him back, but he only shouted more.

"Warden! Please don't do this to me! Warden!"

The guards pulled him away and down into the mines. He fought and thrashed as he saw the long corridor to his cell. To his empty cell. The door neared, open like the mouth of a beast. The guards threw him onto the hard floor and a loud metallic crash came from behind. Darkness swirled around. He was back in his cell. Alone.

He pounded against the door, again and again and again. He screamed and shouted, but no one answered. Tsuran felt it coming. He couldn't stave it off. Tsuran crawled to his cot, wrapped himself with a blanket, and pulled out the small stone statue he kept hidden in his shirt. It fit in the palm of his hand and he gripped it against his chest as his body deteriorated from the inside out.

His ears muffled all sound, his eyes glazed over with a stinging sensation, his body became hot. All of his senses were dull and on fire at the same time. The world pressed in on him from all sides, and his body wanted to explode from within. He rocked his body back and forth, huddling deeper and deeper into himself. If only he could fall asleep. As long as he was asleep, Solitude couldn't touch him. Asleep he was safe. Tsuran squeezed his eyes shut, trying to will himself to sleep.

Only Solitude came.

4

PRISON ARRIVAL

Return to the Plateau, Soilshifter. It is time. We have realized that the meager sacrifices we have offered have not been enough. My Path had said as much before, but I failed to heed its guidance. No more. This drought must end. This war must end. Our people's suffering must end. And so it will. We have seen what is necessary, seven-hundred souls must bear the evil of all hells, a hundred for every cycle of an ordîn's life. I grieve the loss of Swiftrider and Weaver, but this is the Path the Luminous has set before me. I walk the Path of Sacrifice, so Sacrifice I shall walk.

My only consolation is that the child of Death shall be rid of. May the Luminous smile upon us.

- Luminar Stargazer, in the 2897th Lunar Cycle

The cabin moaned as the beast continued its ascent into the mountains and towards the prison where Nasna's target stayed. The goat's every step up the rocky terrain jolted the passengers. Prisoners sat shackled together, but the guards had also strapped them into their seats, ensuring an uncomfortable but inescapable journey to the prison. The seats were hardwood with no give, meaning each step shocked through Nasna's bones. With no other choice, she endured it.

A minimally constructed cabin, the only light came in through cracks from the wood boards, which also let the frigid air blow around her. Though, her clothes did little to protect her and the wind blew through her. She wrapped her arms around herself, but the prison remained a long and cold distance away. None of the other prisoners made much noise except for the occasional grunt. No one was in a talking mood.

They traveled throughout the day and into the half-night without stopping. Some prisoners attempted to sleep, though Nasna found it difficult to even try. But she needed it and so attempted to. After several efforts, sleep came. It wasn't restful. No time seemed to pass between closing her eyes and being awakened by the guards. The only sign she'd slept was the light surrounding the cabin and the stiffness in her neck.

"Wake up, human. We're arriving."

Not long after she awoke, the light dimmed again. But this was not the darkness of night, but shadow. The wind stopped howling. Stillness filled the air. The hoofsteps of the beast echoed around her.

They were entering the mountain itself. She'd made it.

As confirmation, voices cried from outside the cabin and the guards went to the doors, grabbing the handles to keep themselves steady. After a few moments, the beast stopped and Nasna prepared herself, taking in a deep, slow breath. No going back now. Once she stepped out, she wouldn't go back until she completed her mission.

The guards slid the doors open and a wooden bridge connected. One by one, the guards unstrapped and escorted the prisoners off the transport. Nasna was the last out. It was still cold inside the cavern but there wasn't any wind, so that was good. She took in her surroundings. The ceiling loomed high above, more than twice as tall as the transport beast, and the width was even greater. A pit had been dug into the ground to allow the beasts to descend so that whatever carriage or coach it carried would be level with the floor instead of dozens of feet in the air. Guards lined the room, the tone of their blue and violet skin showed most to be late in their green cycles. A single ordîn stood on a balcony, his arms behind his back, staring at the newcomers.

Four ordîns worked a large crank which opened the iron doors, the stone groaning around the hinges. Bright light poured out from behind the doors and she shielded her eyes. The doors opened, a resounding crash accompanying the large amount of light. Nasna's eyes adjusted and behind the two doors was a long hallway, and it looked to be constructed with only lightstone. The ordîns marched her and the other prisoners forward. Guards lined the walls of the hall, a swathe of dark blue amid the white light. Here most were violet in green cycle or red in cyan cycle. Though, a few young ordîns were here too, with skins of yellow and orange. A dull but loud crash sounded behind her. She glanced back. They had shut the iron doors.

Doors open inward and are locked from the outside, she thought. *It would take tremendous force to open it from this side. Better to look elsewhere for an escape route.*

The hall emptied into a rectangular cavern lined with guards, tables, a stairway, and several connecting rooms. Rushing water and a soft heat emanated from one room, a welcome respite from the mountain cold she came from. Though the sound of water was curious inside the mountain. If she had time, that would be something she'd want to investigate. Each adjoining room had short hallways made of lightstone, similar to the hallway behind her though not as long. A preventative measure against Lightless escaping, no doubt. She'd have to keep that in mind.

"Welcome," a voice said from atop the stairway, "to this Iron Mountain Prison." All the guards stood at attention, their fists striking their chests in an echoing salute.

"Now begins your repayment to the world for your crimes." Nasna followed the voice to an ordîn descending the stairs, body straight, dark blue wings tight against his back. "It is here you will work to the end of your days. To repay the debt of every life you have taken, every life you have ruined, every life you have caused to suffer in this world. You shall feel their pain one thousand-fold before we let you drift off of Vicoluntas and into the Abyss."

Nasna looked the speaker over. Male ordîn. Age: blue in cyan cycle. Warden of the prison. Exorcist. Expression, unreadable. The speech so far suggested a Path of Justice or maybe Law.

"I am the Warden," he said, stopping a short distance away. "And I am the Oligarch here. During your stay, there are simple rules you shall abide by. Those who follow and behave are rewarded. Those who disobey and misbehave are punished." He gestured to the tables of bundled clothes and wool blankets. "Each of you will grab one of these. For non-tatzons, cots will be available to you tomorrow. For the tatzons, your cells will have hanging bars for each of you."

The guards led the prisoners to the array of tables. Each grabbed their new belongings and at the end spoke with one cyan-colored ordîn with a large ledger. This guard recorded their name and assigned them a number and cell. As she stood in line, Nasna took in as much information as she could. There was no telling how often she would be here.

To one side stood two archways larger than the others. A group of guards came out one, escorting what looked like two dozen prisoners, all tatzon. Those prisoners had amused expressions as they watched the newcomers. The guards led them past Nasna's group to the hall the running water had come from.

She eyed each prisoner, making mental notes about each of them as they passed by. But she stopped once she'd checked each of their markings. Tatzon markings were unique to each individual, no two ever being entirely the same. She saw markings that looked like leaves, paw prints, waves, lines, circles, even splotches. None matched her target.

"Hold up, Con-None. Stand there," a guard said to one prisoner. This prisoner protested with a glare but otherwise stayed where he was. Nasna glanced him over and turned back to examine the room. It was tall, much taller than the first... wait. She looked back at the secluded prisoner. She needed to look at him closer. There was something... wrong about him.

Male tatzon. Age: late twenties, early thirties. Posture and expression denoted Guardian attributes. Three arms made him a body-possessor of one possession or mind-possessor of two. His hair was straggly and his beard unkempt, yet he somehow looked less wild than most of the prisoners. His markings were strange, though. Black crescents scattered across his skin, but only on the right half of his body, with the other void of any marking. Not something she'd ever seen before. In her experience, markings always covered the whole body, so this was an unusual sight. But that wasn't what was wrong about him. There was something else. But what? She surveyed his body carefully. Besides his markings, he seemed just like a typical... her gaze stopped on his shoulder. That was it. He had three arms, but only one connected to a shoulder. His right shoulder sloped off and descended until his next arm.

He was missing his priarm.

But there was more. Another reason he looked so wrong. It was his skin. Most likely, it was a dark gray on a given day, like most Rajals, but he was a sickly ash color. His eyes were bloodshot and twitched toward any movement. He was grabbing one hand, itself shaking. This tatzon had been enduring Solitude.

No doubt about it, they would punish only a dangerous individual like that. Her gut told her to be wary of him. And she'd learned to trust her instincts.

"Name?" a voice said, pulling Nasna's gaze from the tatzon. It was her turn in line and the ordîn in front of her did not seem pleased.

"Name?" the guard said again.

"Sitora Whitestone," Nasna said. The ordîn jotted the name down and Nasna glanced over. The Exorcist from before whispered to the Warden. Both looked at her.

"Looks like a solo cell for now," the ordîn in front of her said. "You are in cell number—"

"One moment, scribe," the Warden said, walking over to Nasna. "Whitestone is it?"

Nasna nodded.

"I have been informed you have the hans."

Nasna only nodded again.

"Her papers, please."

The Exorcist held up the papers he carried and handed a couple to the Warden. Nasna stayed put, not fidgeting while the Warden read. There wasn't any reason to worry. She'd already filed the paperwork. It'd been the last preparation she'd made before venturing to the prison. Once assigned to her cell, the actual work would begin.

"Murderer, I see," the Warden said more to himself. "Fiery temper, but with a solid head on your shoulders it appears." The Warden glanced at the ordîn marking the roster. "We are making a minor change."

Nasna froze. What was he talking about? Without a change in his expression, the Warden beckoned over the priarmless tatzon.

"What do you want, Warden?" the prisoner asked. "Don't I have a penance to pay? Or did you just miss me?"

Nasna glanced at the ordîns, waiting for the clubs to come out. The guards didn't even react. Either this prisoner was an idiot people ignored or a person they respected. Looking him over, she guessed the former.

"Con-None," the Warden said. "I have two things to say to you. Listen well." The prisoner, Con-None, crossed his arms, though with a shaking arm it didn't appear as rebellious as he may have hoped. "First, as part of your penance, you shall introduce these convicts to the mines and guide their first day here."

Con-None groaned and stared at the ceiling. "Can't you find someone else?"

"Yes, I can"—the Warden's voice remained even and composed—"and I will not. The decision is made, Con-None. Will you reject it?"

The prisoner held his shaking arm tighter and shook his head.

"Good. Then, for the second reason you are here. I give you a cell-mate."

The tatzon's expression was blank for a moment until it formed into a look of relief. This faded when he looked at Nasna. Her stomach twisted. This was not a part of the plan.

"Wait, you don't mean with this, right?"

"This will be your new cell-mate, Con-None. She was assigned to a solo cell, I am not sure why. I made no such order. However, since you require a new cell-mate, I think it best to place her with you."

Not good.

"Why her?" Con-None asked. "There's plenty of tatzons here. Just give me one of them."

The Warden didn't look at him as he wrote something down on the ledger. "Are you not in need of a new cell-mate?"

"Come on, you want me on the hunting team as much as I do, and I can't with a human."

"You are not getting back on either the hunting or furnace teams. Not until you finish your payments." The Warden finished writing on the ledger. Nasna needed to speak up, otherwise, things were about to become complicated.

"Warden, if I may," she said. "The tatzon doesn't want to room with me, and I'm fine keeping my cell—"

"There is no argument here," the Warden said, his voice as unchanging as his face. "Con-None, you are one of my more gifted Guardians and yet you also are troublesome. This human also has a reputation. It would be good for you both to keep each other in line." The Warden walked away, glancing over his shoulder. "I warn you, Con-None, to not kill this one." The Warden looked over his shoulder at Con-None. "Despite her being Unhallowed."

Air lodged in Nasna's throat, realizing how much of an idiot she was. She'd known Whitestone was a murderer, but not an Unhallowed. That was perhaps the worst crime for Nasna to have.

Regardless of nation or culture or class, every tatzon in the entire world had a Partner, it was a part of their very core existence. Every tatzon society revolved around this. In many places, the Partner was the second half of a person and the bond between Partners was more sacred than ground touched by gods. To break that bond, to desecrate it by killing one Partner and leaving the other alive was the single greatest evil a person could commit. This belief seemed ingrained in the very marrow of what it meant to be tatzon.

And now, a prison filled with criminals believed her to be this Unhallowed.

Tension rose in the air and other prisoners. All glared at her and Con-None. The Warden returned the way he'd come, leaving the guards to deal with the prisoners.

"Damn him," Con-None said under his breath.

Nasna, despite herself, agreed with Con-None. With one action the Warden had complicated her entire mission. Not only had he made her a target, he threw her in with a cell-mate... she would have to figure something out. Perhaps this Con-None would encounter a strange accident sometime soon. However, the thought caused a twinge of pain in her stomach. Her Path did not dictate an accident, so she was free to find a different option. She would have to wait and see.

The guards prodded the prisoners in the back. "All of you move along. You too, Con-None."

Nasna glanced at Con-None who gave her a quick glare before marching off past the guards, not waiting for them to grab him or escort him. The guard with the ledger told her the cell number before moving on to the next prisoner.

They led Nasna's group through one archway on the side and they walked down a short hallway into a wide gallery that differed from the previous room. Several wooden machines stood around the room which appeared to work the various pulley systems here. Along the walls, an array of equipment sat in organized piles ready for mining. Next to each machine was a large shaft with an opened iron grate, bright light filtering out of them.

"For those in cell block ninety-one through one-hundred ten, over there," one ordîn said, pointing to a shaft. "For those who are in one-hundred eleven through one-hundred thirty, come here."

As he rattled off the cell block numbers, the newcomers splintered off to their section. Nasna followed Con-None. Once he reached his shaft, he ignored the guards and threw himself over the side, grabbing onto the ledge to make his descent. By the guards' expression, this was not protocol. They made each prisoner drop their belongings into the shaft first before having them clamber over the side, though Nasna had to wait for Con-None to finish his descent. The shaft didn't have ladders. Instead, handholds had been dug into the wall which Nasna had difficulty getting a good grip on. With her hands wrapped they felt as if they were on the verge of slipping out and dropping her the rest of the way. Not wanting such an event, she took her time descending, much to the annoyance of the guards.

The shaft itself had strips of lightstone embedded on all four sides. No shadows existed inside the shaft. This might have suggested she was being brought to an area with Lightless, except none of the other prisoners had been Lightless and they were all being sent with her. For the time being, she'd remain patient.

At the bottom, she picked up her bundle and took in her surroundings. The shaft had been long, yet breathing remained easy in this area. A glance around showed all the shafts from above led to this gallery, which was much taller than she had expected. Tall enough for a tatzon to stand on the shoulders of another and still have some room above them to jump. It was also wide, even wider than the gallery above. Every several feet stood a pillar of unmined stone which must have helped support the structure of the gallery and prevented it from collapsing. These pillars also had lightstone attached to them creating light for the entire area, especially in the center of the gallery where there were many more shafts in a line. Like the gallery above, each had pulley systems next to them with several wheelbarrows and baskets. There were a few guards in this gallery but not any other prisoners. However, iron doors lined along the walls and had to be the cells of the prison.

"All newcomers come here," a guard said. The prisoners gathered and the guard handed out small lightstones attached to leather straps. "These are your sources of light for the duration of your time here. Whenever you head to the mines, wear them. They'll be your only source of light besides fires. Fires will make breathing harder so we suggest using these more."

After handing over the stones, the guards gave each of them a leather sack with various mining equipment. The sack had a shoulder strap, as if that'd help decrease the weight for Nasna.

"These are your tools for the day. You'll return them at the end of each workday. We will take anything broken out of your payments."

"The other prisoners will teach you how to use your equipment and what you should look for," another guard said. "You'll learn all the rules in a short time. But here are the absolute basics you must know: first, everything you have is a privilege. Second, every privilege can be revoked. Third, every privilege can be earned. And fourth, your lives are at the mercy of the Warden."

Nasna looked around, half-expecting one prisoner or another to speak up, to roll their eyes, to show any sign of resistance. There was none. All looked down at their equipment and stones, their new lives dawning on them.

"Drop your belongings into your new cells," the guard continued. "Con-None will then show you to the mines. Welcome to the end of your lives."

Not all the prisoners moved at first, but Nasna didn't have time to care about the inner feelings of criminals. She slung the leather bag across her shoulder, taking a moment to adjust to its weight, and tucked the blanket under her arm. With her cell number in mind, she walked along the gallery wall to find it.

The oval gallery looked to have several branching tunnels leading off into dim-lit passages. Results of past generations of prisoners following certain iron veins from the looks of it. Each of the doors had numbers carved into the stone with a small lightstone above to shine on it. All the doors were unlocked and opened. The numbers were in an ascending sequence, so she followed along the path looking for her cell. This led her into one of the branching tunnels, which had less light than the rest of the gallery. There was only a single lightstone embedded near the start of the tunnel so she held up her new necklace to guide her. If even on the first level there was a difficulty with light, she would need this. Even with all her skills, she couldn't see in the dark.

Along the tunnel walls were more cells and at the farthest end, a fair distance from most others, Nasna found hers. Her necklace shone around the small two-person cell. It was tall—likely to accommodate tatzons who might have a dozen arms—but not as wide, perhaps only six feet, though it was much deeper. Next to the door sat a foul-smelling bucket and in the far corners were two straw mats.

She placed her bundle and sack by the door and examined the blanket and mattress. Strange. Tatzons didn't sleep on the ground. She glanced up at the ceiling and shone her light toward it. There were still two sleeping bars embedded above her, and handholds went up the wall for any tatzon too short to reach them. Either this cell came with two mats or Con-None didn't use the sleeping bars.

She shrugged. It didn't matter. Nasna grabbed her blankets to decide where she'd sleep for the rest of her time.

"That corner is mine," a voice said behind her. She turned to Con-None leaning in the doorway with his three arms crossed. "You can put your stuff anywhere, I guess. Just don't touch my things and I won't touch your things. Somehow we got to make this work."

Nasna nodded and dropped the bundle next to the opposing wall. She looked back at her new cell-mate. Neither said anything for a moment. Neither did they move. She wished he'd leave. How was she to act like Whitestone every day? Tatzons clung onto the nearest person, so how could she explore with him being a constant presence around her? Her Path started adjusting to him, deciding what to do with him.

"I guess we're cell-mates now," Nasna said with a smile. He wouldn't be able to see the smile behind her wrappings, which meant it was one of the few times she could get away with it. Sometimes she missed smiling.

The tatzon scoffed and looked away.

"The name is Whitestone, what should I call you?"

He glanced over at her. "For a murderer, you're talkative."

The word hit her in the chest and she stopped smiling. "Since when have those two things been exclusive?"

"Fair enough." He straightened and dropped his arms to the side and his full height towered over Nasna. "But let's set a few basic rules here. Just because we're cell-mates, doesn't mean we need to be friends."

Nasna crossed her arms. Of course, they wouldn't be friends. Friendship was something forever forbidden to her. She hadn't been thinking about it, nor was it a part of her plan, but the words still stung. They always did.

Con-None sighed and ran his hand through his dark hair. "Unfortunately, it means neither of us can leave each other's side."

Nasna frowned. That was the opposite of what she needed. "I don't see how it does."

"You've been outed as an Unhallowed. Inside here are hundreds of tatzons, all of which will want you dead when they know."

"Only a handful of people know. I don't plan on telling everyone."

"But the Warden is. He'll make sure your crime is known throughout the entire prison."

Nasna opened her mouth but shut it. Her shoulders slumped. This would complicate things.

"Why would he do that?"

Con-None leaned back against the doorway. "I can't guess what goes on in the idiot's mind, though he is a twisted bastard. I just know this: if you go anywhere without me, the others will try to kill you. And I'm not going without a cell-mate again. Even if it's you."

"But there's guards everywhere. No one would try killing me with so many around."

He looked away and out the door. "No one protects an Unhallowed. No one pities them, not even the guards."

Nasna looked away, but he was right. Damn it all, how was she supposed to get anything done with Whitestone's reputation here?

There was no sense in complaining. She was already here and couldn't undo what'd been done. Either way, free movement around the prison didn't appear to be an option any longer. Not only would she have to contend with guards at every corner, but now she had to deal with a prison of tatzons who'd want her dead.

She glanced at her new cell-mate, her Path itching for control. "Are you wanting to kill me?"

He sighed and shook his head. "You'll face punishment here. I don't need to render justice. Doubt such a thing exists, anyway." He looked away from her, but Nasna caught the pained expression on his face. It only lasted for a moment, but it was there. He turned back to her. "Grab your gear, it's time to get to work."

He made it look as if he would walk away, but Nasna knew better. They were now cell-mates. He would be at her side at all times. A new complication.

5

———◆◆◇◆◆———

NEW CELLMATE

I do not care what it takes, you must find those two! Send out every troop and every family if you must. The sacrifice is not complete until you bring back Swiftrider's daughter and the child of Death. Their escape will doom us if they are not returned. We already marked them, we cannot choose others and the Luminous frowns upon failure. They cannot fly, so search fast across every cracked ground and broken pillar. You must find them. Without them, we die.

- Luminar Stargazer, in the 2897th Lunar Cycle

Despite everything, Tsuran had to admit that the Warden knew what he was doing when he doled out punishments.

Tsuran looked over his shoulder at his new cell-mate, Whitestone something or another. She came to his shoulder and had a small build, average for a human. Cloth wrappings covered the rest of her body, hiding her appearance and likely her deteriorating flesh. Humans enjoyed being infected with every disease they could get their hands on, and while tatzons were resilient to most of them, the hans was a different story. Even Tsuran could become infected with it. He'd need to be careful with this one.

Along with giving Tsuran a new cell-mate who could be the death of him, the Warden gave him a job. Tsuran had to be the welcoming committee to all these newcomers.

And he might be—no, he was the worst choice for this. He hadn't even worked in the mines since he first arrived. And even back then he'd paid little attention. He scratched his chin and sighed. It's not like he had much choice here. Tsuran needed to be on the Warden's good side again, so if he had to do this he would. But he'd do it in his own way.

The Warden hadn't said how Tsuran needed to introduce the new residents, which meant he didn't need to take long. The sooner the introductions were over, the sooner he'd be able to get back to his own work. There was a lot of work ahead of him if he were to find a new crystal to buy his way out again. And now he'd have to deal with a dying human by his side.

He glanced at Whitestone as she walked behind him, her mining sack on her shoulder. She'd acted tough earlier, but something about her, her size maybe, told him she wasn't one for acting tough. If he didn't keep her near him at all times, this mine would kill her in no time. But if it did, perhaps Tsuran could get a tatzon to cell with.

He shrugged off the idea. It was unlikely the Warden would give him another cell-mate soon, even if she died. He had no choice but to make sure she lived. But then again, why they sent humans to this prison was anyone's guess. He hadn't known many that survived longer than a month or two.

"Alright, follow me," Tsuran said to the entire group as they gathered back together. "I'm Con-None and today I'm to show you your new lives."

Several of them didn't pay attention to him, each stood around their new cell-mates murmuring among each other. They didn't want to listen to him, which was fair. He didn't want to talk to them. He shrugged again and picked up his mining bag. If none followed, it'd make his job easier. Especially with many of them glaring at Whitestone.

"For those who don't want to die in their first month here, grab your bags and follow me." He turned to Whitestone and said quieter, "You go down first."

She stared back at him for a moment, nodded, and descended the next shaft. Tsuran moved right after her, not letting anyone in before him. He slipped over the edge and climbed to the next gallery. He kept his lightstone hanging around his neck since there would be no lightstones embedded in the shafts from here on out. They landed in a room which had some lightstones here and there to cast a dim light around the large space, but overall it lacked the light of the gallery above.

"Are those other cells?" Whitestone asked, nodding toward the many doors along the walls.

Tsuran nodded. "The first two galleries are just cells."

The two walked to the second shaft they would descend, which was one of several bunched together near the center of the room.

"The galleries have many shafts, I see," she said.

"Yeah, helps with airflow. It also helps keep traffic moving with mining."

"And the pulleys?"

He gave her a side-glance. It'd been a joke earlier, but she was pretty talkative. Then again, maybe he just wasn't used to people asking him questions.

"You'll see. It's still early in the day for them being used on this level yet. Don't worry, you'll get plenty of use out of them before the day is through."

By this time some other prisoners were filing behind them from the shaft. Some had yet to put on their necklaces, the idiots.

"Any not wearing your lightstone put them on," he said. "Once we go beneath this shaft, they'll be your only light."

"There's no lightstone down there?" one prisoner asked, sounding insulted by the idea.

"There are some deposits here and there. It is something we're mining for. But we are mining it, which means the ordîns don't care to keep any of it down in the lower levels for visibility. It gets dark fast."

A crash came from the shaft behind them. It looked like a few prisoners had fallen part of the way down. No one else reacted beyond looking at them, so Tsuran walked over. They had not dropped from a high distance and didn't appear injured as they groaned on the ground.

"Better get used to climbing the shafts without falling," Tsuran said. "When you're heading back you're also hauling a sack full of rock."

The prisoners seethed with an *I'm-going-to-kill-you* kind of look. It was a look he was familiar with.

"Also, before we go any further, there's something else I think you all ought to know." Tsuran turned so all the prisoners could hear him. "I know you're all hardened criminals who're itching to bleed someone, but the folks above don't tolerate murder here. The more prisoners alive means more food and drink for everyone. Every death means less for the living."

This caught their attention. He'd meant it to. It wasn't true, but they didn't need to know that yet. For now, it was best to deter the more stabbing-inclined of the group. Some had already been glaring at him with eyes of murder. Even if it was their first day, he wouldn't put it past any of them to try killing an Unhallowed.

"Our lovely guards are not fans of prisoners killing each other. If there is even a suggestion that any of you have killed another prisoner, they'll place you in solitary confinement for the rest of your days here."

That part was mostly true. Solitary was a punishment for serious crimes unless there were good justifications—though the Warden never shared what made up a "good justification"—and this ceased every glare and murmured threat among them. Silence enveloped and the criminal tatzons drew closer to their cell-mates. Tsuran smiled to himself as he returned to Whitestone. That would keep the tatzons in line. It always did. It was what had kept so many from killing him.

He led them down two more shafts before stopping. As they delved deeper, they started running into resident prisoners who were busy going about their mining. Some were already filling baskets with rock and ore, and others waited to hoist them with the pulleys to the higher level.

Once they arrived at the fifth level, he led them to one of the other passageways where there was active mining. None of the galleries were as excavated as the first two so there was always more to mine, even in the higher levels.

"Be sure to keep your lightstones in front of you wherever you look," Tsuran said. "Once you've been here a while you'll have memorized where all the shafts are. Until then keep a watchful eye. One wrong step could be your death."

This was where they were to learn the intricacies of their work. How to hold a pick, whether to use a pick or a gad, what to be looking for in the rock. But Tsuran was not planning on being the one to teach them. The Warden would understand.

"Welcome to prison," Tsuran said and turned away, nudging Whitestone along with him.

"What're we supposed to do?" a prisoner called out. "Hey, where are you going?"

"Sorry, can't stay and chat. A pretty girl's waiting for me, hate to keep her waiting."

He ushered Whitestone back toward the gallery and along the walls seeking a new tunnel. A quieter one. Though, he wouldn't find one on this level so he walked to the descending shafts.

"Where are we going?" Whitestone asked.

"Deeper into the mines."

He hoisted himself over the edge of a shaft and climbed down, Whitestone following.

"How deep does the mine go?"

"I think there are some twelve levels right now. But we won't be going all the way today."

He stopped at the bottom and took in a breath. Breathing was still doable, but with every shaft they descended the air became thinner and warmer at the same time. If they went to the eighth level, there would be access to fresh air. But he wouldn't bring this human there. It'd remain his secret area.

"Alright, we'll work here," he said and headed toward one of the quieter tunnels.

"Will we be safe?"

Tsuran shrugged. "As safe as a mountain mine filled with criminals can be."

"Reassuring."

"I aim to please."

Unlike the higher levels, the gallery here was busy. Dirt covered prisoners moved past them, shouting to one another, laughing, and working away as if it was real life and not some trapped existence. Tsuran's ears flooded with mining, hammering, and the cracking of stone. Miners shouted, barrows wheeled past, rocks tumbled, and prisoners dumped everything into baskets ready to haul up to the next level. Amidst the noise, there were also fires along several of the walls attended by mining crews. Whitestone pointed to them.

"Didn't the guards say no fires?"

"For light, yeah. They use the fires to heat the stone and then when it's hot they splash water on it. It causes the rock to crack."

"So mining's easier."

"As the theory goes. But it uses up breathable air, so it's only done a few times a day."

"Doesn't setting these fires weaken the structure? What about cave-ins?"

"They happen. The deeper you go, the more frequent the cave-ins. Part of the reason most rarely delve deeper than this level. Oh, this one will do." They moved past most of the active working and found a dark tunnel without fire setting nor much noise, which meant it had little iron. This was fine with him.

"We're heading down there?" she asked.

"Sounds empty. Perfect for keeping us both out of people's thoughts for a while."

They headed deeper into the tunnel, leaving behind the other prisoners and surrounding noise. They passed a few people at first, but by the time they hit the end of the tunnel they had gone several minutes seeing no one. The air was unpleasant to breathe and had little circulation. A glance at the rock showed no traces of iron nor anything useful to them, but he also didn't know what he was doing. He was a Guardian, not a miner. Even when he first arrived, he'd only mined long enough to buy his way out.

He eyed Whitestone. It'd be trickier to do that this time. With her around, he had no chance of getting onto the hunting team. But the furnace team was still an option. No idea how it'd help him get out of here, but he'd figure that out once he got there.

He sighed and sat onto the ground next to his sack.

"What are you doing?" Whitestone asked.

"Sitting."

She dropped her sack to the side. "I see that. I meant why. Aren't we supposed to be mining ore or something?"

"You eager to mine, or something?"

"Well, no, but isn't that what—"

"Look"—Tsuran spread his hands to the surrounding walls—"if you want to break rock, go right on ahead. I won't even stop you. But that's a lot of energy I don't want to waste."

She looked between him and the wall. "Won't the ordîns punish us if we don't mine?"

He leaned against the wall. "Can't punish what they can't track. Besides, they only care about getting crystal. Iron can buy you some stuff, but crystal is the real currency around here."

"Then why aren't we—"

"Because I don't want to?" He scratched his head. This woman seemed confused about not working. One would think an Unhallowed would jump at the opportunity to laze around out of other's sight. Though, this brought up a worry he'd been pushing aside for the sake of nullifying Solitude. He cleared his throat. "Just take a seat. I got a few questions for you, anyway."

Her attention jerked toward him, her posture becoming more rigid. Seemed she was looking forward to this as much as he was.

"I don't think we have anything to talk about," she said, her voice stern, cold. Or at least, she was going for that. It sounded more like she was imitating someone's imitation of a grouchy elder.

"We're cell-mates now," he said. "We have to talk whether we like it or not."

She hesitated but sat across from him. He half-expected her hand to drift toward one of the mining tools, just as his drifted to the hidden pocket in his shirt. Instead, she sat upright, legs beneath her, hands open. If it came to a fight between them, he'd win even without his secret. The way she kept her body motionless was disconcerting, though.

"There's not an easy way of going about this," Tsuran said. "But I have to know. Why did you kill someone's Partner?"

She fidgeted. "I thought you didn't care."

"I said I didn't plan on killing you. Didn't say uncaring." He leaned forward. "I care a lot. I care about you not stabbing me at night."

"I won't."

Tsuran snorted. "Well, I'm filled with confidence." He leaned back, keeping a hand near his chest, and looked her over again. She remained motionless and quiet. With her face covered he couldn't gauge her reactions or expressions or anything. Only her voice and movements.

Maybe she wouldn't stab him, but there was no telling with an Unhallowed. Of all the monsters he'd fought and known in this world, there was only one worse than an Unhallowed.

He narrowed his eyes. "Why did you kill a Partner?"

With their small space and distance from all other workers, her breath reached his ears. Subtle, but audible. It quickened. The only sign his words affected her at all since she remained still. After a moment, she said,

"They double-crossed me."

"How so?"

"We'd made a deal. A deal on another crime we committed. But he took my share and so I killed him."

"What was the crime?"

Her fingers, before straight and relaxed, rubbed against each other and her head bobbed as she spoke.

"We robbed some rich people. And, it was all my idea. I found the pair and saw that we could get a lot of money from them. So, I made the deal with the tatzons and together we robbed and got the ivories. But then when we were back at our hideout I was double-crossed. They took my share, and I didn't like that and I got angry. And I killed the Partner and took what was mine and... and then I was caught and brought here. End of story."

She scratched the back of her hands and looked away.

"Anyway," she said, "I won't kill you if you won't kill me."

Tsuran blinked and his hand faltered. For the last three years, convicted criminals of all stripes had surrounded him. He'd heard story after story. Even before that he'd had dealings with the underbelly of Rajalend. Never in all his years had he ever met someone like this.

Someone so horrid at lying.

Tsuran had met children who lied better than this woman. There was no single moment where it even sounded as if she believed what she was saying. Tsuran didn't. But he wouldn't call her out on it. She was an Unhallowed. Maybe this was just a part of her insanity.

Besides, he didn't like her stillness from before. It was a trained stillness. A stillness few criminals had. One that could be deadlier than all the lies she spouted.

But through it all, there had been one thing she'd said that had sounded genuine, the only thing she'd spoken with what had to be her actual voice. She wouldn't kill him. But one should never trust an Unhallowed.

"I just need to be clear," he said. "It was just that one tatzon, right? Don't have a personal vendetta against all tatzon or something?"

"Not all tatzon." Her fists clenched and her voice hardened. Tsuran reached underneath his shirt into the pocket, feeling the cool touch inside.

"And how do I make sure I'm not one of those tatzons?"

She looked back at him and paused. Tension crackled through the air. A familiar tension he knew well. It was the same kind he'd feel right before a fight with a beast. The kind he felt before he faced death.

Her hands relaxed, and she stood up. He tensed.

"You won't be," she said. "We'll just make a deal ourselves."

"Yeah? And what's that?" He rose to his feet, keeping his arms crossed to disguise the fact of having a hand in his pocket.

"Deal is that we leave each other alone," she said. "You don't kill me or turn me over to other tatzons and I won't kill you. You stay out of my business and I stay out of yours."

Now she was talking like a real criminal. "Fine. But realize that a part of this deal is that you aren't leaving me in Solitude, got it?"

She huffed but nodded.

Neither held out an arm to each other. Both looked at the other. She turned from him and picked up her pickaxe.

"With that out of the way, can you show me how to mine?"

"I thought I was clear I didn't want to."

"You were," she said. "But it doesn't seem as if people like you here. I've already made enemies of tatzons here, I'd rather not do that with the ordîns. I'll mine something today."

Tsuran stared at her and shook his head. "I don't get you. A criminal with a work ethic? You know this isn't a genuine job, right? This is punishment. This is a prison."

She took her pick and hit against the wall, letting the iron clang in the tunnel. "And I'll make sure they don't make it worse for me." She hit again, and again it clanged and bounced off.

After watching a few more attempts, Tsuran took his hand out of his pocket and sighed. It didn't look like she'd try to kill him. But if he didn't show her how to hold the pick, she just might cause a cave-in that would kill him.

And he would not let her be the death of him.

6

FIRST DAY OF PRISON

S targazer, it is time to let go. The war is over, we lost. Finding the *missing sacrifices will not change that. The Luminous does not favor us any longer. I and the people with me have found a mighty island far south of the Meadowlands, we call it Tifre. There are many ordîn tribes here, primitive but they have no wars with tatzon. I seek to consecrate this land and these peoples, unite them under one leadership, but I am not you. I and my Path confirm we need your leadership and your guidance. Forget our old home, come and help make a new one. You have asked sacrifice of so many others, it is time you do the same of yourself.*

Please note, as we are a new people, I have chosen a new name. I hope to see you soon.

- Naresh the Soilshifter, in the 2912th Lunar Cycle

Since arriving to this mountain hole, little had gone according to Nasna's plan. She was supposed to be finding her assassination target, but she was stuck pretending to be an Unhallowed human around an unhelpful tatzon.

She and Con-None mined away for what had to be most of the day without stop. Or, at least, she did. He spent a fair amount of time idling by the wall and didn't seem to take her concerns too seriously. But she knew ordîns. She wouldn't give them any reason to place any focus on her.

She filled her sack with what rocks and small metals she found and together they headed to the gallery to unload before going back and repeating the process. The hardest part was how much easier it felt to breathe in the gallery compared to the tunnel, though even then it wasn't similar to breathing in the open air. Nasna had no sense of time, but eventually, Con-None decided they worked enough for the day and she desired genuine air just enough to agree. They headed back to the gallery and made their way back up the levels. With her arms tired and sore, it was the last thing she wanted to do, and, to the audible annoyance of Con-None, she needed a break after each shaft. In the past, her physical training prepared her for every situation. Mining all day seemed to be an exception.

Despite her fatigue, she remained alert and attentive. Whenever she passed a female tatzon, she checked over their markings, looking for her target. Nasna knew it wasn't likely to find her on the first day, but she looked anyway. She was so close. She stood in the same mountain as that woman.

The contract had been vague on various details, specifically, the "why", but Nasna focused on the target's description: female tatzon, undisclosed age, markings resembled circles with broad lines striking through. Found among the Lightless and said to have light blue eyes, an extremely rare occurrence in tatzons. That had been all she needed to know to demand the contract. Her Path dictated her to accept the contract. The detail about the markings had been wrong, an unusual mistake for the Strikers, but Nasna knew the target.

Female tatzon in her mid-forties. Ovals around each light-blue eye with a broad stripe descending from them. Enjoyed sweet mushroom pies. Sung a lullaby before she slept. A Lightless.

For twenty years Nasna had looked for her. She'd come close over six years ago, but Valerija disappeared. Then, six years of nothing. Now, nothing stood to hide Valerija from her. Nasna would kill her. Death would come soon.

The thought did not make her smile, though. Because there was still that small part of her, that weakness in her, that kept wanting to hold onto the person Nasna had once been. The part that still wanted Nasna to be the sister she had been, not the assassin she was.

Ignore that, her Path whispered in her heart. *Walk the Path.*

Obedient, Nasna pushed all thoughts of her weakness out of mind, though there was always a sliver of it she couldn't dismiss.

The second level appeared busier than the third somehow, even though there didn't seem to be as many people working. Everyone stood in a line, a long line. She glanced past them to the shafts on the opposite end. There were guards at each shaft who appeared to be searching every tatzon. The ordîns waited for the tatzon to remove their shirt before they inspected the full torso, not caring whether the tatzon was male or female, and sent the prisoner along.

She took in a quick breath. Not good. Would they have her remove her coverings? No, they couldn't find her out. Not on the first day.

"What are they doing?" she asked Con-None. With the surrounding noise, he must not have heard since he kept walking, not even heeding the long line which continued to build. She kept close to him, noting again the glares she received from near everyone in the room.

Con-None walked to one shaft and, ignoring all the prisoners and the guards, climbed to the next level. The guards glanced at him once and did nothing. They also ignored her so she followed behind, her breathing easy again.

At the top of the shaft, dozens of guards stood with food and drink. There were more lines here. This time, Con-None stood in one so she stood next to him. Even he couldn't cut past this one.

Some prisoners in front handed over full sacks to the guards, heavy by the looks of them. But they could have dumped them into baskets like everyone else. It seemed odd they'd carry it all this way just to give to the guards. But many of the prisoners did this. Not only that, but the guards gave different food portions to those with sacks to hand over compared to those who didn't. One ordîn stood by and wrote away in her bulky book as the sacks passed by her. When they opened, light poured out and Nasna's eyes widened. They were handing over crystal.

It was Con-None and Nasna's turn, but he shrugged and showed his empty hands. The guards handed them both their food and Nasna frowned. Of all the portions she'd seen handed over, theirs was hardly enough to call a meal. While others received even a strip of meat, all they got was a small bowl of mush. Her stomach lurched. For all the planning she'd done, she forgot she'd have to eat this while she was here. Later, she'd have to ask why they didn't get meat as the others.

They dropped off their equipment near where they grabbed their food, though they kept their lightstones. Once done, Con-None headed straight to their cell, apparently not wanting to socialize with other tatzons. Nasna didn't complain. With the looks she was getting, she preferred to be alone. Or, at least—she glanced at her cell-mate—as alone as she could be.

They left the main throng of prisoners and Nasna walked close to Con-None. "Why didn't we get a better meal?"

Con-None smirked. "I told you before, crystal is currency here. No currency, no extra food."

"Even if you mined iron all day?"

He nodded. "If you got a lot of iron, maybe. But even a little crystal is better."

She stared at her bowl and frowned. "And we can't get crystal because..."

"Because that's where all the people wanting to kill you are."

Looking at the bowl, she almost wanted to face every single one of them. If she had to live off this long, she just might. She looked up.

"Hey, why were guards inspecting prisoners earlier?"

"Oh, that? They're checking for new arm growth."

Nasna cocked her head. "What?"

"You know we tatzons can grow new arms, right?"

"Of course I do, I'm not stupid. But why would it matter how many arms you've got?"

He sighed and ran a hand through his hair. "It's not the quantity they care about, it's the type of arm." He set his bowl aside and leaned forward, holding out two of his hands, the right one covered in black crescents, the left empty. "You know of the Seven by Sevens, yeah?"

Of course she did. However, Nasna doubted Whitestone would, so she shook her head.

"Thought as much. It's a summation of tatzon magic. There are seven types of possessions, and within each type is seven layers of power. For instance, Guardians possess statues. That's the type. The first layer of power is their ability to mind-possess the statue, where they put their consciousness in the statue but not their body. After that, they can body-possess, and then they can body-possess with empowerment. The layers after that are pretty rare. They're powers more of legend than anything.

"Anyway, the point is this: every layer of every type is a new arm." He held out his upper left arm. "This arm gives me the power to mind-possess statues." His right arm. "This is body-possession." The last left. "Body-possession with empowerment. All are of the same type. I can't use any of these to, say, body-possess a tree or something. I'd first need an arm to mind-possess plants and build from there."

"That's the point of the priarm."

He nodded. "More or less. It's the only arm that can access all seven types. It only allows mind-possession, but that's how tatzons get to choose what they'll specialize in, if they remain active."

"You said they don't care about how many arms a person has, but the type. What type would they care to check for?" Even as she asked it, she looked to the darkened areas of the tunnel. "The shadows. They're checking for Lightless."

"Yeah, in our area the ordîns want to be sure there aren't any Lightless."

Nasna looked back at him. After a pointless day in the mines, she was hearing something pertinent.

"They keep Lightless on the other side of the prison. Too easy for them to escape here. The ordîns constructed this specialized area to keep the Lightless where they are. I haven't been myself, but I've heard they made the whole gallery with lightstone. Prevents any shadows from forming so there's nothing to possess."

Nasna nodded. That mostly made sense, but not all of it. "If there aren't Lightless here, why check for arm growth?"

"As long as someone has a priarm, they can learn any of the possessions. So anyone could start learning shadow possession if they wanted to. The chance of escape is a risk, so, at the end of each day, they check the tatzons for any new arms growing. If any show even a hint of arm development, they're sent to the Lightless area. And never seen again." He looked over at her. "Guess it's good you humans can't grow arms, yeah? If we had to check your diseased body every night, everyone would lose their appetite. Wouldn't be real nice of you."

Nasna rolled her eyes and looked ahead. They reached their cell, but Con-None didn't enter. Instead, he took a seat next to the door and ate. Nasna also sat down, but she wouldn't eat yet since it'd require moving the wrapping around her mouth and with the light from their necklaces, Con-None would see her non-diseased skin. She held her food in her lap.

"But you can't tell just by looking at an arm what it can possess," Nasna said. "So how do they know if the new arm is for possessing shadows? What if it was something else?"

"What else is there to possess? The only statues are above with the ordîns, and there aren't beasts or plants in the mines. I suppose there's a chance someone could try possessing spirits, but becoming a Soulborn is difficult and I doubt any of the criminals in these mines can do that or would even want to. That only leaves you with shadows."

Nasna sat back and stared at her food. He was right, and there was no reason to dwell on it, they were all just criminals. But it didn't sit well with her. Forcing someone into an even more isolated place just because of mere suspicion. Even as criminals, they'd still be taken from any bonds they'd made in the prison, away from any new friends they now had. Perhaps it was just. Perhaps it was wise. Either way, it sat in her stomach like a spoiled mushroom.

"What about the other two possessions?"

Con-None laughed. "You mean dreams? Allow me to let you into a little tatzon secret: nobody possesses dreams. Maybe to try it out once or twice, but it's a useless possession to grow an arm for."

"But they could possess the dead." Nasna's voice quieted. She never enjoyed thinking about Disturbers.

His laugh died and he frowned. "Maybe. Some here might try, but people don't die around here in ways that usually allow possession to work. Collapsed rock ruins a body."

"But why'd they ignore you?"

He stopped eating mid-bite and brought his food down. His face looked pained. She shouldn't have asked.

"I don't have my priarm," he said, his words deliberate and forced. "None of these arms possess shadows. So, without my priarm, I can't grow Lightless arms. They know this and so they don't check me."

Nasna looked away from him. This was a sore spot, that was clear. She needed to apologize and encourage— no, she would not do that. This, her Path dictated. She'd remain quiet. She was an idiot for asking and an even bigger idiot for caring. Better if she just changed the subject.

"They split Partners around prisons, right?"

"Typically."

"Do you know where yours is?"

He rose to his feet, discarding the rest of his food. "I'm going to sleep. Shut the door when you come in." Without even glancing at her he went inside and laid on his bed.

Only then did she realize her mistake. His name was Con-None. Literally that none was his Partner. She imagined there were many Con-Nones out there as a result of the war.

Now alone, she ate her food in silence and thought back over everything she'd learned, doing her best to not think of the questions she'd asked him.

If what he said was true, Valerija was in the other prison area. Now, Nasna just had to find a way there. However, if it was an area for Lightless, they wouldn't take her there regardless of what she did since she couldn't grow arms like a tatzon. She wasn't a possessor. She was more.

She set aside her bowl, hung up her necklace, and went inside, shutting the iron door behind her. Darkness covered the small room. Some light filtered in through the cracks around the door edges, but otherwise, blackness surrounded her.

Her eyes adjusted to what light there was, though she couldn't make much out. Con-None, wrapped in his blanket, turned away from her. He didn't even stir when the door closed, a clear sign their interactions for the day were over, which was fine by her. But she frowned. He used the cot instead of the sleeping bar, and she hadn't even asked him why... but she'd likely already received her answer. Tatzons used their priarm to hang from the bars and the other arms didn't have the strength.

Considering the sensitivity of the topic, it was a good thing she hadn't asked about it.

Nasna felt her way to where she'd dropped her bundle and laid out the blanket. It wasn't much, but the air was not too cold so she didn't worry about freezing to death. Trying to keep her eye on Con-None, she laid on the ground and draped the blanket over her, but the ground here was hard like the rock she'd been mining all day. No feathered beds for her in this prison. And sleep was hard in coming. She'd traveled a long distance without stopping and then mined rock for an entire day. Her body was ready to rest. Her mind, however, was as active as ever.

She undid her head wrapping just enough to pull out her lockpicks she'd strapped to the back of her head. After hiding these under the blanket, she reached under the wrapping on her arm and pulled out the long string she'd hid there. The ends remained tied together, so she took the string and weaved it around her fingers. With the darkness, she couldn't even see it, but she didn't need to. Her fingers moved on their own, moving in and out of the string, creating designs and figures she couldn't see but knew so well her mind pictured them with total clarity. Once a figure was complete, she moved onto the next in the sequence. The memorized movement calmed her, focused her.

Her sister had taught her these, all those years ago, and the part that still wanted to be a sister clung onto this string, onto this memory. Only for right now was her Path quiet.

But it would not be forever.

Valerija waited for her. Death waited.

7

COMPLICATIONS

I understand your plight, Naresh. I do not envy you trying to corral those primitives into a holy nation, and stop expecting me to come aid the attempt. If even the rest of you Luminars have forgotten who you are, I have not. I am close, too. I have tracked the sacrifices to Tutchal, and it is here I shall end what we started. The Luminous will smile on us. I shall make sure of it.

- Luminar Stargazer, in the 2940th Lunar Cycle

Nasna let the punch hit her.

She fell to her knees, the side of her face pulsing. Her eyes remained downcast. If this satisfied them, they would leave her alone and she wouldn't have to kill them.

"Damned Unhallowed," the three-armed prisoner said and spat on her. Two others grabbed her by the arms and hoisted her against the wall, giving her a full view of her assailants.

They were the same four she'd caught trying to follow her and Con-None the last few days. This despite Con-None choosing a different level to work on each day. And this all began not long after Whitestone's crime had become common knowledge, so Nasna dismissed it being coincidental. Everywhere she went, death-glares followed. Con-None said the two of them would have trouble at some point and it turns out he was right.

Of course, this hadn't stopped her from losing him at every given opportunity. Never at a time where he'd be alone to face Solitude, but when they returned to a gallery. She had her mission to think of and needed him to be accustomed to her disappearing for long periods of time. Whenever they dropped off a sack of iron, she'd leave him with their tools and duck behind another group of miners. The galleries gave her little to explore and after an hour of her being gone, she'd make her way to find him again. It wasn't a hard task since he always stayed inside the gallery near the pulleys. He met her with a glare and a further complaint. This had been another of her wanderings with nothing to note of. And then they showed up.

She looked them over. Three female tatzons, one male, all about mid-age. Two in their early to late sixties, the other two looked to be in their seventies. Only the female hitting her had three arms, all others had two. None had been active possessors or had been in the prison a long time since none had any possessor posture. Markings varied in color and shape, though one's resembled a water ladle. Interesting. But on each of their scarred necks was a crude symbol they must've given each other. A line broken by an X. A vow for blood.

The symbols looked fresh.

The three-armed tatzon rolled up her sleeves and sneered at her, looming in and ready to strike. If Nasna fought, she'd kill or at least severely injure them with ease. That would put a bigger target on her, something she wasn't all too eager to let happen.

She took in a breath and narrowed her eyes. She would take as much as her Path allowed.

They pinned her arms against the stone as three powerful fists pummeled into her. She gritted her teeth and took it. She tensed her muscles, giving her strength against the strikes. It helped little. She'd trained herself as an assassin, not a brawler. Aches covered her body and the side of her face was swelling. If she wasn't wearing the wrappings, she'd have spat. And the assault didn't waver. It built. The attacker grabbed her shoulders and drove a knee into her, knocking the air out and blackness flashed across her vision. They threw her to the ground, giving her battered body a moment of reprieve, though it brought little but coughing. Breathing only made everything worse. But all her limbs still moved, so fighting remained a possibility.

A crowd gathered. Her attackers assumed beating her in the middle of the gallery wouldn't have bothered anyone. They were right. All the gathering tatzons looked pleased with what they were witnessing and a few smiled as if they also wanted a turn. Nasna was strong enough to take a single beating, but if others were being planned, she'd have to do something.

The prisoner turned her onto her back, straddling her, ready with another onslaught, much to the delight of a now cheering crowd. Nasna glared at her. She was ready. But the tatzon stared at her, eyes growing wide. Nasna squinted at her, but a coolness, a brush of air, caressed her cheek. Her exposed cheek. Some of her wrappings must've shifted during the attack and now revealed the flesh beneath. Revealed the crimson skin.

Nasna's breath left her.

The tatzon pointed at her. "You... you're a—"

Kill.

Nasna struck, grabbing a droplet of energy within the heart and released it. The woman toppled to the side, body still and lifeless. Nasna turned away from the crowd and fixed her wrapping so no one else would see. So she wouldn't need to kill anyone else.

The crowd became silent. Nasna sat up and stared at the dead woman beside her. Another step into darkness. Her gaze fell to her hands. They remained wrapped. She couldn't see them. Couldn't see them covered in the blood of yet another. She closed them into a fist to prevent them from shaking. She would not shake here. Even if her weakness ached, she would not let it show. She stood, body aching, and faced the other assailants.

They, like the crowd, were quiet, mouths dropped. They rushed to their friend and checked her over. Nasna positioned herself so none of the prisoners were behind.

"She's dead," one said and glared at Nasna. "You killed my cell-mate. You killed another of us." The crowd got over their shock and murmuring grew, as did the angry looks. Nasna's eyes scanned the gallery.

Not counting the three here, there were twelve surrounding her. Only one other three-arm, the rest were two-armed. Most appeared middle-aged, seventy to perhaps eighty, though one seemed younger. They'd be strong but not too fast. There was movement to the side and her attention jerked over. A couple were moving around the columns, trying to get behind her. This wouldn't happen. She looked for a way of escape

Running is a temporary solution, her Path said. *Death is permanent.*

Seven tatzons approached her and their eyes told her they didn't want to teach her a lesson. They wanted to rip her apart.

She closed her eyes. She had no choice. Nasna raised her hands, ready to do what she needed to.

"Hey, hey, hold on! What in the Abyssal's name is going on?"

Heads turned and Con-None pushed himself through the crowd toward her. As she watched him, a quiet sigh of relief escaped her lips. He panted, as though he'd been running around the gallery, and glanced between Nasna and the gathered crowd. He didn't seem put off by the many convicts surrounding him with murder in their eyes, but again something was off about him. It was more difficult to see with the necklaces being the only source of light, but his skin looked discolored. There was a pang in her chest, and it had nothing to do with her assault. Not meaning to, she'd left him alone to Solitude.

"So the Unhallowed lover appears," a prisoner said and everyone else stirred, glares drifting between Con-None and Nasna. Con-None walked past them, his gaze dropping to the dead tatzon and then to Nasna. His eyes said it all, *Why are you doing this to me?*

But instead of saying those words out loud, he pushed himself between her and the rest of the prisoners.

"I think we're done here, everyone. The mine's not chipping itself away."

"Shut it, deserter," a larger prisoner said. "That scum just killed a tatzon, a cell-mate here. We can't ignore that."

Nasna stepped forward. "If anyone else touches me, they'll end dead like her."

Two prisoners took a step forward, but Con-None pushed her back and shot her a glare. As if she could help it. Her Path was in control now, she had no choice.

"Who attacked first?" Con-None asked.

"Out of our way or we'll kill you too."

"Do that and the Warden will crack hard on you."

The crowd stopped. The angry looks didn't disappear, but hesitation flitted behind a few eyes.

"You all know better than I that killing others is not something he likes here. And us disappearing will not go unnoticed."

"But... but she killed first!" One pointed right at Nasna. "The Warden will understand us—"

"Are you real close with the Warden, then?" Con-None said, crossing his arms. "I don't think so. From the looks of it, Whitestone here killed in self-defense, something even that ordîn would acknowledge is within allowance. But a gang of you teaming against her?" He shook his head. "Just imagine what he'd do to you all. The Pits. The Chair. Solitary. He's got plenty of options."

The crowd was less sure of themselves at those words. They looked between each other, his words seeming to get to them. Nasna looked at Con-None. He stood firm, a little color returning to him, but his grip on his arm was tight.

"Besides," Con-None continued, "even if he punishes her, he'd never let you be one to do it. You even try to attack us and you will have him to deal with before the week's out." He grabbed Nasna's arm and pulled her away. She let him. "So unless you want an angry ordîn to deal with, we'll be leaving now."

He led her to the side, away from the others. Nasna watched them. Their anger did not dissipate. It built. Some shouted after them, cursing Nasna and Con-None's ancestors.

But none followed. Their fear of the Warden outweighed their hate for her. For now.

Con-None led her to the nearest shaft, only letting her go to have her climb down. Once at the bottom, he pressed her on to descend two more shafts, deeper than they'd gone before. At the bottom, he glanced around and took her down a tunnel as far as it would go. He said nothing, and she didn't want to encourage him to. However, in his haste to get them away from the others, he hadn't gone back to pick up their equipment. Not that he used it at all, anyway.

When they had gone as far as the tunnel went, he groaned and ran his hands through his hair. He looked to be about to say something but stormed to the other wall, taking in some deep breaths. He turned and walked up to her, finger extended toward her face. His finger shook in front of her. She leaned back against the wall and crossed her arms.

Con-None's hand closed into a fist which he pressed against his forehead.

"This," he said. "This is why you don't go running off on your own. I get you don't like tatzons, but what were you thinking?"

Nasna stared back.

"Are you trying to get yourself killed?" he asked. "I wasn't kidding about the Warden, you know. I don't know what he'll do to you if he learns about this. And then me! What'll happen to me?" He walked away from her, hands in the air. "Of all the people I might have celled with, of all the idiots, why one with a death wish?"

"I'm not an idiot."

He must've not heard her since he kept talking. "Picking a fight with a—wait, no. Even before that, you left me. Again, you left me. And what happens? You kill a prisoner and make enemies and now I got to take extra care to watch you and"—another groan and he dropped his hands—"Lamia would be thrilled to see me like this."

He didn't seem to talk to her anymore, so she let him continue his rambling. She massaged some of her less acute pains. She'd have to redress her wrappings later tonight after Con-None fell asleep and before she ventured out of the cell to continue her explorations. One benefit of being with Con-None over anyone else was that Solitude didn't affect him while he slept, which wasn't common among tatzon to her knowledge. From her understanding, Solitude didn't care whether a tatzon was sleeping or not, if they were alone that was all it needed. Yet, this wasn't the case with him. Normally, that would have piqued her curiosity, but for now this allowed her to leave their cell each night without killing him, so she'd focused on that. Last night she'd finished the gallery her cell was on, so tonight she'd venture to the second level. Nothing of interest yet, but there was no such thing as being too knowledgeable of an area.

"Are you listening?"

She focused back on him. His hands were on his hips and he scowled at her. Nasna shrugged and Con-None sighed.

"Look, if you want to die, then fine just do it. But if you want to survive, stop doing this. Keep me by your side. Because when it comes down to it, the other prisoners aren't your biggest problem. The Warden is."

Nasna pressed her lips into a thin line. She didn't want to admit it, but he was right. Prisoners, she could deal with. Con-None she even tolerated. But if the Warden decided she needed prison correction, he'd learn the truth about her. Then this mission would unravel before her and she'd have only a single resort: fight until either everyone else was dead or she was.

"So, what's it going to be?" he asked.

Nasna checked with her Path. It demanded death, but it desired Valerija's blood over all else. Her actions must not prevent this.

Nasna nodded. "Fine. I won't do it again."

Con-None let out his breath and sat on the ground. "Good. Good. We'll wait here for a few hours before heading back to our cells. Figure it's best we don't run into anyone else for a while."

Nasna sat opposite him and the two remained there in the warm tunnel for the rest of the day. Neither spoke. They let the distant mining be the only noise around them. At one point, Nasna wondered if Con-None had fallen asleep, but he rose and told her it was time to return.

They made their way past the other tatzons, all finishing their day of work, but not any from the earlier crowd. The rest of the tatzons sent similar glares as the two walked, anyway. Hate was plentiful throughout the levels. Con-None had them move through the gallery as fast as possible, being quick to grab their food and drink. When questioned about his equipment by the guards, he made a rapid comment Nasna didn't catch before he pushed her off to their cell.

Over the next few days, Con-None kept a closer eye on Nasna, much to her dismay. And he also had them stay at a lower level than most, also to her dismay. The air was thin and warm and it grew more so whenever he moved them deeper into a tunnel. But Nasna didn't complain. Working at the pace and hours he had them work meant they didn't encounter other prisoners often. Besides, she found that exploring at night to be more beneficial than anything she did in the day, so she let herself do less mining. This got her a smirk from Con-None, but nothing more.

He didn't talk to her much during those days and she didn't engage with him. They found a rhythm of silence that suited her. She preferred not getting to know him since it'd only make it harder if her Path told her to kill him.

Today he worked, or rather tried juggling rocks, a short distance from her, so she sat back and stretched out her legs. She flexed her arms and fingers, smiling. The fatigue of the work didn't come as fast as before and climbing the shafts every day was getting easier, especially with all the exploring she'd been doing. Her body strengthened, but she still had no ideas on how to get to the Lightless area. Last night, she tried getting into the main body, but they locked the grates on top of the shafts. Her arms were thin enough to reach through the holes in the grate, but only one arm stretched far enough to get to the lock. Her picks wouldn't help her there since she needed both hands to use them. Unfortunately, only energy would get her out, but that'd be much too loud. That remained as a last resort only.

Sighing, she eyed Con-None as her hand reached for the string in her wrapping. She stopped. This was no place to be doing that, though she could use the focus they brought. She needed to figure out a way to open the grates. There had to be a way. She was just not seeing how—

A tremor shook the wall and a loud crash filled the air. Some rock broke and fell above her and Con-None. He yelped and she covered her head as they moved out of the way, further into the tunnel. A crack sounded above her and she jumped to the side, dodging a sizeable chunk of rock. It rolled past her and she flattened her body against the wall as the rumble echoed through her ears. And the trembling stopped. The echoes died down. They looked at each other and Con-None's face paled. He cursed and ran toward the noise with Nasna rushing behind him. The air was scorching and breathing was difficult, as it always was, but was it getting worse? No, it couldn't be. It must not be.

The loud crash finished its last echo as the two of them came to the source. Light from their necklaces revealed a cloud of thick dust in the area, surrounding piles of rocks and boulders blocking the way.

The tunnel had caved in.

Con-None slammed against it shouting, "No! You can't do this to me."

Nasna ran up to the new wall. This wasn't happening. She tried to find a way through, but her lightstone wasn't able to pierce through the dust and rock. She grabbed some rock and tossed it aside, but more seemed to take its place.

"This happened on purpose," Con-None said. "A perfect way to get rid of the Unhallowed." His eyes met hers. There was a wild look in them. "Why'd you have to go piss people off?"

"You think other prisoners did this?"

The faces of the tatzons who ganged on her came to mind. As did the face of the one she killed. She cursed herself.

"Just find a way out," he said.

She searched, still tossing aside anything movable. Nasna coughed in the dust and groped around, needing to find something, anything. She found nothing. The rock was large and solid and who knew how thick. There wasn't any visible way out. Trapped. Completely trapped.

"Can we move the rock out of the way?" she asked, but it was a desperate question. The rocks were too massive. There had to be a way out. She threw aside stone light enough to pick up, pushing over what wasn't. Her breathing became more haggard and shallow. There was no way through the wall. No, there had to be. She needed there to be. This wasn't how she was to end.

A loud crack sounded beside her. Nasna turned, but instead of Con-None, there was a stone statue. It wasn't tall, a little shorter than her, but had four arms. And it was pummeling the stone. She paused. Where did he get a statue?

No sense in dwelling on it. This could do it. With a statue, maybe he could break through. She held her breath as he pummeled away at the stone. More dust and rock flew into the air. She turned aside and coughed. The air was thickening, or was it thinning? Either way, it wasn't good.

Con-None stopped hitting the boulders and unpossessed the statue, which itself seemed to disappear from view. Con-None slammed all three of his fists against the stone and cursed.

"Why are you stopping?" she asked. "Keep going."

"It's no use. The rock here is too strong for my statue... mine would break before this would."

Nasna stepped back. This couldn't be how she died. It wouldn't be. She needed to complete her mission.

"Are there any other ways out?"

He shook his head. "This is the only path."

Nasna ran against the other walls searching for anything. But in the back of her mind, she knew there was no point. She'd kept track of the tunnel as they'd come in. Con-None was right. There wasn't a way out.

She turned to him. "What do we do? Do we wait for someone to get us out?"

He didn't turn to face her but slumped to the ground. "No one is coming. This darkness is our end."

She huffed, lightheaded, but she needed to breathe slower. No knowing how many more breaths she would take. Her hand moved to the lightstone hanging around her neck. She would not die here. She knew what she needed to do.

Nasna walked behind Con-None and placed a hand on his back, feeling his energy. She calmed the river within him, letting it drift slower.

Sleep.

At first, it appeared he tried to resist, tried to deny her command. But no one could resist since it began in their river of energy. His breathing eased, and he toppled over.

Taking in a breath, she ripped off his necklace and held hers in the other hand. Neither were large crystals, nor were their rivers strong, but together they'd be enough.

Nasna positioned herself in front of the fallen stone. With any luck, she wouldn't make this worse. She forced her breath to ease as she reached into the energy of the crystals, feeling it course around inside them. She grabbed onto all the energy, not letting a single droplet escape her grasp, and drew it into her.

The power surged into her and built within her entire being, flowing in through her arms like the waters of a burst dam. The energy pressed against her body from the inside, wanting to leave, threatening to burst out of her. It strained in her bones and muscles, all aching and crying out. This energy was not the most intense she'd felt. But even this insignificant energy would rupture her body and kill her if she held on to it for too long. It was the reason her master always cautioned against this. But she held it within long enough to refocus it.

As the last of the energy left the crystals, the light dimmed away from them, enveloping Nasna in darkness. The air thinned, and she held her breath. The energy built and expanded within her, tearing her body apart. She channeled it all into her fist, giving relief to the rest of her body while risking her losing her hand. With a scream, she slammed into the stone, releasing all the energy at once. Pain spiked through her arm as the energy ruptured from her hand in an explosive boom, shattering through the stone, pulverizing it to dust. The force threw her backward and into the wall with another loud crack. The surrounding tunnel shook, and the boom echoed.

Nasna collapsed to the ground and the surrounding tunnel seemed to fall apart again. But she couldn't move with the pain in her body. No telling if her senses were even working properly. Everything quieted and stilled. She tried to look up into the darkness, but something hard fell and struck her head.

Greater darkness took her.

8

TRUTH UNCOVERED

I have failed. Truly failed. My heart pounds I struggle to hold this pen, but I must tell you. I found them, Naresh, I found them. I came at them with all my men. It was to be over. Over. But then she stepped forward, the daughter of Swiftrider, and she struck my guard. I do not understand what foul magics she learned, but the guard died. As did every one she struck. She held out her hand and killed the Luminars one by one. She was no child. She had become a demon. We slew her, but we did not find the child of Death and there are so few of us now. Even my Path agrees, we cannot continue on any longer.

The war... we have lost, haven't we?

- The once Luminar Stargazer, in the 2947th Lunar Cycle

Both Tsuran's head and the world itself spun while he tried to make sense of the high-pitched ringing. He coughed, spat, and coughed again. Dust hung in the air still, thicker now, if possible. He wiped his mouth and rubbed the back of his head. Some rock must've dislodged and hit him, causing him to blackout. But his head didn't hurt especially worse than anywhere else. Or maybe it did. A strange fogginess remained over his mind. Hard to think straight. Had to be why it seemed darker in the tunnel now.

His eyes opened more, but the darkness didn't leave. There was a bit of light up ahead coming out of an exposed lightstone vein.

But that hadn't been there a moment ago. He paused. That was the only light. He reached for his necklace. Gone.

He groaned and pulled himself up from the ground and looked around. The dust stayed heavy in the air but the white-crystal showed one thing with full clarity: a gaping hole in the middle of the cave-in. They had a way out. But how? He stared at it. The moments before he blacked out, what had happened?

His eyes widened. "Whitestone."

She did it. She must have made the way out. Where was she? He scanned about but her lightstone wasn't visible. He leaned against the wall. She hadn't left him behind, had she? No. She wouldn't abandon... well, no, she would. She was an Unhallowed.

As the thought hit him, the familiar sensation of a distant presence rose in the back of his mind. Solitude.

Tsuran jumped to his feet and frantically looked around for that damned human.

A groan. From behind. He spun around. It was Whitestone and he rushed to her. "Please don't be dead. I can't survive another night of Solitude."

He crouched and tossed off the rock covering her. He looked her over, breath held behind his teeth but he eased it out. Her chest rose and fell, so she was alive. He sighed.

"Well, I do not know what you did, but when we get back to our cell, I'll give you the biggest—"

His words died in his throat and he shuffled away from her, his breath stolen. His heart raced, his breathing shallowed. Her wrappings had come undone around her face and laid limp beside her. But he must have seen wrong. It had to have been because of the lack of light. There was no way he'd seen right. But if he had...

Not wanting to stir her, but needing to be sure, he grabbed her arms and pulled her until they were under the veins of lightstone. It revealed this impossibility.

Bright red skin. Pure white hair. Gods above, she was an ordîn.

He knelt and stared at her. What was going on? Why was there an ordîn in his cell and why was she posing as a human? They'd told him she had the hans. That's why she covered herself in wrappings.

But that was a lie. It was to hide her race. And the Warden, did he know about this?

Tsuran shook his head. No. The Warden would never let something like this happen. Deception wasn't his thing. But there was an ordîn right in front of him. Not a spy, since that wouldn't make sense. Maybe she was some criminal they wanted to keep alive. No, that wasn't it. They were strict about executing any ordîn criminals.

Tsuran slapped his face twice. He was losing it and he knew it. He wasn't even sure how to think about this. Though, it didn't help he hadn't recovered from whatever had hit him... or whatever she'd done to him. He stared at his mysterious cell-mate.

"Who are you?"

She didn't stir. Whatever she'd done seemed to have drained her or maybe a rock hit her. He grabbed the loose wrappings and reapplied them to her head, making sure she could still breathe but covering her skin and hair. What would he do now?

He sat upright.

The Warden would want to learn about this. He might even reward this information. No, he would reward this. He might even let this pay off Tsuran's penance, or, better yet, count this as equivalent to yellow-crystal. Tsuran would get a tatzon cell-mate, another Guardian, and he'd be back to the hunting team... and then, with some careful planning, he could run out of these mountains and out of Rajalend forever.

He smiled. At first, the cave-in looked like it'd be the end of him. It turned out to have provided him his key to freedom.

Tsuran picked Whitestone from the ground and held her in his arms as he returned to his cell. He left their equipment for the time being, since this was much more important. Besides, he wouldn't be needing them soon. As he walked past other mining crews, they gave him surprised looks confirming what he'd suspected. He smirked at them.

Their surprise became glares, but only for a moment. It switched to looks of satisfaction once they saw him carrying a limp Whitestone. As far as they could tell, she was dead. And Tsuran didn't plan on correcting them.

By the looks of it, he had several hours left in the day. Plenty of time to see the Warden. But he didn't want to wastes time and so he headed to the nearest shaft, ignoring the stares from those around. Typically, if someone died in the mines, others left them alone. No one carried the dead back up. And this was quite the image: a tatzon carrying a dead human up through the mines.

Once at the shaft, he held her with one of his lower arms and climbed with the other two. It was more difficult to maneuver the shafts while holding her, but she was light. Just like all ordîns. He smirked and continued to ascend the shafts until he reached the first gallery. He laid his ordîn cell-mate in their cell and shut the door on her. Best no one got to her before he came back.

"What are you doing Con-None?"

Tsuran turned to two guards approaching him.

"What's wrong with your cell-mate?" one of them asked.

"That's for the Warden to hear," Tsuran said. "I need to meet with him. I've some information he'll find very helpful and very interesting."

The guard crossed her arms and flexed her wings. "Just tell us what you want to tell him. We'll pass it along."

He shook his head. "It's for his ears only. And believe me, he'll want to know. It's to do with prison security."

The two guards looked at each other. "One moment."

They walked away from Tsuran, deliberating between each other. Tsuran leaned against the iron door and waited. It would be some time before they made their decision, but then they would stick with it. It was the way with ordîns. They didn't sneeze before taking a half-hour to think about it but then nothing in all the world could stop them from sneezing.

After what felt like days of waiting, the guards came back. "We'll bring you to the Warden. Come now."

Tsuran raised a hand. "Actually, I need one of you to stay here and guard my cell-mate. I want to make sure no one kills her while I'm gone."

The guards nodded and one positioned herself in front of the door. A quick decision so they must have already discussed this point. He didn't even try to hide his smile as the other led him to a shaft to the main level. The guard squeezed his wings behind his back and climbed with Tsuran right behind. It must've been inconvenient for these ordîns in the mines. No room for wings. Why they'd choose this restriction instead of being someplace they could fly all day was anyone's guess.

The guard reached the top. "It's Thirds, I have a prisoner to see the Warden. Open the grate."

An ordîn moved above them and the iron grate creaked and whined as it opened. Several guards surrounded the shaft hole, two of which placed hands on Tsuran. He waited as the guard from below explained. None of these ordîns argued or deliberated with him but nodded and allowed the guard to pass. He led Tsuran to the central body where guards stood watch, hissing and clanking poured from the furnace room, and prisoners lugged carts of ore across the bridges high above. Looked like everyone was working hard. He smiled. Just yesterday he'd dreamed of being on the furnace team, but with what he had now, the Warden would for sure put him back on the hunting team. And then Tsuran would be back on track to escaping.

The guard led him up the stairs to the higher level past a dozen ordîns. Though, this was not his first time being brought to the Warden and so most ignored him. They passed through the halls and stopped in front of the Warden's iron-plated door. The guard knocked hard. It echoed down the hall. A calm voice spoke from within,

"Enter."

The guard grabbed Tsuran's arm and pulled open the door, taking him inside.

The Warden's room had few furnishings. A desk and stool faced the doorway, a set of bookcases stood opposite the small but pristinely made bed, itself positioned beside a fireplace cut into the stone. A lively fire burned there, giving some light to the room. lightstone fixed into the walls provided the rest of the light, with each stone having a sliding panel to cut off the light when needed. To the side was a second door, prisoner's confiscated goods inside, and behind the desk was an opening to the large balcony which oversaw the entranceway to the prison. There on the balcony, overseeing work below, stood the Warden.

The guard and Tsuran stopped halfway to the desk and remained silent. Even Tsuran held back from speaking up. He needed to do this right. Even a grateful Warden would still punish Tsuran for acting out a bit too much. The Warden turned and faced them, his blank gaze offering no change from his usual expressionless face. Forever unreadable. Forever unsettling.

"Con-None," the Warden said. "Why is he standing before me?" The Warden brought his wings tight against his back and left the balcony.

"Con-None claims to have information about prison security."

The Warden stood before the desk but did not sit on the tall stool. He kept his arms behind his ever straight back, his eyes unblinking as he stared at Tsuran, who tried to return the gaze.

"Is that so, Con-None?" the Warden asked.

Tsuran nodded, but his attention drifted to the desk. On top of a stack of papers, acting as a weight, stood a small, faintly glowing, red-crystal statue a little taller than his hand.

He hadn't seen it since the day the ordîns had wrenched it from his grasp and there it stood mere feet away. The Warden never had it in the open any of the other times they'd brought him here. And now it sat on display like some trophy. His hands clenched, but he tried to keep his face neutral. He didn't take his sight off the statue.

"Focus, Con-None," the Warden said and Tsuran's eyes snapped to the ordîn. "Do you have anything to say? Or did you wish to give me a reason to place you in solitary?"

"No sir," Tsuran said. That was strange. He never called the Warden "sir".

"Well then," the Warden said, taking a perch on his high stool. "What do you have to say?"

"It's about my cell-mate, the human you gave me," Tsuran said, trying not to smile. This was it. In only another moment, Tsuran would be free of the mines.

The Warden folded his hands onto his leg and, now sitting on the stool, opened his wings. They blocked the entire view of the balcony, as if they were a wall in themselves, and extended around the desk like grasping arms.

"Do tell."

Tsuran kept a straight back and gazed forward. The Warden would not intimidate him, not on a day like today. Besides, the Warden's true strength didn't lie in his size but his voice, his command. That, and he was an Exorcist who, if the tales were true, once hunted renegade possessors brutally. Hunted them with his large wings, bulked muscles, and impressive height for an ordîn.

Alright, so maybe the Warden's size was disconcerting, but Tsuran needed to focus. He was here about Whitestone, an ordîn much smaller and more manageable to think about. Why, she was even smaller than... than....

He stiffened. How had he not realized it, yet? Whitestone was an ordîn, her red skin and white hair proved that. But there was one thing she was missing. Something separated her from all the other ordîns.

She didn't have wings.

Tsuran glanced between Warden and the guard next to him. Both of their wings folded against their backs, but even then the tips of the wings touched their heels and went above their heads. There was no way she could wrap hers enough to hide underneath her clothing. Was it because she was a female? No, that wasn't it. There were just as many female ordîns in the prison as males and they all had wings. No, there was only one reason she wouldn't have wings. She'd been clipped.

His hand drifted to where his priarm had once been and he grabbed onto the hollow emptiness. A pit grew in the center of his chest as the faces of dozens of children flashed across his vision, culminating in the faces of Tamara and Baz with Dazh standing over them.

"Con-None?" the Warden said. "Con-None, stop drifting and speak."

Tsuran looked back at the Warden. "I..."

Idida came to mind. He didn't think of her face but felt the impression of her. Not a memory of her appearance, but of how the air tingled with joy when she was around. Of the resolve he admired.

He exhaled. "I'm sure this is what you had planned, but a lot of the other prisoners want to kill my cell-mate."

"And I am sure you are doing everything you can to keep that from happening."

Tsuran nodded. "Yes, but that'll only work for so long. Just today some caused a tunnel collapse in attempts to kill both me and her."

The Warden blinked but didn't speak.

"She and I escaped. However, I don't expect this to be the last attempt. You telling them she's an Unhallowed, a bastard move, I'll add, is not only endangering us two, but it's endangering your prison. Cave-ins aren't good for business, which I'm sure you already know."

"Do you know which of the prisoners caused it?"

"I don't know names, but I could tell you their faces and markings."

The Warden pulled aside a piece of paper and ink. "Describe them. I would very much like to... converse with them."

"More than happy to oblige there, but I don't think that's all we need to do, Warden. I want me and my cell-mate on the furnace team." Tsuran paused a moment for the Warden to comment. No comment came. The Warden, as always, showed no expression. So, Tsuran kept talking. "It keeps me and my cell-mate safe from other attempts on our lives, which will then help prevent more catastrophes in the mountains. And you'd have me up here ready as a backup hunting member whenever you need. I know I'm still on probation, but we also both know you need someone like me on the hunting team for some of those more tough beasts."

The Warden leaned back on his stool, keeping his balance by placing his wingtips on the ground like legs. "Your skills as a Guardian notwithstanding, you have stated it yourself: you are still on probation."

"Yes, but if I'm on the furnace team, as soon as I'm off probation you can use me right away."

The Warden didn't speak for some time, his eyes remained fixed on Tsuran while he likely debated in his mind about this. After several minutes he spoke again.

"You are a valuable asset to the prison, Con-None. However, that is not reason enough to put you and your cell-mate on the furnace team. Your request is denied."

Tsuran frowned. His ramblings usually worked with this ordîn.

"I cannot place a prisoner on the team so others don't kill them," the Warden said. "Otherwise, I would have to do so for most of the prison. I must not set a precedent. If you wish to be on the furnace team, you must earn your way. Much like how you earned your way onto the hunting team."

Tsuran straightened. "You mean I can still purchase our position?"

The Warden nodded. "Just as I honored your service for getting onto the hunting team, I will honor it again to get onto the furnace team."

"And how do I make sure me and my cell-mate aren't dead before we get you some yellow-crystal?"

The Warden tilted his head toward Tsuran. "That, Con-None, is a part of your probation to figure out. Now, please give me the markings of those who caused the cave-in and you may be on your way."

Tsuran shared the markings of the tatzons. He wasn't sure what the Warden had in mind for them, but hopefully, it'd be just painful enough for others to keep a wide berth around him and his secret ordîn.

The Warden wrote each of the markings and looked up. "And is there anything else that you would like to say to me?"

Tsuran hesitated and then said, "That's it."

"Then you are dismissed. Keep in mind that until you have yellow-crystal with you, do not presume you can call on me."

"Wouldn't dream of it."

The guard escorted him out of the room, away from the Warden and away from his statue. Back to his cell with an ordîn he knew nothing about.

Hopefully, he hadn't just made a huge mistake.

9

A PROPOSAL

N aresh, I have thought long on your proposal, and I accept. I fear much for my life in these strange lands, and it would be good to see an old friend once again. I have already spent too much time with these tatzon, I need the companionship of other ordîn. However, I come only as a guide, not a leader. We have already seen where that brought us. But I shall help you guide the land of Tifre and tame the primitives under a holier vision. In doing so, the Luminous may forgive me.

It took much deliberation, but I decided that I too shall have a new name.

- Yavahush the Stargazer, in the 2948th Lunar Cycle

Nasna's eyes fluttered open and shut. The darkness faded away and lucidity returned. Though, that may not have been a good thing since it brought the pain from her ripped arm to the front of her mind. She coughed and winced. Even her insides didn't feel great. Yet, if the pain meant anything, it meant she lived. And the air was easier to breathe now. Even the heat was bearable. It was even a little chilly.

She groaned as she sat up, but something surrounded her, something flexible and long. A blanket. She had a blanket around her. They hadn't brought a blanket with them. What was going on? She shook the grogginess away and looked around. She wasn't in the tunnel at all, but her cell. And across from her, with a lightstone in his lap lighting the room, sat Con-None. He must've carried her back here.

"You're awake," he said. "I brought you some food. You must be hungry after today."

Nasna rubbed her neck but winced. The same hand she drew energy with. Best she did not use it for a time. She looked at Con-None.

"What happened?" she asked. She did not reach for the food. She wouldn't eat until she awoke more.

"I found you unconscious on the ground, so I picked you up and brought you back here. You've been out for the rest of the day, everyone else is already asleep."

Instinctively, her hand flew to the wrapping around her head. It remained intact. But it felt different. It must have shifted from the release of energy or from being thrown backward. Or... she eyed Con-None. He sat cross-legged, his hands folded together in his lap, and leaned against the wall. None of his usual smiling, but a serious look on his face. Nasna's heart beat faster.

She readied herself. If guards stood outside ready to storm in to take her away, subtlety would be pointless and she'd then need to fight her way to her target. Because she was not leaving until Valerija laid dead. Not until Death took a firm hold of Nasna's heart.

"Did anything else happen while I was out?" She looked between him and the door. He opened his mouth but closed it again. Nasna tensed. If needed, she could reach him and rupture his heart before he cried out.

"I told the Warden about the tatzons that caused the cave-in," he said. "He'll see to them. So, we won't need to worry about anyone troubling us anymore."

She narrowed her eyes. He saw the Warden and told him about the cave-in. What else had they talked about?

"That's good," she said.

He nodded and looked to the side. She listened outside the door, but there wasn't any movement out there. If guards were standing outside ready to bring her in, they were impressively quiet. But if he had found out about her being an ordîn, they would have come for her while she was still unconscious. No reason for them to wait. Nasna released some tension in her body but focused on Con-None.

"You should eat," he said. "You'll need your strength for what's next."

She glanced at the bowl of food at her side. "And what is going on?"

He cleared his throat. "I've decided"—she tensed again—"I'll help you do whatever it is you came here to do. And then you'll help me escape this prison."

"What are you talking about?" She slid her feet behind her, subtle enough he wouldn't notice. He looked to the ceiling and took in a breath.

"I know you're an ordîn."

She pounced.

She grabbed his throat and forced him onto the ground, taking hold of his energy, paralyzing all of his body except for his head. His eyes widened and his heart beat faster under her palm. She leaned in close to him.

"Time to speak, Con-None. Who did you tell about me?"

He didn't look at her, but instead tried to glance at his body. "I... I can't move. What'd you do to me?"

"I'm asking the questions. Who did you tell? The Warden? Tell me how many guards are coming or I'll end your—"

"Oh, get off of me, will you? No one besides me knows your little secret, alright? I went to the Warden, and I planned to turn you in. But guess what? I didn't. I made a little gamble. So, either kill me or get off me. This... I don't enjoy this."

Nasna glared at him. She had a firm grip on his energy and there had been no sign of lying. But all that meant was he had told no one else. It didn't mean he needed to live. Then again, he said something about helping her, so maybe that could be a reason for him to live. Her Path had not demanded his death yet, so she released his energy and moved off him. Though, in the recesses of her mind, she felt something begin to strain.

He rubbed his neck and sat up. "Thanks."

"You have one minute to convince me not to kill you. You know my secret so why should I keep you alive?"

Her eyes narrowed. Both she and her Path waited for this answer. Nothing could keep her from Valerija, so nothing less than a compelling reason would save his life.

Deep inside her, beyond where her Path could hear, the weakness inside her whispered,

Please, please give a compelling reason.

Con-None crossed his arms, one hand sliding underneath his shirt, to that secret pocket he thought she hadn't noticed. "And I thought you were prickly as Whitestone. I think my goods looks are enough to not kill me." He grinned and, despite the situation he put her in, she rolled her eyes. "Nothing? Not even a groan?"

"The only one who will groan is you if you don't give me a proper reason."

"Oh, so ominous."

Nasna's eye twitched, and she was honest enough to know that this annoyance came from her and not her Path. Was he this nonchalant about dying?

His grin faded, though did not disappear, and he leaned forward. "Let's start with the basics. No matter what jokes I made before, the guards don't want prisoners ending each others' suffering too soon."

"Except, people hate you," Nasna said. "They'd award me instead of punish me."

"True, but killing me will draw attention to you, something I get the sense you want to avoid."

"I don't need to announce it."

"If you hadn't noticed, I stand out around here. People will notice when I disappear. And besides, that still leaves you pretending to be an Unhallowed inside a prison of tatzons. You want to do that alone?"

"I can handle myself."

"You did almost die today."

"Without you I don't have to be that careless."

"So what? You plan on just killing every tatzon that tries to get you? The Warden will ignore one or maybe two killings. Once you impede his business, he will search for you."

Knowing he couldn't see, she let herself a small smile. Yes. That was a good point. She couldn't kill him without being caught. That had to be good enough to let him live.

But her Path remained as it was. It still waited. It still wanted more death.

Her heart faltered. If that wasn't reason enough to keep him alive... a sickness grew in her stomach. But if her Path told her to kill, then she had to. The straining inside her worsened as she dared push back against her Path.

But, she thought, *he's right. Killing him is a bigger risk than letting him live.*

You speak from weakness, her Path said. *Yours is the Path of Death. Walk it.*

She swallowed, but pressed. *He didn't turn us in, so maybe he could be helpful.*

A long moment passed before her Path answered. *What does he want?*

"Let's say I don't kill you," she said. "What's your aim?"

"Already told you. I help you, you help me escape this place."

"Nothing else?"

"Well, I have some belongings the guards took I want back."

"What belongings?"

"The kind you don't need to worry about."

She frowned. "If you're wanting to earn my trust, you're not doing a great job."

He shrugged and grinned. "Well, you still haven't told me if you plan on killing me, so we might be even."

Nasna jumped to her feet, fists clenched. "By the Abyss, you're going to make more jokes about this? Do you understand your position? I hold your life in my hands and you haven't given me much to trust you."

Her frustration was all she had to keep her tears back. Did she have to kill again, just because this idiot wouldn't take the situation seriously?

Con-None looked at her for a moment and then rose to his feet and stood tall. "I am Tsuran Con-None, the Red Sword of Rajalend." His voice lost every bit of his earlier levity. There wasn't threat in his voice, but there was danger. "So let me be clear of one thing: you hold nothing. *I* hold my life and *I* am the decider of my fate. I don't need you to trust me. I just need you to realize how stupid you would be to throw away a resource like me."

It seemed her words had struck something in him. Though, his struck even deeper in her, but she would not, could not, admit it.

"And you're willing to do whatever is necessary to help me?" she asked.

He nodded.

"Even at the expense of others' lives?"

"If it's the rabble you find around here, I have no qualms."

She stood staring up at him, knowing he couldn't fathom the storm raging inside her. Her Path demanded death. It needed death. But her weakness, that insignificant part of her heart that dared rebel, wanted him to live. Back and forth, the two voices vied for dominance inside of her. The voice of her Path was stronger, but her weakness was sweeter. They argued around and around in her head. Demand after demand. It was enough to force her into madness. And the straining inside worsened, a strain that only came from fighting her Path, a strain that could break her. Very few times did these forces fight with such vehemence. She wanted to cry. She wanted to scream.

Instead, she pulled out her string and formed the familiar figures with it. With her eyes closed, Nasna moved through her sequence, her fingers weaving in and out, pulling and releasing. Figure after figure formed in her hands, and if Con-None spoke, she didn't know it. The figures quieted every voice in her mind, quieted her very heart.

In the quietness, Nasna found her voice.

Valerija's death is most important. Only hers is necessary. I could use him. And if he becomes a liability or a problem, I can kill him then. But... let's wait and see.

Her Path rumbled to the surface of her mind. *You still speak from weakness, despite your reasoning. You are to walk the Path of Death, and it demands pain, suffering. It desires only to kill, to destroy. Your heart betrays you.* Her Path stirred through, growing stronger inside her, and she knew if it wanted to, it could take over and force her to kill. But it stopped, and this Path, this spiritual guide, smiled. *If this man is to live, then another must die. Your weakness, must die.*

Nasna's finger froze, string falling limp between them. Her weakness... the last part of her not given over... the only part still resembling Clear Sky's sister.

How... how could it die? She thought.

Just complete your contract. I will do the rest.

She nearly killed Con-None right then. But her weakness, that which couldn't help but want to protect, begged for Con-None and not itself.

Holding back tears of what would come, Nasna agreed to the deal.

She put her strings away, took in a breath, and faced Con-None. "I'm an assassin with the Shadow Strikers. I'm here to kill a Lightless."

His face looked blank and expressionless. Then he relaxed against the stone, interlacing his hands on his belly. "Makes sense."

"Makes sense?" she said, narrowing her eyes again. "That's all you have to say?"

He smiled. "Not sure how you'd want me to react. All I'm saying is I couldn't figure out what you'd be doing here, but an assassination makes sense. Lots of bad people here, you know."

The levity with which he took this information should have upset or unnerved her, but she formed a slight smile before wiping it away.

"You still want to help me with this? Killing one of your own kind?"

Con-None sighed. "I'm a criminal you know. How do you think I got here?"

"Then... I'll help you escape."

Silence in the cell. Con-None smiled widely.

"But," Nasna said, raising a finger, "only if you help me kill my target. That's our primary task. Escaping is second."

"That's fine by me. But in return, I also expect you to not leave me alone anymore. I am still a tatzon who needs a cell-mate."

"Deal."

He clapped his hands together and closed his eyes for a moment. For that brief second, he looked... peaceful.

"You still haven't told me your name," he said, snapping his eyes open.

"Why do you care to know my name? Whitestone works just fine."

"Except it's not your real name. And if we're going after a Lightless, I figure we might as well have a small amount of trust."

"Thought you didn't need my trust."

He shrugged but kept his smile. "Maybe a little."

She took a deep breath. "Call me Nasna."

Con-None, or rather, Tsuran, dropped his smile and blinked. "Nasna. You're Death's Touch. Thought you were just a story."

"Still want to work with me?"

"Well, can't say I've worked with too many myths before, but"— he leaned forward with that stupid grin of his —"I guess we have someone to assassinate." He held out his crescent marked hand. She went for his hand, but stopped, making a second dangerous decision.

She reached for the wrappings around her head and removed them, letting the air caress her skin. It was strange to unwrap in front of him, but this was important. With her head uncovered she looked him in the eyes and clasped his arm. It had been a long time since she last trusted anyone, and the last time she had was the reason she was in this prison now. Now she would trust, even if only to a small degree, a criminal she'd recently met. One whose words still rung in her ears,

... I am the decider of my fate....

"Here's to not killing each other," Tsuran said with a smile.

Despite herself, she snorted and smirked.

"So you can smile," he said. "I will say, it's a little weird seeing your face."

"Don't get used to it. It's just for the moment."

But she wasn't sure if that was true. Even as she spoke those words and clasped his arm, she had to fight down how pleasant it was to not hide her face. To not kill.

10

CRYSTAL CAVERNS

I have completed our contracts with the Oligarchs of Rajalend. You were right, they were all too eager to hire our ordîns as mercenaries and police. They even offered to pay more when they learned Veirzen employs our mercenaries as well. So, we shall fight both sides of this war and reap the benefits. I will be on my way back to Tifre shortly, though our next problem is to deal with Farhata of the Rising Coast. He has opposed our rule from the start and has a way of influencing the people. He is a dangerous enemy.

- Naresh the Soilshifter, in the 2950th Lunar Cycle

The guards unlocked the cell door and Tsuran opened it, glancing back at his cell-mate. "Alright, let's get going, fast."

The ordîn, Nasna, looked at him through her wrappings. "You seem eager today."

"As eager as beast mold. Come on."

He left the cell and hurried down the tunnel to pick up their tools and meal for the day. The other prisoners were taking their time, which was fine by him. With the attempted murder yesterday, they'd all think Nasna was dead, so seeing her would cause a commotion. A deadly commotion. Best he and Nasna get down into the mines before anyone else.

Plus, best no one else learned where they were heading.

He grabbed a sack of tools and tossed it to Nasna. She stumbled back under the weight and her head snapped up to him. Her face probably had an intense glare right then. Next time, he'd just hand it to her. He straightened, glancing over her. A few tatzons were looking in their direction. They looked surprised. And not happily.

"Let's go."

He led Nasna down the levels, deeper than he'd brought her before. At each gallery, he hurried her to the next shaft and headed down. At the bottom of the fifth gallery, she headed off down a tunnel, but he rushed past her.

"Not yet, still going deeper."

"Deeper? Where are we going?"

Tsuran placed a finger on his lips and made a slight head nudge toward a group of prisoners entering the gallery.

"I'll say when they can't hear us."

She huffed but headed into the next shaft. Tsuran eyed the other tatzons a moment. They didn't seem to notice him so he followed her.

They descended another two levels. The air grew warmer and staler with each step. The galleries also shrank, though most remained substantial. At the bottom of one shaft, Nasna grabbed his arm and turned him toward her.

"We're seven levels deep now," she said. "Isn't this dangerous? I thought the mines become more unstable down here?"

Tsuran nodded. "I know, but the reward is worth any risk. You'll see. Just one more level to go."

Nasna stepped in close to him, her voice lowered. "I'm not taking another step unless you tell me where we're going."

Tsuran sighed and glanced around. No other prisoner had come to this level yet, though some would soon. He'd learned not to trust the darkness.

"We're going to the key to our problem," he said, leaning down. "All I'm saying until we're there. Just... trust me."

Nasna crossed her arms and looked at him. With her face covered in her wrappings, he couldn't tell what the ordîn was thinking, but she didn't object anymore. Tsuran took this as meaning she'd attempt some trust.

Not that he didn't understand her trepidation. Cave-ins were more likely to occur the deeper they journeyed, and they just had their own harrowing experience with one yesterday. Wariness was fresh in his mind too. But if they were to succeed in what they needed to do, and if he was to succeed in his plan, there was only one place they could go. Besides, with her Tsuran stood closer to his goal than ever before. If he had to face a few more cave-ins to achieve his aim, he'd pay such a small price.

They descended the next shaft, entering the eighth gallery whereupon Tsuran led Nasna to the furthest end and into a narrow tunnel. The tunnels this deep were only wide enough for them to walk side by side. But the ceiling remained a few feet above Tsuran's head, meaning they meandered down the winding path without difficulty. It'd been years since he'd last been in this tunnel, but it was unmistakably the correct one. The air stirred with a chillness and vitality he didn't experience elsewhere in the mines. He took in a deep, fresh breath.

"We're almost there."

They turned a corner, and the tunnel straightened. Nasna stopped. "What... what is that?"

The tunnel narrowed to a point where only one could proceed at a time, to an end with light shining in.

Tsuran smiled. "Our key to freedom."

He pressed himself through the narrowed passage, the chill building in the air, and the fresh delight building in his lungs. The tunnel ended, and he stepped out into the massive cavern filled with crystal. Various kinds of crystal deposits covered the walls and ceiling. lightstone dominated, though there was also blue, green, and even some red-crystal throughout. They stood on a path branching in two directions. One path followed a wall deeper into the cavern, going far beyond their sight. The other led to a wide-open space with a high concentration of crystal forming on the walls and floor. In the middle of the cavern, separating the two paths, sat a clear lake that reflected the light of the crystals.

"What is this place?" Nasna asked.

"I've always called it the Crystal Cavern. Not imaginative, but it works. A group of prisoners discovered it a hundred years ago, though only two lived long enough to tell anyone else. My old cell-mate had been one of the lucky few told and by the time I came here, he was the last one aware of the place."

Nasna turned and looked at him, her wrappings still covering her face. "Does this cavern lead to the Lightless area?"

He shook his head. "No, that's not why we're here. But it can help us get there."

"How?"

"You see over there?" He pointed to the area of dense crystal. "Over there is a deposit of yellow-crystal, a rare crystal with a high price point."

Nasna crossed her arms. "So, now you want to mine?"

Tsuran grinned. "A little."

"I know the value of yellow-crystal, but how's it help us here?"

"Because of how the Warden runs this prison. He wants to motivate prisoners to bring him crystal, so he allows them to purchase 'privileges' with any crystal they find. People buy clothes, food, more equipment, things like that. But with yellow-crystal"—Tsuran's grin broke into a wide smile—"we can buy our way onto the furnace team."

Nasna placed a hand under her chin and nodded. "Furnace team? Yes, that'd be good. We'd be out of the mines, able to attain better intel, even find a way to the Lightless entrance... this might work."

She walked further into the cavern, her head bobbing around as though she tried to take in every inch of information. Tsuran leaned against the wall, watching her. Sure, he'd been with her since she'd arrived, but now she was like a different person. Well, probably because she was. She was an ordîn and not a human, and that was just the start. He didn't know how long this team-up would have to last, but it wouldn't be boring, at least.

He looked at her wingless back, and a hand drifted to his armless shoulder. A clipped ordîn. There was a story there. Perhaps someday she'd tell him, but if she was anything like him he'd never hear it. He dropped his hand. No need to hurry to find out. With all the work to do in this cavern and the furnace team, they'd have plenty of time to get to that if they ever did. Well, that was if she didn't change her mind and kill him outright. Not the worst of options, but not so soon. Best he got on her good side and stayed there.

"Hey," he said and Nasna turned toward him. "No one else ever comes to this cavern, so we'll be safe from other prisoners here. No one else will know what we're doing or about your secret while we're here."

"Good." She nodded and turned away. Not the reaction he'd been hoping for. Seemed being indirect with her wouldn't work. Tsuran cleared his throat. She turned back. "Yes?"

Tsuran rubbed the back of his neck. "I was trying to say you don't have to wear those wrappings here. I mean, if you don't want to."

She didn't move. She stared toward him, her expression hidden.

"Why do you want me to take off my wrappings?"

"I didn't say you had to. Just can't imagine it's comfortable to wear. I was just offering."

"Why do you care if I'm comfortable or not?"

Tsuran fought the urge to roll his eyes. Why would he care if she was comfortable? He'd already seen her face, it wasn't as if he were trying to trick her into revealing it. It was just a nice sentiment, a consideration.

She stared at him for a long time—damn ordîns and their excessive deliberation times— and then reached for her wrappings. She stopped midway.

"How long do you think we'll be in this cavern?"

"Days. Weeks. It depends."

She kept her hands in midair. It didn't look like she would move and Tsuran feared he'd have to wait a half hour or more before she decided what to do. But after less than a minute, she moved.

Whatever war she waged in her mind, one side won and she took the wrappings off. Besides the crimson red skin and short white hair, her face wasn't what he expected. No stern expression, hollow cheeks, or even furrowed brows. No marring, affiliation tattoos, or broken nose. She looked nothing like what an assassin should look like. She looked like... well, a normal person.

Her eyes, though, gave him pause. One was a light gray, typical for an ordîn, but the other was split top to bottom with one half being dark blue and the other a deep green. Now that was something he'd never seen. Though maybe it was a common ordîn trait, and he'd just never noticed before. But if it was, why? They already had their color-changing skin, did ordîn need more color in their—

Those split colored eyes met his.

"Should I put these back on?" she asked and Tsuran averted his eyes. He must've been staring.

"Sorry, I've never seen eyes like yours before."

"It's a family trait. It signifies my lineage."

"What lineage is that?"

She paused and, for a flash of a moment, she looked sad. She cleared her throat and took off the wrappings from her arms. "I don't know the lineage. I left my homeland before anyone told me."

"You're taking them all off?" he said, looking at her arms. Time to change the subject.

"I haven't been able to examine my arms since yesterday."

Tsuran waited for her to elaborate, but she didn't. However, he didn't need her to. She took off the wrappings and revealed arms with cuts running up and down them as though someone had taken a knife and sliced her open.

"What happened to you?" he asked, taking a step closer to look at them.

"This is the price I paid to not die yesterday."

He glanced up at her and back at her arms. This must've come from whatever she'd done to clear the cave-in.

"Will you be alright?"

She nodded. "It'll hurt for a while. I hadn't taken in... well, I'm not as injured as I might have been."

"If you say so."

Nasna folded her wrappings into small squares and laid them near the entranceway. "I can't do any heavy lifting until these heal more"—her gaze darted between him and the heavy sack of tools he'd thrown at her earlier—"but I'll do my part. Where's the yellow-crystal?"

"This way."

They took the path toward the high concentration of crystal Tsuran scanning the room as they walked. There was one problem with the place he hadn't mentioned to her yet, but he'd be sure to before they left. For the time being, he didn't see any of those complications. A stroke of luck.

"Is the water safe to drink?" Nasna asked.

"It was the last time I was here."

She looked up. "When was that?"

"Something like a year ago. I got yellow-crystal from here to buy my way onto the hunting team back then."

"Ah, so that's how you know this will work."

He nodded. "I do wish we could get onto the hunting team, though. I miss taking down a beast."

"As soon as we're done with my task, you'll be hunting beasts to your heart's content."

Something in her voice made him glance over at her. Now able to see her face, what he found surprised him. Her eyes were downcast and her lips formed a slight frown. Even her steps slowed for a moment before she caught his gaze and straightened her back and face.

He shouldn't pry. It'd be best to let it drop.

But he couldn't help himself.

"So, tell me more about this assassination of yours. What'd they do?"

Nasna stopped in her tracks, but her gaze remained fixed on the crystal in front of them.

"No need for you to know any of that."

"Why not?"

She turned to him. "Because it's not your contract."

"But I'm helping you with it."

"Doesn't mean you need to know anything about my work."

Tsuran grinned. "Would knowing mean you'd have to kill me or something?"

Her fists clenched, her jaw tightened, but this tension didn't reach her eyes. She almost looked to be on the verge of tears. She looked away from him.

"Maybe," she said. Tsuran's grin faded. That wasn't a threat. It was something else. Resignation, perhaps. This couldn't be helping his position with her, so he needed to just shut his mouth for the time being.

But his mouth kept moving.

"So, why did you keep me alive? It looked like you'd kill me, so why didn't you?"

Nasna's body tensed. Possibly stopped breathing too. She swallowed. "I can change my mind if you don't enjoy living."

"I thought ordîns didn't do that? 'A decision made is a decision followed' or something?"

Her eyes closed, and she took in slow breaths. "My Path decided you were worth more to me alive than dead. That's all."

She marched forward and Tsuran frowned. "Right. Your Path. Of course. Makes sense. Though I have one follow-up question: what does that mean?"

Nasna glanced over her shoulder but didn't stop. "What?"

"Your Path. What is that, your assassin code?"

"Oh. No, nothing like that." She walked on, no longer looking at him. Though, this only intrigued him more and he hurried up beside her, giving the most expectant look he could muster. After a moment, she spoke, though tentatively. "When an ordîn dies, their soul does not leave into a world beyond. Their soul travels throughout the heavens until they find an ordîn child to live in. This child becomes their host and they intertwine themselves with the child's soul. It's their job, their duty, to guide and direct this child in how to live and act. Thus my people called these wayward souls 'Paths'."

"Sorry, stop. What?" Tsuran had heard strange things, unbelievable things, throughout his life. This was... well, it wasn't the most unbelievable thing out there, but given how little ordîns shared about themselves, this was among the least expected. "You're telling me that your kids get possessed?"

"No, no. It's not possession." Nasna pursed her lips. "It's like you have a distant relative coming to stay with you. They live in your home and can talk to you and share stories and wisdom. But it's still your home and you decide how to decorate or what to eat."

"So, you have a dead ordîn living in you, but they don't control you?"

She slowed, her eyes dropping. "For most. Things are... more complicated when you're clipped." Her voice shuddered at her next words, "Some relatives are more demanding than others."

She walked toward the crystal again, faster this time, and Tsuran didn't press any further. The crystal deposits on the ground came up to Tsuran's knees, begging for someone to harvest them. But he was after the bigger prize and led Nasna around the crystal to the wall where the vein of yellow-crystal broke through the stone.

True to its name, this crystal was a deep yellow color, but unlike most other crystal it was opaque. It emitted little light, so no one used it like lightstone. However, it was the most durable of all the crystals, only red-crystal had any chance of even cracking it. It remained the only crystal able to cut through any spirit or take the full brunt of a Colossal beast attack again and again without strain. It had once saved his life while defending a village in Rajalend. Now, it would save him from the mines for a second time.

Nasna went to the stone and examined it. "How much is here?"

"Hard to say, but I'd imagine a lot. At least enough for the two of us."

"How do you expect us to break it, though? It's yellow-crystal."

He gestured back to the entranceway. "Near the exit, I've hidden a gad I used last time. The tip is made of red-crystal. It'll take a couple of precise strikes, but it'll do the job."

She cocked a brow, turning to him. "Where'd you get that?"

"From my old cell-mate. No idea where he got it though. Stolen or handed down from someone who stole it."

She let out a breath and nodded. "Well, if that's the case, let's get started."

The cavern echoed with a moan and the two froze. The moan grew louder and a few more joined. Tsuran turned around. Several spirits moved out of the walls from the other side of the lake and headed toward the two of them.

"This could be a bad time to bring this up," Tsuran said. "But the main reason most don't know about this cavern is because of spirits being here."

He looked over his shoulder. Nasna glared at him.

"And," he said, "spirits are attracted to crystal and quite protective of it."

"Stop talking, they're getting closer."

"Here." Tsuran handed her the gad he'd held onto. "Hold this between you and them as we walk back to the entrance. Walk slowly."

The two walked back as the spirits crowded the area with the yellow-crystal. A few stared at Tsuran and Nasna, and for a moment Tsuran worried he'd have to sing, but the spirits let them go.

"We'll be safe near the entranceway," he said. "That wall is heavy with iron so they stay away from there."

"Why wasn't this the first thing you mentioned?"

Tsuran shrugged. They were far enough for him to turn his back on the spirits, so he turned toward the entranceway. "It wouldn't have changed anything. It's a minor detail."

They reached the entranceway, and both leaned against the wall.

"That's not a minor detail," she said. "That's a big problem."

"We'll figure something out." He gave her a grin. "We're a team now. Right?"

She glanced at him and then looked back toward the spirits. "Right. A team."

11

MINING AWAY

C *hange is difficult for me, Naresh, you know this. Change is hard for*
an ordîn in my cycle, and yet I change most unexpectedly. I fear
saying much to you other than this: I have someone who is dear to me.
And were we back in Oushwala, were we still true Luminars, I would die
for this forbidden desire. But the Luminous have already abandoned us,
and if I am already to dissolve in the four vortexes of hell, then why should
I deny a moment of happiness? She helps me forget and even dream.
- Yavahush the Stargazer, in the 2951st Lunar Cycle

Six Common spirits and two Smalls roamed the cavern. Some on
the ground, a few in the air. All in Nasna's way.

The spirits stayed close to the crystal and away from the iron,
so she surveyed the situation without them bothering her. She
sat at the water's edge close to the cavern's entrance and studied
the spirits. She watched their habits, their patterns, looked for
anything that would be useful. The spirits came and went, being
replaced by a different spirit every so often. They'd leave by either
floating up through the ceiling or by drifting deeper into the cavern
and out of view. The number fluctuated, their sizes moved between
Small and Common, but there was always at least three spirits
right next to the yellow-crystal.

They needed a method to keep the spirits back. Nasna had one idea, but there wasn't any guarantee it'd work. With nothing else to try, she and Tsuran returned to the main gallery and collected various mining equipment. Gads, hammers, a pick or two, whatever iron they could get their hands on. She pilfered from other prisoners, and he tried seeing if the guards would give him some. After a few days, Nasna had gathered a sizeable pile and Tsuran had gotten a sack. So, for the rest of the week, she worked on gathering more iron and he hung back, never close enough to draw attention to her, but close enough Solitude didn't settle in.

At the end of the week, a few prisoners grumbled about missing tools, and rumors about thieves started soon after, so she stopped. They had a fair amount, anyway. The two moved the stolen goods down to the cavern during the night, avoiding all unwanted stares and questions.

The next day, they were ready to act.

As soon as they entered the cavern, she went to the pile of iron tools and gathered some into her arms. "Alright, let's see if this works."

"Well, even if it doesn't, we got a pretty collection building now."

"Just grab some tools."

They walked along the path to the spirits and the crystal. The spirits glanced over. She and Tsuran stopped. The spirits didn't look away, but also didn't attack. Nasna took a few steps forward. Still no movement from the spirits.

"Is it working?" she asked. "Spirits are aggressive, right?"

"I mean, not really. The only times I've ever seen them go into any kind of frenzy is when there's a beast nearby or if there's harm done to a crystal."

They took a few more steps. One Small looked away and crawled through the wall. Nasna let out a breath and strode forward. The two came close to the crystal, and the spirits nearest them all moved away. They came closer to the yellow-crystal, yet the spirits kept moving back. Using all the stolen goods, the two created a tight circle around the yellow-crystal deposit, keeping only a set of tools for mining. And they waited and watched. Spirits came and went, changing in size and the number present, but all now avoided this circle of iron. Tsuran let out a sigh.

"I can't believe that worked."

"Will this hold?"

He shrugged. "I've never tried this before. But I imagine if they're avoiding it now they'll avoid it as long as nothing changes."

"Until we mine the yellow-crystal you mean."

He nodded. "We're not in the clear. They're still watching us. Like they're waiting to see what we'll do."

A shiver ran down Nasna's spine. The spirits seemed to keep their gaze fixed on the two of them. One disappeared through the ceiling, but its eyes were the last part to float through. One spirit, a Common looking to be half the size of a Large, came near, though it did not proceed past the iron. It stood perhaps ten feet away from the pair and Nasna stood straight, determined that her knees wouldn't buckle.

"Is it safe enough to try mining?" she asked.

"Third rule," he snorted. "As long as we're in this cavern, 'safe' is not a word we get to use."

"But we can mine?"

Tsuran sucked in a breath and looked over the yellow-crystal. "Well, there's not enough exposed for us to take it right now. This much would buy one spot for us, but not two. We must uncover more of it first before we go for the crystal."

"Will that put them in a frenzy?"

Tsuran furrowed his brow as he gazed back at the surrounding spirits. "I think... I think as long as we don't strike the crystal we should be fine. From what I've seen, they don't care about rock and stone, only the crystal." He groaned and shook his head. "Abyssal's tail, this will take forever. We need to be careful with where we strike and with how much force and all that."

"It can't be helped," Nasna said picking up her tools. "We have to get this crystal."

"I know, but"—he looked over his shoulder—"I don't like that one just staring at us."

She eyed the larger Common. "Think it'll come over the iron?"

"No, I just don't like its eyes. They look so sad and doe-like. As if I'm its disappointing son who brought ruin to the family."

Nasna cocked her head to the side. "What?"

He shot a grin at her. "Just trying to lighten the mood. What with death literally standing and floating feet away from us."

Nasna suppressed a smile and rolled her eyes. "Let's just work."

As Tsuran said, the work was slow. They took turns working on the stone while the other would rest and keep their tools ready for any floaters that might drift from above. Nasna was glad he was right about the spirits not caring about rock. Though, he was also right in that if they struck too hard or too deep, they might hit the crystal. Then it'd be over. This made the work slow. When they'd finished their day, they'd only finished a small part of their task. Nasna worried about leaving their work unfinished, afraid the spirits would somehow overcome the iron if they left the circle for a night. Tsuran smirked.

"The iron keeps them out, not us. I doubt they care if we're here our not."

Nasna resigned, and they left for the main gallery, tired but hopeful. When they returned in the morning, everything was as they'd left it, with the spirits still outside the iron circle. Their plan might work. So, they returned to their work heedless to the number of spirits in the cavern with no more trepidation or hesitation. They now had a small haven amongst the deadly forces watching them day after day. Their progress remained slow, forcing them to return for several days, though Nasna stopped caring to keep track. Time became irrelevant in these caverns of rock with no sun or moons. There were no days, nor any half or full-nights. Here inside this crystal cavern, she let go of weeks and months. It didn't matter if they'd been mining in this place for a few days or a few weeks. It only mattered that they were here doing the work.

The two talked occasionally, though finding ongoing subjects of discussion was awkward for her. She'd never needed to chat this much on a mission and she wasn't sure if she enjoyed it or not. But she found Tsuran open to many of her questions, though she never probed too deep. This was the first time she spent extensive time with a tatzon, so she asked something that never made sense to her.

"For tatzons, each of your arms gives you certain powers. An arm to mind-possess, a different one to body-possess. But I read once that you needed to practice the next layer of power in order to grow an arm for that layer."

Tsuran nodded. "You read right."

"How can you practice a layer of power you don't have an arm for?"

"Every arm grants you access to the next layer in order to practice. It's painful to do at first, but once you've finished growing your arm for it, that layer is as easy as the rest."

"Have you practiced your next layer?"

"Next for me is total-control. I... I don't know many people who've even figured out how to do it. Maybe I will one day. When the time is right."

They continued in this manner, small talk that stayed away from anything too personal. When she didn't mine, she watched the spirits while going through her string figure sequences. Spirits weren't as common in Rajalend as in the north toward her homeland, but even then they'd been something she'd avoided. She'd never been this close to any nor spent this much time being able to watch them. It was an opportunity she didn't want to waste and so studied them as best she could.

Though their size changed with every new batch of spirits, most were in the Common-sized range, anywhere from fifteen to twenty feet in height alone. The largest she'd seen remained to be the doe-eyed spirit from their first day, well over twenty-five feet, perhaps even nearing a Large size. It also never left the cavern, always sitting close to the iron circle with its gaze set on the two. Time to time a Small, which stood eye to eye with Tsuran, would come near, but the iron had a stronger affect on the smaller ones.

Nasna kept a watch out for any Larges entering the cavern. If one came, their meager iron would hold no protection for them.

When she looked beyond their size, the sheer variety of the spirits exceeded what she'd seen with beasts. Some floated, some crawled, some walked, and others flew with arms like wings. A few spirits looked to be nothing but a ball of limbs while others had a strong resemblance to beasts, though they remained hairless and smooth. The only constant was the blue, semi-translucent bodies that glowed and shimmered. And, they all shared the same white eyes, which gazed at Nasna and Tsuran. Yet, after a cycle of time, those white glows no longer seemed like those of hungry monsters bent on destruction. She didn't drop her guard, not for a moment. But there were a few she smiled at. Surely her Path wouldn't care if she smiled at a spirit.

But at one point, while she watched the spirits, Nasna sat up. She blinked as Tsuran's hammer strike echoed through the cavern.

"Tsuran, stop for a moment."

He paused and turned toward her. "What is it? Are they moving?"

"No, listen." She craned her head to the side and closed her eyes. The last of the pick's echoes died away, and she heard it again. A subtle, quiet song hummed in the cavern.

"Do you hear that?" she whispered and glanced at Tsuran. His jaw clenched and his shoulders tensed. His gaze turned back toward the surrounding spirits.

"Yeah. I do."

"Do you know what that is?"

He stiffened and moved from the wall. "I think I'm ready for a lunch break."

He put down his tools and pulled out their food and drink, handing over some to Nasna. She huffed but took it as he sat next to her. Not looking away from him, she bit into her food. He looked straight ahead. He was not going to say anything.

Nasna crossed her arms and tried giving him her best stern expression. There was no way he was getting away with this one. He looked over at her and his eyes widened before he laughed. Heat rose in her cheeks and she leaned forward, but he raised his hands.

"Alright, fine, yeah I know what it is." He gazed back out at the spirits, his smile fading. "It's the spirits talking to each other."

Nasna's brows raised. "They talk with each other?"

"Yeah."

Nasna looked back at the spirits. None had what looked like mouths and she couldn't see anything inside their translucent bodies that could create sound. This song, this speech apparently, was unlike anything she'd listened to before. The more she focused, the more the wordless song grew in her ears. It was so melodic, so calm, so lovely. The longer she listened, the easier it became to hear it. If she listened long enough, maybe words would form and then one day she'd understand it. She'd understand the spirits, perceiving what they say and what they desire. She'd be unlike any other ordîn, the first to communicate with the spirits and perhaps one day to even befriend them. By knowing the song, by befriending the spirits, she would learn their secrets and know their power. Throughout the world, none would withstand her. All the world would become formed to her balance, to her order. She'd be the greatest ever known and her Path would be—

Tsuran clapped next to Nasna's ears, and the sound echoed throughout the cavern and through her head. None of the spirits reacted, but Nasna glared at Tsuran as she rubbed her ear.

"What was that for?"

He took a drink and leaned against the rock behind them. "Don't pay attention to their song. Don't let it into your head. It... changes you. Puts ideas into your head that seem so natural, but are a trap."

Nasna squinted at him, but then her heart raced. Was that what just happened to her? She'd never before cared to speak to spirits or befriend them. Standing up to the world was not in her plans, and yet just moments ago it had seemed like the greatest truth. Her eyes widened as she stared at the spirits.

"What was that? What happened to me?"

Tsuran let out a sigh. "I don't know how it works. But I know their songs have power in them... the power to change things. Try not to listen to them."

"Why didn't you warn me before?"

"Didn't know if you'd hear them. Not everyone pays close enough attention to do so."

"Do you hear them?"

He paused, and there was a change in his eyes. It looked like pain, or perhaps anger. He looked away so she couldn't decide.

"I can. But I shut it out."

About a dozen spirits moved around the cavern with fluid movements, seeming to wander aimlessly and yet with some communicated purpose between them. Light from the crystals reflected through them if one meandered close to them. Or rather, the light seemed to fill them since when they drifted away from the walls, soft streams of light trailed behind, connecting them to the crystal. And this borrowed light enhanced their natural glow, either making it brighter or by giving it a hint of red or green. It only lasted a moment before they returned to their original ethereal selves.

As Nasna watched, the song remained in the air, ready to fill her ears and mind with its deceptive melody. But Tsuran was right. As long as she didn't focus on it too much, shutting it out was a simple task.

These creatures. For so long she just thought of them as a different beast type. But they were something else entirely.

"It's strange, you know," she said. "When you look at them, spirits are fascinating and beautiful creatures."

Tsuran leaned forward to look her in the eyes. "You're not listening to the song, are you?"

She shook her head. "No, I'm just saying. They look elegant."

He shrugged. She looked back at the doe-eyed Common in front of them. It had a long serpentine body with two long arms coming out its... neck? Hard to say since it had little of a head. Only a face forever set toward Nasna.

"It's just so strange how something so beautiful and calm can be a source of such chaotic destruction."

She sighed and took a drink of water. Out of the corner of her view, Tsuran had the beginnings of a smile.

"What?" she asked.

"You're..." He shook his head and stood up.

She stood as well and crossed her arms. "I'm what? If you have something to say, say it."

Tsuran grinned at her. "You're just different, is all. Didn't expect such a pretty statement from an assassin."

Nasna hesitated and her Path whispered to her. It was time to return to work and leave their too-comfortable chat.

She pushed past him and picked up her tools. "I'll work for a time."

"Fine with me. Just remember to ignore the spirits."

That wouldn't be a problem. Now that she learned of the song, ignoring it would be easy. He was the real problem. He couldn't be ignored, but he needed to be. Her Path stirred inside her. He was alive because he was useful. If he became more of a hindrance, then he'd have to go.

For his sake, for her own, she shoved the song and him from her mind. Especially him.

12

DANGERS OF SPIRITS

W orry not, my dearest Starlight, I will not be gone for much longer. Naresh and the others have almost all the tribes under the name of Tifre, only a few resist. Soon, Naresh will sit upon an ordîn throne and rule as queen, and when that occurs she won't require my help any longer. I'll be free to come to you and protect you. I have also heard the same rumors you have, but I will not let her find you or hurt you. Only a few more months and we can go where no one can find us and we can be together.

- Your Yava, in the 2952nd Lunar Cycle

When something becomes familiar enough, it takes on its own form of invisibility. It is mundane, and so the eyes gloss over it without even noticing. Nasna had experienced this throughout her life, but it amazed her when she realized this was happening with a cavern filled with more wealth than all of the Dragon's Maw, and with the spirits that inhabited it.

As she and Tsuran continued working on their task, this Crystal Cavern became more and more what was normal, what was familiar, and the rest of the prison was strange and unknown.

She tried her best to ignore Tsuran, to keep him at an arms length away, but as their time passed in the cavern, talks picked up again. At first, it was only about their work, about where to break rock, and what to leave intact. It changed to topics about the crystal around them and the kinds of crystal either had seen in their lives and in the ways they've seen it used. This led to talks about Rajalend and some inconsequential memories about it. The topics always revolved around the areas they'd been too and never on themselves. Yet, after both laughed over a story Nasna had been telling, her Path had her shut down all the conversation once again. Her throat closed up, and she stopped talking mid-story. Tsuran prodded for her to finish, but she turned away and said nothing more. They spent the rest of the time in total silence. This silence continued, her Path forcing her mouth shut.

She understood her Path's reasoning, but sometimes she just wished it'd let her laugh, if only for a little time. This wish came from her weakness, and her Path could not shut that out. For now.

During one of their days of silence, a loud crack echoed around the cavern and Nasna turned to Tsuran who'd been working on the stone. He froze, his gaze set on where he hammered. Nasna's eyes darted to the spirits. None moved. Her Path loosened her tongue, and she turned back to him.

"Tsuran?"

"I think," he said, looking at her, "I think we're ready."

She paused. They were ready? She rushed over to the yellow-crystal. He was right. There was enough uncovered now for both of them. With this, she'd take one more step toward her target. Toward the end of Valerija and the end of Red Dawn.

"Now comes the hard part." He glanced at the surrounding spirits. Nasna looked too. "As soon as we strike the crystal, we'll be in trouble."

"So we must be fast. We'll both strike together, break the crystal off, and run faster than any of them."

Tsuran rubbed his forehead. "I don't know. There's more spirits today than usual. We should wait until—"

"We're not waiting." Nasna picked up her hammer and positioned herself beside Tsuran. "We've come too close to wait any longer. We're doing this and we're getting out of these mines."

Tsuran pursed his lips, looking between Nasna and the yellow-crystal. He stared at the ceiling and let out a heavy sigh. "If you kill us, I'll never forgive you."

Nasna couldn't help but smile. "I'll keep that in mind. Ready?"

Tsuran brought up his crystal gad. "For spirits to gruesomely kill me? Always."

He placed the gad onto the thinnest neck of the crystal and she looked back at the spirits. They didn't react. The tall, doe-eyed Common remained close, well within striking distance. That would be the one to attack first.

"We'll need three or four good swings to crack through," he said. "Then hit hard and fast."

Tsuran nodded. Nasna's heart thudded in her chest and her mouth dried. This was it.

She took in a breath and raised her hammer.

Sweat trickled down her temple. She evened her breathing.

In rapid succession, they struck.

The spirits screeched.

The piercing cry erupted throughout the cavern, coming in from all directions. It drowned out the strike of the hammer and the crack of the crystal. Some spirits changed into grotesque shapes while others had fire or lightning crackle around them. The serene beauty they had a moment ago disappeared in an instant. But though cracked, the crystal had not broken off. She raised her hammer again. Tsuran yelled and shoved her away into the wall. The doe-eyed Common's clawed arm cut into the stone wall and another clawed through the ground, breaking the circle of iron.

"Nasna, run!"

He pulled her to her feet. She cursed, and they both ran. There was no way of getting to the yellow-crystal now. There was only escaping and living.

Flame and lightning struck the wall and water on either side of them, sending sprays of water and stone against them. Nasna looked over her shoulder. A dozen spirits charged toward them. And they were fast.

One spirit burst through the water, another careened overhead bursting with falling flames. Fire shot toward them. Nasna dove away from the flames, but the heat followed. She and Tsuran weren't fast enough. They weren't even half-way to the entrance tunnel. The spirits were at their heels.

A bolt of lightning struck the ground underneath her and threw her into the wall, air stolen from her lungs. Her ears rang, but she picked herself up. Another claw heaved the stone floor underneath her and she flew again.

Her vision blurred and she smacked against stone. There was only a blue glow around her. Something warm and wet dripped down her cheek. Nasna pushed herself to her feet. No sign of Tsuran. Only spirits.

Fire and lightning soared toward her. She dove. Rock and stone shattered and exploded around her. She rose to her feet as spirits surrounded her and blocked her path to the tunnel. Nasna took in the area before her, looking for a way out.

The walls. They had blue-crystal. Less common than lightstone and also possessing less energy, but that was fine.

She placed a hand on the crystal and drew the energy into her. To her surprise, the spirits reacted with another high-pitched screech. They dove toward her. She turned, channeling all the energy into one arm, and punched toward them, unleashing the pent up power. The force pushed her against the wall but had a greater impact on the spirits. The nearest ones, mere feet from her, burst apart while the force threw the further ones back. This did not deter them and they rushed toward her. Nasna drew in energy and released it again, gaining similar results. She halved the number of spirits present, though her arm hurt and a part of it split and bled.

She rushed past them and back to the path. A dozen screeches followed her. She glanced back. More spirits entered the cavern. Spirit after spirit passed through the far wall nearest the crystal, and there didn't appear to be an end to them.

She turned back to the entrance and ran. The blue glow behind her intensified as the many spirits flooded the cavern after her. She just needed to make it to the tunnel. The iron in those walls would protect her. Still no sign of Tsuran, though.

The crystal veins diminished. No more energy for her to fight with. Only sprinting now.

The walls and floor around her burst, but she pressed through, trying to ignore the flame. Just a little farther. She neared the entrance.

A tremendous power gripped her body. Air left her chest and blood spurted from her mouth. She glanced down and her body became like ice. A spirit had grabbed her.

It was strange. For being called "spirits", Nasna had always imagined that they were always intangible beings, always phasing through the material world without substance. Yes, the stories always said differently, but it was another thing to be held in the hand of this monster. Whatever these creatures were, they felt very corporeal right now.

It was the doe-eyed Common, and its eyes were now like fire. It squeezed. Nasna cried out, or at least tried to, but no air escaped her. Pain broke through her as the grip crushed her. She struggled against it, but it was so tight she felt as though her limbs would burst off, much like what energy tried to do inside her.

Wait, energy. This was a spirit, it had energy too!

She thrust her hands onto the spirit, which felt like thrusting into soft mud as her hand went inside the spirit. Nasna ignored the strange physical sensation and focused. There was energy. Strong, and yet so similar to all other energies. Still a coursing river. She had thought it'd be different, but right now was no time to be contemplative. She just needed to live.

She grabbed onto the energy, a large amount too, and erupted it. The spirit burst in a spray of... glowing blood or some ethereal ooze, and the eruption flung Nasna into the nearest wall. She hit hard and slumped to the ground, taking in haggard breaths. It was difficult to move. The spirit almost broke her leg. Good thing being clipped didn't take her strong bones away. She pushed herself up, only to collapse onto the ground. Rock fell behind her. She pounded her fist onto the ground and tried pushing herself up. She had to move, had to get out of there. Other Commons headed her way. Her leg gave way, and she fell against the wall. There wasn't crystal near her and the other spirits would kill her before she touched their energy. But she couldn't die here. She couldn't leave her work unfinished.

The spirits surrounded her. Flames and lighting coursed between them. There was no way out.

I'm sorry, Clear Sky.

She closed her eyes and waited for the end to come.

But the spirits didn't strike.

She peeked through her eyelids. The spirits were around her, still grotesque and misshapen. She opened her eyes and looked around, though her vision remained blurry and unclear. The intensity of their white eyes dimmed and their bodies morphed back into their normal shapes. The fires and lightning dissipated, and the cavern quieted.

Except, not quite. There was something else in the air. A song. A wordless song, much like the spirits'. Yet, this wasn't the spirits'. And it grew louder and louder until it seemed to emanate from right beside her. She looked up, the haze in her vision lifted.

Tsuran stood next to her, his eyes on her. And he was singing.

He helped Nasna to her feet and semi-held her as they walked back to the entrance, all the while keeping his song going. The spirits swayed to the melody, almost as though they danced, and parted ways. None followed.

His song wasn't as easy to listen to as the spirit one was, but he didn't have an awful voice. But this song, it was different. It wasn't just spirits that had songs with power in them.

They passed unhindered to the exit, but it wasn't until they were in the tunnel that he stopped his song. He let go of her, and she fell against the wall, her leg throbbing.

He glared at her leg, grabbed her by the arm, and walked away. "Let's head back to the cell and get some rest."

"Hey, wait—"

"There's no point in staying here," he said, his voice hard. "They'll leave, but I saw more and more coming in. We can't get the crystal until they're gone. We'll check tomorrow. Come on."

Nasna eyed him. He didn't want to share his secret, did he? Fine. For now, she'd drop it. But that was one secret she wanted to know. Because it might be the key to getting back to the yellow-crystal.

13

SECRETS

C ounselor Yavahush the Stargazer, I regret to inform you in this way, but Queen Naresh the Soilshifter has been murdered along with all your kin from the north lands. I have only a couple reports from the few surviving guards, but their descriptions show the Shadow Strikers were involved, though we cannot be sure who hired them to carry this out. At this moment, the land of Tifre is in a fragile state and Farhata of the Rising Coast is already making motions to seize power. The Queen had orders that with her death, you were to take her place.

Her dream is in your hand, Tifre is in your hands, King Yavahush the Stargazer.

-Counselor Ordal of the Long Night, Loyal Servant to the dream of Tifre, in the 2953rd Lunar Cycle

Tsuran sighed. Even after three days, there were still too many spirits here. And several were closer to the tunnel entrance than he liked. He pushed himself back through the crevice and made his way into the tunnel where Nasna waited for him. She wore her wrappings since they were not in the cavern itself and, although this was how he'd met her, it looked strange.

"How's it look?" she asked.

He shook his head. "Just as many as there was yesterday. Some still hung around the entrance, so I wasn't able to get a good look, but I think they're the same spirits."

"I thought you said they would leave."

"I'm not an expert on their schedules. They might leave today or they might leave in a month. No way of telling."

Nasna groaned and leaned up against the wall.

"There's nothing we can do about it," he said. "We'll just have to keep checking in until we can go in again."

"Isn't there something you can do? We can't be wasting time like this."

"There are over twenty spirits and I don't even have a blue-crystal statue, let alone one that'd help. What do you expect me to do?"

She glanced up. "Can't you do that thing you did last time? That song?"

Tsuran straightened and looked away. "No. That wouldn't work."

"But why not? It worked great last—"

"It just wouldn't." His tone was harsher than he'd meant it to be, but he didn't intend to apologize. "For now, let's head somewhere else and do some mining or something. No point in staying here."

Nasna sighed but followed as Tsuran headed out of the tunnel. Waiting was the best option for them. If he had his red-crystal statue back, maybe he could take on that many Commons. But with just his little one? Not happening. And even though she'd taken on a big Common by herself, she had survived by luck alone. No, fighting all those spirits wasn't a possibility. They'd have to either wait or come up with another plan.

Neither spoke as they moved through the gallery and past other tatzons. No one else knew about the cavern and it was best to keep it that way. Not that they'd be able to steal the crystal from the spirits, but they could close off the cavern with a cave-in. Prisoners were petty like that.

The two ascended a level and headed down a random tunnel. Tsuran glanced behind him. No one seemed to watch or follow them. He nodded to Nasna, and they delved deeper into the dark passage.

Since the cave-in, they'd had no major run-ins with other prisoners, a much-welcomed reprieve. And Tsuran still had seen none of the tatzons he'd told the Warden about. Rumors circulated the prison, but since no one talked to either him or Nasna they didn't learn what the rumors were. But people left them alone, a fine enough answer as any.

The tunnel was quiet as they walked since no one mined in here. An empty tunnel, like so many others. Except, something itched in the back of his mind. This level. This side of the gallery. A quiet tunnel.

He smirked and shook his head as they turned a corner.

"Looks like we're back to where it began," he said. The passage ahead became almost blocked by fallen rock and boulders. Almost, except the large hole in the middle. Without having meant to, he had led them back to the cave-in that revealed her secret to him.

"What are we doing here?" she asked. "I don't think this is a good idea."

"I didn't plan this. Just happened. But it will be fine. Probably."

"Probably?"

"Yeah. I get we have poor memories here, but this tunnel is just as safe as any other tunnel we've been in. I doubt people will try killing us here a second time. They could kill us anywhere."

"I'm more worried about the stability of this place."

"It hasn't caved-in again since we were last here. But if you want to find a different tunnel, we can—"

"No. I'm sure it'll be fine." She started for the hole but stopped. "Just in case, though, let's stay on this side."

"Fine by me."

With the dust having settled long ago, it was easy to see how deep and thick the cave-in had been. Its width seemed to be more than twice his size. A smaller Common beast or spirit would fit nicely. He whistled as he peered through.

"Still can't believe you can do this," he said glancing over at her. "If you can do this kind of destruction, why not kill all the spirits down there?"

"Why don't you just sing to them?"

Tsuran clenched his jaw and looked ahead. Using the song had been a mistake. Relying on that power... it was as if he relied on Dazh, and he tried to move on from that thought.

"That's not how it works," he said.

"And neither does my power."

Keeping the hole in view, he dropped his equipment to the side and massaged his arms as he leaned against the wall. Nasna sat opposite of him and took off her head wrapping. She then pulled out her strings to do her... she called them string fingers or something. He watched her hands weave through unique designs, her face a show of deep thought.

"So, master assassin, what's the plan?"

She didn't answer. He waited a few moments. Still no answer. He tapped his fingers along the wall, trying to find a rhythm, but that didn't ease the itchiness in him. So, he took slow steps around the tunnel. And she still didn't even look up at him.

He sighed and reached into his secret pocket and pulled out his little stone statue. His thumb ran along the familiar grooves, the smoothness of the touch taking him away from Nasna and their current situation. The statue was small, fitting in the palm of his hand, and he kept it in a upright standing position. It had four arms, which he had shaped himself after receiving it. But the face, the face he never shaped or changed. The carving was crude, but he never even thought of changing that.

Nasna shuffled in her place. "Are there any other areas where we can get some yellow-crystal?"

He scratched his chin. "Not off the top of my head. I mean, I'm sure there are plenty of places where there's yellow-crystal deposits throughout the mountain. But I'm unaware of any current tunnels reaching them or how we would find them. Not aware of rumors about any being discovered, either."

She nodded, continuing with her string. "I feared that. And are you sure we have to get yellow-crystal? We can't get any other crystal?"

"Not if we want to get on the furnace team. Not with... well, not with how much I owe the Warden."

"So, for us to buy our way out of the mines, yellow-crystal is our only option." She thought for another moment, but she eventually looked up at him, though she kept her string thing going. "Then tell me about the statue."

"Statue?"

"Yes. You had a statue down here last time. Yet, I hadn't seen it until you possessed it and I haven't seen it since."

Tsuran sat down in front of her, showing her the stone figurine. "That would be this."

Her hands slowed and she cocked her head to the side. "I don't understand."

Since it was easier to show than explain, Tsuran winked at her and possessed the little statue. As it fell through the air, he empowered his possession, growing it until he was as large as Nasna. She kept her expression neutral, but he liked to imagine she was duly impressed. He shrank the statue back and unpossessed it, materializing in a squatting position.

Nasna picked up the figurine. "You can possess statues this small? I didn't know Guardians could do that."

"Most can't. Not sure how it is for other possessions, but with statues people start out only able to possess statues the same size as them and then they train to control larger and larger ones. I didn't do that. I went the other way. Never met a single other Guardian who has."

"I suppose in a war against Veirzen, small statues aren't as helpful."

"You'd be surprised." He took the figurine back and tucked it away.

"How big can you grow it?"

He shrugged. "About as big as you saw it now. Trying to grow much larger than that gets dangerous."

She frowned. "I guess that wouldn't be very useful against spirits then." He nodded in response and she picked up her string again, returning to her figures. "With that being the case, explain to me why you can't use the song from the other day." She pointed her gaze at him. "The effect you had on them was incredible and we need a trick like that."

Tsuran crossed his arms and looked away. "I already told you everything I plan to."

"That's not good enough. We have to get out of the mines and into the Lightless area. Our best chance is with yellow-crystal that's guarded by dozens of spirits who were all frozen by your song. So, tell me how it works, if you can empower it or anything. I can't make a plan without knowing everything we have."

Tsuran's hands tightened over his arms. He'd been a fool to reveal the song to her. A bigger fool to use it at all. He was sure that in whatever hell Dazh was in, he was laughing his head off.

But what was he supposed to do? Let them both die?

Tsuran did not glance at her. He kept his gaze fixed on the darkness of the tunnel outside of the range of the lightstone necklaces. His gaze followed the dark tunnel to the small lightstone vein that illuminated the cave-in hole. His muscles relaxed and his brows raised.

"So you want to learn the secrets to my song?"

She nodded. "We need to know everything we have."

"Well, how about a trade?" He turned his gaze toward her.

She cocked her head to the side. "Of what?"

"Information. I tell you the secret of my song, and you tell me how your power works."

Her body tightened, becoming rigid. Tsuran stared back and grinned. Either he wouldn't have to talk about Dazh's song or she'd explain her magic. He won either way. From her posture, it seemed she realized this too.

"Fine," she said. "We'll make a trade."

They stared at each other for a moment. She gestured at him.

"Well?" she asked. "Tell me about the song."

"Why do I have to go first?"

"Because this was your idea, and I asked first."

"And how do I know you'll tell me if I go first?"

"How do I know the same about you?"

"I'm not the one who has to wear a head wrapping."

She sighed and looked him in the eye. Or at least he guessed she did since her eyes hid behind the wrappings. "Tsuran Con-None, I promise I will tell you the truth about my power after you tell me about yours. No tricks, no lies. On my honor as an ordîn."

Tsuran paused. That was unexpected. An eye roll, sure. Maybe even exasperation or an annoyed threat or something. It'd been a joke, anyway. But she made a promise. She was serious about this. Which meant he'd have to be too.

"Alright, but understand no word of this goes out to anyone ever," he said.

"Likewise."

He nodded. "Alright, I didn't sing..." He hesitated. "Remember how I said the spirits communicate with each other through those songs of theirs? Well, we can do the same with them. We can talk to them using their language."

"Really?"

Tsuran shrugged. "Sort of. I'm not a Soulborn so I can't say how much of a chat we can have. But certain songs exist that can control spirits to an extent."

"How much can you control them? Is it like possession?"

His brows raised. She sounded intrigued and interested in this, more than just understanding a new tool she had. He smiled.

"No, nothing like possession at all. Remember when you listened to their song?"

She nodded. "Yeah, it was like new ideas were pouring into my mind. They seemed real, but now ridiculous."

"My song works in the same way, but for spirits. My... someone I once knew, a Soulborn, learned a lot of these songs, even taught me a few. The one I sang the other day calms spirits and tricks them into thinking you are one of them. But it's not perfect. I can only affect Smalls and Commons, nothing bigger." He wriggled his brows. "Guess my voice doesn't cut it for the Colossals of the world."

Nasna gave a subtle head shake with a most delightful rolling of the eyes. Which helped him talk about this. Somehow, sharing with her about this made the song less about Dazh. Not by much, mind you, but less.

"But why can't you use this song to clear the cavern?" she asked.

"If I could've, I would've. The song calms them, but doesn't tell them to leave. And remember how it was easier for you to ignore their songs when you had something else to focus on? Same with them. If we break off the crystal and run away with any, they'll ignore the song."

She leaned back against the wall, her hands weaving through her string with greater speed now. "Are you sure?"

He smirked. "Remember, this isn't my first time getting yellow-crystal. Trust me, once we get it, nothing will stop them from trying to kill us."

Nasna sighed.

"Do you have any other songs that might help?"

He shook his head. "Nothing for this situation. Again, not a Soulborn. This is the best I got."

"I guess it doesn't help us right now." She finished one of her figures and moved into a new one. There didn't seem to be any shape she didn't make with her simple string. And no matter how quick she weaved, her fingers never went where they weren't meant to. At least, if they did he couldn't tell.

He cleared his throat and she glanced up.

"What?"

"It's your turn."

"Oh, right."

She let out a quick breath, tucked her string away, and sat straight up, looking Tsuran dead in the eyes. His smile widened, and he folded his hands onto his lap. Finally, he'd understand what kind of power she had.

"How much do you know about ordîn magic?"

He shrugged. "There are two different types. You got the Exorcist who can banish a possessor from a possession, and you have the Sensor who can, well, sense whenever a possessor is active nearby."

She nodded. "And that's what most people believe about it... but that's wrong. Even ordîns believe that's all our magic can do. Few realize the depth of our power." She rose from the ground and paced. "Our power has nothing to do with possessors. It's a natural side effect of what we do."

"Is that so?"

"I wasn't aware of our true power for most of my life. It wasn't until me and my... anyway, at one point, I met an ancient ordîn who taught me the secrets of our power. Taught me the secrets of energy."

"Right... what's that?"

"If you would just listen, I'd be getting to that." She took a breath, but still didn't look at him. "Energy exists in all people. It also exists in crystal and spirits. It's this power and life that connects to the living being. In one sense it is raw power and an ordîn can connect to it and control it in some ways. It's this energy that allows you possessors to use your magic."

Tsuran cocked a brow but said nothing.

"There's a certain energy within you tatzons that allows you to possess the things you do. Ordîns don't have this kind of energy and so we can't possess. But we can influence the energy, control it, manipulate it, guide it. That's what allows us to exorcise possessors and sense a possession. It's because we're sensing your energy or removing your energy from a possession."

"But how does it make you able to punch through solid rock?"

She paused, reached for her string, stopped, reached for it again, and started up her figures.

"I'll be honest, Tsuran, I don't understand what energy is. Even my master didn't. In one sense, it's a life force. Except that energy doesn't exist in plants or even beasts, but it does in crystal. In another sense, it's pure power. Except that we can manipulate it to affect a person's body and emotions and state of consciousness." She looked down to her arms, as though she held something there. "Without it, a person would die, and yet it's not something physical in them. Except that it can physically affect them. I can make you sleep or cause paralysis throughout. Sometimes I can even make body parts move against your will. But more than that, I can sense emotion and intelligence within the energy. My master even heard of someone who sensed another ordîn's Path. It's... I don't know."

She placed her hands over her necklace, blocking some light from it. "And"—her gaze shifted to the cave-in down the passage—"as for punching rock, one of the forgotten abilities of the ordîn is that not only can we affect energy within another, but we can draw that energy into ourselves. By doing this, by removing the energy from its original container, I unleash the outstanding power trapped inside of it. Energy becomes unstable. It's raw power and if I release it, an explosive force erupts."

Tsuran leaned forward. "So you took the energy from our necklaces, right? And then used that energy to break the rock?"

She nodded. "That's correct. But at a cost."

They both glanced at her arms. "Drawing in the energy cuts you?"

"When removed from its original container, energy wants to expand and burst out. The longer I hold energy inside of me the longer it will cut me open from the inside, trying to escape from my body." She turned back to him. "That's why I can't fight so many spirits with this power. Either I'd have to draw in a lot of energy to kill them all, or I'd have to touch each one. Both can kill me and one of them can destroy all the surrounding crystal."

"Hm. And you said beasts are different?"

"They don't have energy like a person or a spirit. I don't know why. But it means that while I could paralyze you, I couldn't do that to a beast."

"Then what would happen if you unleashed energy on a beast?"

She shrugged. "They'd still get hit by the energy. It'd be messy."

Tsuran took another drink of water and rested his head against the rock. "Tell me, are assassinations ever simple for you?"

Her body stiffened and her gaze fell to the ground for a moment. She turned away and cleared her throat. He squinted at her. Strange reaction for an assassin.

"Are you sure there's no other place to get yellow-crystal?" she said, recomposing herself.

"Don't know. The mine is huge. Lots of tunnels and levels and I haven't been to all of them. I know the deeper into the mine you go, the more likely it is to find crystal. Down to the…"

Tsuran blinked. His mouth fell open. He was such an idiot. The biggest idiot. How had he not remembered this? Sure, it'd been a few years since he'd heard the tale, but this wasn't an easily forgotten rumor. He groaned and dropped his head into his hands.

"What? What is it?" Nasna asked.

He took a deep breath and jumped to his feet. "I think I may have realized the solution to our problem."

"Really?"

He nodded. "Yeah, I may have remembered something. Now don't get mad, but I just remembered that there might be a second way into the Lightless area."

Silence seemed to echo in the tunnel as Nasna stared at him.

"Tell me," she said.

"Now this is just a rumor, and I only heard it once years ago."

"Tell me," she said more forcefully.

"Well, I heard that on the twelfth level, the deepest place the mine goes, there is a place where the two sides of the prison meet."

Nasna's arms raised, and he wasn't sure if she'd hug him or hit him. She might not have known herself because she froze and did neither. She stepped back, cleared her throat, and picked up her equipment.

"Then let's go. Show me the way."

"Again, just a rumor."

"I don't care if it was a rumor or someone just sneezed and it only sounded like it. If there's a possibility we don't need yellow-crystal, we should explore the option. Besides, it might be a while before the spirits to leave the cavern, anyway. This beats waiting around and doing nothing."

She had a point there.

"And what if there is a way?" he asked. "What if there is another way to the Lightless area?"

She paused, the tension in her body returning. She shook herself. "We'll deal with that later. First, I want to see if it's true."

Not waiting for him, Nasna marched off toward the gallery, rewrapping the cloth around her head. Tsuran hurried after. No telling if this rumor would pay off, but this sounded better than waiting for another cave-in. Although, cave-ins were more likely the deeper they went. But they only had to go five more levels. Hardly comforting.

They left the remains of the cave-in, and he looked over the hole Nasna made with newfound knowledge. If she did this to solid rock, what did she plan on doing to her target?

It sent a shiver down his spine, so he shook it off and headed out of the tunnel.

14

---◆○◆---

THE BRIDGEWAY

*K*ing of Tifre,

I represent gods who have taken interest in you and that land you create. We have watched from the shadows, seeing your rise and your falls, your losses and your gains. You wish to create something that can withstand what destroyed Oushwala, we have similar aims. You have few allies and without careful planning you shall lose all your friends have made. We can help. We have power deep in Rajalend and beyond. We can establish Tifre's power among the nations, and we can even help rid you of Farhata of the Rising Coast.

Go to the terebinth tree during the Moonless night. The six of us shall meet with you then.

- Nimat, the Void Within

Every mine shaft they descended brought them deeper into the maws of death. And they descended them all.

They climbed down into the eleventh level and Nasna glanced around. The smallest one yet with only two shafts in the floor. The pulley system hadn't made it this far, and the mining was quiet, perhaps only a handful of prisoners down here.

But strangely enough, it seemed like she could breathe easier now, as though the air had become fresh and alive again.

"I think we've just about made it," Tsuran said. "You want to take a break here or just keep going?"

Her arms ached from all the climbing, plus they had not brought their food for the day. But this wouldn't be a long trip since this was to see if the rumors were true and that was it. Resting would only be an unnecessary delay. She walked to the next shaft and Tsuran followed.

She peered over the shaft, looking for the handholds, and paused. For most of the levels, the only light came from their necklaces. All else was pitch black. But the bottom of this shaft had a faint blue glow. She held up a hand. Tsuran knelt beside her and peered over.

"Spirits," she said.

"Could be," Tsuran said. "Though, lots of blue-crystals can give off a similar glow."

"Wouldn't people have already mined any obvious crystal?"

"Maybe."

"Why wouldn't they?"

He gave her a sidelong glance. "Because of spirits."

Nasna sat back. They had climbed all the way here. It would be pointless to climb back to their cell without having found out any new information. They'd known there were risks of encountering spirits down here, and that wouldn't change with a day or two. Besides, if they needed to get out, he had his special song.

Tsuran leaned further over the shaft, his ear turned to the ground.

"What are you doing?" she asked. He held a finger to his lips and ushered her over. She brought her head over, trying to listen too. There wasn't anything. She closed her eyes and held her breath.

She heard it. Besides her heart, there was something else. It was quiet but distinct. Someone mining below.

"So there are people down there," Tsuran said. "I guess that means it's safe enough to go down."

Nasna nodded. "You go first, just in case."

"Your concern for my well-being is heartwarming."

"You're the one with the song, not me."

"It doesn't provide complete and total protection, you know."

But he still shimmied over the side and descended with Nasna following right after him.

Crisp air flooded her lungs as they approached the next, and likely last, level. The heat which had been building throughout the galleries washed away and a coolness wrapped inside her. For so many levels, the air had felt as if it were trying to suffocate her but this air was fresh and encouraged levity. The difference was so sudden and stark she became light-headed and almost lost her grip on the handholds. She steadied herself and took in slow breaths, acquainting herself with this delicious relief. Fresh air was a good sign, it meant there was an airflow. And an airflow meant there was another way out other than this shaft.

She stopped halfway and watched Tsuran descend the full length, waiting for him to usher her down. He dropped to the floor and turned toward the gallery. He stopped as if he'd become stone.

Not a good sign. She thought to ask what was wrong but closed her mouth shut. Any noise could put him in danger. But that wasn't the only problem. Her arms shook holding the stone ladder. Up or down, she needed to move soon.

Tsuran looked up, his expression odd, and beckoned to her. She let out a breath, joined him on the ground, and turned to see what had made him so...

She took a step back, her mouth falling open. The gallery looked similar to every other level at first, open space with columns supporting the ceiling. But it opened up into a massively wide tunnel, wider than even the main body of the prison, with blue light pouring in from the end. Blue, white, and green-crystal covered the walls and ceiling of the tunnel, all jetting out of the rock like jagged pillars. Even the smallest was four times the size of Tsuran. There was more crystal here than she'd ever seen or even imagined. And it was bright. Not just the white lightstones, but even the blue and green-crystals were dazzling. And, if possible, this brilliance only increased as the tunnel proceeded.

Nasna readjusted herself, swallowed, and walked forward. "Let's go."

There were no spirits inside the tunnel and she wanted to move through before they showed up. But there was still a subtle caution in her steps. Crystal surrounded her and appeared to be an easy mine and yet it remained untouched throughout all these centuries. The only reason prisoners would stay so far away from such a deposit was that the risk far outweighed the reward. If Tsuran was right, this place should be a prime gathering spot for spirits. Nasna's eyes darted from side to side, expecting spirits to come out of the walls at any moment.

Tsuran paused and fell behind her. She glanced over her shoulder, but he was staring at his arms.

"What is it?" Nasna asked.

"This air isn't natural."

She raised a brow. "What do you mean?"

"You haven't noticed it?" He looked both ways around them. "Open the wrapping on your arm."

"What?"

"Just for a moment."

She eyed him, but his expression was strange, something between confused and pleased. Nasna unwrapped a part of her arm and let the air caress it. And she felt what Tsuran did. With her wrappings covering her so tightly she hadn't noticed it at first but it was obvious now.

The air was contradictory.

If she breathed it in, it was fresh like spring water. It brought clarity to her mind and ease to her lungs. Yet, it breathed warmth against her skin. It almost seemed warmer here than all previous levels. To her skin, the air felt like a summer's day outside of the forests, while to her tongue it was like an autumn evening. It tasted like it too. She opened the wrapping around her lips and took in another breath. Her eyes widened. The air was fragrant and almost sweet. Someone had to be boiling autumn tea, or perhaps there was a luscious garden nearby.

She glanced to Tsuran. "Is this... a good sign?"

He looked down the tunnel. "Only one way to find out."

They continued to the end of the tunnel where their steps ceased. Neither spoke. The unexpected view before them silenced words. They did not stand at the entrance to a new cavern similar to the one they'd left or like any they'd been in before. They stood on a ledge overseeing an expanse that could have swallowed a nectar tree like Al'Rajak whole.

The ledge dropped off for thousands of feet to a ground that expanded out for what looked like miles because there was no end to it. Crystal deposits of various colors and massive sizes were plentiful along the walls and ceiling, creating enough light to rival the midday sun. Crystal veins etched their way along the ground, creating walls and pathways. The entire cavern looked like one enormous maze. Rock and crystal intertwined in a complex structure that staggered Nasna's imagination and understanding. None of it looked accidental but constructed. Yes, a maze, but also a design. The crystal on the ground created the image of a seven-pointed star, and each point was itself a seven-pointed star.

She tried looking closer, but squinted due to the bright light, which seemed too close. She looked down. This blinding light came from her necklace. Somehow this place had increased the intensity of her lightstone to the point she'd need to stop wearing it. She took it off and turned to Tsuran, but he must've also noticed since he took his off too. Nasna paused as she glanced at him. Perhaps it was because of the intensity of the surrounding light, but his iron color had drained. His eyes narrowed and his jaw set. He had the demeanor of recognition. And not the good kind.

"Tsuran, what are we looking at?"

His voice was a whisper, as though he feared to utter his thoughts. "We've entered the spirit realm."

A cold shiver shot through her. She looked back out over the massive cavern, or rather the land, before her. Tsuran had to be wrong. It wasn't even possible.

"You're kidding," Nasna said, her voice matching his. "That's impossible."

"Well, we're not quite in the realm itself. They call this a Bridgeway. If you manage through the maze to the far end, you'll descend into the world of spirits."

"You mean this prison has been sitting on top of this Bridgeway for centuries?"

"For thousands of years, most likely."

"Is that why the crystal is brighter here?"

"I guess. I'm not an expert. Just things I remember."

Nasna stepped away from the ledge and examined her surroundings again. To the side of the ledge was a crude stairwell that curved along the wall down into the maze below. But if they followed those stairs, it would be too easy to lose their way down there. However, one could traverse the cavern if they flew. No impediment, no restriction. This maze ceased being dangerous if only they could fly... if she still had her wings.

Nasna's eyes fell to her feet. Why think of things like that? Her stomach knotted as memories clawed their way into her mind. Her head spun, and she walked back to the tunnel wall as the voices of her past poured in.

"For the sake of the Luminous!"

"No, mother!"

"It's alright, Red Dawn. We'll be together again."

"Let go of my family!"

"Everyone, grab those two! Don't let them escape!"

"... you doomed us all... Death's Touch...."

"Nasna?"

She stood upright and blinked away her blurring vision as she turned toward Tsuran. For once, she was glad for the covering.

"What do you want to do?" he asked. He must not have noticed her reaction.

She took a quiet breath and cleared her throat. "We haven't found a way into the Lightless area. As interesting as this place is, I don't think it will help us much."

He nodded but glanced over the ledge. "That might be true, but look at all the crystal here. There is more than enough here for us to bribe our way into anything. It'd be easy to find some yellow-crystal. And it appears I'm not the only one with that idea."

Right. The mining. There were other miners here. And not just one or two people. It sounded like there were plenty of prisoners down there.

"How many do you think are mining down here?" she asked.

He shrugged. "Impossible to tell. Though, the thing I'm wondering about is how long they've been mining down here.

With so much crystal, you'd think news of this place would be more common, right?"

Several loud moans swept through the cavernous land, silencing all the mining. The farthest end blazed with brilliant light and glowing bodies emerged from it. From her distance and vantage point, coupled with the fact she saw them, the emerging spirits had to be all Larges and Colossals. And there were ten of them. Some hovered, others slithered like snakes, while others trudged forward with dozens of limbs. All had the same blue-white translucent and glowing bodies, yet even they seemed to glow brighter in this place than elsewhere. They all headed toward the miners below, and by proxy, toward Tsuran and Nasna.

"Will your song do anything?"

Tsuran shook his head. "It only works on Smalls and Commons. Wouldn't work on anything larger. I can't do anything."

"So the miners will die?"

Tsuran quieted.

"They had better not die. They still owe me for my services."

The voice came from behind Nasna and Tsuran, who both pivoted. A tall cloaked tatzon stood behind them, but where had he come from? Nasna hadn't heard his approach at all.

"Though, as long as they follow my instructions, most of them won't die today."

The newcomer did not glance at either but held his gaze out toward the spirits. Nasna looked him over. Male tatzon. Cloak prevented sight of arms but judging by his size and how he towered over both her and Tsuran, he had several. Age: indeterminable with his hood up.

"And who are you?" Tsuran asked. The newcomer walked toward them, Nasna tensed but he went past and sat down on the ledge, draping his legs over the side.

"You would think by now they would know how this works," the tatzon said. "I tell them again and again, don't strike the crystal until I say to. Again and again, I tell them. And yet, they seem to not listen."

"Are you meaning the miners down there?" Tsuran asked.

"This is not the first time they've done this either. I'm guessing one of them ceases to listen to me anymore. Well, if that is the case, the spirits will weed them out soon enough."

"Who are you?" Nasna asked.

"Me?" The tatzon turned toward them, his gaze boring into them. "I am the Warden of these caverns here. I am the Guide under the Crystal Light, I am the Watcher of Spirits. I am in charge here."

"What makes you in charge down here?" Tsuran asked.

"What makes me in charge," the tatzon said, standing tall so even Tsuran had to look up, "is that I, and I alone, know this maze's secrets. How to maneuver it, where to hide, how to mine. How to survive."

The man spread out his nine arms—four emerging from either side of his torso and one coming from just behind his left shoulder—and threw his head back, letting the hood fall backward revealing a bald tatzon in his mid-eighties. His markings resembled triangles that alternated between brown and black coloring. He smiled down at the two of them.

"You may call me Dalvinder. Dalvinder Ealhhere Bosede Con-Orinda, and if you have any desire of mining here and surviving, you will need to employ my services."

"Services?" Tsuran said with a smirk. "Have to say that's a new one."

Dalvinder nodded and gestured out to the maze. "This here is the greatest and most plentiful place to find crystal deposits in the whole of the mountain. Here you may find the rarest of crystal, the most luxurious, the most powerful. But as you can see, spirits also traverse this place, more frequently when there is mining going on. But I have watched the way, I have seen the paths, I know the hidden places."

"That's great," Tsuran said. "But I think we'll be just fine on our own."

A scream rang out in the cavern. Nasna looked toward the maze. One spirit descended into the maze, its scythe-like hand cutting through the rock. The screams silenced. Most of the spirits moved on, searching for new prey. But one Colossal stood in the middle of the cavern, its gaze set on the ledge with the three of them.

"The Colossal sees us," Nasna said. Dalvinder spun toward the ledge.

"Well, Stone Cutter is here. My, he doesn't look pleased today."

"You named the spirit?" Tsuran asked.

"Of course. He's such a constant nuisance that it seemed fitting to give him a name. It is easier to hate what is named."

Tsuran cocked his head to the side. "I suppose."

"Never mind that," Nasna said. "Perhaps we should retreat into the mines."

Instead of doing that, Dalvinder sat back down on the ledge. "Oh, you need not worry about Stone Cutter there. None but Smalls and Commons ever make it up this far. Why, if that were not the case, they would have invaded the mines, rampaged through the galleries, killed everyone."

The Colossal continued its gaze toward them for a moment more before, as if to acknowledge Dalvinder's statement, it redirected its attention to the ground beneath it.

"How many miners are down there?" Tsuran asked.

"Oh, about two dozen. But how many will live all depends on whether they listen to my instructions."

"Instructions?" Nasna asked.

"Even if the spirits attack, even if they come into this place, even if they search far and wide, that doesn't have to be a death sentence. I have been in these mines for a very long time, and this place especially. That means I have found the ways to live and to survive, and for a price I share them"—Dalvinder abruptly turned in his seat toward them though he remained precariously on the edge—"but we haven't had introductions. What may I call you?"

Nasna glanced and Tsuran. He shrugged and stepped forward. "I am Tsuran Con-None."

"Con-None? A sad tragedy. A devastation. A true loss." Dalvinder looked him over, a strange expression on his face. The moment passed and with a polite smile, Dalvinder turned toward her.

"Sitora Whitestone."

"A pleasure to meet you both," Dalvinder said and then stood up. "So, how would you like to discuss the services?"

"As we said, we don't need your services," Tsuran said.

"Oh, don't you now? I doubt that. The maze is confusing enough if you have not memorized the places you must go. But even if you somehow traversed it, you will not find the prime places to mine, the prime places to avoid, the prime places to survive."

"We'll just have to make do," Nasna said.

"Well, I cannot force my services, I only come recommended by all who live." Dalvinder put on a saddened expression. "Though, I am curious, what do you look for in these mines?"

"Yellow-crystal," Tsuran said without hesitation. "Just trying to buy some better privileges, that's all."

"Is that so?" Dalvinder said and laughed. "Well, who isn't down here? Though it is odd to see such a pairing as you two. It's not common for a tatzon and human to be working alongside each other with such—oh, what's the word—amicability."

"We do what we must to survive," Nasna said. "Besides, where is your cell-mate?"

"Him? Oh, imagine he is on the far side in the mine somewhere."

"You don't keep your cell-mate by your side?" Tsuran asked.

"I don't see why I need to. As long as anyone is by my side, Solitude doesn't affect me. No one here is my Partner, I see no reason I should treat them as one."

"I see," Tsuran said.

There was silence between them as the three watched the spirits below search for prisoners. There weren't any other screams, but that did not mean people weren't dying.

"Do you think the others will be fine down there?" Nasna asked.

"I'm sure the Lightless are already in safe places." A sly grin spread across his face. "Though, I am more concerned about the others. Nervous for their harvest. Anxious they won't pay me."

Nasna and Tsuran straightened and looked at each other.

"Did you say Lightless?" Nasna asked.

"Oh yes," Dalvinder said, lazily gesturing toward a far wall. "This maze connects both sides of our prison home. This is a Bridge to many places, I suppose you could say. A connecting bay of outcasts. A crossroads of criminals. A path of the damned."

Nasna rushed the edge and peered across, her heart pattering in her chest. There was another way into the Lightless area. Now they just needed to find it. She looked around for another ledge high above like the one they stood on, but there wasn't any. The entranceway might be inside the maze somewhere. If that was the case, things looked grimmer.

"But if there's a way across," Tsuran said, "why don't we ever see any Lightless in our mines?"

"Just because an opportunity exists doesn't mean one should take it," Dalvinder said. "There is no benefit for them to go to your side, only detriment. Punishment. Solitude."

Nasna caught Tsuran's attention and jerked her head in the tunnel's direction. Tsuran nodded.

"Well, it's been a pleasure, but we must go now," Tsuran said and Dalvinder glanced at him. "Though, do you need us to stay longer? I don't want to leave you alone."

Nasna glared at Tsuran. She didn't want to stay any longer than... oh. Tsuran didn't want to leave a lone tatzon to endure Solitude. No tatzon would put another through that, even a stranger.

Dalvinder paused. His eyes fixated on Tsuran with an expression Nasna couldn't decipher. He smiled and stood.

"That's unnecessary. I think it is time I check on those below. But before you go, are you sure you do not wish for my services? I promise what you find here you will not find elsewhere."

"We'll think about it," Nasna said, joining Tsuran by the tunnel exit.

Dalvinder bowed to them both. "Well, until then."

He turned and jumped off the ledge. Nasna and Tsuran rushed to the edge and peered over, watching him fall. Dalvinder waved at them both and vanished. Nasna took in a breath, widened her eyes, and looked again. But there was no sign of him.

Tsuran pulled away from the edge. "I think he was a Lightless. Don't know what else he could have possessed down there besides shadow."

Nasna closed her eyes. He was a Lightless. There was a way to the other side. There was another way to Valerija. She looked up to Tsuran. "Let's head back and think up a plan. We've found just what we're needing."

15

---◆○◆---

A NEW OPPORTUNITY

*F*arhata, I am sure by now you've heard the libraries of Al'Rajak have *accepted both of your nieces to study there and I wanted to write you personally to congratulate your family on such an achievement. However, I must admit I may have had a hand in this. I knew how important it was for them to go, and they have such brilliant minds, that I spoke with the Oligarchs myself about allowing their admittance. They informed me they would allow it on the stipulation that you would oversee one of their many mining operations, since they've heard of your exceptional leadership skills.*

I do hope you will accept their offer. It would be such a shame if your nieces' dreams were crushed so.

-Yavahush the Stargazer, King of Tifre, in the 2954th Lunar Cycle

Tsuran wasn't one for gods, but sometimes he wished one would show up and grant him a wish. Right now, he'd wish for a full-body massage.

Tsuran let out a long breath and set his pickax down against the wall. He pulled his shoulders back and massaged an arm. He cast a glance to the other half of their Crystal Cavern where near two dozen Common spirits and a handful of Smalls still lingered. They no longer crowded the area near the entrance, being heavy in iron, so Tsuran and Nasna could enter again. Though, those spirits still guarded all the yellow-crystal. No way of getting to it, but they enjoyed the privacy and fresh air the place provided and so they kept returning.

Tsuran stretched but Nasna continued to mine away at her side. He smiled. Determined little thing. There was iron in these walls, which they might use against the spirits, though it was a long shot and meant he had to do actual work. Nasna had been mining hard those past few days, so it must have helped her think or something. Her endurance kept building, especially compared to how she was when she first arrived. But she pushed herself too hard, especially this week. And, even if she wouldn't admit it, she'd been having trouble sleeping. Then again, so had he. Nothing about their situation was good for his health.

"Hey, time for a break," he said. She turned, wiping the sweat away from her brow and breathing deep. He pulled out one of the water flasks and handed it over.

"Thanks." She took a drink.

"Come up with any new ideas?"

She shook her head, leaned back against the stone, and took out her string to make her little designs. "Without knowing how to find the Lightless entrance, there's little we can do. It wouldn't be easy to maneuver through the maze, especially with spirits around. Just give me some time. I'll figure something out."

The same answer as yesterday. Ordîns were notorious for needing ages to decide things, but she continued to hit against the same problem and it was doubtful they'd ever find a solution. It had been almost a week since they'd discovered the Bridgeway and had yet to venture back because of these exact problems. Harvesting the yellow-crystal remained as elusive as before. It was right there, so close. Just a couple more strikes with the crystal gad and they'd have all they could wish for. But on both fronts, there were just too many complications.

Tsuran drank some water and pulled out his small statue from his pocket, a comforting yet unhelpful item at the moment. He sat on the ground and leaned against the wall, pulling out a small slab of dried meat from their meal pack. He stared at the meat. It hadn't been too long ago that he'd been on the team providing food to the mines. It wasn't good that he missed possessing those shoddy statues, yet it was difficult not to miss being on the hunt.

But he wouldn't trade this time with Nasna for any amount of time out hunting. After all, soon he'd be well on his way out of these mountains and out of Rajalend. The past would leave him alone, at last.

"What?" Nasna asked.

He looked at her, blinking. Had she been talking to him?

"What?" he asked.

"You were frowning. What was that about?"

"I was? Oh. I guess I was... it's nothing, don't worry about it. But I was thinking that if you aren't coming up with ideas here, maybe we should go back to the Bridgeway. Might be easier to memorize the place."

Nasna stared at the ceiling, still doing her string figures and not stopping or missing a step.

"The place is a maze. A lot of the turns were hidden from view, so we couldn't memorize a path if we wanted to. We'd get lost if we tried. Besides, we don't even know where in the Bridgeway we need to go. I didn't see any place that resembled an entrance to the Lightless."

"Well, then why don't we try just using Dalvinder? He seemed willing enough."

Nasna rolled her eyes, something that shouldn't have made him happy, but it did.

"Yes, why don't we just tell him we're trying to kill a Lightless? I'm sure that'd go over real well."

He shrugged. "I didn't say we have to explain everything. We could say we want to get to the Lightless area and that's all. No need to tell him why. If he asks we can tell him we're seeing a friend or something."

Her hands sped up with her string. She pursed her lips and closed her eyes for a moment. Yet, she still didn't seem to miss a single step with her figures. She breathed out and shook her head.

"It's too risky. We'll figure something out, but I don't want to involve other people."

"That's quite a pity. I was becoming intrigued by you two."

Tsuran and Nasna froze. Someone else was in their cavern. Jumping to their feet, Tsuran gripped his pick and statue while Nasna raised her hands. They turned to the voice and saw Dalvinder leaning against the wall as if it was the most natural place to be.

What was he doing here? How had he even found—

Nasna launched herself forward, hand outstretched toward Dalvinder. Tsuran's eyes widened. Either she'd paralyze him or, more likely, kill him. She'd removed her wrappings when they'd come in here, so he now saw her as an ordîn. Saw their secret.

Nasna was fast but without even flinching, Dalvinder vanished.

"He's possessed the shadows," Tsuran said. Nasna turned and narrowed her eyes. There was a fury in them, a rage that looked unlike anything he'd seen in her.

"Now, we have no need for that." Dalvinder's voice came from behind Tsuran. Again, Dalvinder leaned against the wall, arms spread out, and a subtle smile on his lips. He seemed unconcerned by Nasna's attempt to reach him. "I just came to talk."

Nasna rushed forward again, but Tsuran was ready this time and grabbed her arm. "Wait."

She glared at him with such intensity that he nearly let go. But he understood prisoners. Dalvinder wasn't about to turn them into the Warden and by doing so expose himself. No. He wanted something else. They needed to find out what.

That and, though he only half-admitted it, he didn't enjoy seeing her like this.

Whether she had the same thought are not, Nasna stopped struggling and turned her glare toward Dalvinder.

"What are you doing here? You have one minute to justify yourself before I end up killing you." Her voice was unlike her usual self. It was hard, guttural, and sent a prickling feeling over Tsuran's body. Dalvinder chuckled.

"My, perhaps you are an interesting sort."

"Speak."

"Again, there's no need for threats or hesitation about my presence here. I didn't come here to fight or reveal your secret."

"Why are you here then?" Tsuran asked. "How'd you even find us?"

"Well, I suppose the real reason I'm here is that I wanted to find out the truth." His eyes narrowed on Nasna. "I wanted to see if you were an ordîn or not."

Some breath left Tsuran. He'd already known? Were rumors going around? Impossible. There was no way anyone could have known her secret. And if they had, they would have told the Warden long ago.

"Don't worry, at the moment I am the only other one in this entire prison who knows your little secret," Dalvinder said, as if he could hear Tsuran's thoughts. "And I intend to keep it safe, for now."

"How did you know?" Nasna asked, taking a step toward him.

"The same way I discovered your cavern here," Dalvinder said and raised one of his arms. It grew from his back, a sure sign it was one of the newest arms grown.

"Possession?" Tsuran asked. "What kind?"

"It's a Dream Walker arm."

Despite himself, Tsuran laughed. "You're kidding."

"I know, no one considers dream possession a useful category to explore. But I've been here in the mines for a long time and after a while one gets bored. I have Builder arms, Guardian arms, and even a Wrangler arm, but those are all so useless here. So, I explored dream walking, experienced it, lived it, grew it. And through dreams, I learned all I needed to about you two."

"How?" Nasna asked, taking another step toward Dalvinder who still seemed unconcerned about her approach.

"Dreams tell much, little ordîn. Over the last few nights, I've been entering your dreams. It intrigued me why a human and a tatzon worked together and so I explored. In your dreams, you are shown as who you are, nothing is hidden, all is revealed." Dalvinder folded his arms and leaned forward, still smiling. "It may not seem as useful as all other possessions, but you would be amazed at the power of a dream."

"But why spend all the time and effort growing a dream arm?" Tsuran asked. "I'd imagine developing further Lightless arms would be more helpful."

"As much as I would love to discuss dream possession with you, I think we are getting off-topic," Dalvinder said. A look from Nasna showed she agreed.

"And that's it?" Nasna asked, looking back at the Lightless. "You just wanted to find out if your dreams were right?"

Dalvinder shook his head. "Not just that. There is only so much I could learn from your dreams. I wanted to know more, specifically why an ordîn doesn't have wings and why she is here in prison. I did not expect the answer to be an assassination."

Tsuran gripped his pick tighter. Nasna tensed. Nothing Dalvinder said so far showed that he planned on turning them in, but he was a Lightless. A condemned Lightless at that. They were not the kind you automatically trusted.

"So what do you want?" Tsuran asked.

"Yes, yes, I suppose a direct statement would help ease your tension. To put it simply, I would like to offer you my services."

Tsuran blinked. He wanted to offer his... wait, what?

"What do you mean by that?" Nasna asked.

"Simple, I would like to guide you to the Lightless area, and, even better, I would like to guide you to where your target is."

Dalvinder leaned back against the wall, waiting for their response. Tsuran and Nasna glanced at each other. This was what they needed. Yet, there was something else. Something unsaid.

"You'll bring us to the Lightless area?" Tsuran asked. "Just like that?"

"No, not just like that. I offer my services, but not free."

Tsuran snorted. And there it was. He wanted something from them. A true Lightless.

"Not interested," Nasna said and her arms twitched as though she were readying herself to attack again.

"There are only two ways into the Lightless area," Dalvinder said. "Either through the maze below or the ordîn entrance above. Spirits will kill you before you maneuver through the maze and ordîns will kill you before you make it through the top levels. I offer to bring you to where you need to be. I think you should be a little interested."

Tsuran gritted his teeth. That was the situation they were in. And he would have been lying to himself if he didn't admit he was interested. But that all depended on what Dalvinder wanted in return. That would be the crucial fact.

"What do you want in exchange?" Tsuran asked. He kept his attention on Dalvinder, not wanting to see what kind of glare Nasna had for him at the moment.

"Ah, that's more like it. Cooperation, one of the finest attributes of any tatzon." Dalvinder took a few steps toward them and they raised their fists and pick. Ignoring them, Dalvinder walked along the walls tracing the veins with several fingers. "As you know, crystal is a very useful currency. Especially in these mines. However, not all crystal is equal. Not all hold the same significance. Some crystals carry greater worth than the whole of the prison, mountain, or range we find ourselves in."

Tsuran and Nasna shifted their stances, making sure Dalvinder was always in front of them as he spoke.

"When I first arrived here, I had a crystal that held great significance to me and the Warden confiscated it. Our service exchange is very simple: retrieve my crystal for me and then I will bring you to the Lightless."

Tsuran paused. The request was simple in theory, but in actuality, it was a difficult thing to accomplish. He glanced over at Nasna, but except for her narrowed eyes, she was unreadable. So irritating. There was already the Warden with his unknowable face. After all this time, Tsuran should be able to know what's going on in his cell-mate's head but she was closed off right now. No way of knowing what she was thinking. Icy Abyss, it was hard knowing what *he* was thinking. They had to get to the Lightless, but stealing from the Warden? That was insane... well, except he had been planning on stealing from him anyway, so... Tsuran sighed. Sometimes there was too much insanity in his life.

"And where is this crystal?" Nasna asked.

"It is amongst the many treasures the Warden hoards."

"If you know where it is, why not get yourself?"

"And how would I do that? I am only a Lightless. Even I cannot sneak out of the mine."

"What is so important about this crystal?" Tsuran asked.

Dalvinder stopped and his gaze turned away from them. "It belongs to my Partner. It is the last thing I have of him."

Tsuran felt the statue in his hand. In this, he understood Dalvinder. The Lightless looked back at the two of them, a smile returning to his lips.

"What you do is up to you. I shall return to the Bridge. If you ever wish for me to bring you to the Lightless area, bring me my crystal. Otherwise, I have no reason to see either of you again. Have a good day."

He disappeared, possessing the shadows and leaving the room. Silence replaced his presence as both Tsuran and Nasna stared at the entranceway. Water dripped around them and in the back of the cavern, the Small spirits moaned to each other in their strange whispers. But it didn't look like Dalvinder was coming back.

Tsuran turned to Nasna. "So. What do we do?"

Nasna walked toward the entrance, raising her hands toward the shadows. Tsuran watched as she moved without a sound, watched her checking the place Dalvinder had been. Nasna stood upright and looked back at Tsuran,

"I don't trust him."

Tsuran nodded. "Can't say I don't agree. However, it doesn't change the fact that he has given us an offer."

"Do you think he'll turn us in?"

"I doubt it. There's nothing for him to gain by doing that. A Lightless shouldn't even know we exist, so if he turned us in he'd also be revealing himself and his Bridgeway racket down below."

Nasna faced the entrance again. "Do you know where this crystal of his would be?"

Tsuran scratched his chin. "I think so. There is a room connected to the Warden's office where I've heard he keeps all the good stuff. My guess is it's kept in there."

"Is it guarded?"

"The whole level up there is guarded, Nas."

"Right."

Tsuran folded his arms. "You thinking of breaking out and finding it?"

"It's an option, but I don't prefer it. I don't know the layout of the upper prison, nor any schedules or anything like that. I hate going into a place blind."

"Well, if you want, we could try breaking into the Lightless area from above, though I doubt that'd be easy to do."

"Nothing we're trying to do is easy."

She pulled out her string again and delved into her designs. Tsuran looked back to the spirits and waited for her. The spirits remained in the far back, hovering and crawling around the yellow-crystal as if it was their warmth against the mountain cold. One spirit, a thin Small with long fingers, looked up and stared at Tsuran with its glowing white eyes. Tsuran didn't blink and hardened his grip on his statue. The spirit's whispers reached his ears, reverberating inside his mind. Whispers he couldn't understand or decipher. Whispers like those that drove Dazh into his insanity. Whispers Tsuran hadn't been strong enough to save his family from.

Tsuran closed his eyes and refocused his breathing, reigning it back under control. He eased the tension off his statue since it'd cut into his hand. He let his gaze drop to the small stone figure.

"My target is only part of our problem," Nasna said, and Tsuran jumped a little at her voice, though she didn't seem to notice. "Escaping is another issue. And that requires information that's best gotten from freely walking around the upper levels. If I had access and didn't have to worry about guards catching me, I could formulate a better plan than from here."

Tsuran cleared his throat and pushed Dazh out of his mind. "So regardless of whether we work with Dalvinder or not, it seems our next step is to get on the furnace team."

Nasna gazed over to the spirits. "Which means we have to get the yellow-crystal."

He looked toward the dozens of spirits. "Yeah. And, as much as I hate to say it, that'll be the easiest part of this whole thing."

16

ONE LAST GAMBLE

I wish to thank the six of you for your hand in opening Tifre's trade to the Dragon's Maw, for it will bring even greater wealth to our budding nation. It has been a hard many years since my kin died and I do not believe I could have ruled as I have without your help. I am still unsure if I am the right man for this throne, but that's beside the point. I will visit Rajalend soon, but I doubt I shall have time to meet with any of you. There is someone I first must see. I made a promise, long ago, and I will keep it.

- Yavahush the Stargazer, King of Tifre, in the 2959th Lunar Cycle

Nasna didn't like their plan. Too many variables, too many problems might arise, so much might go wrong. The worst part was knowing they had to go through with it. The yellow-crystal was key to any next steps since without it they were stuck. She took a deep breath and finished tying her wrapping. Somehow, it itched more every time she put it back on. But once they put their plan into motion, she wouldn't be staying in the cavern long, so wanted to be sure it was snug.

She looked over at Tsuran as he pulled out the small statue he kept in his pocket, the one he held when he thought she wasn't paying attention. It had to be the one he'd used back during the cave-in incident, but she hadn't seen him use it since. Neither had brought it up either, so she knew little about it or how he'd sneaked it in. However, if he could possess a statue that small, it was impressive. She'd have to remember to ask him about it later. If they survived the insanity of this idea.

"Ready?" she asked.

Tsuran's typical grin returned. "Well, when death is the worst-case scenario, I'm always ready."

"Right."

She took another look around. They hadn't wasted time after Dalvinder's departure, deciding to proceed the same day. Over two dozen spirits remained in the room, gathering near the yellow-crystal. Getting them away from the crystal was their, or rather that was her, first task. She patted the hammer and gad at her waist.

"Alright, I'll keep my song up for a few minutes," Tsuran said. "It should give you enough time to cross to the other side. Remember, don't move until I give the signal."

Nasna nodded.

"Well, good luck."

"You too." She walked away but stopped and looked back at him. "Don't die, alright?"

Tsuran smiled and began his song.

Nasna took the other path of the cavern, the one that drifted along the other side of the lake. It took her further away from the entrance and even further away from the main ground in the cavern. This path only had the small walkway next to the water, but it did not taper off or disappear. Instead, it continued along the wall further into the cavern. It ran parallel to the area with the high concentration of crystal, but crystal also lined the walls here. However, since there wasn't a lot of room to stand, Tsuran hadn't wanted them ever to harvest crystal along this path. A wrong step or a miscalculated swing could send her into the cold water, and with spirits around here that could mean death. If she had to run, it'd be tricky.

The path widened as she walked, but the amount of crystal lessened so the place grew dimmer with every step. Peering to the farthest end, the path disappeared into the darkness, but the cavern looked to continue beyond it. Nasna had no need or intention of discovering what awaited them that far into the mountain. All she needed was to be as far from the spirits as possible.

There wasn't much crystal left on the walls, so she looked back. It looked far enough. She pressed her back against the crystal and looked straight across the body of water to where Tsuran was. From her distance, it was hard to even see him. The only way he stood out was with his moving necklace. However, she couldn't miss the spirits. They were all Commons, and yet even at this distance, they looked massive. If there had been a Large here... no, she wouldn't think about that. Only what was in front of her.

Nasna gripped the hammer and gad. She leaned her head back and tried to relax her breathing, taking in one deep breath after another.

You've got this, Nasna. Trust Tsuran to do his part and follow through with yours. We'll make it.

The song stopped. Tsuran had possessed his statue. And she waited. Tsuran said he'd need several minutes to get into position. She counted the seconds, which were slower than the rhythm of her beating heart.

Breathe. She needed to breathe. She'd faced plenty of challenges in her life, fought many powerful people. But these weren't people. These were twenty Common spirits. No one did this. It was suicide. Leave it to Tsuran to come up with a plan to kill them both. And she was an idiot for going along with it. And really, what was taking him so long?

"Ready!"

His words echoed toward her but the spirits didn't react, just as Tsuran had said. As far as signals went, this was the least subtle. She placed the gad on top of the blue-crystal, keeping her back to the wall so she continued to face the spirits. She raised the hammer and took in one last breath.

"Come and get me."

She struck the gad, cracking into the crystal.

All the spirits turned, their white eyes glowing brighter. Lightning crackled around some and fire burst around others.

Their bodies twisted and their once beautiful visage became replaced by nightmares. Their glow dimmed in all but their eyes. Eyes set on her.

A high-pitched screech rang through the cavern and the spirits charged toward her, some flying, the rest either pushing themselves into the water or climbing on the ceiling. Waves splashed her feet, drenching them. Fire struck the water's edge in front of her and lightning broke into a nearby wall.

Nasna didn't move.

She kept her hand on the crystal and her attention on the spirits that shot lightning and fire at her. These moved slower than others. Not that it was a great comfort. It wouldn't take long for all the spirits to reach her.

A spirit neared and raised a ring of fire. She drew in energy from the crystal wall and channeled it into her arm pointed at the spirits. She released the energy.

The force pushed her hard into the wall, but most of it burst away from her and hit the spirits. It struck a few, but she hadn't taken in a lot of energy and they weren't too close. So all she did was push them back and disrupt the fire. However, her drawing energy seemed to enrage the spirits even more. The waters churned with the Commons breaking through them, rock from the ceiling fell as the spirits dug into it, and a few spirits screeched again.

The spirits bolted toward her.

She stood firm.

Water and rock shot around her.

She stood firm. She had to trust Tsuran.

The spirits reached her ledge.

Nasna grabbed the energy in the wall. But the spirits stopped. Their lightning still crackled in the air and their flames danced around them. But the spirits no longer charged.

Another screech and the spirits turned away from her and bolted away. Away from her and back to Tsuran. He must've finished breaking the yellow-crystal off the wall.

They rushed away from her and as they did, she hurried back along the path. Nasna focused on her steps. Tsuran's empowerment was fast enough to get the yellow-crystal to safety.

To get him to safety. She couldn't run on the ledge she was on, but she tried. The rage of the spirits around gave haste to her feet.

She glanced over. Tsuran's statue rushed toward the entranceway, a faint yellow emanating from him. The spirits sped toward him with greater speed than before. She had to give him more time, but it'd hurt. Throwing her hands onto the crystal, she drew the energy into her. Another screech and several spirits turned toward her. She did not hold on to the energy long, but it still tore through her. She channeled it into her arms and directed the blast toward the closest spirits.

Her head knocked against the stone and a white light flashed across her eyes. Her vision returned, and she was falling to her knees. She grabbed onto a rough part of the wall and shook herself. That had been risky, but it had ripped into a few spirits, so now she distracted them from Tsuran. Keeping one hand on the crystal wall, she rushed down the path until it widened and she had more room to run.

Flames burst in front of her, rock shooting into her face. Her arms came up. Lightning struck the ground beneath her, shattering it and sending her into the wall. She fell to the ground, groaned, but got to her feet.

Another strike of fire missed her. Behind her, four spirits floated toward her. She grabbed the wall, drew in the energy, and released it in their direction. Her breath was heavy, and the wrappings on her arms looked red. Parts of her arms split.

Even though she was not letting the energy remain in her body for very long, repeatedly doing this was cutting her up. But it pushed three of the spirits away and sliced another in half. She had no choice but to do this. She risked losing an arm, or worse, her life.

She scanned for Tsuran and found him on the far path. Several of the largest Commons surrounded him. Fire struck the ground around him, but it looked like he dodged. Did he still have the crystal? It was so hard to see.

Another spirit burst out of the water next to her and landed in front of her. Watching Tsuran would have to wait.

The spirit was three times her height and its mouth was wide and shining with light. Bright white fangs dripped with some mucus that sizzled when it touched the ground.

It lunged at her. She jumped out of the way. That vast mouth chomped onto the ground, cracking the stone. She regained her footing and launched back to erupt its energy. But the mouth moved around the body as though it were independent of it and bit down.

Nasna dodged again. The spirit ravaged the ground. She pushed herself back at the spirit, thrusting an arm in it before its mouth could move toward her. This spirit's insides gnawed at her arm, eating it away. She screamed and erupted the spirit's energy. Glowing blue blood splattered across her and sent her flying backward, crashing along the floor until she stopped and coughed up red blood.

A loud crack and explosion boomed through the cavern and Nasna turned toward the source. Several of the spirits had combined their lightning and flames and shot it right at Tsuran. Shattered rocks flew. As did Tsuran.

"Nasna, the crystal!"

Her eyes widened. She saw it. A yellow glow flew in the air, away from the explosion, away from Tsuran. It arced in the air and dropped into the water.

She pushed herself off the ground. "You've got to be kidding me."

She ran to the water and looked into the clear, dark waters. The glowing crystal fell deeper and deeper. No telling how deep the lake was, so she had to act fast.

The cavern quaked beneath her. Nasna glanced over and groaned. A spirit descended from the ceiling on a far end of the cavern and it filled a good portion of the space. A Large. Larger than five combined Commons. It wailed as five arms burst from its back, all ablaze with green flames. These arms crashed into the ceiling and the walls, shaking the cavern and cracking rock everywhere. The other spirits also attacked the surrounding stone, throwing all of their flames, lightning, and glowing claws into whatever was near.

Walls and ceilings broke off and fell, crashing against the ground and water. Nasna froze. A cold sweat built over her body. The spirits wouldn't let them leave. They'd cause this cavern to collapse in on itself before they allowed Nasna and Tsuran to escape.

But she wasn't leaving without a yellow-crystal. She rushed back to the crystal wall and drew in all the energy. She gritted her teeth against the pain, turned toward the watery depths, and leaped into the cold.

The water wrapped around her body, pressing in like iced daggers. She pointed herself toward the yellow-crystal, which still looked as though it was falling, and released energy from the soles of her feet. The force shot her through the water like an arrow through air. Water pressed in from the outside while the energy pressed out from within. Both tried to crush her.

A large section of the wall or ceiling fell into the water next to her, pushing her off her trajectory and swirled her around. More rock fell around her, crashing much too close. But she pressed herself toward the yellow-crystal, releasing another small burst of energy to shoot herself toward it. The crystal continued to fall into the dark depths while the cavern collapsed above her. The deeper Nasna went, the more her lungs burned. Not only was the energy, falling rock, and freezing water trying to kill her, but she also didn't have any air left.

She struggled forward, arms reached out to the yellow-crystal. She was almost there. The water churned as more rock crashed around her. Arm after arm she pressed herself forward. The yellow-crystal was within reach.

She tried to grab it.

It slipped from her fingers and fell further into the water.

She wanted to gasp for air, to open her mouth and let in the water. Her lungs screamed inside her, and her body bellowed for release. She didn't flail but pushed herself forward one more time. She reached.

Her fingers wrapped around the yellow-crystal and she pressed it against her chest.

The surrounding water flooded with a bright blue glow. In front of her, the Large spirit emerged from the rock. The rock would prevent Tsuran and Nasna from escaping, but the spirits could still move through them if they wanted. A clawed hand of fire boiled the water as it careened toward Nasna while the other arms crackled in green light. This could kill her. She didn't have enough energy to fight back, but, then again, she didn't need to.

This would hurt.

The claw hit her. The last of her air left in water-filled screams. She clenched her teeth and shoved her hand into the arm, grabbing onto the energy within it as the flame boiled her. She drew the energy from the spirit into her. A muffled screech ripped from the spirit and the flames extinguished. She drew in more and more energy until the arm itself dissipated. Another flaming claw sped toward her, but it wouldn't touch her. Not this time.

She channeled the energy into the soles of her feet and released it. There was a dull boom below her and her body shot through the water, past falling rock and emerging spirits. All of her body hurt from the pressure of the water, the lack of air, and the pain from the energy. But she held the yellow-crystal tight, refusing to let go.

She broke through the water and soared into the air, gulping in a deep breath before she plunged back into the lake. The waters thrashed around with the walls and ceiling collapsing around her. The cavern was dark with only her necklace and the yellow-crystal giving light. She swam forward as more and more of the cavern broke above her. Waves hit her on all sides, spiraling her toward one end and another. She gasped. Where was she? Which way to land?

"Nasna, quick!"

Over there. Tsuran stood waving his necklace. She swam toward him.

The cavern boomed with the falling of rock and the screeching of spirits. Needing one last push, she drew in energy from her lightstone and released it from her feet. She sailed through the water and crashed onto the land. She gasped for air, which hurt just as much as having nothing to breathe. But she still had the yellow-crystal.

Tsuran came to her side and picked her up. Everything around them shattered and broke. He held her up, and they ran for the exit.

All the cavern collapsed around them.

Tsuran shoved her into the entranceway and she pressed herself through. The entrance and everything else quaked again.

"Run, just keep running," he said.

She broke out of the entranceway and he followed just behind. He grabbed her hand, and the two rushed away as the entranceway fell behind them and the surrounding tunnel broke apart. What had started in the cavern followed them into the unstable tunnel.

He pulled her along as the walls of the tunnel collapsed in on them, rocks hitting them from every direction. He pulled her aside as a chunk of ceiling fell and almost crushed her. She pushed him forward as the floor broke beneath them. Together, they pushed and pulled themselves through the toppling tunnel. They kept running until they burst into the gallery, themselves now collapsing. The gallery shook and echoed with the booming sounds of the destroyed cavern.

Several moments passed and everything quieted and settled.

Somehow, they had made it. They could never go back to that cavern again, but they had made it.

Coughing and gasping, the two sat up and stared at each other. She looked down. They were still holding hands, so she took hers back. There were shouts from other prisoners in the gallery, but who knows what they said. Didn't matter. The two had their yellow-crystal. Tsuran tried a tired smile, and it resulted in him laughing. Nasna's heart still raced, but she smiled and laughed too.

Tsuran's idiotic and reckless plan had worked out. Now they would get onto the furnace team. And she'd be one step closer to killing Valerija.

With this thought, Nasna's laughter died in her throat.

17

DAZH CON-TSURAN

Yava, you have a daughter. I didn't want to tell you before, since I didn't know if she'd survive the birth, but she's alive and healthy and beautiful. There is little time since the Rajals are sending us away from here and I don't know what hole they plan to bury us in. I've asked nothing of you before, but I ask you now to keep your promise and take us far from here. Please come save your daughter.

She has the most beautiful eyes, by the way. They are so bright.

- Your Starlight, 363 of Our Eighth Age

Tsuran and Nasna stood still as the Warden examined the yellow-crystals they brought him. They stood in the main prison body, the clanking of furnace work in the distance and the watchful eyes of guards nearby. But Tsuran smiled and breathed in the surrounding air. This was so much better than the mines.

"This crystal for permanent places on the furnace team, is that correct Con-None?" the Warden asked, though he did not turn his gaze from the crystal.

"That's right," he said. The Warden handed the yellow-crystal off to another ordîn who headed to the stairwell with them. The Warden faced Tsuran and Nasna and nodded.

"I shall keep my word. It is done. I will inform all the guards of your new station. For now, you may return to the mines. Furnace team begins tomorrow." The Warden turned and walked away from them and the other guards escorted the two back to the shafts. Tsuran's smile widened. Even if they didn't get Dalvinder's crystal or if they came up against other major obstacles, at least they wouldn't be in the mines anymore.

They thanked the Warden and were escorted back into the mines, just in time for dinner. They grabbed their food for the night and retreated to their cell, long before curfew. But there was more comfort in their cell than in the common area of the gallery where dozens upon dozens of prisoners would love to make another accident happen.

He brought his necklace in with them and closed the door behind. Nasna was already removing her wrappings. Tsuran stretched his arms with a yawn, sat down on his bedding, and pulled apart some meat from dinner. He closed his eyes and memories of life outside the mines swirled in front of his mind. He sighed and smiled.

"I know it's all a part of our plans here," he said, "but to be honest, I am looking forward to not mining rock day in, day out."

"Right, because you did so much mining before. Is working on the furnace team all that great?" She removed the last of her wrappings and placed them beside her bed. "You're still a prisoner. Is there any pleasant job?"

"Oh, I wouldn't say pleasant. But being on the furnace team is better than down here. I'd like to be back on the hunting team, but that's not happening as long as you're my cell-mate."

Nasna sat opposite him and ate her food. "What's the furnace team like?"

"There's a bunch of furnaces, for starters. Other than that, I'm not sure. Never worked on it myself. From what I've picked up it's straightforward: pour rock into it, make sure it's boiling inside, then you let the heat do the rest. I doubt they'll have us go without some kind of training."

Nasna nodded and bit into her food, but her attention still seemed elsewhere.

"You excited to get out of these mines?" he asked.

Nasna shrugged. "It's the next part of the job, that's all."

"Well, yeah, but you must be happy to finish this up and head home, right?"

"It's just what I must do. Nothing more."

She looked away. She had the same expression she always did whenever the assassination came up. Something bordering sadness and determination. She tried to hide her face, like every other time, but there was no hiding those downcast eyes. Tsuran had once met a bounty hunter who refused to talk about her work. But that seemed more like a professional attitude than anything else. Nasna here... it was different. Despite what she said, this was more than a job to her. And if he didn't know any better, it ate away at her.

And for whatever reason, he cared.

Despite his best efforts, he enjoyed her company. Honestly, it would be hard to give up the times they had in the Crystal Cavern. They'd talk, they'd laugh, she'd freeze up like a statue and try to act all serious again.

He smiled. Genuinely smiled. And that was another thing. She kept making him smile these genuine smiles. He didn't want to lose that, lose any of this.

He pulled out his statue and held it, feeling its familiar and comforting touch. The light from his lightstone reflected off the carved gray face. It smiled. He always made sure it smiled. Helped make sense of the world.

"Tsuran?"

"Yeah?" he said. She had her strings out again but didn't do her figures. Nasna didn't glance at him and bit her lip.

"I've wanted to ask for a while," she said, her words slow and hesitant. "But what's so special about your small statue there? You reach for it when you're uneasy or need to think. I also know you look at it every night before you fall asleep, even if you try to hide it. It seems more important than a simple tool."

Tsuran paused. He hadn't realized she'd noticed that much. Instinctively, he put the statue away, his mind coming up with reasons to go to sleep or head out in the gallery or anything to get him away from here. But he looked at her eyes, at her split blue-green eye, and found himself unmoving, not even needing to move.

"It is special," he said. "This... my kids made me this."

"You're a father?"

He nodded, a heavy smile ladening his lips. "Tammara and Baz." His gaze did not leave the small statue, did not leave the last thing he had of his children. "Their mother and I were out at sea during the Hashan Raids, keeping the Veirs back. When we had some leave, we came back to find these two had made each of us little statues that, I guess, were supposed to look like us."

Nasna put her strings aside and leaned forward for a better look at the gift. "Creative kids."

"I've always guessed it was Baz's idea. He always was more the dreamer than his sister. Always turning rocks and plants into stories. I was so sure he'd grow up to be one of the great bards in the courts of the Oligarchs. But, even if the idea was his I know Tammara was the one who did the actual work. That's just the way she was. She loved working with her hands. The more dirt involved, the better. A perfect duo, those two. He imagined wonders and she made those wonders real."

Nasna smiled. "They got your face right."

He laughed. "Yeah, guess they did. Though, they didn't do the eyes. Idida did those." Nasna glanced up, brow cocked. "Oh, sorry. Idida looked after the kids in my absence. I always felt so lucky, you know? Idida was my lover, yet she loved those two as if they were her own."

Nasna frowned a moment and shook her head. "Even after all these years I've lived in Rajalend, I've never gotten used to the fact you Rajals separate lover and spouse."

Tsuran smiled. "Idida would've liked you. She came from Tutchal and I guess there the two are the same. It was an argument we had a lot. She always said she wanted to be my wife and that made no sense to me. I get her customs were different, but here she was asking for a less important place in my heart. She wanted to have a lower status."

"Yeah, that's not how the Tutchalan see it."

He nodded, still with a big smile. "I know. Sometimes I wonder if I didn't marry her just so I could see her flare up like that."

She smirked and sat back. As she did, her smile vanished and she fixed her gaze on her strings. "Tsuran... you talk of your family, but use words like 'was'."

Tsuran glanced at her but said nothing.

Nasna leaned away. "You never talk about your Partner."

"No, I guess I don't."

"Did they send him to another prison?"

"No"—Tsuran folded his hands around the statue—"I killed him."

The air thickened as if they were down in the depths of the mines. He closed his eyes and fought against the memories, against the days that led to Dazh's death, of the day it happened, of the days that followed. But fighting was useless. They always flowed so easily into his mind. His jaw clamped down, almost biting his tongue off. He squeezed his kids' statue. He said the words. The words that forced every memory to break into his mind like a stampeding beast. He had no defense against it. Everything erupted within him.

The forests of Rajalend towered around them, two Partners facing each other. Tsuran stood with his crystal statue, Dazh with his spirit. The light of the three moons bled through the canopy, only giving enough light to show the ground littered with bodies that stained the forest floor red. Idida's mangled body covered what remained of Baz. Little Tammara laid dead next to Tsuran's wife and her Partner. All of their blood pooled on the ground, leading up to Dazh, his face lit with a stained smile. Then there was the fury, the disgust, the shame.

"Just do what you do best," Dazh had said. "Run."

The scene changed and fresh blood dripped onto the ground. Dazh's blood. Tsuran stood outside his statue, standing over his dying Partner. Blood fell to the ground like teardrops.

In the far distance, a single sparrow cheeped. A steady, serene, lonesome call. In the wide forests of Rajalend, no answer came.

The chirping stopped and silence became absolute.

Tsuran stood alone. Alone in a black forest void of all light, an endless and starless sky stretched above him. It all bore down upon him, crushing him into nothingness. The darkness stabbed through him.

Sharp pain in his ear drew him away from the forest and the dead and brought him back to the cell. His heart raced, pain throbbed in his chest, and his mouth tasted dry. He glanced up to see Nasna pulling her hand away from him and he stared at her.

"Did you just pinch my ear?"

"I flicked it," she said, turning her gaze away from him. He rubbed his ear and tried regaining control of his beating heart.

"Why would you flick it?"

"I didn't know what else to do. You went away." She turned her gaze back to him. Pain pooled behind her split colored eyes. "You looked in pain so I tried bringing you back."

His breathing eased, and he wiped his forehead. "Well, unusual method, but thanks."

She pulled her legs up and placed her face on her knees. Tsuran watched her, unsure of what to do. Unsure what to make of what even happened between them. This... was not how he thought his evening would go.

And more so, he did not expect what he did next. He did not leave her or try to sleep and end the conversation.

Instead, he stayed and he spoke.

"His name was Dazh Con-Tsuran, and he and I were Partners since our seventh year. He was a gifted Soulborn and he was the one who taught me the spirit songs. And we were Partners but... we saw the world differently. We didn't have a good childhood and he wanted to see the world hurt for all the hurt it gave us. I just wanted to move on, to leave the past to be the past and just keep moving on." He took in a heavy sigh, the statue in his hand and the softness in Nasna's eyes the only reason he could press on. "I couldn't stand his tirades and I wanted more from life. That's when I met my wife. We were both Guardians who had Partners that weren't, so we made a marriage contract of being a Guardian pair. And then we went to war. But Dazh..."

It was hard to talk. The lump in his throat threatened to squeeze out any access to air and his heart felt like a lump of burning coal behind his chest. Nasna sat and waited.

"He started killing people, hundreds of people. They called him the Harvester."

Nasna's hand went up to her mouth. It seemed she'd heard of him.

Nausea built in Tsuran's stomach as he spoke. "During that whole time, I knew nothing. Some ten years he enacted his cruelty and barbarity. And I knew nothing, because anytime we came close to arguing or bringing up the past or future or anything, I left. Went back to the war effort. So I heard stories of the mass killer, but never, not for a moment, suspected the tatzon that held a piece of my soul within him.

"He kept getting worse. The things he was saying, the things he believed... and then I found out. I don't remember when I made the connections, but I realized who he was. And I panicked. I grabbed my kids, my wife, Idida, everyone. I had them pack up and we left for Tutchal. I didn't know what else to do, but I had to get them safe and I couldn't face him."

Tsuran's voice burned in his throat. He didn't want to speak anymore, but he had to. He needed to finish. "But he found us. He followed and... he killed them. My wife, her Partner, my Idida... and my kids. He killed my little Tammara and Baz. The bastard saved them for last, too!" And through the darkness, through the heavy pit in his stomach, a growl rose through him. "He was my Partner! We shared souls and history and pain and life. And he... he murdered them... tortured their minds with those spirit songs and then he..." His hands shook and he wasn't sure if it was from fury or overwhelming sadness. "For me. He did all that for me. Thinking that would change me, put me on the 'right path'. I'll never forget how surprised he looked when I rammed my crystal through his heart."

He was there again. The dark, unending forest covered in death. All he wanted was to collapse next to them, to pull his two little ones into his arms, just as he had that night. He had cried and screamed and wailed for so long. Solitude had tried to claim him that night, but sorrow had been stronger. The grief came all again.

And then, warmth.

He opened his eyes to see Nasna kneeling beside him, her hand holding his. It wasn't much. She merely held his hand, and yet her presence was like a small torch amid the blackened forests of night. So small, so insignificant, yet amid the oppressive darkness of his soul that chilled his body and obscured the light in the room, she stood as a haven of radiance.

He cleared his throat and took his hand back, backing away from the haven and returning to the night. "Let's not talk about this anymore."

She nodded and returned to her side of the cell. "I'm sorry, Tsuran."

"Yeah, well, thanks, I guess." He shook himself. Time to change the subject as far from Dazh as possible. "Enough about me, what about you?"

"Me?"

"Yeah, how did you come to be a part of the Shadow Strikers? It's not an organization I'd expect an ordîn to join."

The ease in her body disappeared and she looked as tense as she had the night he proposed their teaming together. Didn't seem like a topic she wanted to discuss, so he added, "Never mind. It's better we sleep." He turned over on his side, closing his eyes and wishing upon every wish he'd be able to sleep tonight without dreaming of the story he told. Those nightmares were ones he could live without.

"It's because I'm clipped."

Tsuran looked over. Nasna sat still, legs tucked into her chest, her hands going through her string figures. She didn't look at him.

"What?" he asked. She didn't speak for a few moments, but Tsuran waited. She spoke slow at first, as if speaking were a struggle.

"I'm a Shadow Striker because I'm clipped," she said. Her voice was devoid of strength or joviality. It sounded empty, defeated. "It's the only place I'm welcome. It's only with them I can follow...." She shook her head. She shoved her legs away from her, tossing the blanket over her and turning away from him. "It doesn't matter. This is who I am now. Who else besides assassins would welcome a mur... a clipped ordîn like me?"

Their cell became as silent as the rest of the gallery, with only the faint steps of the sentries echoing in the distance. He gazed at her, but she didn't stir and didn't speak again. He turned over, her words in his ears, his chest stirring with feelings and hopes he didn't understand. With just a single moment, he understood her, understood how different she was. Understood what she could mean to him. And as he closed his eyes to sleep, her question swirled in his mind. Who would welcome a clipped ordîn?

He didn't realize he whispered. He didn't realize the words came out of his mouth.

———————◆○◆———————

Idiot. Idiot. Idiot!

What was she thinking? What kind of insanity was she getting into? She'd almost told him the truth. Nasna kept her blankets over her and looked straight at the wall.

Get a hold of yourself, Nasna. Don't forget your Path. Don't let him confuse you more....

Confuse more? It was all confusing. Why had she asked about the statue or his Partner? Why did she even care? She didn't. Of course, she didn't.

But then she'd come close to telling him the truth of why she was here. Of who she truly was. Why mention being clipped? This was dangerous and wrong. She had to tell him to not get the wrong idea. He couldn't start asking questions or probing deeper. They were getting way too familiar with each other.

But... what if she had told him? What would have happened?

That was easy. He'd realize she was just as much a monster as his Partner had been. Then he'd have to... have to....

She wanted to kick herself. Why did she care? She was a Shadow Striker. This was her Path, her destiny. What he thought of her didn't matter. He was a tool to help her, nothing more. Just a tool. Just a—

A faint whisper reached her ears. Not from guards outside or her Path within. It was Tsuran. He'd said those words. An answer to her question of who would welcome her. A question she didn't think had an answer.

"I would."

She turned toward him but he didn't look back. Was she meant to hear those words? Did he mean—

She shook her head again and glared at the wall. No, she didn't care and wouldn't care. She was a Shadow Striker. He didn't change this. Nothing did. Why... why was he making this so complicated?

Those two words hit her in the chest, leaving her breathless. They couldn't be true. Not if he knew the whole truth. Not if he knew the Path she walked in. She shut out the words. She wouldn't let them in.

But try as she might, there was a single thought she couldn't fight back. One she couldn't suppress. Try as she might, this whisper from her weakness made its way through the walls of her Path.

And I would stand by you.

18

HIDDEN WAYS

N imat, I know you all have significant influence in Rajalend, will you not help me in this? I know they are in Rajalend, they could not have been sent far. I only need information, contacts, locations, anything that you can spare I will accept. I was foolish to leave her so destitute, but I could not have imagined a child coming from our union. How could I know it was even possible? But I am a father now and must do something before my opponents discover her and the child. No one will follow me if they know I've coupled with a tatzon.

But... my daughter has Bright Eyes... she needs me.

- Yavahush the Stargazer, King of Tifre, in the 2960th Lunar Cycle

The allure of the furnace team wore off after the first wheelbarrow of ore.

Tsuran glanced over the side to the furnaces far below. Nasna worked away, letting the iron magma flow. That damn girl and her work ethic. Sure, he'd become accustomed to the rhythm of the team as much as she had, but where he tried to prolong every action, she wanted to pull double duty. She couldn't have been enjoying the work. It had to be an ordîn thing. He smiled. They'd have to chat later about her not showing him up.

He passed from the warm air of the furnace room into one of the darker tunnels that led out from it. A few other workers walked in front of him, all pushing the wheelbarrows, while others passed them going back to the furnaces, their barrows filled with coal and ore. The tunnel led out of the furnace room and over the main body to a single large chamber above the mining shafts. Throughout the day, a few furnace workers had to hoist all the mined ore from the shafts to the higher level. His least favorite job, but he wasn't having to do that today.

But he'd have to do it tomorrow. That was a big downside to this team: there wasn't any way for him to get out of work. Down in the mines, he could go down a single tunnel and disappear with Nasna for hours upon hours and no one would be the wiser. Not here. He'd complain to Nasna about it again tonight. And, just like every night so far, she'd just roll her eyes and keep doing her string figure thing. It was a ritual he was looking forward to.

Tsuran followed the path into the wide chamber where they stored the iron ore and coal. Some prisoner years ago had dubbed the place the Dump Room, due to the towering piles of ore and coal scattered throughout the room.

Once in the chamber, he shoveled a mix of ore and coal into his barrow, but his mind went to the reason they were on the furnace team. The Warden's office. That elusive and untouchable sanctum. It'd been a while since joining the team and still no plan. There weren't any obvious ways to the ordîn level besides going up the stairs, but that wasn't an option.

None of the pathways up here led anywhere expect the mining shafts and the furnace room. Though, one section of the walkways opened up to the main body. One wrong step there meant a fall to the death.

The only other exit was the dark hole the water flowed into in the furnace room. The guards always were sure to keep prisoners away from it, though it didn't seem likely any would throw themselves in. There was only rushing water crashing into rock and descending into darkness. And everyone knew where it led to. The Pits.

A shiver ran down his spine and he pushed his now full wheelbarrow back with the other works. There were too many rumors and thoughts about what awaited people in the Pits.

Beasts. Spirits. A giant ordîn who ate tatzon flesh. No one knew, but no one sent down ever came back.

He returned to the furnaces and the ordîn monitor directed him on the iron to coal ratio. Once done, just like every other time, Tsuran turned right back around and headed to the Dump Room. He groaned to himself. Three more hours and he would trade with Nasna.

The prisoners he walked with made their way into the Dump Room first, taking some easier spots right near the front. Not wanting to be too close to them, Tsuran wheeled his way deeper to the far corners where few rarely ventured. He didn't go far enough to where Solitude had a chance of settling in, but he could go further than most. Solitude had always affected other tatzons quicker and with greater ferocity than it had to him. He hated to admit it, but his parents' experiments had worked.

The corner was darker than the rest of the chamber, his necklace being the only light around, and the mounds of coal and iron hid him from view. He needed to hurry with his work. The shovel flew in a frenzy, digging into the black mounds and tossing the ore into the barrow. Coal scattered around as his shovel swung through the air. The room was a mess anyway, so it didn't matter. As long as Solitude didn't come in, he'd be fine.

He turned to shovel iron from next to the wall and paused. His necklace cast light over the black wall, revealing an even darker space. Inspecting it closer, it looked like this section of wall had a large fissure running from the ground up. Rock and debris littered the ground next to his feet, including a small boulder that stood below his waist. It sat against the crack, covering the bottom, but something about it seemed off. He examined it again. The stone didn't appear as if it'd dropped. It leaned at an angle against the wall, over the fissure. An intentional placement.

Tsuran grabbed the boulder and pushed it aside with great effort. He crouched down and light shone inside the wall. The light did not hit any wall deeper inside but revealed the crevice ran into the mountain, a crawlspace of sorts.

No... a passage. A hidden passage.

The voices of the other prisoners drifted further away, out of the room. They were leaving without him.

No time to think about it, he took out his kids' statue and placed it inside the fissure. He grabbed his barrow and rushed back to the others.

Through much difficulty, he reigned in his giddy smiling and focused on his work until midday arrived. As soon as the guards announced a break, Tsuran descended the ladder and hurried over to Nasna. She had already gathered their lunches for the day and handed one to him when he arrived, which he dug into.

"Hey, take it easy," she said. "Eating fast won't help you much."

He nodded and moved to the farthest corner and sat down. She joined him. After a moment of eating, he leaned in close to her.

"Hey, are you able to exorcise?"

She leaned back, head tilted. "What?"

"Can you exorcise like other ordîns?"

"I'm sure I already told you I can... but why?"

Tsuran smiled. "I want to do a little exploring." He settled into the far corner trying to make himself as invisible as possible.

Nasna scooted in. "Exploring? Don't tell me you're going to try possessing right now?"

"I found this big hole in the Dump Room that seems to just keep going. I want to find out if it goes anywhere."

"Are you insane?" Her voice dropped to a whisper. "They have Sensors everywhere. You possess here and they'll come for us."

"Not all of them have that great of range. And besides, if you think they're suspecting me or are getting too close, you just exorcise me and bring me back."

"You're mind-possessing?" she asked, and he nodded. She let out a sigh and rubbed her forehead. "We shouldn't be taking risks like this, Tsuran. We have to figure out other things."

"We should seek every useful bit of information, right? Might lead somewhere good."

"How are you even going to get your statue to the Dump Room without being seen?"

He smiled. "It's already there."

She raised a finger. "But... don't you need to see it?"

"When you possess a single thing enough times, you can sense it. You can possess without seeing."

She shook her head. "This is reckless."

"I sure hope so."

And with a grin, he reached out to his statue and mind-possessed it. His mind whisked away from his body toward the statue and he no longer sat on the floor of the furnace room but stood as his statue in total darkness.

Mind-possession remained a strange experience. He was here and yet not. His spirit moved the statue and yet his body remained on the floor next to Nasna. Mind-possession felt more invasive, more unnatural, to him than body-possession, though he didn't understand why. Regardless, he rushed down the hole in the wall. He wanted to explore but he would have to be fast. Not only would some Sensor feel him possessing, but if he stayed too long Solitude would become a problem. In reality, he had little time to explore. Now that he was here, it might have been a better idea for Nasna to explore this place. Oh well.

He held out a stony hand in front of him and one against the wall as he ran. Without lightstone, he had no way of telling where he ran or how far. His size meant he fit inside, but this also meant he would run for what seemed like miles but it'd only be a few yards. Mind-possession didn't have empowering capabilities, so he settled with running through the ever-continuing darkness. But there didn't appear to be anything special about this space. It just kept going into the mountain. With all the hundreds and thousands of prisoners who lived here over the centuries, there had to be secret passages. And he needed this to be one of them.

The pitch-black that surrounded him was so all-consuming he couldn't tell if he moved at all. For all he could tell, the statue kept running in place.

Wait... there, down the way. That might be... it was. A glint of light. The light grew brighter as he came closer and the passage curved. He reached the corner and turned around it. So much light. And beyond it... he smiled. He'd been right.

He fell to his knees and gasped, his self being wrenched and ripped from the statue. Someone pulled Tsuran out, dragged his mind through air and stone, and thrust him back into his body.

His eyes snapped open, and a gasp escaped his lungs. Nasna had a hand on his chest and pressed the other to his mouth, stifling his gasp. But her gaze remained steady on the entranceway. From there, several guards entered, and they gazed around the room.

"Good timing," he said in a whisper. She nodded and looked back at him. Her wrappings were open just enough for him to see her different colored eyes. They were not happy.

"You are an idiot," she said. "You almost ruined everything just now."

Tsuran shrugged. "But I didn't, and I think you should be grateful."

She crossed her arms and brought her gaze back toward the guards, who didn't seem to glance in their direction, yet. Sensors, trying to determine if possession had occurred or not. With them here, he wouldn't possess again. But as long as he wasn't actively possessing, they couldn't trace it back to him.

"And why should I be grateful?" Nasna asked.

"Because," Tsuran said, grabbing his food, "I may have found a way to the Warden's office."

Her attention snapped back to him. Her eyes were wide behind the slits in her wrapping, but he didn't need to see them to know he had her undivided attention.

"What? Are you serious?"

He nodded and then paused. "Well, maybe. You brought me back before I investigated further. But I think I found a secret passageway in the Dump Room." He told her about the crevice in the back of the room. Nasna nodded.

"And?"

"Once I was far enough in, I turned this corner and saw a hole in the floor."

"A hole? What do you mean?"

"You brought me back before I was close enough to see, but there was a lot of light pouring in from it. But that's not the best part"—he leaned in and so did she—"I heard guards in there."

Nasna brought a hand to her chin. "What does this mean?"

"Not sure. But I think it's worth investigating further. I shouldn't do it again since there are Sensors around, so when you're up there, check it out."

She pulled away. "Well, we've had no other good lead so far so it's worth checking out, I suppose. But"—she raised a finger at him—"no more possessing. That was too close."

He raised his hand. "On my life."

A grin broke across his face. She shook her head, then stopped. "Tsuran."

She pointed to his raised hand, and he looked over. It shook.

He frowned. "Oh." He brought it into his lap to hold it still. "I guess I was alone long enough for Solitude to come in." She kept gazing at his hand and he tried to smile. "I'll be fine. Not alone too long so this isn't a problem. It'll be over before you know it."

She returned to her food and added nothing more. It was not long before they had to get back to work. This time she headed to the upper levels, and he worked on the furnace below. There was nothing else for him to do with the time so he tried to focus on the work in front of him. Though, he kept glancing up above trying to see when Nasna would come back.

When she finally came back into view, she didn't look down at him. She kept working, not giving him any sign of anything. Tsuran sighed. Either she had found nothing, or he wouldn't hear about it until later when they were back in their cell.

It was a long day.

At the end of their work, the guards escorted the furnace team back into the mines. Tsuran stayed close to her, but she still didn't say what the light had been. Inside the mines again, the two grabbed their dinner and rushed back to their cell. Seeing her in such a hurry brought a smile to his lips again. Once in their cell, he had to stop himself from shouting as he turned toward her.

"What did you find?"

She placed her food and water onto the ground and let out a controlled breath as she unwrapped the cloth from her head. And yet, this time, it seemed she took her precious time doing this. Tsuran began tapping his foot and crossed his arms.

"Well?"

"It was a tight fit, but I crawled into the space," she said, folding her wrappings into neat squares and placing them beside her. "And to begin I found this." She held out his statue to him. His arms unfolded, some tension released from his body, and he took it. He felt the familiar form in his hands and tucked it back into his pocket.

"Thank you."

"I also found the light you were talking about. And when I looked closer it was just like you said. That passageway leads to a hole that opens up to the ordîn level."

Tsuran sighed and smiled. He knew it.

"Then I guess we found our way to the Warden's office," he said.

"Almost," she said and sat down, pulling out her string. "We can't be hasty about this. We should watch the movements below the hole. See if there are any routines, patterns. We should learn as much as we can before we make any plan."

"Fair enough, but it must excite you to have a lead."

She nodded but seemed to become lost in thought as she went through her string figures. Tsuran let himself do the same as he ate. It had been a hunch, a gut feeling, and it had paid off. It had been a passageway, and it was what they were looking for. He agreed with Nasna about watching and learning all useful information before they made a move. However, he doubted she realized she'd have to be the one to do all of that. From her description, he wouldn't fit in the hole, anyway. Besides this, him watching would cause Solitude to settle in. Perhaps he could delay it if he kept seeing an ordîn, but he didn't want to risk it. Tatzons never spied alone. He'd admit it was one fault of his kind.

"Tsuran?"

He looked up from his food. "Have a plan?"

"Hm? Oh, no." She stopped her figures and placed them in her lap, though she didn't look at him. "I just wanted to thank you."

Tsuran paused. He put his food down. "For what?"

"Everything. You've taken some colossal risks in helping me, some of which were downright foolish. But you've continued to risk so much." She looked at him, but her gaze fell. "I understand you're doing this just so you can escape. But I want you to know I appreciate all you've done. I doubt I would have made this kind of progress without you. I haven't been the warmest of people to be around, but I'm..."

She hesitated, her mouth hanging open. She took in a breath and looked him straight in the eye. "I'm glad they put us together in this cell. I'm glad to have met you, Tsuran Con-None."

She held the gaze. But not long. It dropped to the ground, and she resumed her string figures.

"I'm only saying that once," she said, her voice trying to become gruff, and failing. "But I thought I ought to say it. Anyway, goodnight."

She took her food and turned away from him.

Tsuran remained as still as he had been when she first spoke those words. He hadn't smiled, hadn't blinked, hadn't made a sound. He wasn't even sure if he'd breathed or if his heart had beat at all.

She was glad to have met him.

He opened his mouth, to say the same, but Dazh's voice drifted in his ears, *"Run."*

Tsuran clamped his jaw tight and turned away from her and faced the shadows in the the cell. It... it was time. He'd held up his end and helped her get what she needed. Now she'd help him get what he needed. Then he'd leave. He'd leave it all behind.

With or without her.

19

THE WARDEN'S ROOM

Y our personal plight does not interest us, neither does the search for a common criminal. Our power is great, but are we to stop all our activity, all of the work we do for the world, and search on our hands and knees for such an insignificant outcome? Our aims, your aims, are much higher and greater than this. Do not become distracted, Yavahush. Keep focused on the trade agreements with the quintal. It is a precarious thing, yet it is vital for our plans to succeed. You are king first, and everything else second. Do not forget that.

- Nimat, the Void Within

Nasna wished she could wipe away the sweat from her brow. The heat from the furnace blared and remained constant. Sweat drenched her head wrapping, which made it itch without relief. Tsuran volunteered to do most of the furnace work close to the heat during their shifts. But for this morning they'd switched, so he worked on the higher level hauling in the coal and ore. They would switch again after midday when he finished his preparations. She continued her diligent work in their corner where the guards still had a blind spot. The morning lumbered along, despite the work. The plan engrossed her mind. They only had a ten-minute window of opportunity. But ten minutes would be more than enough for her.

A guard announced the break for midday. Nasna grabbed Tsuran's and her food and headed over to their corner. A few moments later Tsuran joined her.

"Ready?" he asked, looking over his shoulder.

She nodded. "Is everything ready on your end?"

He didn't answer, still looking behind him and rubbing his hands together. Nasna flicked his arm, and he jumped a little as he glanced back at her.

"What?"

"Everything ready with you?" she asked, tilting her head.

"Yeah, it's in position. We're ready when he's out."

"Alright," she said, looking him over. Perhaps it was his nerves, but he'd been acting off the entire day. He needed to relax and focus. This was a big day. But he didn't look like he needed a reprimand. Maybe some reassurance. "Hey, Tsuran, are you alright?"

His attention snapped to her. "What? Yeah. Why you ask?"

"You haven't even tried to annoy me all day. You seem nervous."

"Do I?" he said, putting on a smile. "Guess it's just that we have a lot hanging on today. I haven't broken into the office before either. So... yeah, just a little nervous."

She looked up at him, frowning. "Hey, maybe we shouldn't do this today. Don't need your nerves throwing us off."

"What? No, it'll be fine. We'll be fine."

"I'm serious Tsuran. You don't seem in the right mindset. We can just do it tomorrow."

He flicked the side of her head before she swatted him away. With a wry smile, he took his food to the side to sit down. "It'll be fine. Stop worrying so much."

Nasna sighed. She stretched her arms above her and sat in the furthest corner where she could adjust her wrappings to eat without being seen.

Perhaps he was right. Perhaps she was the one with the nerves. She chewed on a dried piece of mountain rat and watched him do the same, his smile remaining plastered on his face. She put her food down and rubbed where he flicked her. He was right. They weren't waiting for tomorrow. They knew the plan. Now, they just had to do it.

She finished her food and gulped down her water. "I suppose I'll get in position."

"See you soon."

As she passed him, she hesitated, but flicked his ear in retribution. He shot her a look and she felt rather satisfied by it. Nasna walked to the ladder in the middle of the room and climbed. The Warden would start his lunch soon and Nasna wanted to be sure the guards saw her working before anything happened. On top, she grabbed one sack and threw it over her shoulder and ignored the wheelbarrows as she had the entire week. It was easier to hide a sack than a barrow and using a sack meant they'd expect her to take longer than others.

She walked along the narrow paths and bridges, keeping herself in plain sight of guards whenever she could until she reached the Dump Room. Nasna filled her sack and marched back to the furnace room where she dumped the contents in the furnace's top under the watchful eye of the ordîns.

She repeated the process as many times as time allowed, but never brought full sacks since she didn't want to wear herself out. She needed to appear like she was working, though she made sure she did not do any of this too fast.

Since this plan had come into fruition, both she and Tsuran had worked slower than the others. Not slow enough to get punished or draw the ire of the guards, but slow enough to set their own pace. Enough to create the expectation that they'd disappear without being seen for several minutes at a time. If one or even both of them were missing for ten minutes, no one would suspect anything.

Her third pass back, she picked up a small rock and let it drop below her to where Tsuran was. He looked up, and they nodded to each other. It was time.

She made her way back to the Dump Room, passing a few of the other furnace workers. She filled her sack, keeping a sideways glance toward the other prisoners in the room and waited for them to leave. When the other two wheeled their contents out of the room, Nasna acted.

She ran to the back of the room behind the large piles of coal and ore. Past much of the rock and to the far wall where the small boulder laid against it, waiting for her.

She rolled it to the side, hid her sack behind, and, before any other prisoners entered the room, dropped to her belly and crawled into the pitch darkness. The muted stillness of the passage continued to send prickly chills up her spine, but she pressed on, careful to not cut herself on the jagged sides of the crevice. The light from the ceiling opening came into view and she slowed her movements, making each one careful until she reached the edge.

Peering over, a couple of guards patrolling beneath came into view. A male and female. Young for guards, both orange in green cycle. Seeing them meant Nasna had about a minute before the Warden would leave his office. Once he did, she would have to act fast.

She looked to the side of her shoulder and grinned. Tsuran's statue stood with all four arms saluting her. It wasn't moving at the moment so he wasn't possessing it yet. She gazed at it.

Get here soon, Tsuran.

A large door shut below and she looked through the hole. She couldn't see the office from where she was, but it wasn't long after that the Warden walked beneath her. She held her breath.

It was now or never. She glanced over. The statue remained motionless.

The Warden was now past her place and made his way down the hallway. As soon as he turned the corner, Nasna would have three minutes to get into his office unseen. From there she would have the rest of the seven minutes to find what they were looking for and to get back into this passage. But there was no moving if she didn't know Tsuran was beside her. She had no way back if he wasn't here.

Something tapped her shoulder, and she looked over to see the small statue waving at her. She could almost feel his smug expression smiling back at her. They would talk later about his timing, for now she moved.

She pulled herself through, keeping one hand on the ledge as she nimbly moved her body out until she dangled halfway from the ceiling to the floor. She dropped several feet, landing softly. As soon as she touched down, she sped through the hall toward the doors of the Warden's office, pulling out her lock picks.

She arrived at the door and worked away. It was a competent lock and gave her pause for a moment. But the footsteps of the next patrol were coming from just around the next corridor. She needed to hurry. She had to ignore the sound and focus on the lock.

A solid click came from the door and she swung it open and moved inside.

Seven minutes.

She rushed to the second door in the room, going past the bookcases and desk, and went to work unlocking it. This didn't take as long as the first had and she was in within a moment. The door opened to a large storage room filled with rows upon rows of shelving and dozens of crates, stacked and otherwise. The Warden filled every shelf with the various items he'd taken from prisoners over the years, though what he did with any of it was anyone's guess. However, that wasn't her problem. Her problem was the fact it'd take hours to search through all of it.

But she didn't need to. As she walked into the room, there was a strange sensation that swept through her. She knew where she had to go. Nasna rushed to the back of the storage room, ignoring the shelves full of different trinkets, jewelry, clothes, books, and even weapons. It was amazing what prisoners tried to sneak in. Such idiots.

There was so much in the room. Plenty of things to hold the crystal in, yet something in her, her instinct perhaps, told her to keep going to the back. She had an image of a black box with a tree emblem emblazoned on it. She shook her head. It was a strange thought. She hadn't considered it before, but now it made so much sense.

A lightstone in the ceiling lit the room, so she wasn't groping around in the dark. She reached the back of the room. And there, on a shelf next to a set of books, sat a black box with what looked like the emblem of the Ethereal Tree. Ten silver tree trunks twisted around each other and then sprouted ten branches that curved and entwined with the roots to create a perfect silvery circle.

Except, oddly, this emblem only had eight trunks and branches. She opened the lid and green light filled the room, pouring from a green-crystal the size of her fist. Yet it looked different from other green-crystal, brighter somehow. She placed a hand onto the crystal and felt an immense amount of energy, even more than the yellow-crystal. A small crystal, yet there was an intense power within it.

No wonder Dalvinder wanted this back. Doubtful sentimentality had much to do with it. It didn't much matter. She had the crystal. It was time to go. She turned toward the office when the door to the hallway opened and shut.

She froze. There should still be time. The Warden was never back this early, and it'd only been a few minutes. Had someone seen her?

She took slow steps toward the door, her ears listening to the footsteps which seemed to belong to only a single set and not a whole patrol of guards. She crept to the open door and peered outside.

"Tsuran?"

He looked at her and smiled.

"What in the Abyss are you doing here?" She walked out of the storage room but looked at his hand. He was holding a small figurine made of red-crystal, about a hand tall. He must've found it on the Warden's desk.

He held up the figurine and smiled. "Since we were retrieving things the Warden had taken, I figured I might as well take something he'd taken from me."

That figurine had belonged to him? She shook her head. "Tsuran, just go, we don't have a lot of time anymore."

"Sure thing. Made sure the crystal is inside that?"

She rolled her eyes. He was wasting time, but she opened it to show him the crystal. He smiled and reached for it. But he stopped, his eyes widened, his mouth fell open, and he stumbled backward. Nasna closed the box. "What is it?"

"Nas, we can't bring that back to Dalvinder." His voice was low. What was he talking about?

"Tsuran, we don't have time for this, we can discuss this—"

"That's a spirit vessel. There's a spirit in that."

Nasna glanced at the box. A spirit vessel? Why would Dalvinder—no, it didn't matter. Only getting to Valerija did.

"Tsuran, we'll discuss what to do with it later but for now we have to go." They were wasting time. Even if it was a spirit vessel, it was no more dangerous than being caught trying to steal it. Nasna tucked the black box into her clothes and rushed toward the door. With a groan, Tsuran followed behind her. She'd wanted enough time to lock the doors to keep out suspicion. Tsuran was slowing everything down.

"What I wouldn't give for a key," she said. A small jangle came from behind her. She turned and he held up a chain of keys. She grabbed them, ran outside, and locked the door behind them.

"Where'd you find this?"

"On his desk. I figured he wouldn't miss a few keys here and there."

They rushed back to the opening in the ceiling, though she wished Tsuran would be quieter. She was unsure of how much more time they had. However much they had, they needed more.

"Give me a boost," she said. Tsuran folded his hands together, giving her a place to step onto. As she stepped, he tossed her upward, and she grabbed a hold of the edge of the passage. Nasna struggled to pull herself up but almost stopped, hearing the next patrol coming from down an adjoining hallway. In less than a minute they would see them.

Tsuran cursed and jumped, pushing her with the boost she needed. But as she pulled herself up, the black box caught on the edge. She pulled herself into the crevice but it slipped out of its holding. Her upper half was inside the passage, so she couldn't do anything. It dropped, along with her heart. She paused, waiting for the clatter on the floor. Instead, Tsuran said,

"I caught it. Go, just go."

She wasted no more time and pulled herself into the crevice and crawled through.

"Tsuran, don't get caught. And don't you dare lose that crystal."

20

---◆○◆---

PAIN OF FAILURE

*I am leaving for Rajalend. I have found some leads on where they've
taken the two of them and I will investigate. I understand this will
displease the six of you, but understand I have no gods any longer. But I
can have those two. And do not think I neglect my duties. I have arranged
for Ordal of the Long Night to attend the trade talks with the quintal. He
is more than capable and thus I am not needed there. This task of mine
is too important, and if you shall not help, then I shall go alone.*

-Yavahush the Stargazer, Lover and Father, in the 2961st Lunar Cycle

Tsuran watched Nasna disappear from view and cursed himself.
The guards were just around the corner so he didn't have time to
even try getting himself up there.

He grabbed the red-crystal statue and threw it up at the ceiling.
It hit against the wall of the opening and bounced against the
stone. The crystal clanked against his kids' statue, knocking it loose
from its perch and sending it over the edge. He cursed and caught it.
What he wouldn't give to have an arm to possess multiple statues.

He glanced up. The crystal statue rolled to the edge, threatening
to teeter off. Tsuran held his breath. The guards turned around the
corner. No more waiting to see if it fell.

He possessed his small statue but did not empower his size,
instead falling to the ground with the black box held above his tiny

form. He fell quite a distance, at least in his perspective, however, he landed without a crash and rushed to the wall, empowering his speed. Tsuran threw himself against the stone wall. Thank the gods for his statue matching the rock. Without looking for him, they wouldn't see him.

Tsuran watched the giant bodies of the ordîn guards walk down the hallway to where he stood. He prayed they would ignore him, ignore the black box, and that the red-crystal wouldn't fall. He remained motionless as they approached.

One stopped and she stared right at him.

"Possessor!"

Without hesitation, both guards charged.

Right. He forgot about the Sensors. Time to run then.

He turned and empowered his speed down the hall. The shouts of guards came from behind him as he rushed through the hallway, other guards from far down the corridor also taking up the call.

Even with empowering his speed, the statue stayed small so he ran about as fast as a regular person. To him, he sprinted down the hall with the speed of the wind. But in reality, all the guards closed in on him.

His statue was too small for them to grab, but he had to get away with the box and out of sight before he unpossessed. If he was going to get away with this, they couldn't see him unpossessing.

That's if he could get away with this. And it was a big "if".

He slid down one side of the hall as he tried turning to face the stairway, a descent reminiscent of a mountain. The whole place became chaotic with the number of guards coming into the main area. It'd be tricky to maneuver around all of them. Trickier still deciding where he would go. But no stopping now, and he descended the stairwell, or rather jumped from step to step.

The ordîns followed behind and awaited him at the bottom. But they weren't the only ones he needed to worry about. Nasna was still in the crevice. If they caught him before she got out.... Tsuran ground his stony jaw. Get his statue and get out. That had been the plan... but not this. He hadn't meant to endanger her. They were supposed to have more time. How had he timed it so poorly?

Dazh's awful laughter filled his ears, "*Run, Tsuran. Just run.*"

Tsuran looked ahead, seeing the long hallway of lightstone. Past there was freedom. His mistakes couldn't follow him out there and he would not let his foolishness today get Nasna caught. He'd need to distract them long enough for her to get out, long enough for her to have an alibi. So, he'd have to run.

Tsuran looked around as he jumped each step. With every moment it seemed the guards increased their numbers, and all of them seemed to know where he was. As long as there were Sensors around, he wouldn't be able to outrun them or hide from them.

He maintained his empowerment and rushed down the center of the wide cavern toward the bright light pouring from the main entrance hall. The surrounding guards tried stomping on him, smashing him with their clubs, grabbing at him, but he was small and fast enough that they were like lumbering giants. It was a little fun.

One guard hit him with a club, sending the box sliding away from him. He left it. A spirit vessel was not worth being caught.

Halfway to the doors, a voice boomed behind him. "Close the doors. Do not let the prisoner out."

Ordîns took off in flight, soaring above him into the hallway. Tsuran ground his teeth. If he made it through the doors, he'd have a chance. But above all, Nasna would have the time she needed. So, he had to risk it. He empowered his possession and grew his statue to his full height, which made his speed even greater.

He raced the guards, his stony feet crashing against white-crystal, a flurry of wings beating around him as dozens of ordîns flew as fast as they could, shouting out to those on the other side of the doors.

A loud clunk sounded through the hallway and Tsuran saw the doors closing.

He doubled his speed. Tripled it. He neared the doorway to life.

It slammed shut.

Tsuran skidded to a halt, his heart dropping. Before he could dwell on that, guards descended upon him, so he turned and ran back into the prison's main body. But he stopped at the edge of the lightstone hallway. Guards stood at each entrance and blocked every pathway. They surrounded him. They trapped him.

On top of the stairs, the Warden watched with an unconcerned expression. Tsuran's eyes went further up to one walkway leading from the Dump Room to the furnaces.

Nasna stood there, looking down. To him, she stared right at him, expectant of some miracle. And she was out.

He shrank his statue, but a swift hand slammed into him and he felt a force grab onto his soul and pull him from his statue. He materialized onto the ground and several guards, including the one who'd exorcised him, jumped him, shoving him onto the ground and his face into the stone floor. A different guard held down each arm with several more striking him with their clubs. They were not taking any more chances with him. They pulled him up onto his knees and continued to beat him.

"Hold," the Warden said and the guards stopped.

Tsuran spat blood onto the ground while the side of his face felt warm and wet. He lifted his head. The Warden walked toward him, no sign of hurry in his steps. One guard handed him Tsuran's statue, which was about a foot long now. The Warden looked at it with a seemingly uninterested gaze.

"It seems you have been busy, Con-None."

Tsuran didn't open his mouth. Not this time. Anything he said would only worsen his situation.

"I did not even know you had this. It is curious, you are still the only Guardian I have ever met who can possess such a small statue. I am impressed." He gripped the statue and stared at Tsuran. "But this is not tolerated here. Unauthorized possession is not tolerated. Trespassing is not tolerated. Attempted theft is not tolerated. Escape is not tolerated. You shall reap the punishment of your crimes in full, Con-None."

The Warden turned to the guards in charge of the furnace area. "Where is his cell-mate? She must have had a hand in this."

"She's on the upper level of the furnaces, Warden," one guard said.

"I see her," the other said pointing. The Warden followed the direction to Nasna standing in the open walkway.

"How long has she been on that level?"

"Since after midday. She hasn't descended since then and I've seen her continue to do her work."

"I see," the Warden said. "Bring her here. I want to question her." He watched Nasna for a moment before turning back to Tsuran. "Before she arrives, tell me, Con-None, how did you two get into my office?"

Tsuran lifted his head and spat. "Don't you dare insult me. As if I'd ever team up with a human. I snuck into your office all on my own, I didn't need any Unhallowed's help."

The Warden raised his brows. "Is that so? That is hard to believe. Now, lying to me, I believe that."

"Oh, shut it. If you're going to punish me, do it already. But don't dirty my name saying a human helped me. I'd rather have my eyes burned out than for anyone to think I'd stoop so low."

Tsuran sucked in his breath. Poor choice of words.

The Warden straightened his back and gave a curt nod. "As you wish. Bring him to the furnaces."

The guards dragged him into the furnace room, other guards clearing the way for the Warden. Tsuran didn't have the strength to fight, and any struggle would worsen his fate. He should have been more careful with his words. But then again, Tsuran would rather have his eyes burned than endure Solitude, which would be in store for him if the Warden didn't believe he suffered enough.

Prisoners in the area gathered to watch, but the guards pushed them to the side. They had looks of curiosity and pure satisfaction. The deserter was at last receiving his due. He dropped his gaze. In some small way, this was justified.

The Warden had Tsuran thrown in front of a furnace. A moment later guards brought Nasna down before them. Her expression remained hidden behind her wrappings, but he was sure she was furious with him, it was the only possibility. Tsuran looked away and stared at the Warden. He wouldn't give anything away. Not a glance to tie Nasna to this. It'd been his idiocy that brought this onto him.

"Beat him," the Warden said. The guards pummeled Tsuran again, this time with even greater fervor, greater pleasure. One always kept a hand on him and Tsuran dared not fight back for fear of worse retribution. All he could do was take the abuse.

There wasn't a part of him their clubs did not strike. They dropped him to the ground and drove their weapons into him. He tried to ball up, to cover himself, but others pulled his arms and legs apart. The beating continued until he was sure his whole body bled and bruised. Another guard struck the side of his head and a ringing sounded in his ear and his sight dimmed.

Dazh laughed in his ear.

The beating stopped. The Warden must've ordered it, but the ringing drowned out all other noise.

His head pulsed, ached, and bled for sure. He wasn't sure if his eyes were opened or closed with the world so blurred as it was. But the cruel world came back to him in painful detail.

The guards pulled Tsuran onto his knees, bringing in several waves of pulsating pain through wherever they touched, and everywhere else. Through a swollen eye, Tsuran lifted his limited gaze to the Warden, now holding something he hadn't before. It was an iron rod they used to break the metal out of the molds. The Warden pulled it out of the furnace, the metal glowing red. Tsuran breathed heavier. His gaze drifted to the hot iron.

"Did this human help you?"

"No."

The Warden drove the hot iron into Tsuran's leg, searing it. Tsuran screamed and his vision blurred even more. He saw Dazh, sneering at him as his songs kept Tsuran frozen and paralyzed, unable to stop what was to come.

The Warden held the rod in his leg for what had to have been an eternity before pulling it away and back into the furnace.

"I ask again, did this human help you?"

Tsuran gritted his teeth, trying to keep his tongue behind them. "I would never... never with a human...."

The Warden drove the hot iron into his chest and Tsuran's screams filled the room. Guards held him firm against the blazing fire that seared into his flesh. The Warden didn't press hard enough to pierce through, only enough to mar, enough to torment.

But it was only the torment of Idida that he saw. Dazh seemed to have a particular hatred for her as his songs twisted and warped her, before his spirit came in and—

The Warden pulled the rod away and Tsuran gasped, trying to draw in even a mouthful of air. His heart raced, his breathing rapid and shallow. The Warden shoved the iron back into the flames, took it out, and plunged into his leg again.

Again. And again. The rod went into the furnace and then into Tsuran. Again. And again.

Dazh's laughter echoed on into forever, as though it encompassed everything. Tsuran just wanted that laughter to stop. That pain to stop.

"Run, Tsuran. Just run."

Tsuran had no more voice, his throat ripped bare by his screams. This... this was too much. He needed to confess. That's all the Warden wanted. Just a confession. If he confessed, it'd stop. He could even put all the blame on Nasna, say the ordîn forced him to do this. They'd believe that. She was clipped. An assassin. Just... confess.

"Do what you do best...."

"One last time did this human—"

Tsuran's voice rang out in a broken and hoarse shout, "I would rather die than associate myself with a human! I may be a thief and a deserter, but I am still a proud tatzon."

The Warden paused, staring at Tsuran without a change to his emotionless face. He pulled out the iron and brought it close to Tsuran's eye. The heat blazed off of it, biting into his cheeks, hovering just a small distance away. Tsuran clenched his jaw, as time seemed to slow. This was the last thing this eye would ever see.

Yet, he realized he'd do it. He would lose his eye, his life, before betraying Nasna. In a strange way, he hadn't lied. Maybe at one time it would have been a lie, but not here. Not now.

As she came into his mind, Dazh's laughter diminished and the scene of the forest faded away. Not entirely, but imagining her there in the forest with him... it made it bearable.

The Warden lowered the iron, his face unreadable. Tsuran's heart pounded against his seared chest as the Warden lifted Tsuran's statue. "A proud tatzon? Well, then I suppose we must break your pride." In a fluid motion, the Warden threw the statue into the furnace.

"No!" Tsuran tried to lunge forward, reaching for the flames, but the guards pulled him back and beat him down again. "No, please, don't burn it!"

They answered with a club to the face. He tried to struggle, but they clubbed him again. Before his eyes, his statue, the one given to him by his darling children, burned.

Tammara had spent months working on it, getting the details as good as Baz described. Idida helped with some of the finer work, but it was Baz who had wanted to do the face himself. The only time he had wanted to do any physical work

"We made this for you, daddy," Baz had said with Tammara at his side. "Now, whenever you're away, you have something to remember us by."

Tammara had beamed. Idida had kissed him.

That statue, that remembrance of his family, cracked under the heat and joined the molten iron.

"No...."

The Warden said something about Solitary cells and Tsuran being beaten and paraded before other prisoners. He mentioned Nasna. Possibly. The details of the conversation were pointless. It was all pointless. Only flame swirled in Tsuran's mind now.

He had the vague sense of being moved out of the room, of being shouted at, of being hit. But life had already ebbed out of him. It was as if all light in the world had dimmed, all warmth stolen. All that remained were the frozen bones of people who'd never be laid to rest.

The last fragment of Tammara and Baz in this world had been destroyed.

And it was Tsuran's fault.

21

THEIR ONE FRIEND

For an ordîn that has lived so many years, you are a fool. Your absence has not gone unfelt or unnoticed. The quintal took great offense at you sending your second-in-command and the agreements failed. They have even retaliated with attacking some of your shipping. Tifrans all over are whispering whether you are even fit to be king and I have heard talk of them taking drastic action toward you. And, with all of that, you failed to even find the two you sought. Was it worth it?

I have argued to the others to abandon you, but Boban wishes to give you one last chance. Do not disappoint us again, King.

-Nimat, the Void Within

Nasna stared at the iron doors leading into solitary confinement. The guards who'd just passed hadn't noticed her creep. Her presence here remained unknown.

The confinement cell was in a separate section on the first level of the mines, holed off far away from every other cell and tunnel. She and Tsuran had never gone to this area before and most prisoners avoided the area. The guards only infrequently passed by the long, empty tunnel connected to it, which meant she wasn't rushed as she stood in the open facing the door.

She needed to get the crystal. It wasn't her fault he got caught. He should have stuck with the plan. Thanks to him, she spent almost an hour with the Warden being questioned. Her alibi held enough that his Path compelled him to let her go. However, he'd likely start a thorough investigation soon enough, so her position here became precarious.

But, even with all that, she stood in the silence, not moving forward, not moving back. The rest of the prison had gone quiet with the other prisoners already asleep. The only sound came from guards walking around and the hushed tones of their chatter. Otherwise, the gallery was like a grave.

She reached for the iron door. She stopped.

He's been useful, her Path said. *But his usefulness has ended. Let him be. He was a means, and the end is in sight.*

But she needed to be sure he wouldn't break and reveal herself. What if Solitude caused him to confess? It'd be better that she see to him. This made sense. As did every other excuse and reason she layered together, all explaining why she had to go in. She made every excuse, gave every reason, but she hid the truth deep within her heart where her Path wouldn't see. She kept it hidden. She wouldn't let her Path deny her this. Not this time.

Nasna pulled out the keys Tsuran had taken from the Warden's office and hoped one of them worked on the door. She didn't mind spending the time to pick it, but keys were always simpler.

The second key she tried unlocked the door, and she breathed out. With a push, it opened to a short passage that ended with a second door. She closed the first door behind her, shunting herself off into total darkness.

Nasna placed the things she carried on the ground and grabbed a hold of the blanket and unwrapped it. Bit by bit light flowed out into the room as she unfolded the small lightstone necklace. No guards would see the light at this point. She gathered up the food, water, and blanket and unlocked the second door, which opened to another short passageway, ending with... a third door? Why would there be a third door?

She paused. This design wasn't foolish or wasteful. This was to create complete and total isolation. Not even the sound of others talking or walking by would ever reach the prisoners here.

Solitude would be complete.

She opened the final door and her light revealed a cramped space a little more than half the size of their cell. It had a low ceiling, no sleeping bar, and little air. The floor was rocky and bare.

A thin cracked voice came from the shadows,

"Is... someone there?"

"Tsuran?"

"Nas?"

She took her head wrapping off. "Yes, it's me."

Tsuran huddled in the farthest corner, though it wasn't far from the door. Nasna cast light on him and she gasped before she could stop herself.

His usual iron skin looked more like ash, which accentuated his crescent markings and many bruises. His face and body looked thinned, gaunt, as if they shriveled away. Black and purple bruising covered his neck and side of his face. And his eyes, now colorless, stared widely toward her. One of his arms laid twitching at his side, while the other two hugged his shaking body. A leg curled underneath him. The other endured a spasm in front of him.

He looked as if he would fall apart if she but breathed on him, as if he'd been diseased for months or years. It'd only been a few hours in the room and already he looked worse than when the guards tortured him or when the Warden burned him.

This was Solitude.

Nasna kept her tears out of sight, where they belonged.

"You came," Tsuran said looking at her through empty eyes.

"I brought you food and drink. I also brought you this blanket since I didn't think they'd give you one."

She placed it all next to him but he didn't move from his place, only looked at her offerings. He closed his eyes and the shaking worsened. His breathing became hard, rapid, and shallow. Nasna rushed to his side and placed a hand on his shoulder.

"Tsuran? What's wrong?"

He didn't answer. The spasm shot through his body, and he foamed at the mouth, wavering and toppling onto his side.

"Tsuran!"

His body stopped, and she held one of his hands. His lips trembled. He wiped his mouth and rubbed his cheeks, wet with tears. "I'm sorry."

They locked eyes and just like the rest of him they trembled. She reached out and touched his energy. His river was all wrong. It pushed against itself, having no proper course. Part of it was like icy water moving through mud. Another part spun in a whirlpool that emptied nowhere. Here and there spun small vortexes of a strange energy that crashed into the other pools, breaking them and further disrupting the river's coursing. But saturated into all facets of this broken river was pain and fear. It immobilized him, strangled him, tormented him.

She patted his hand. It wasn't the firm hand she was used to. It was skeletal, fragile. And this was because of her. He was falling apart all because of her. She attempted to smile. "What are you sorry for?"

"I ruined your plan. I almost got you caught."

"Let's not think about that right now. You need to eat and I need to address your wounds."

She moved to the food and blanket, but he grabbed her. His voice shook. "Wait."

He tried to sit up but fell over, so she slipped under his arm and helped him up. He took in some deep breaths and inched his way to the food and drink.

"Thank you," he said and picked up the meat but only nibbled at it. "You didn't have to do this."

She sat near him. "I think I did. Who else can I talk to in this tatzon infested place?"

Normally, that would have gotten a laugh from him, but his face remained somber. He continued to nibble at his food. She folded her wrappings and set them to the side and scooted closer to him.

"Let me see your wounds." She reached for his chest. Tsuran turned away, but she lifted her hand and gently pulled his chin toward her. "Tsuran, let me see them."

A small amount of life returned to his eyes, a hint of darkness amidst pale emptiness. He removed his shirt and this time Nasna choked down her gasp.

The bruising and cuts were worse here. Barely any part of him was unharmed. And the effects of Solitude made it look so much worse with him appearing thinner than she'd ever seen. Her gaze went to the places on his chest and side, all black from being burned.

"I want to try washing and bandaging you. It'll sting a lot."

He didn't argue or say anything, so she cleaned him. Using water and a clean cloth, she made her way around his torso doing what she could for him, wishing she had some kind of medicine. Nothing she had would help ease his pain or aid his healing, but it was better than nothing.

He gritted his teeth and groaned as she worked, despite her being careful. When she finished, she wrapped him with the bandages, which were just extra prison-wear she'd stolen at various times during her stay in the mines. They'd at first been to make her bedding more comfortable and for her to be warmer. She hadn't imagined she'd be using them for this.

"Why are you doing this?" Tsuran asked.

She didn't even glance at him. "Why didn't you turn me in?"

He quieted, taking a small bite out of his food.

She continued to wrap his chest until the cloth covered the wounds. She tied the bandaging off and looked at the searing on his leg. It didn't look any better than the others. She cleaned his leg's wounds and wrapped the makeshift bandage around it. Nasna glanced up, but Tsuran didn't look at her. And a thought, a dangerous desire rose through her. Her Path warned her, but it did not outright demand her silence.

"Tsuran, I want to show you something."

She moved the lightstone between them and turned away from him. With a quiet breath, she pulled up her clothes to reveal her back to him.

"What're you doing?" Tsuran asked.

"Showing you the truth."

Whether it was a gasp or some Solitude inflicted spasm, she could not tell, but she knew he saw the symbol that was emblazoned—no, burned and branded into the center of her back. Four spirals lined vertically down her spine with a spear striking down through them. This brand sat between her shoulder blades, right between two small knobs on her back, the last remnants of what was once her wings.

"I don't come from Rajalend," she said. "The land I was born in is very far away. A land where tatzons and ordîns were at constant war. It's a place where our leader demanded horrific sacrifices from the people. A place where the ordîn gods demanded a sacrifice for victory. Demanded our lifeblood."

She pulled the wool back over her back and faced him, taking out her string figures to calm her heart. Tsuran watched her, eyes not leaving her.

"Many died, it was a very bloody war. In a last desperate attempt by my people to win, they conducted a mass sacrifice. Our religious leaders, the Luminars, gathered family after family, branded them with this symbol—the mark of sacrifice—and had their wings clipped. They then offered all these people as blood sacrifices to the gods."

Tsuran kept looking in her eyes. She wanted to look away, to look away and hide this pain, but she would not. Not from him.

"My family was also chosen. My parents and my two siblings were branded and clipped. Along with me." Her voice cracked, but there was also a fire in her tone. A fierceness that burned behind the pain.

"I watched hundreds of my people killed. Opened onto black stone. Cut by our own leaders. I watched so many friends and relatives die. And then, I watched my mother, my father, and my older brother all die before me. It was only by luck and sheer chance I ran away with my little sister. My little Clear Sky who was still a baby. But I ran and ran from the carnage and the blood-lust. And perhaps because of that, because the last two sacrifices escaped, the gods did not give their blessing. After that, the enemy killed all of my people."

"How old were you?"

She looked down at her figures as she spoke. "I was still in my orange cycle but about to enter my yellow cycle. I had bright violet skin if you'd believe it. In tatzon years, something like fifty years old. A child in ordîn standards." She stayed still for a moment, letting her fingers create the Flying Hare figure before moving into the Lady's Tear.

"Clear Sky and I ran and hid for a long time. I did whatever I needed to protect her and keep her safe. We stumbled upon my mentor, an ancient ordîn in his last cycle. For whatever reason, he took pity and cared for us and taught us the ancient secrets of the ordîn magic." She smiled at those memories. Days of meditation in the middle of a hot rain. Clear Sky teaching Nasna string figures. Both touching energy for the first time. "Clear Sky was a natural, far better than me. I struggled to sense energy when even grabbing crystal. Yet she could feel it and manipulate it without touching a thing. She was gifted."

Nasna gazed off into the shadows and her smile faded. "When our master died, we came to Rajalend hoping for a better life. But we weren't the only ones who made it out of our kingdom. By the worst kind of curse and luck, we ran into the Luminars and their army of followers. I don't know if they had looked for us before. But when they found us they put all their efforts into tracking us. They believed that if she and I died, the gods would bless them, and then they would reclaim their lands. And so once again we were on the run, hiding from place to place until we found a tatzon family willing to hide us. I think we were there for well over a year. Another auspicious time for us. A time where I felt like my sister and I grew and lived real lives."

She balled her hands into a fist and her voice became harsh, deep. She slammed her fist onto the ground. "But I was a fool and dropped my guard. As soon as the family realized they'd get money from turning us in, they sought the Luminars and betrayed us to them. The Luminars came for us at night, after I'd hurt myself misusing energy. I was in no condition to fight, so Clear Sky paralyzed my energy, hid me, and went to face them."

She closed her eyes and sat upright, taking in a deep breath. Her lips trembled and she sniffed, as she held back a tide of emotion.

"By the time I got there... I was too late. I found my sister among many dead ordîn and tatzon, and I held her in my arms. Her blood was red as my skin is now. Her eyes as lifeless as the stone here."

She gestured to the room and held her arms there for a moment, her body straight and rigid, like a statue. Nasna looked back at her strings and tried to form the figures again, but her hands wouldn't move. All she could do was stare.

Tsuran, with considerable effort, pushed himself toward her and took her hands into his. His eyes were not as clouded as before, and so she saw his heart pour through them and the compassion caused her to not push him away but to cling.

"She was still so young. They wanted to kill her as a baby, and they killed her as a child. A mere child." She closed her eyes. "They came for me next. But I would not run. And I would not let them escape, even with my injuries. I wouldn't let them get away with what they'd done. So... I chose my Path, the Path of Death. It gave me the strength and power to fight them. To kill them. I stained that tree with their blood, the ordîns and tatzons both. They all paid the price for my sister's death." She shook her head and wiped away a tear rolling down her cheek. "Some of them escaped. A few of the family members, and some ordîns. That was near twenty years ago and I've been searching for all of them ever since. I'm determined to avenge the deaths of Clear Sky and my family." She sniffed and looked Tsuran in the eyes. "That's why I'm here, Tsuran. The tatzon I'm looking for is the target of this contract. And I must kill her."

There was a stillness that followed her words, one that pressed hard on her shoulders. Yet her heart had quieted as well. She didn't feel it. She felt nothing at all.

Except his hands.

Nasna looked into his dark eyes and summoned the courage to ask once again. "My people betrayed me. My leaders, my gods, and even the tatzons I considered my new family betrayed me. So, Tsuran, tell me now... why did you not turn me in?"

He opened his mouth, but a fit of coughs struck him. She gave him some water and helped him drink. It spilled onto him and some of it spluttered out mid-cough, but the coughing died down and he drank more. Even with Solitude waning, he still looked so weak. She let him calm, deciding not to say anything. He coughed into his hand and something like black blood spurted from his lips.

With a twitching gaze and quivering chin, Tsuran looked at her. As he did, the spasm eased away and he smiled.

"Because I don't betray my friends."

And there it was. The answer to her question. The answer she had both hoped for and feared. For years, she'd prepared herself for Valerija's death and what came next. Her Path had been bringing her to this place for twenty years, and she'd made peace with it. She'd come to peace with knowing Clear Sky's sister was no more and all that remained was a tool for Death. It had taken twenty years, but she had come so close to closing off and forgetting her heart.

And now, with those few words, Tsuran took all that peace away.

22

SHADOW STRIKER

You have a knack for angering gods, it seems. Nimat is so frustrated with you he refuses to write anymore. Things in Tifre are not going well, I'm sure you can admit. It's been three years since you failed to establish ties with the quintal and in that time you've only barely held onto your power. Do you understand how vital a strong Tifre is for the future of this world? You have seen what the Nightmare is capable of and we need Tifre and the quintal to prepare for him. I hope you accept your place in this world. Nimat might just kill you himself if you don't.

- Fidda the Tusked Pack, in the 2964th Lunar Cycle
(Correct me if I have the date wrong. I'm not used to tracking time.)

Nasna took another look behind her to the iron doors of Tsuran's cell. She'd stayed until he'd fallen asleep, though it had taken some time even with her calming his energy.

"I hope sleep comforts you against the Solitude."

She took a deep breath and clenched the keys in her hand. It was time.

Nasna snuck through the gallery, avoiding the guards patrolling, and climbed a shaft to the upper levels. The keys unlocked the grate with a quiet click. For fear the grate would fall open and announce her escape to the whole prison, she didn't push the grate open too much. She slid herself out from underneath it and replaced it, making no further noise.

Nasna scanned the room. It appeared she was still alone, however light filtered in from the shafts and doorways. There was no hiding if any guard came in.

She looked at the pulleys in the room connected to the higher level. Rubbing her hands together, she ran to the nearest one, grabbed onto the rope, and hoisted herself up. If they could pull up baskets of rock and ore, they'd support her ordîn weight. She climbed the ropes until she reached the top level and headed down the hallways to the Dump Room. With no lightstone, the entire room was like sap from a pitch tree, dark and impossible to see through. Going through a mental map of the place, she stumbled around, being sure to know where the exit was.

She groped along the wall until she found the crevice with the rock. She shoved it aside and without a second thought, threw herself into the hole and followed the now-familiar path. The distant darkness met rays of light and grew brighter as she approached.

Once again she saw the opening in the ordîn ceiling. And something else. On the edge, about to fall, laid the red-crystal statue Tsuran had taken. She reached out and grabbed hold. This had ruined today's plan. She sighed and tied it into her binding. He'd owe her for this.

Dipping her head beneath the hole, she tried to get an idea of who was still around. She made out the space in front of the Warden's office and gritted her teeth. Several ordîns stood guard. Looking down the hall showed every door had a pair of guards. Tsuran had been right. They had increased security.

She made a silent curse and backed away. No way of getting to the door the way she had last time. She'd need to find another method. Nasna scratched an itch under her ear and let out a slow breath. She knew where she needed to go.

The Warden's office led to a balcony overseeing the entranceway to the mountain and the balcony wouldn't have any guards. If she found a way there, she wouldn't have to deal with the sentries in front of the office. At the very least, she had to try.

She came to the end of the closed-off hallway where it opened up to the main cavern. She peered around the side and examined the room below her. There were guards here and there, but not as many as she had feared. And none of them seemed to be in a static position. They all kept moving around, nightly patrols, most likely.

Wait, no. The guards pulled small carts with crates. Odd. Where did they come from? She narrowed her eyes. The guards took their loads out through the main entrance and not the other way around. So, the crates came from inside the prison. Which meant... yes. They had to be transferring the crystal and iron ingots from storage to the loading bay. That's why prisoners never did that work. Lower risk of prisoners escaping.

This was what she needed. Staying low to the ground, she crept across the bridge into the furnace room. The guards here all worked together to cart out the crates of crystal and iron. She looked beyond them to the large storage room where they held all the crates, to where she needed to be.

She continued to make her way across the stone bridges above the furnaces to the end nearest the storage room. So far the guards hadn't noticed her. The dimming light of the furnaces, mixed with the rushing water, aided her stealth. She could have run from one end to the other without being noticed at all, but she crept forward and crouched by the edge for a moment. She didn't have time to be overconfident and make a sloppy mistake.

Nasna looked over the edge to the ground floor, a fair drop. The bones of an ordîn were strong, but she didn't want to test just how strong, yet.

She threw herself over the side and grabbed onto the rock wall, grateful it had natural places to grab on to. Her descent was slow, but all her time climbing shafts had strengthened her fingers, so she found it easier than she once would have. Halfway down, she seemed close enough, so she dropped the rest of the distance and landed in a squat.

Guards entered the storage room and she stayed in the shadows. The furnaces continued to blare beside her while the water rushed behind. The doors to the storage room laid ahead, its many crates stacked high.

She waited until the guards took away a crate, then rushed in, staying close to the wall and in the shadows until she reached the end of them. She crouched at the edge of the darkness, looked around, and sped straight into the storage room without a second look.

The storage room remained stocked with crates, though less than usual, and she had to look for one with crystal. It was more valuable, so they would move it first. The labels on the crates made it easier to find one.

Nasna grabbed onto an empty crate and dragged it near the front of the other crates. She moved as fast as she could, but even empty these crates didn't drag well. Satisfied with its position, she jumped inside and shut the lid.

Nasna waited. Outside, guards' voices entered the furnace room again, dull against the rushing water. The newest guards came near to her, talking about strange dreams they'd been having, and grabbed onto her crate and hoisted her up.

She steadied herself against the sides so she didn't wobble around and reveal herself. She took a deep breath, letting it out through her nose.

Light filtered through the sides of the crate as they moved her. At first orange with a bit of white, then pure white light shone into the crate from all sides, even beneath her. This had to mean they were in the long lightstone hallway. It grew colder as they moved through the hall until the light drifted away and the cold became all-encompassing.

The guards put her crate down, though from the elevating movements it seemed they placed her crate on top of another. As long as they put nothing on top of hers, she'd be fine. The guards walked away and Nasna took in a few chilly breaths. She didn't hear other guards close by, so she opened the lid and peered out.

The guards walked away but there remained other guards in the entrance moving crates around. She was on top of a single set of crates and there were a few lightstones around. She took in a breath and left the crate, dropping behind the stack.

Nasna waited for a heartbeat. No one shouted an alarm so she glanced around. She was near a wall perpendicular to the balcony and the balcony itself sat right above the lightstone hallway, the most lit area in the cavern. If she wasn't careful, the guards would spot her as she climbed there. She examined the surrounding walls. It wouldn't be easy.

Nasna ducked down as guards came with another crate. They left, and she crept to another side of the wall where she found a fissure ascending through the stone. She crouched and examined it, being sure to keep herself in the shadow. The fissure was climbable. The problem was if she'd climb fast enough between crate deliveries.

Nasna rolled her shoulders. She'd have to be fast enough. Failure wasn't an option.

Ascending the fissure was not like climbing a shaft with handholds. She had to be methodical with her hand placements, applying pressure so she didn't slip and fall. She wasn't moving fast, but she pushed herself to keep moving.

Hand by hand, foot by foot, inch by inch, she scaled across the wall to the balcony. Her whole body ached, but her fingers, which held her entire weight, felt as though they were about to snap off.

She was close to the balcony. She might just jump from here and get it over with.

No, that wouldn't end well. One false move meant total failure and death. No hasty movements. Slow, steady.

The balcony was close. With one last strain of energy, she landed onto it. She let out a slow breath and slid against the wall to the floor.

Never again. She was not doing something like that ever again. Her lungs were ready to erupt inside her and the thumping in her chest had to be echoing throughout the whole of the prison. She looked at her hands, at her crooked fingers.

She'd done it, she'd damaged her fingers beyond repair. Now she wouldn't be able to do her string figures again. Not with these frozen claws... no, she could open them.

Nasna sighed. She needed to calm down, this wasn't the time to be so dramatic. She might have had spent too much time with Tsuran.

She paused and leaned her head back.

Tsuran.

He was back in the cell, still sleeping and dreaming of some good time in the past. Not enduring Solitude.

She stretched her fingers and tried to relax her legs. Yes, she needed to get the crystal, but she also needed to hurry and return to him before he awoke. She would not leave him to Solitude again.

She glanced to the wall she'd just climbed. There was no way she'd climb it again. She'd have to find a different way out, but she'd think of that later. First, she had to find the crystal again.

She double-checked no one had noticed her before moving to the balcony doors. She pressed an ear to the crack, but it was quiet on the other side, as she'd expected. It was late enough for the Warden to be asleep.

She opened the door and moved inside, being in the Warden's office for the second time today. But this time was different. She heard the guards— felt them—outside the door, ready to move at a moment's notice. The room was darker than earlier, but the small amounts of light from the door and balcony provided enough for her to know where to go. But she glanced to the corner, to where the Warden slept.

He laid with his wings wrapped around him like a cocoon, shielding him from the terrors of the world as an ordîn's wings should.

Nasna stood still for a moment to be sure he slept. His body remained still and his breathing even. Asleep, but she shouldn't push her luck with any loud noises.

She moved once again to the storage room and used the keys to unlock it and went inside. She didn't even bother to look around but headed back to where she found the crystal the first time.

The black block box sat in the same place as before. She smiled. The Warden was as much a creature of habit as most.

She cracked open the box and green light poured out. The crystal was there. Now she just needed to find a way back to the mines without being caught.

She took a moment to tie the box tight against her body. This time it wouldn't fall anywhere. She left the storage room and, with faint hope, examined the ceiling, looking for any holes like the one in the hall. She scanned around the room for crevices or cracks or anything that might lead to a passage. But they had smoothed the room's stone when constructing it and there was nothing to help her.

Nasna monitored the Warden as she searched further. He did not stir, but she didn't dare drop her vigilance, the Shadow Strikers had taught her that much.

Convinced there wasn't a single secret passage in the room, she returned to the balcony and peered over again. She didn't have enough strength to climb the wall again. If she had a rope, then she could climb down. But she would be in full sight of the guards. There would be no hiding then.

She crept back into the office and looked at the Warden's desk. She didn't have a way of getting out, but there were still other things she needed to learn. Also, she returned the keys to the desk, figuring she wouldn't need them anymore.

On the neatly organized desk sat a large ledger opened to a page with several columns and rows of squares, each with differing numbers. The first row had lines crossed through them and every box had written notes. A Rajal calendar. Nasna looked at the newest crossed out date.

This must have been today. She read across the next few days and found she was looking for. They expected the transport to arrive tomorrow to collect the iron and crystal and to drop off supplies. The next transport wouldn't arrive for another two months.

Nasna's heart sunk. She had just tomorrow to fulfill what she needed to do. No way she could stay here another two months without the Warden questioning her. There wasn't time to waste in this office. She again looked around the room trying to see if there's anything that she might use. But the Warden's office offered no help.

Perhaps she'd find something back in the storage room. She went back and looked around the confiscated items. Most were useless. Her breathing became hot as she scoured through useless trinket after useless book. There had to be something that could help her. But besides the spirit vessel in her clothes, nothing in here had any power or usefulness to her.

Nasna stopped, a small pendant on a shelf stood out. A faint light glowed from it.

She examined it closer and her mouth opened. Some jeweler had made it with yellow-crystal and the river still coursed within it. Not enough to be frightening to her, but enough that perhaps it could serve as a distraction.

She took the pendant, headed to the balcony, and looked down to where the crates of crystal were. Holding the pendant in her hand, she judged how far she could throw it. She'd have one chance at this before she would have to turn and run inside to hide. If this worked, all the guards would be on alert, the Warden would awake, and there'd be enough chaos for her to get out of here.

She grabbed ahold of the energy within the pendant and twisted it in the opposite direction of its natural flow. The river resisted her, but she was stronger. She kept turning and twisting the energy, feeling the river building and straining against the crystal walls that contained it. Nasna brought it to where the river itself was in so much flux and turmoil that the river was more like a tiny storm, wanting to be unleashed. She kept it there.

Taking careful aim, she threw the crystal toward the crates, ran inside, and dove underneath the desk just as a thunderous boom erupted from outside. It was followed by a series of explosions that bled into one another as one concussive roar shook the mountain prison.

Nasna pressed herself against the side of the desk. That was more than she'd expected.

Regardless, the result was as she hoped. Guards burst into the Warden's office as he flung himself to his feet. Nasna stayed underneath the desk, hidden.

"Report, what is going on?" the Warden asked.

"I'm not sure, Warden. We heard an explosion and came in to—"

"Find out what is going on."

"Sir!" The guards left the room, and the Warden rushed to the balcony and bellowed to the guards below. There were replies, but Nasna ignored them and crept out from underneath the desk. The office door was open and there weren't any guards. This was her chance.

"What in the Abyss' name is going on?" the Warden said. Nasna froze.

She turned, her heart pattering in her chest, but he wasn't facing her. Instead, he faced a glow coming from the entranceway. Blue and white light illuminated the entire cavernous room. Nasna's breath caught in her throat. There were—

"Spirits!" the Warden said. "Guards alert all personnel, take out all crystal weaponry. Do not let the spirits take the crystal."

Nasna ducked beneath the desk and the Warden turned and rushed into the storage room. If he thought it curious the door was unlocked, he ignored it as a moment later he reappeared brandishing a spear tipped with red-crystal. He rushed to the balcony and unfolded his massive wings just as a dozen spirits, some Small, some Common, rose in the air facing him. The Warden flew toward the spirits.

Nasna took this chance and dashed out from the desk and toward the hall. She peered around the side but there weren't any guards. If word was spreading, they would all be heading to the entranceway to fight the spirits. She hadn't thought destroying crystal would have summoned spirits like this, but she would take the opportunity they provided.

She sprinted down the hallway to the stairway, meeting no other guards on her path. As she turned the corner to the stairs, guards rushed toward the lightstone hallway brandishing crystal weapons, just like the Warden. However, none of them were looking in her direction, so she dashed down the stairs and headed to the shafts. None stopped her. Doubtful anyone even noticed her. There were spirits to take care of.

She ran over to the shaft she'd come out of and looked down. With all this noise and commotion, the guards below would come and investigate. But she didn't see them yet. Nasna opened the grate and went into the shaft. However, the grate closed with more noise than she'd wanted and she cursed. Putting it out of her mind, she descended into the mines. The time for subtlety was over. She ran to the solitary cell, passing column after column. Ahead of her, the guards came into view.

Though she ran, her steps were still silent, so they didn't even notice her. She grabbed onto them, paralyzed their energy, and dropped them, leaving them on the ground and hurried to the cell.

She crashed through the last door and Tsuran bolted up, wide-eyed.

"Get up, Tsuran. It's time to go."

"What? Now? What's going on?"

"What's going on is that we have to kill someone and escape. And we have less than a day to do it."

23

———◆○◆———

THE LIGHTLESS

T he quintal have answered me and will start up talks again, but they are hesitant. It seems for such short lived creatures, they hold onto slights with a forceful grip. More so, their demands are much steeper than they had been. Relations are tense at the moment as I struggle to figure out what we should do. Ordîns have hundreds of years for a plan to come fruition, so working with a time line of a tatzon is not something I am equipped for. And I know the Tifran people watch my every move, waiting for my next misstep. For a king, I feel very trapped.

-Yavahush the Stargazer, Prisoner of Tifre, in the 2965th Lunar Cycle

Solitude does not attack like any bodily disease. There is pain, yes, but it goes far beyond that. Outwardly, people can see how Solitude warps the body through the limbs that curve unnaturally, the skin that loses all color, through the seizures and the violent thrashing and coughing of blood. Always so much blood that has turned black. But these outward signs are mere afterthoughts to the truest pain.

Tsuran felt it now, just as he had every time Solitude had ever sunk its parasitic claws in him. With every step he made, every stumble he had, Solitudes power rattled his entire being. Because Solitude began in the soul. It was a disease of the spirit, but one that did not end there but spread to the mind and the body until there was nothing left but something twisted, something dead.

But Nasna helped. He held onto her as tightly as he could, but his body was that of an old man now, aged for two hundred years and left to rot away in the sun. He stumbled forward more than walked, but she kept him from smashing his face on the stone floor. Solitude could not consume him whole with her there, but neither did it leave.

She brought him to the shafts and dread took what remaining strength he had.

"I've an idea," she said and brought him to the shafts with pulleys. She tied the ropes around him and lowered him down into the dark depths. Back into the grips of Solitude.

A choking spasm gripped his body and a silent scream scratched through his throat. Darkness clawed his eyes, bit at his chest, burned the useless legs the Warden attacked.

"Tsuran." Nasna's voice echoed down the shaft, overwhelming the darkness, making it shrink back. "Listen to my voice. I'm here, I'm still here."

"...Nas..."

The journey down the shafts was not pleasant. The ropes dug into his weakened flesh, his burned legs buckled and spiked with intense heat, as if the Warden had plunged the heated metal into them again, and Tsuran felt Solitude waiting just beside him, readying to pounce and kill him.

But Nasna spoke to him through it all. She did not leave him. Even when the light from the lightstone did not touch him, he felt her beside him, a barrier to death. Yes, her voice carried something heavy in it and there were obvious hints of exhaustion as she lowered him level by level, but she did not let up. Never once did she drop him or leave him alone for long at the bottom of a shaft.

However, once they reached the Bridgeway, neither moved further. Neither could. Exhaustion, pain, and an untold number of other things took their toll on both and they fell asleep beside each other.

But sleep didn't bring rest or peace. There were only nightmares.

Longs blades scraped against bones, which snapped and cracked. Screams filled a void of his own making. He tried to close his eyes, tried to look away and stop. The smell of the severed flesh wafted into his nostrils, yet he couldn't turn away. But this couldn't continue. He had to stop this.

"You can do it, Tsuran child," his mother's voice said.

No, he couldn't. He wouldn't. This wasn't right.

A powerful hand rested on his shoulder. It had to be his father. "Tsuran, listen to us. Do it."

But... the screams. Hundreds screamed in his ears. And the stench was too much. He had to stop.

"Do it, Tsuran child," his mother said, in the way she always did when her smile became too wide. His father grabbed Tsuran's hand and held it up.

"You've done so well so far. Just a few more today. That's it. Very good."

Tsuran opened his eyes and stared at the tatzon girl strapped to the stone table, her priarm extended away from her. He gripped the long blade tighter. Father was right. Tsuran had done well so far. He'd done so many. What was one more?

He sliced down.

Tsuran sat up, sweat covering his body, his breath heavy. He looked behind him, but Nasna was still and quiet. Seeing this eased his breathing, though he was glad for not waking her.

"Bad dream?"

Tsuran started at the voice and turned to see Dalvinder sitting close to him.

"Dalvinder, what in the Abyss?"

"I didn't wish to wake you, and so waited for you to awake."

Dalvinder tossed something toward Tsuran and he caught it. It was a slab of meat.

"You might as well eat up. With you two being down here I expect you didn't have breakfast."

Nasna moaned and Tsuran glanced over his shoulder. She'd turned and her eyes opened. She gave him a small smile but then bolted upright at the sight of Dalvinder.

"We have your crystal."

"I would hope so," Dalvinder said, tossing her a piece of meat. "I had already conveyed I wouldn't render my services unless you brought me the crystal. And finding you on the floor, I suspected."

"How long have you been here?" Nasna asked.

"Not long. The morning has only begun."

So, they'd slept, more or less, until the morning. At least they hadn't wasted too much time. Tsuran bit into the breakfast provided by Dalvinder and Nasna handed over the black box. Tsuran kept a close eye on it as Dalvinder opened it, green light washing over him. He had a wide smile on his face.

"It's been so long," Dalvinder said. "I haven't seen this in over forty years."

"And what do you want with a spirit vessel?" Tsuran asked. Dalvinder raised his brows at this.

"You're aware of these? How interesting, not all tatzons are."

"My Partner was a Soulborn. I am well aware of what it is."

Dalvinder nodded but kept his smile. He tucked the black box into his cloak and rose. "What I plan to do with it has nothing to do with our services. But I don't wish to do much with it. It's the last thing I have of my Partner. Having it close to me is all I need." With several arms, he gestured toward the Bridgeway. "Shall we, then?"

Nasna helped Tsuran to his feet and they followed Dalvinder to the stairs leading down into the maze. She paused at the top.

"Oh, I almost forgot," she said. "Here." She pulled out his red-crystal statue.

"You found it."

"I tried going through our little tunnel before. It turned out to not be a good plan, but I found this. Figured you'd want it."

He held the crystal in his hand, light from crystals reflecting through it. Tension released throughout his body like a sigh he'd held in too long.

"Thank you, Nas. Thank you." He traced a finger along it, his vision captivated by the familiar and the memory.

The stairs were tricky to maneuver. They weren't proper stairs, only cut rocks with enough room for one person at a time. One false step meant a long fall to a quick death. Nasna had kept some of the rope she'd used to lower him down the shafts and kept some of it looped around his chest. He figured that if he fell, he'd just take her with him, but she shut him down when he brought it up.

"I'll keep you up," she said.

At the least, the stairs were not slippery and had decent grip. Dalvinder descended with little care for falling, since the shadows would catch him at the bottom. When they made it to the ground floor without a major problem, Dalvinder wasted not a moment before taking them into the maze of crystal and stone. It did not take long before Tsuran realized how they would not have been able to make it through without a guide's help. The maze twisted, turned, stopped, dropped, and spun every few steps. The crystal was bright, the stone cold, and everything looked like the place they just came from. Yet, the Lightless walked without hesitation, as if he were taking a morning stroll through a fluorescent floral garden.

Being around two people helped abate Solitude, but he still sensed it inside him, not entirely gone yet. Besides that, he still had his physical injuries slowing him down. At one point, Dalvinder glanced him over.

"You do not appear well this day. A tired man. A sickly soul. An unfortunate companion."

Tsuran smirked as best he could. "What a compliment. Thought I was just a dead man walking."

"He just came out of being in Solitude for over an hour," Nasna said. "He hasn't gotten better yet."

Dalvinder looked back. "Twenty minutes alone kills most tatzon. And you still live?"

Tsuran shrugged. "Slept through most of it."

The Lightless stared at him as they walked, and there was something about that stare that irked Tsuran, but Dalvinder turned away and said nothing more.

They left the maze, Dalvinder leading them into a tunnel that led to a bizarre device. A large wooden platform sat on the floor of the tunnel, several ropes tied to it and rising through a massive shaft.

"What is a lift doing here?" Nasna asked.

"Ah, then you know of such a thing," Dalvinder said.

"I saw similar things in the Tutchal cliffs and beyond."

"Yes, it is not as common in the Rajal lands, but not all Lightless here are Rajal."

Nasna had said "lift", but this looked nothing like any lift he knew of. How could a Builder possess this? Tsuran looked between them. "I don't get it, what is this?"

Dalvinder motioned to the platform, "Let me show you."

The three of them stepped onto it and Tsuran noted that the wood was not rotten or too old. Had the guards given these criminals fresh wood? Before he could consider it more, Dalvinder pulled hard on one rope, which resulted in a loud *thunk* and the platform rose with the sound of squeaking pulleys and grinding rock. Somehow, without possession, this wood rose.

"Someone's pulling it from the top?" he asked.

Dalvinder smiled. "Had I the knowledge to explain the system, I would need to have the care to understand that which does not interest me in its existence."

Tsuran blinked and looked to Nasna but she only shrugged, which elicited a short laugh from the insane Lightless.

"Be glad you need not climb these shafts," he said, gesturing to the stone around them. "A Lightless long ago decided that the pulley systems of the ordîns was an inferior way to live. He developed these lifts, for there are many, because he would not live as others lived here. A starving wreck. A failing heart. A disgrace of tatzon kind."

"A Lightless made this?" Nasna asked.

"Not all criminals are fools."

The lift took them up quite a ways before stopping inside a gallery as wide as the first few levels on the other side of the prison. And it did not look like a gallery at all. Tsuran saw a village.

Shacks and stalls of wood, bone, and hide filled the place. Tatzons walked back and forth, with wheelbarrows and short carts, laughing, talking, helping, constructing. It was such a jarring vision Tsuran was sure that Solitude had made him see phantoms, but Nasna gasped and put on her head wrappings before someone noticed.

"What in the Abyss," Tsuran said. "I... how?"

Crystal was everywhere. He saw deposits in the stone walls, but he also saw them in sconce-like constructions around the prison village, giving the place light and shadow. He heard mining in the far distance, and far it was because he could not see the end to the gallery.

"Come, you're quarry is not here." Dalvinder motioned them forward, toward a set of lifts that ascended up multiple enormous shafts. As they moved past the Lightless... villagers, very few gave them any notice. Some nodded at Dalvinder, but the rest moved on with their day.

When they were on the second lift heading up, Nasna pulled Dalvinder toward her. "Why didn't you warn us there would be people so soon? They almost saw me."

"Ah, perhaps it slipped my mind. Escaped my grasp. Didn't even occur to me."

Tsuran took Nasna away before she attacked the man. "You want to explain what we just saw?"

"I told you, there was a Lightless who came here who did not wish to live as the others did. A criminal he was, but a visioneer at heart too. He was not content on dying, so instead, he created a small nation."

"A nation?" Nasna asked.

"Of sorts." Dalvinder smiled. "On this side of the mountain, there are only four levels. With lifts such as these, the shafts can be larger and deeper, so the Lightless can excavate every level they touch. And they have. The Bridgeway aside, much crystal, much iron, and even other precious metals have been found, mined, used, sold. The ordîns had once been in control, believed they had the upper hand, but deals were made. Promises kept. A trade established."

Tsuran scoffed and leaned back, only to realize the wall behind him was ever moving. "You mean the Lightless bought off the guard? That seems far-fetched."

"And yet, you have seen the truth. The Lightless hold great power here, because we hold all the crystal, and the ordîn cannot touch it, cannot find it, cannot have it. Trust me, what you have seen so far is but the poverty of the place.

Dalvinder's words proved true. On the following level, the constructions were less crude and ramshackle. Tsuran saw what almost appeared to be streets with hanging braziers of crystal. Finely constructed homes stood tall in clusters of neighborhoods here and there. Dalvinder pointed out a market where goods and arts and services were sold. The people here wore clothing made from leather and hide, which looked finer and more comfortable than the regular prison garb. With everything Dalvinder explained, Tsuran only heard descriptions that were saved for civilization, not prisons in mountains. Tsuran had always considered Lightless to be the most devious and untrustworthy of possessors. Yet, they somehow made all of this.

There were even guards though most stood around the lifts. With a few words from Dalvinder, the guards let them by and they ascended to the next gallery, and Tsuran could only imagine what awaited them.

"I still don't get why the Oligarchs would allow this," Nasna said. "Someone would put a stop to this."

"Do you suppose they know?" Dalvinder asked. "Perhaps they do, perhaps the ordîn keep it to themselves. After all, the criminals are still kept away, trapped within this place. What does the rest of the world care if they are comfortable, as long as their evils do not touch their homes?"

The lift continued to creak ever upward, and Tsuran saw light drift in from the top of the shaft.

Dalvinder also looked up. "As we approach our destination, I should warn you of the current leadership of this Lightless nation. Sent here some years ago for multiple murders, Alboin Anghar Sigil Con-Ebru made a name for himself among the Lightless here. He is one of only four among the Lightless that can empower his possession, thus making him formidable as an opponent. Yet, he is also quite charismatic and thus was placed in charge of the nation. An ambitious one, with plans to oust the ordîn and claim ownership of the entire Iron Mountain. Many have challenged his right to rule, and no one has yet lived from such an encounter. He is brutal, he is calculated, he is hot-headed."

"I don't see why we should care," Nasna said.

"You should care, because the very person you seek to kill, is the very person he calls 'lover'."

The lift stopped and the three exited into the second to last gallery, and, as Dalvinder had implied, it was grander than the previous floor. It was much the same: tall homes, stores and markets, crystal everywhere. But there was much also not the same. In a word, everything here was decorated. Homes were constructed with hide and bone, but they gilded much of the bones with silver. People wore jewelry of ivory with small crystal insets. Crystals of various colors laid together to create mosaics as walkways. And the air, it smelled of cooked meat and something else, mushroom perhaps. Most bizarre of all, was the music in the air.

Yet, everyone he saw was a criminal. How was this just? Murder someone or rob a family, and they were punished with a life far better than anything they had in Rajalend.

Dalvinder led them toward one of the taller constructions, where several Lightless gathered, talking with a large tatzon of four arms and markings like a series of dark brown horizontal waves.

"That's Con-Ebru," Dalvinder said. "Hm. He does not appear to be in a good mood today."

Tsuran looked to Nasna, but she had stopped moving. She stood frozen, staring toward Con-Ebru.

"The woman. Next to Con-Ebru," she said.

Tsuran looked over. Standing next to the man was a middle-aged woman with markings of ovals around each eye, vertical lines descending from them.

"That's her," Nasna said. "That's the woman I must kill."

24

VENGEANCE

Naresh left me with her dream of an ordîn nation. You six came with an offer of help and the knowledge of the threat of this Nightmare. I understand Tifre's importance, the vital role it plays in the future, and yet I struggle to not distract myself with thoughts of my daughter. In six years, I have not received a single whisper of her whereabouts, and I know it is likely they both have died by now. Though, I doubt I could be the man I must be for Tifre if she lived, so perhaps it is better this way. Every family I have had, I failed to save. I have been forsaken, and I have forsook. Perhaps that it is all I am.

-Yavahush the Forsaken, in the 2966th Lunar Cycle

The world dulled around Nasna. Every sound, sight, and smell blurred into the background. All her focus centered on the woman. People stood near her, moved past her and around her, but the only distinct person was Valerija.

Nasna dropped her necklace and stepped close to the walls. The Lightless had shadows everywhere, some places darker than others, and though she wasn't a Lightless, she was a Shadow Striker. They'd trained her how to disappear. The shadows enveloped around her and, in her own way, she became one with them. As the rest of the world became unfocused to her, so she became unfocused to the world. She didn't need to possess the shadows to walk in them. To strike from them.

Her heart thumped in her chest but she moved with slow, undetectable steps. Everything culminated in this moment. No rushing, not a single mistake.

Valerija left Con-Ebru's side and went into the home behind. A beautiful home. Something that usually must have been a benefit to her, but now it'd be her downfall. Inside that construction, Nasna could do what she needed to without being seen.

Staying in the shadows, she moved to the door, making sure none noticed her, not even Tsuran. If she took out her target before Con-Ebru finished chatting with the others, then she could leave with no one knowing what happened. She wouldn't have long. But she didn't need long.

Twenty years. She'd been hunting for twenty years. Now Clear Sky would rest.

The door had closed behind Valerija. Nasna tested it. No lock. A final glance behind and she opened the door and slid inside, shutting it behind. She turned and looked around the room. The image that came to here was Tutchal. Fur rugs covered the floor, colorful curtains hung from the ceiling, wooden furniture even adorned the corners. Crystal, ivory, silver, all signs of wealth filled the place, decorating the stairs to the second floor. All quite impressive, and it provided plenty of space to hide. She crept down behind some chairs and listened.

She waited for a moment. No noise from outside. Only Valerija humming inside. Nasna gritted her teeth. She knew the song. The same song Valerija sang at night while putting Clear Sky to sleep. She'd sung it every night Nasna and her sister stayed with the family. Did she sing it that night twenty years ago? Did she sing it before they killed Clear Sky?

Something like a fire grew in her stomach, but not a warm flame. Instead, it made her cold but strong, and it seeped into her being. Strength from her Path.

Nasna stepped away from the chairs and moved to a curtain and peered around it. Valerija sat on the opposing side, sewing something. The scene was strange to see inside of a prison. A woman humming to herself in a home, as if this was the most natural place for her to be. She sat in prison and yet lived an almost normal life. A life she'd stolen from Clear Sky. The icy fire flowed through Nasna's veins like ice.

She sidestepped out from her cover and lunged toward Valerija who looked up, her eyes widening, her mouth opening. Nasna laid a hand on her and paralyzed her energy. The woman froze, unable to make a sound, unable to scream for help.

Nasna's heart thudded hard against her chest, as if it'd break through her ribs. Her teeth clenched around hot breath. The last of the tatzons who betrayed her, betrayed Clear Sky, was in her hands at last.

"I found you, Valerija." Nasna leaned forward, grabbed the wrappings around her face, and pulled them down, showing her face. She came close to the woman, and a flash of recognition flew across Valerija's eyes. "Remember me? My sister? How you sold us out?"

Nasna grabbed Valerija's throat with both hands and squeezed. When she spoke, Nasna's voice didn't utter the words. A dark voice rumbled from her throat. She'd become the mouthpiece of her Path. The mouthpiece of Death. "Twenty years I've wondered why. Twenty years I've been trying to find answers. Now that I see you... I don't care. It's time I send you where I've sent the rest of your family."

The woman's throat crushed beneath Nasna hands, the icy fire aiding her strength. But she let go. There shouldn't be signs of struggle. Nasna returned the wrappings to her face, placed a hand on Valerija's chest, and grabbed a hold of a droplet of energy within her heart. With this, Nasna would avenge her sister. With this, she would, at last, kill the weakness inside and embrace the Path of Death and her life as a Shadow Striker.

Nasna paused. On Valerija's face, something came down her cheek. Nasna squinted at it closer. But what she saw made the icy fire lose some of its vigor.

A tear.

Not only one. Two. No, three... now streams. Crying. Was she... feeling guilt? Remorse?

Nasna ground her jaw. No, she cried for her own life. A selfish creature to the end. The only one who mourned her death was herself. Nasna wanted to spit. Such a pathetic creature. Nasna was not only doing herself a favor but the entire world by ridding it of this....

Something made a small quiet sound and her gaze snapped up. The door wasn't open. No one had come in. Must have been a trick of the mind. But... Valerija's lips...were they moving?

"P... please...."

Nasna let go of the energy and jerked away. Impossible. Nasna had paralyzed her energy. Movement should have bee impossible, let alone speaking.

"... Please... don't...."

Nasna's mouth dropped open. She stared, unable to blink. Nasna had paralyzed all of her energy, especially her voice, no doubt about that... had Valerija fought through the paralysis to speak? Not possible. No one had ever done that. Not even Nasna had ever broken energy paralysis.

But this tatzon, this betrayer, had.

And she begged for her life.

Nasna shut her mouth and grabbed Valerija by the collar, jerking her. "Is that what my sister asked? Is that what she pleaded before you butchered her?"

Tears continued down Valerija's face. "I'm...sorry..."

Nasna lost her breath and let go of the woman. All the icy fire died out in an instant, leaving her colder than the icy sensation that ran through her. In its wake remained only a large painful lump in her chest and throat. Every time she'd imagined this moment, every time her dreams brought her to face Valerija, there had never been remorse coming from the woman.

Twenty years. Nothing to an ordîn. But to a tatzon, that allowed a whole new person to grow. Had she regretted what she and her family had done? Had it driven her to a life she wasn't proud of? Was that why she was here in prison now?

Something in Nasna strained, cracks appearing along with it. It had strained before, every time she made deals with her Path, every time she found a loophole for her weakness. Now everything prepared to snap. Her life prepared to end. There were no loopholes this time, no workarounds. Only a choice.

Nasna placed her hand on the woman's chest. "Sorry doesn't bring Clear Sky back."

She grabbed ahold of the energy within Valerija's heart and released it.

Valerija's eyes showed no pain, only sadness before glazing over, one last tear falling to the ground. Nasna stood up, staring at the last of the tatzons who'd betrayed her, and the straining inside of her eased away. She'd done it. Only the final Luminar remained. And Nasna would find him. She had found every other one of them. None could stop her. She was Nasna. She was Death.

Nasna let out a breath. She finished it. After so long, it was almost strange to think this part of her journey over. Yet, staring down at the body, the same nausea from every other kill swirled in her. The same emptiness crept in, the same turmoil. But why? She'd chosen and followed her Path, just as every ordîn must, and yet she remained like this. Why, after all her work, after all her years of searching, and even after her accomplishing her goal, why wasn't she satisfied? Why didn't she feel... happy?

She brought order to the world. This was her chosen Path. And yet, why did her body revolt against the action? This should have killed her weakness. It should have been dead. Why did it still hurt so much?

Her hand wandered to her chest, touching the choppy waters of her own river. Was her weakness still fighting to live? Still struggling for her to live differently?

She clenched her fists. It was too late for her. This was who she was... whether she liked it or not.

A soft gasp came from behind. She spun, raised her hands, and expected to see Con-Ebru standing behind her. She stopped. Nasna's eyes grew wide and something thick lodged in her throat. Standing before her, holding a blanket to her chest, with a terrified expression, was a small tatzon girl. Maybe seven years old, having no arm besides her priarm. The child had been behind one of the other curtained-off rooms, Nasna hadn't even noticed her before.

The child looked between Nasna and Valerija on the ground, her skin turning pallid. Her skin with... no, that was impossible.

"Mom?" The child ran past Nasna shook her mother. "Mom, get up."

Nasna turned and looked at the child again. She had to have seen it wrong. This couldn't be right. She knelt and grabbed the child, turning her around. She needed to have a clear look. The girl pushed back, but couldn't get out of Nasna's grip. Tears streamed down the child's face. Down a face with unmistakable markings and light blue eyes. Nasna fell backward as she pushed herself away from the girl, her heart racing and breath gone. It couldn't be. The contract had gotten the detail wrong, that's what Nasna had believed. That's what she'd told herself again and again. Nasna's body froze with only her thoughts being able to function.

Those markings... circles with broad lines striking through them... the markings of the contract... Valerija wasn't the assassination target at all. This child is.

"What did you do to my mom? Why won't she get up?"

Nasna couldn't move. She forgot how to. This was all wrong. She was here to kill Valerija. That was why she had taken the contract. Why she had begged for the contract. It was supposed to be just her. There wasn't supposed to be a child. There wasn't supposed to be... a family.

A shiver ran up through Nasna's skin and she stared at the woman again. Valerija cried. She begged. She broke through paralysis. But not out of a selfish desire to live. Not out of cowardice or fear for her own life. She hadn't cried and begged and apologized for herself. It was all for her daughter. For her child. A child Nasna had stolen family from. A child the Shadow Strikers sent her to kill.

The girl cried over her mother and Nasna's memories flashed across her mind. Images as bright as day flashed across her eyes. There was the blood mixing with the surrounding fires, the cold dead eyes of her parents, and the screams of her baby sister. The world had been nothing but shadow and smoke and flame. An empty world. A cruel world that had taken her family. A world she had become.

"No, this is all wrong." Nasna scrambled to her feet, running into a small table, knocking over what was on top. The child cried, louder and louder. The world spun around Nasna and her vision blurred in and out. She wanted to vomit. But she had to go. She had to run. She rushed to the door, pulling it open and ran into the Con-Ebru as she burst out.

"What the Abyss is this?" he said. "What you doing in my—"

He tried to grab her but Nasna darted past him, going straight to Tsuran. She could hear Con-Ebru shouting at her, but the world had grown dull again. She looked up. There was Tsuran, familiar, safe Tsuran. She ran to him, almost into him.

"Hey, what's going on?" he asked. "What—"

"We have to go," Nasna said. Her voice choked and words were hard to get out. "I made a mistake."

Con-Ebru's voice bellowed out around the gallery.

Tsuran grabbed her hand and ran.

25

---◆○◆---

RUN

A re all ordîn as dramatic as you? You seem to choose the worst times to embrace sentimentality since you stand on precarious ground right now. There is still the faction who wishes to dispose you, to find Farhata and place him on the throne. A single misstep, a single mistake, and these people will abandon you, and we shall have no need of you at that point either. Stay focused on the quintal, because we are close to laying claim to that wondrous island of theirs.

So, for your sake and ours, no more surprises.

- Fidda the Tusked Pack, in the 2966th Lunar Cycle

The little town erupted into a tumult of shouts and curses, followed by the thrum of hundreds of tatzons rushing toward Tsuran and Nasna.

Time to leave. His body objected to movement, every step breaking through him. He still hadn't recovered from Solitude, let alone everything else his body had been through. He wouldn't be able run for long.

"Don't let those two escape!" Con-Ebru said, his voice booming through the streets. Tatzons appeared out of the shadows in front of the lift leading down. Tsuran made a sharp turn toward a second one, pulling Nasna behind.

Several Lightless appeared near them and swung at Tsuran. He ducked, pulling Nasna to the side. One came out of the shadow at his feet, but Tsuran shouldered through her and ran past them. Tsuran pushed and pulled Nasna toward another shaft. She wasn't helping. He needed to keep them alive. Hard to do that with her like this.

"Nas, snap out of it. We need to go."

He pulled her out of reach of a hammer strike. Too close. And it grew worse with each passing moment.

The Lightless had the closest lifts guarded now, so not an option any longer. If he didn't do something, and fast, the Lightless would overwhelm them. He gripped his statue and struck the nearest tatzon, slicing into her face.

The column next to Tsuran cracked and exploded, sending shattered lightstone and rock at them. Black tendrils broke through the column and shot toward Nasna.

Tsuran dove to the side on top of her and the shadowy tendrils coursed above him. He scrambled to his feet, pulling her with him.

A figure cloaked in shadows walked toward them, those tendrils spread out from them like branching arms. Tsuran's eyes widened. The figure wasn't in shadow. It was shadow. It had to be Con-Ebru, empowering the shadows.

Tsuran could fight all the other prisoners if he needed to. It'd take time, but against his red-crystal, they wouldn't pose a challenge. But an empowered Lightless was a different story. This was an actual challenge, an actual danger. And who knew how many other tatzons here could empower their possession. Tsuran did not want to wait around to find out. He had to get out and make sure Nasna lived.

He possessed and empowered his statue.

The statue, no larger than his hand, enlarged to his regular size, and he struck the nearest prisoners. His arm broke through their chests and tossed them several feet back.

Everyone stopped. He stood to his full height and empowered each of the statue's four arms into blades.

He saw it, saw it in their eyes, the dawning realization that they faced a Guardian in red-crystal. The pain in his body was gone, left to be dealt with outside the statue. He had no fatigue, no limp, no lack of energy.

He glanced over. The lifts to the upper level were unguarded. And substantial amounts of light illuminated all of them.

He pushed Nasna. "To the gallery above, go."

She didn't argue. They rushed to the shaft. The prisoners rushed and pushed themselves out of his way now. A few brave idiots ran at him with their iron picks, as if that would do anything. The picks bounced off, and the tatzons died with Tsuran's arms slicing into them. It was almost cute how they thought their hammers and picks would harm him.

Nasna arrived at the shaft but glanced back at him. He pointed up with his blade-arm.

"Go!"

Something large and heavy struck him from behind and he stumbled forward. He turned.

Sledgehammers. This Lightless towered over him despite only having three arms. Each arm held a sledgehammer with crystal spikes embedded in the iron. Iron against his statue would do nothing. But iron with crystal would be a problem. Worse, it was green-crystal. This wouldn't bounce off. If it hit, it'd hurt.

The large Lightless attacked with all three hammers. Tsuran jumped back, two missing him, one hitting his side. An acute pain jolted through the statue. He steadied himself and gritted his teeth.

"Didn't even feel that."

The prisoner swung the hammers again. Tsuran lunged forward, caught the hammers with two arms, and struck out with his others.

With speed surprising for his size, the prisoner sidestepped away from the attack and struck Tsuran's legs.

His legs swept out beneath him and he crashed onto the ground. At that moment, a couple of Lightless jumped past him to follow Nasna, whose lift inched upward. Tsuran gritted his crystal teeth. That wouldn't happen. It was time to stop messing around.

Empowering his speed, he rolled out of the way and jumped to his feet. He sped past the two going after Nasna, cutting them off.

A sledgehammer sped toward him out of the corner of his eye. He ducked and dodged to the side. Another Lightless joined the fray, also wielding a hammer with embedded crystal.

Prisoners shuffled behind him and he turned. Tsuran narrowed his eyes at a third prisoner with a hammer, except this one had a single spike. A red-crystal spike. If that hit, it would crack his statue.

The three attacked, with far greater coordination than he expected, with practiced ease of fellow soldiers. He frowned. Nothing in him wanted to kill a soldier, but more than that, more than anything right now, he would not let these three or anyone else get to Nasna.

He was the Red Sword.

He fought as such. As he did, the ruckus, the chanting and cheering of the crowd, even the confident glints in these Lightless' hearts, it all died down. But, as he pushed them back, it returned, the thrill, the euphoria of the fight, of the hunt.

These Lightless were decent fighters, but he was a warrior.

They were fast. They were strong. He was faster. He was stronger.

Tsuran blocked their multitude of attacks, returning with his own swift strikes. When they thought they cornered him, he shrank the statue out of their grasp and then enlarged, slicing at legs and hitting one in the chest. They growled and switched to a defensive stance, but he sped behind, arms like scythes cutting through rotten mushrooms. But the Lightless disappeared into the shadows beneath their feet, his strike missing them, and then they returned, grabbing their weapons and launching with ferocity at him.

It brought it all back. He heard battle, felt the creaking and shattering of ships, smelled the salty brine in the air.

Tsuran couldn't help but grin as he slid beneath two attacks, shrinking and then enlarging behind the larger Lightless, cutting deep into his inner thigh. "Come on, then!"

Tsuran darted his eyes to the side to see a few others trying to climb after Nasna. He sliced up, cutting the shaft of one sledgehammer before he leapt back, shrinking and unpossessing his statue. His body materialized beside it, and in a fluid motion he caught the small statue in midair, turning, and threw it toward Nasna's lift. It left his fingers and the Lightless rushed him.

He winked at them and possessed the statue as it, as now he, hurtled through the air like a diving sparrow. Tsuran empowered his size and slammed into a Lightless on the shaft wall, arms slicing into her. Tsuran dropped and slit the Lightless beneath him. He landed on the floor and turned. The Lightless who had been climbing fell to the ground next to him.

Shadowy tendrils crashed into Tsuran's side. He flew into a column and it broke around him. He pushed himself up. Con-Ebru stood in front of him, body-possessing and empowering the shadows. This wasn't good.

Tsuran stared the shadow figure down. The tendrils sped toward him. He dashed to the side.

Rock and stone shattered behind him. The other prisoners cheered. He lunged toward Con-Ebru and struck. But Tsuran's arm slid through the shadow as through air. Not good.

The shadows wrapped around his legs and spun him around through the air, crashing into the floor, the ceiling, the walls, though not through any of the homes. The statue broke through lightstone embedded pillars, and hitting this crystal sent jolts of pain into him. Everything moved too fast. Nothing stopped.

He shrank the statue and fell out of the shadow's grasp. Tsuran flew as though flung, unable to tell which way was up and which way was bad. But he needed to act fast. He unpossessed, grabbed his statue, and flung it toward the lifts, repossessing it as it left his hand.

He landed on the ground in front of the shaft and empowered his size. Nasna had to be at the top by now. No reason to stay here.

He leapt and dug his arms into the wall and pulled himself after her. Shadow tendrils came after him, wrapping around a leg. He shrank the leg and climbed faster. The shadows didn't follow. Not into this shaft of light.

He crested the shaft into a gallery starkly different from the one below. The entire chamber was pure lightstone, reminiscent of the main hallway into the prison. Shadow didn't exist here. Con-Ebru would have no power here.

Tsuran wasn't looking forward to what awaited him outside the statue, but it was best he did not possess when he didn't need to. He left the statue and dropped to the ground, all the pain and injury returning in full.

Groaning and cursing, he tried to get up onto a leg, but nothing in him wanted to move. He collapsed back onto the floor.

His breathing was hard and raspy, but he tried to push himself up again. A hand gripped underneath an arm and he looked up. Nasna held onto him and helped him up, but she didn't glance at him, didn't even seem to be aware.

"Nas, you alright? You hurt?"

She only looked at him.

Voices echoed up through the other shafts and he glanced over to them. It wouldn't be long before the Lightless arrived. And at that point, they'd be trapped. The only other shafts led up into the main area, to the ordîns.

Nasna looked away and returned to her silence.

He grabbed her by both shoulders and shook her. "Oh no, you are not freezing on me."

She broke out of his grip and slammed a fist into his sternum. He stumbled backward until he fell. But he glared back. She'd had enough time to pout or daydream or whatever in the Abyss she was doing.

"What was that?" she asked, her voice raised and eyes narrowed.

Good. She was angry. About time.

"That was your wake up call. I don't know what's going on with you, but I need you to snap out of it. We have prisoners on all sides coming up, guards above us, no way of getting out, and I can't fight all of them by myself. I was just thrown around like a child's toy down there!" He wheezed and coughed hard, blood spattering against his hand. "I need you, Nas."

He coughed again, trying to take in gasps of air in between them. It just would not end. That was the problem with having an actual body. With statues, he could always leave when he'd pushed too far. Not so with a body. It'd always be waiting for him, weak, broken, and unable to continue.

Nasna knelt in front of him, her face softened and eyes downcast.

"Tsuran, I... I'm sorry—"

"Apologize later. First, we need a plan."

Shouts poured from around the gallery. The prisoners came out of the other shafts. They all had picks and hammers, and though none appeared to have crystal, it was only a matter of time before that behemoth made his way up. Nasna helped Tsuran to his feet.

"What's the plan, Nas?"

"Why do I have to come up with a plan?"

A sharp pain in his neck. He reached up, but the world blurred and he dropped to his knees, shaking his head with everything spinning and spinning. He wanted to vomit.

"Tsuran, what's—"

She quieted. She collapsed beside him, groaning.

Other prisoners yelled and ran about. Or did they stay put? Hard to tell. Shouting? No, something else. Like wind. Gushes of air or something. No, that's not right. Flapping. Flapping wings. That meant the ordîns were here.

Chaos erupted all around him as the guards flew down and subdued the prisoners. They shoved him onto the ground, and something bitterly cold clasped around his wrists as several guards kept a firm grasp on him. He turned, trying to look for Nasna. She was also the ground with several guards on top of her.

A familiar voice spoke above him, one Tsuran hadn't been too eager to hear again.

"Con-None. Why am I not surprised?" the Warden asked. "Do you enjoy pain this much?"

⎯⎯◄◊►⎯⎯

Weakness through limbs. Dizziness. Vision blurring in and out. Had to be venom from a sandstone viper.

Someone grabbed Nasna, pinning her head to the ground, and clamped something solid around her wrists. Her vision ebbed in and out of clarity, though everything remained more or less distinguishable. Several guards held Tsuran down—though with the drug it wasn't necessary—and the Warden stood above them while the rest of the guard pushed the prisoners back. But even that wasn't needed since the Lightless didn't seem to be in a rampaging mood anymore.

However, the Lightless weren't her key problem anymore. Now, she and Tsuran were in the hands of the Warden. And he was all out of mercy.

"Chance after chance I have given you," the Warden said. "And at every opportunity, Con-None, you have chosen the path of death."

The guards on top of Tsuran slammed their clubs onto him. He groaned and she tried to reach to him. A solid club cracked onto her shoulder. She grunted and jerked her body again—the most she could do—trying to get close to him.

"And you," the Warden said, turning toward her. "I had my definite suspicions of your involvement with him, but I think this is all the proof needed. You shall both be punished."

Nasna wanted to push against those on top of her, but her body struggled to heed her commands. If they injected her with another dose of their drug, she would pass out. She needed energy. And she laid on a floor of lightstone. Only a little energy would do it, just enough to get her mind in order. Just enough to fight back.

The Warden grabbed her head wrappings and pulled her head up.

"What is this?" Nasna tried to fight back, but the Warden tore the wrappings off. "An ordîn. A clipped. What is the meaning of this?"

The usual composure the Warden wore vanished, replaced by what all proper ordîns reserved for those like her. For a clipped. He stared at her as if her very presence filled him with bitter nausea, as if she had poisoned him and all his loved ones. Nasna glanced down at his clenched fists. The Warden stepped back toward the shaft hole, so if he'd wanted to hit her he showed a fair amount of restraint.

"Bring her to the Chair. I want her questioned."

"Sir!" the guards said and pulled Tsuran to his feet. "And what of this one, sir?"

"I am done giving him chances. Throw him to the Pits."

The guards saluted and dragged Tsuran off toward the wall. They unfolded their wings and flew upward with him in their arms.

Grab energy, that was all she needed to do. She wouldn't let them take Tsuran from her. Nasna closed her eyes and searched for the energy in the floor. She never drew energy from anywhere but her hands, never needed to, but as long as she was touching the stone, she could do it. She searched and searched, but the drug seemed to create a wall between her skin and the energy. A jab in her back broke her concentration.

"I do not know who you are," the Warden said next to her. "Nor do I know why you are helping Con-None, but we will pull every secret from your body. And then you shall be erased. An abomination like yourself will not continue to—"

A loud shattering crack sounded behind Nasna and the ordîns. Vibrations ran through the ground beneath her. The guards all turned, and she looked behind, squinting through the haze.

More than a dozen shadowy tendrils reached out from one shaft, despite it being filled with lightstone, and battered the crystal in every direction. They smashed into the ceiling, floor, and walls, cracking and shattering all the crystal and upturning the stone. Wherever they struck, they destroyed lightstone and shadows formed.

"Stop that prisoner," the Warden said and several guards rushed forward to exorcise the possessor.

But they did not get far. The shadows became like spears and burst through the air. The guards didn't make it within even a dozen feet of the shadows' origin. They dropped dead to the ground, black shadows pulling out from their chests.

The Warden bellowed out other orders and several more guards rushed forward to take down the prisoner. This had to be Con-Ebru, coming for her.

Ten guards charged the shadows. The tendrils retreated into themselves like a ball of shadow. Or rather, like a coiled serpentine beast that struck with sharp needle-like tendrils when a guard came too close. Ordîn after ordîn fell as the shadow speared through their skulls. Some guards dodged the shadow while others went into the air and sped down to the center of the shadow. But the shadows kept them at bay.

One guard was faster than the others and used the other guards' deaths to get behind the shadow possessor. The ordîn cried out and slammed his fist into the shadow body. All the shadows froze.

Silence filled the room, and all gazed at the inconceivable. The guard hadn't exorcised the possessor. Con-Ebru remained a shadow, the tendrils still flowed out from him. The guard who'd struck him did so again.

The Lightless remained as he was and did not leave the possession. Without hurry, Con-Ebru turned and faced the guard, who gawked. The guard shouted and drove both hands into the Lightless.

Again, nothing happened.

Nasna took a step back.

"What is this?" the Warden said. "This... this is not possible."

Nasna agreed. It wasn't possible. It shouldn't be possible. But it also shouldn't be possible for a Lightless to keep possessing shadow inside a room with this much light.

A shadow tendril sliced through the guard and Con-Ebru faced the Warden, Nasna, and the remaining guards. She glanced over to the Warden. On his face was a third impossibility.

All composure, gone. All poise, gone. There was only one thing etched into his blue face.

Fear.

"Warden," a voice echoed from the shadows. "Your days of ruling are over. This mine belongs to the Lightless now."

Two dozen tendrils shot from the shadow possessor, smashing into the lightstone all around him. It was like a tornado of shadow and wherever it struck, light vanished and shadow remained. Prisoners ran for cover, columns snapped apart, floors cracked and scattered. This level, designed to prevent Lightless from escaping, was being destroyed by a show of power Nasna hadn't ever imagined.

"All guards return to the upper level!" the Warden shouted. Nasna left the ground as the ordîn guards holding her took off in flight toward the shaft exit. As they flew higher, Nasna's mind cleared more. The prisoners shouted, even cheered, in an ever-increasing din, and charged after the retreating ordîns.

The shafts to the Lightless area were much wider than the ones to the other mine. These were large enough to allow the guards to fly upward with Nasna in tow. Air rushed past her as the guards flew higher and higher until they bolted into the main Lightless entryway, the huge iron grates crashing and locking behind them.

The Warden shouted orders to all the guards running back and forth, but in the chaos, combined with the venom, it was hard to figure out what was going on. They pulled her out of the shaft area just as shadows burst through one grate, broke it off of the stone floor, and tossed it to the side.

Guards, all wielding crystal weaponry, rushed past her into the room as her guards pushed her out. They pulled her into the main body and she looked around for Tsuran, but no luck. The Warden had said the Pits, so she just had to get there. They wouldn't have thrown him in yet.

The guards holding her threw her aside against a wall and turned back into the shaft room. They must've received new orders, but her head remained in a constant battle between clarity and dullness so she had heard nothing. She laid on the ground—her face at an awkward angle against the wall—and struggled to gain control of her legs. She needed to get up and run. But the drug remained strong enough that her legs wouldn't heed her commands. The Lightlesses' shouting grew louder. A real fight, a proper battle, had begun. And it didn't matter who won that fight. She was in trouble.

Tsuran leaned against the stone wall. The guards who had been dragging him to the Pits received orders to return to the shafts. They seemed to forget him.

He stood in the hallway to the furnace room. Clanging and shouting echoed around him, but he wasn't clear on what was happening. Not that it mattered because the guards took Nasna off somewhere, and he was being brought to the Pits. Plus, he barely could move his body, likely the only reason the guards felt fine leaving him. He wouldn't have long before the guards came back to finish out their task. And then it would be too late.

No, he had to act now. He wouldn't just let them do whatever they wanted to her.

He quested out for his statue. This was difficult with the drug dulling his connections to everything, but it didn't sever his connection like Solitude did. It took longer than it should have, but he found the statue. But it was too far away from him to body-possess it.

He groaned and hit his head on the wall. He needed to get it closer. No way he'd be moving to it. And mind-possession, although it had the range, would leave his body helpless. If the guards came back to find an empty body, they might just kill him with no more hesitation. He only had one last option. One last thing to try.

Total-control.

It did not have the range of mind-possession, but it went further than body. It would have to be enough.

The drug was a pain to deal with, but he pushed himself, trying to find the statue, trying to have total-control over it. Using a power he hadn't grown an arm for yet, he pushed his being far from him.

He split.

He hated this sensation. It seemed like half of him was being smashed while the other became steeped in flames. But everything counted on this. So he pushed total-control further out, splitting his being more, sending half out for his statue while keeping the other half inside his body.

He found his statue. A vague and dull familiarity almost out of his range. He poured all of himself into this last push.

Total-control possession.

His being split. He no longer just leaned against the hallway leading to the furnace room. He also laid on the ground in his statue, somewhere in the Lightless entranceway. The furnaces crackled far behind him and guards and prisoners fought over him. The stone wall was cold against his fleshy cheek while the floor shook underneath his crystal body. It was as if he was no longer a single person, but two.

And it hurt. It hurt a lot.

Nasna pushed herself onto her knees, though she almost fell over from the effort. She shook herself and tried standing up, using the wall next to her to stabilize her.

The fighting behind her was getting worse. No way of telling who was winning, but it didn't sit right that all those guards hadn't ended it yet. That meant the prisoners were holding up their end in the fight, though perhaps it was just against that single possessor.

She ran forward, though it was difficult keeping her balance. As she moved, the effects of the drug dimmed. She took step after careful step, scanning the room. She needed to find Tsuran. They'd said the Pits, which had to mean that waterway in the furnace room. Another few steps and she faced the furnace hallway.

And there he was.

"Tsuran!" Nasna ran forward. One leg wasn't as fast as the other and she tripped, catching herself at the last moment. Tsuran glanced up, his face contorted, his skin flushed. Not as bad as when he'd been in Solitude, but this didn't look good.

"Nas?" he said with a strained voice.

The sounds from the Lightless area grew louder and Nasna turned. Guards poured out, many of them bloodied and struggling to stand, with prisoners rushing after them, many now carrying the weapons the ordîns had brought in. The guards were losing the fight. There weren't any shadowy tendrils to aid them, but it didn't look like the prisoners needed them. There was enough shadow all around this room for them to use. And they did.

Dozens of ordîns fell dead. Their bright blood splattered across the floor. The tatzons clove through their captors and Nasna looked away, her legs shaking.

They were there again, bellowing in her ears. The screams. The ordîns who fell, bloodied.

She was there again. The great wide altar. The sacrifices. The countless slain ordîns. Her family.

No, she wouldn't go there. That was cycles ago. This carnage was now.

The Lightless poured out from their prison and forced the ordîns up the stairs away from them. The prisoners had won this fight.

The main body filled with the escaped Lightless, and many surrounded her and Tsuran pointing sharp weapons at them. She took steps back until she met Tsuran's body and she leaned against him. Even if the drug made standing difficult, she would shield him as best she could.

A figure appeared in front of them, rising from the shadows. The shadow faded as Con-Ebru unpossessed it. He stood amongst all the prisoners and glared at Tsuran and Nasna.

"So what'll we get to do with them?" another prisoner asked.

Con-Ebru smirked and slammed his fist into Nasna's face. She fell to her knees and blood spluttered from her mouth.

"Nas...." Tsuran said but moved little. He still looked as if he were about to keel over himself.

"I think the Warden had the right idea," Con-Ebru said. "Let's bring them to the Pits."

More chuckling amongst the prisoners and they grabbed Tsuran and Nasna and pulled them into the furnace room. She tried to struggle against them, the effects of the drug almost worn off. But damn it, she still couldn't feel their energy. They dragged her and Tsuran to the far end, to where the water flowed down into the black tunnel. To the endless darkness.

Con-Ebru turned Nasna around and grabbed her by the face, pulling her close. "You'll die for my lover's death. But thanks. Had it not been for you, I don't think we would've ruled these mines."

He spat in her face. They lifted her and threw her into the water and it swept her away into the darkness and away from the light. Away from the furnace room. Away from the prison. Away to the Pits.

26

———◆◆◆———

THE PITS

I *magine my surprise when one of my prisoners approached me with*
a request. She requested a letter be delivered to you. Imagine my
further surprise when the contents of the letter showed that you once laid
with this tatzon and spawned a child together, a child who lives within
my prison currently.

I believe it is time I return to my rightful place among my people and
you flee into obscurity. It would be a shame if something were to happen
to these two, otherwise. The mountains are a dangerous place.

Do not test me.

- Farhata of the Rising Coast, Warden of the Iron Mountain Prison,
in the 2967th Lunar Cycle

The frigid water brought a sudden jolt through Tsuran. His eyes
shot open and his lungs wanted to take in a gulp of air, but he
pushed the urge away and kept his mouth shut, focusing on his
total-control. Tsuran could not afford to break his possession.

Water rushed him down the black tunnel, swirling around him
and trying to drown him. The tunnel sloped, and he descended,
water and air whipping past him, all of it taking him further from
his statue.

He almost bit his tongue from tightening his jaw, but it was all he
could do from screaming. Half of him still ran through the furnace

room inside the statue, growing more and more distant from his actual body, magnifying the splitting of his being. Without the fourth Guardian arm, he couldn't even attempt at empowering the statue's speed or size during total-control, so all he could do was run. Run and not lose concentration.

His actual body sped up.

Not good. If he went too far, he'd lose the statue. He tried to spread his body out against the rock but the stone was smooth and he couldn't get a grip. And if he remained in the water for too long, he'd lose consciousness. This was the absolute worst time to be using an ability he'd not grown an arm for yet.

In the statue, he came up to the wall below the water and climbed. His body smashed against the stone and air escaped his mouth. Vision in the statue blurred. His eyes closed. The statue climbed the wall and fell into the watery rush. As it fell, he lost his connection and returned to his body.

Darkness covered him. His lungs were about to give out.

A burst of light shone around him—igniting a pounding ache in his head—and a freezing wind cut across him, threatening to choke out his last bit of life. The coldness took away his blurry vision and the new air coming into his lungs seemed to wake him up. But this wasn't time to celebrate. He was out of the tunnel, but now he was airborne. And falling.

Water from the tunnel poured down alongside him like a mighty waterfall and cascaded into a large opening in the rock below him. If he didn't do something, he'd follow the same path.

Maybe his statue. No good. Still too far to body-possess.

He plummeted.

He didn't dash against the rock but struck water and plunged through the churning depths, water crushing him on all sides, tossing him around in an icy flow. It shot through him, battering his body and strangling his near-empty lungs.

He needed to breathe, but his body wouldn't respond. Black filled his vision. His mind drifted as everything weighed against him. His body convulsed, a hand reached for his throat, but the rest of him did nothing but drift deeper into the watery depths.

The Abyssal would wait for him now, ready to take him far away from everyone he loved...

No. It wouldn't end this way. He wanted to thrash and fight, but his body wouldn't respond to his determination. It had already given up once he'd hit the water. Only his mind hung on.

Something tickled him inside. An itch. A slight scratch. It pricked at his mind and he turned his attention to this familiar feeling that welled within him.

His statue. His connection grew as it fell closer. Close enough to body-possess.

He reached out and possessed it.

The cold, the pain, the discomfort, it all disappeared from his body and a rush so pure in this crystal statue replaced it. Only it wasn't adrenaline, but a sensation similar, yet more intense. He always felt it when he possessed crystal, as though the crystal itself filled his soul with strength and movement.

The swirling depths still surrounded him, but he no longer drowned. The statue didn't need breath, so neither did he. He empowered the statue, enlarging and flattening his four arms and paddled away. It was awkward swimming in the statue and not natural at all. But it kept him alive, so he wouldn't complain. The arms propelled him forward to the surface, though he kept paddling since the statue wouldn't float.

Some land was nearby, so he made his way to it and pulled himself up out of the water. Leaving the statue meant returning to a cold, wet, beaten, and Solitude tormented body, and that was not something he was ready to deal with. While possessing, his body would stay exactly as it was, neither healing nor worsening.

For now, he looked for Nasna. He surveyed the cavern and then the water behind him. His gaze went past the rocky shore he stood on and across the watery lake. He paused and his crystal jaw went slack.

In the middle of the wide expanse of water sat the giant crystal from his last time on the hunting team. From when Leof had died. This was the Pits? If so, then that meant....

Tsuran scanned the room, looking for any sign of the Colossal beast. His gaze rested on the water where the beast had come from last time.

The water remained still. For now.

He had to find Nasna and get her out of here. Sunlight from the opening in the ceiling mixed with the veins of lightstone and provided enough light to see, but even then there wasn't any red-skinned ordîn lying around.

Staying in his shrunken form, he made his way along the water's edge, eyes darting all around the cavern. He dared not call out to her for fear it'd awaken the beast if it slept here.

"...Tsuran...."

He turned around. That had been her. A weak voice, and if he'd been out of his statue, he may not have heard it. But he did. It came from behind. From across the water. He squinted. On a distant shore? No, and not in the water either. Where could she—there! On the rock lying next to the giant crystal, hard to tell what kind of condition she was in but it wouldn't be good. But she was there.

"Nasna!"

Somehow he had to keep her from freezing to death. He ran toward the water without an actual plan. Then again, he didn't need a plan. He just had to get to her. She needed him right now.

Bubbles burst from the lake, the water churned, and the ground shook beneath Tsuran. He froze in his tracks. The water exploded as the Colossal beast rose from the lake, just as it had all those months ago.

The beast roared as it stepped out of the water toward him and the ground quaked. Even though he was still small, it seemed as if the Colossal sensed his presence. Sensed his crystal statue. Tsuran eyed the tusks and claws of the turtle. All could break through the crystal, through him.

He had his statue back, but this was a Colossal, and Tsuran had no team. No backup, not even a Partner to switch with. Just him. Him alone against something almost fifteen times his size. It was madness. Insanity. A death sentence.

But he did not back away, his gaze drifted to Nasna. Yes, he had no team, no Partner. But he had her. And he wouldn't let that go.

He was a Guardian. About time he guarded someone.

Tsuran empowered the statue, growing to regular size and shaped his arms into blades. He glared at the Colossal beast.

The beast charged, its spikes digging into the stone ceiling causing debris to crash down around its hard shell. The ground rumbled, but Tsuran stood ready. This wouldn't be like the last time. This time he would fight.

The beast clawed at him as it moved forward. He pushed himself back. The paw swept past him and crashed onto the ground beside him. Broken rock pelted his body, throwing him back several feet.

Without a moment lost, he charged forward, jumped, and dug his arms into the beast's paw. The beast grunted, raised its leg, and flung Tsuran off like an annoying insect. Tsuran rolled on the ground and then got to his feet just fast enough to dodge the tusks which dug through the ground toward him as though it were softened earth.

But the beast wouldn't daunt him. He was Tsuran Con-None, the Red Sword of the *Burning Air*.

He dashed forward without empowering his speed, since he was already pushing his limits. Tsuran neared another leg, but the beast raised it and brought it barreling toward him. No time to dodge. No need to.

He crouched and threw his arms above his head. The beast paw crashed down around him, but unlike the last time he had done this, he pierced straight through. His crystal did not crack or waver underneath the weight and strength of the beast but cut through the paw without resistance. The beast roared. Tsuran smiled. He pulled himself through the top of the paw, eliciting more echoing roars from the turtle, and rammed his bladed arms into the leg, cutting deep. If he cut deep enough, maybe he could cripple the beast.

Before he could, the turtle slammed its paw into the wall with power that shook through Tsuran's red-crystal and embedded him into the stone, high above the ground. He grunted. He felt that one. Tsuran broke an arm free just as the beast reared back on its mid and hind legs, snarling. Tsuran watched the beast lunge forward with unimaginable speed, power, fury. With the full weight and power of a Colossal behind these strikes, even red-crystal would waver and break.

Tsuran hardened the crystal right before the claws crashed into him which sent spikes of pain through him. The crystal was strong, but this beast was too.

The Colossal struck again, and again, and again. He continued to empower the crystal, but every strike embedded him further and further into the stone wall. Every strike buried him deeper into his grave.

Nasna watched from the ground, a useless spectator to Tsuran's death.

She'd been lucky to land next to this massive crystal. By drawing small amounts of energy from it into her, she kept herself alive. It didn't negate the cold, but it gave her the strength to continue. It helped her fight off death. If she stopped drawing energy from it, the cold would kill her.

But that didn't matter now as she watched Tsuran die. She needed to help him but what could she do with a frozen, still shackled, useless body? A broken, clipped ordîn with powers beasts were immune to.

The turtle backed up for another crushing blow.

A large blade-like crystal, larger than the beast's tusks, burst from the hole into the beast's arm and Nasna bit her lip. A second blade sliced into the same arm, followed by a third that drove itself into the beast's face, digging into its eye.

The cavern trembled with the beast's ear-bleeding cry. It backed away from the wall and Tsuran's statue burst out. Nasna gasped. Tsuran was now much larger, half the size of the Colossal. To enlarge it so much... Tsuran was going beyond his limits, beyond what was safe. Empowering like that would kill him faster than the Colossal.

Tsuran threw himself into the beast and sliced away. His attacks cut deep into the beast. Blood splattered across both ground and giant statue. But being so large now meant dodging wasn't an option, and, rising on its hind and mid legs, the beast attacked him in a frenzy. Tsuran brought up his arms and took the barrage, the ground beneath him breaking. A tusk pierced through his chest, but Tsuran did not give in. He struck back, his sword-like arms slicing through one of the beast's legs, severing it off. Dark blood gushed from the wound.

"No, Tsuran, stop." Her voice wouldn't reach him, but she had to try. He couldn't do this to himself. "Leave. Go, save yourself."

But even if her words had reached him, he would've fought on. Because the idiot wasn't fighting to kill the beast. He fought to defend her. He fought for her to live. A lump formed in her throat and built until breath stopped.

He fought for her. And he would die for her.

The two giants clashed against each other. A beast bent on furious destruction. A Guardian bent on saving his one friend. Their fight caused the ground to quake and the ceiling to shatter, yet nothing shook more than Nasna's heart as she watched helplessly. He fought so hard for a dying woman. For a dying monster.

"Tsuran..." her lips, frozen and cracked, hurt from even the tiniest movement. But she needed her words to reach him, to save him.

Tsuran made a deft strike into the beast's side, leapt back and...

And disappeared.

Nasna picked up her head, trying to see better. His statue vanished. What did he...

Her eyes widened and her mouth fell open.

Tsuran... he laid on the ground, still, unmoving, and, most terrifying, no longer possessing his statue.

The turtle growled and her heart died.

Get up, Tsuran. Get up and run!

As if he heard her heart, he rose from the ground. He coughed and struggled to stand. Without his statue, he was so small compared to the mountain-turtle. Yet, he picked himself up, fell to his knees, and stood up again. He had his statue in hand, miniature as normal. His body wavered, but he wielded his statue like a dagger and stared up at the beast, and shouted. He did not turn and run. Only stood and shouted, his statue raised to the turtle. The damned fool still challenged it. Still fought it. And he would now die.

Nasna's jaw tightened. "No, I won't let anyone else die for me. Never again."

She was not a helpless clipped ordîn. She was more. She was Nasna, the Touch of Death. And she would not let her friend die.

Heart pounding, cold stabbing, she struggled to her feet and faced the beast. Even if it did not have energy, she would fight it. Because even if it had no energy at all, this giant crystal did. And plenty of it.

She grabbed the crystal, grabbed a hold of the massive river coursing within it, more than she'd ever felt or imagined before, and drew all of it into her.

She screamed and closed her eyes as the energy surged into her, filling—no, breaking through her body. It was more energy than she'd ever taken into herself before, and all of those smaller times had been dangerous. But she continued to draw it in, dragging more and more of the river into her.

A new piercing cry emanated from the beast and the ground quaked. She wrenched her eyes open only to see the Colossal charging toward her. It ignored Tsuran and aimed for her. It didn't like her touching its crystal.

Nasna forced a smile. *Good.*

The light from the giant crystal dimmed as the energy flooded her body. The energy tried to expand and release within her. It was as if air continued to fill her body and if she exhaled her body would rupture.

Out of the corner of her eye, Tsuran faced her. He shouted something, but it didn't reach her ears. He had pushed himself to the brink of death just to save her. It was time to return the favor.

Thank you, Tsuran. For everything.

The beast leaped toward her. She channeled massive amounts of energy into her legs, down to the soles of her feet, and released it. The ground exploded beneath her and the force sent her flying straight to the Colossal.

It opened its massive maw, serrated teeth welcoming her flesh with glee.

She sailed through the air. Her legs shattered, body split open, blood pooling in her eyes. Nasna let out a cry from the depths of her lungs. She didn't fill this cry with the pain from the cold, the energy, or the explosion behind her. Nor was it born from fear, rage, or hate. It came from a single burning desire.

To protect her one friend in the world.

She soared straight into the beast's jaw, through its throat and into its body. The jaw clamped shut. She met the darkness.

27

---◆○◆---

WHEN THE SOUL CRIES OUT

I beg you help me, I know no where else to turn. I have no one here in Tifre that can or would help me, even Ordal would struggle knowing about my dalliance. I have found no sound sleep these last nights and I am ready to break. There must be something you can do, you claim to be gods do you not? You must have power to reach them, save them or even prevent Farhata from acting against them. Please, I will do anything you ask if you would only do this small thing for me.

I cannot let those bright eyes dim. Not again.

-Yavahush the Forsaken

"Nasna!" Tsuran shouted. But it was too late. She'd launched herself straight into the Colossal and it'd chomped down. And she was gone.

This was his fault. If he'd just held out a little longer, if he'd just kept empowering beyond what he knew was safe and had just—

The beast exploded.

A massive force erupted out from it, crashing into the ceiling, the wall, the floor, and toward Tsuran. Pure reflex kicked in and he possessed his statue.

The eruption hit him.

The force threw him to the opposite side of the room, crashing through all rock like it was a thin cloth. He spun fast, breaking through everything he came into contact with, still flying.

Tsuran hit the ground hard and rolled until he collided with a wall, broke through it to the other side, and collided with a second wall. Even inside the statue, blackness shrouded his eyes for a moment. His ears rang with the percussive echoes of the blast. But overall, he seemed unharmed.

Then his reflex hit again, throwing him out of the statue so he wouldn't start growing Remnancy. Cold enveloped him worse than before, and nothing sounded right. Light glared down into his eyes, and he coughed from all the dust in the air. The cough worsened until blood and water spilled from his mouth. The air wasn't pleasant to breathe in.

He wiped his face and grabbed onto the wall next to him and tried to pull himself up. But the rock broke off and he fell face-first onto the ground. One arm was useless, one leg didn't obey. The cold gripped his soaked body, already numbing his toes. Worse of all was the whisper of Solitude. He still felt it in his bones, and he was now alone. It was coming.

Breathing grew harder, but he tried standing again. He had to get up. He had to find Nasna. Solitude be damned.

The wall didn't break this time as he pulled himself off the floor. Though, his only good leg wobbled beneath him and he stumbled forward, falling again. Dust clouded the air, broken rock fell from the ceiling hitting the ground near him, and he almost tripped over a smoldering piece of beast flesh to his side. If he weren't so cold and weak he might have vomited from the smell. But he straightened and looked forward, and his jaw slackened.

The waterfall from the furnace room still fell, but he wasn't close to it anymore. That explosive force had sent him crashing through most of the rooms of the massive cave. Had he not possessed his statue, he would have died for sure. But that wasn't the major problem. The problem was he could see the waterfall. There were no walls of rock impeding his vision, no twisting paths, or myriad of rooms. There wasn't even a ceiling.

That force had destroyed the entire mountain's top.

The cold white light of the sky shone onto ground that had never known sunlight, though until moments ago it hadn't even been ground but rock hidden deep inside this mountain. A mountain with a different shape now. There remained parts of what had been the top on either side of the explosion, creating a smaller twin peak. But in between these new peaks was barren land.

The ground beneath him gave way, and he caught himself from falling into the chasm at his feet. He backed up, gaping. If they ever made it someplace with a good mushroom ale, he'd have to spend some time to get a grasp on what kind of power she held.

First, he needed to find her.

Cold, wet, and legs wobbling, he descended into the new hole of a mountain. He resisted possessing his statue. Possessing now would mean losing his soul and becoming a Remnant. If he were going to die today, it would be as Tsuran, and nothing else.

Though snow fell on him, there were sides to the hole that protected him from the wind, the last thing he wanted to deal with. He headed straight toward where the center of the explosion had been, though Nasna had just rewritten the terrain. Only the waterfall gave him an idea of where to go.

The closer he came, the more he saw bits and pieces of the beast. The ground was a mix of red blood and gray stone. He was getting close.

"Nasna, you idiot, where are you?"

No reply. He shouted again. And again.

Solitude blazed in his bad leg, and even the cold and numbness could not stop him from feeling it.

Solitude will not have me.

He forced his dying body forward.

"Nas! Answer me! Where are—"

He stumbled over a broken claw and fell onto the bloody ground, coughing and adding his blood to it. Shaking his head, he stood up again, though, with the dust settling, more of the beast's body came into view, scattered around. That explosion... it had decimated the Colossal and obliterated the mountain. How could she survive—

No. He refused to think like that. She was strong and alive. She had to be.

He pushed on, getting closer to the waterfall which was spreading its contents around its new container. It would take years before it filled this place, though with the open-air the water would freeze. As would Tsuran and Nasna. He pressed on.

Solitude started to spread like a burning infection up his leg and toward his hip.

Shivering, teeth clattering, he arrived to where the explosion happened. It looked to be the center of the hole. If she were anywhere, she'd be—

A small groan.

"Nas!"

There she was! Rock and dirt covered her, and she wasn't moving, but he found her. He rushed to her side and tossed off the rock and held her in his arms.

Solitude retreated.

"Nas? Can you hear me?"

She didn't open her eyes nor move. She groaned and shivered.

"Oh, Nas." Tsuran held her close to him and she flinched, groaning more. He looked at her and gasped.

All along her body, even her face, her skin had split open in large gashes, with muscle and bone showing inside. It was just like the time with the cave-in, except worse. There was no recovering from this. These wounds were fatal.

Being more careful this time, he brought her close to him. They were both cold, wet, and on the brink of death, so he didn't care if she would be angry with him holding her. If he were to die, it'd be with his last friend nearby.

"I'm so sorry, Nas. This is all my fault. I'm so sorry."

He gritted his teeth to prevent the tears from coming out of his eyes. It'd only make it hurt worse. Some Guardian he was. He couldn't save his family then and he couldn't save Nasna now.

Her lips moved as though trying to say something, but her voice was so small and hard to hear. Tsuran brought his ear to her mouth.

"Sorry, what? I didn't hear that."

Her breath warmed his ear as she opened her mouth. He closed his eyes to better focus on her words.

Something struck his ear, leaving a sharp pain. With the cold, it hurt more than it should have, but he glanced up. She smiled, her hand dropping from his face. She'd flicked his ear.

"I said, I'm glad you had a bath." She shivered and her teeth clattered, but she smiled anyway. Tsuran couldn't help but smile back.

"Is that what it takes to get you to smile? A bath?"

She attempted a shrug, though she winced at the effort. "Can't say it doesn't hurt." Her eyes met his, and she grabbed his arm. "I... I don't know if I'll make it, Tsuran."

He wanted to tell her to stop speaking like that. That she would be alright. There'd be a way out.

But she was still as wet as he was and they couldn't dismiss her wounds. He wouldn't let their last moments be one of false hopes and lies.

"I don't know if I will either, so I need to say this before we're both gone." Tsuran looked into her eyes, her split colored eyes, and smiled as he rubbed the ear she flicked, still stinging in the cold. Tsuran looked deep into her eyes, never looking away. "Before we die here, Nas I have a question to ask... would you be my Partner?"

Nasna's eyes widened, and it appeared her breath left her.

She stared at him, both of their bodies shivering against each other. Her mouth opened but darkness crowded around his eyes. He wasn't able to stay awake any longer. He toppled over into the starless night.

28

──◆○◆──

A FINAL OFFER

I have argued many chances be given you, despite the other five wishing to abandon you. They say that you do not have the heart to defend the lands, and I tell them again and again that you do. But since before we found you, alone, lost, without kin, you had already hid from who you truly were. When you lost Oushwala, you thought you could hide from your failure by abandoning all that it was to be a Luminar. This family you made, it is something you must cut from you, leave it behind irrevocably. This world needs Yavahush the King, the Leader, the Luminar. It does not need another father.

-Boban the Scultped Overseer

Images whirled around without focus. Distant memories, all clouded in fire. Bodies scattered across the ground, some dead by the hand of Luminars, others by Nasna's. The images swirled into one another, forming a new vision, but it was all the same.

From the moment of her birth, never far behind her steps, death followed. Death worked alongside her. It flowed from her. She was Death's Touch.

The strange dreams and visions faded in and out, some of recent events and others from a time long ago. The ones she hated most were silent, devoid of all sound but filled with the image of her approaching tatzons and ordîns alike, bringing death in a single touch. Smoke, fire, and darkness encased all the visions.

Nasna gazed at each image, each dream, seeing every death in her life surrounding her and morphing into each other, bleeding into one another.

The cut open bodies of her parents swirled into the motionless body of Valerija, which then became the sight of a dozen slaughtered tatzons, all at her feet. It did not stop. It all sprawled out before her like a horrific painting, and she was the artist.

She tried to look away but every place she looked, new images appeared. And they were all the same. They all revealed who she was.

This was her Path. This was how she as an ordîn would bring balance and order to the world. Through Death. There was no light, no coming dawn. All was darkness and smoke and fire.

There was a sharp sting on her ear and she turned, but nothing was near her. The images were far from her, but something struck her. A subtle pain lingered there. Then it spread.

She reached for her ear but it seared her fingers and she pulled away. This pain crept around the side of her face and spread further down her body. The pain built in intensity and welled within her. But as it did, the darkness wilted back, the smoke cleared, and the fire dissipated. They were all being pushed back by a light emanating from her.

Soon the pain reached around her arms and she looked at them. They were on fire. Pure white flames engulfed her. They were consuming her.

Her dream-self screamed. She had a vague awareness of it being a dream, but she didn't know how to wake up. She wasn't sure if she could wake up. These flames could be her end.

This white fire continued to roam around her body until it culminated and surged onto the outer shoulder of one of her arms. The light was intense, as was the scorching pain. The fire seared itself into her upper arm, flooding her body with the flames.

Heat spread throughout her and—as though the fire was energy—expanded. Breathing stopped. Movement ceased. She wanted to panic, to do anything. But none of her body would respond. The intensity flared through her chest, coming up her throat and filled her head. Even her tears burned her skin as they poured from her eyes.

But the darkness, the visions, all the death burned away. It dissipated as if it had never been there. All Nasna saw was the burning white fire embracing her eyes.

And it built evermore.

It scorched, it burned, it blazed, and yet, it strengthened. It did not turn her to ash, but bolstered her, flaring through her fortified body. It would not kill her, but restore her. The heat intensified until it burst from her back. She gasped—the air breathed like molten iron—and looked back. The white fire burned out of her back in the shape of wings.

The fire showed her the world around her. Shattered ground, opening up like a blossoming flower, with a chasm of black beneath it. The flames seemed to prod her, to encourage her. She should jump.

Because if she did, she would fly.

Nasna bolted upright, her breathing irregular and alternating between too shallow and too deep. The dream still swirled in her mind, but soon gave way to the coldness of the cavern and the distant rushing of water. And the crackling of the fire.

Nasna paused and looked over. A fire? Where did that come from? And wait, where was she?

With her mind clearing, she looked around. She sat inside a cave, but not the one she'd been in. This one had a gaping opening to the outside of the mountain and in the distance, there was the... wait, was that the Pits waterfall? What had happened to the rest of the... her hand went to her mouth.

The mountain top... she'd destroyed it. Nothing there but an empty bowl, snow covering it.

She looked down at herself. She wore different clothes and had a blanket wrapped around her. To her side laid Tsuran, also wrapped in a blanket. This made little sense, but at least he breathed. It meant he lived, as did she. Dry, warm, and alive.

"And so you're the first to awaken."

She glanced up and sitting on a fallen boulder near her and Tsuran, was Dalvinder. He also sat wrapped in a blanket, but not shivering as much as she. She pulled the blanket tighter around her and scooted closer to the fire.

"Dalvinder? What are you doing here? And how are we—"

"Alive?" Dalvinder said. "That would be because of me. I may have gathered clothes, blankets, food, and brought them here. I had figured the waters wouldn't do well for your health."

Nasna looked at the clothes around her and touched the warmth against her skin. "You put us in the dry clothes?"

He jumped from the boulder and sat next to the fire opposite her. "I also brought some wood. I knew you would need to be warmed up some way."

"Thank you. I think we would've died if not for you."

"You most surely would have. The only reason you survived at all is because of how quickly I got here. Not an effortless task. Not with the prison in the upheaval of this moment."

Nasna stared at the fire. They had almost died. Their lives saved at the last moment, but her mind went to the moments before she had blacked out.

She looked back at Tsuran. Partner? What could he be thinking? She wasn't a tatzon. She didn't do that. Yet, she couldn't help but smile at him.

"I must say," Dalvinder said, "I find it impressive that you two could defeat a Colossal beast by yourselves. As well as… well"—he gestured to the remains of the mountain—"all that. It's a wonder either of you live."

Nasna glanced to the side of Tsuran and saw his crystal statue, the only thing that could have saved him. She only survived because she was the source of the energy release. The very center of it.

"There are few able to fight and survive so well," Dalvinder continued. "I'm surprised you didn't fight all the prison before."

"They drugged us," Nasna said.

Dalvinder folded his arms in front of him. "Ah. Anyway, I'm here for more than just being a kindhearted person. I have a last service I would request of you two."

"Of course you do. What could you want from us now?"

Dalvinder smiled. "I would like you to escape."

Silence between them. Nasna blinked at him, her only other movement being a subtle shiver. She'd heard him correctly, but this made little sense. Nasna tilted her head to the side. "What?"

"More precisely," Dalvinder said as he pulled out something underneath his cloak. "I would like you to bring this out of the prison to a specified place for me." He held the black box she had stolen for him, with the spirit vessel inside.

"Why?"

"Why what?" Dalvinder asked. "Why do I want you to bring this out of the prison? Why you two? Or why should you do this for me?"

"All three."

Dalvinder smiled again. "The answers are simple and follow as thus: I no longer wish for this to be in an area where people can abuse it. I want it returned to a special place where it may remain buried and hidden. A memorial for my Partner if you will.

"Why I choose you two, it's because you already have a desire to leave and you both seem skilled enough together to accomplish this goal.

"Why you should?" There was a mischievous twinkle in his eye. "Setting aside the fact I have saved your life, if you accept I will provide you with a way of escape." Nasna looked between the box and Dalvinder. If he told her the truth, then perhaps it was not too late for her and Tsuran to get out.

Her and Tsuran.

She wasn't even thinking of escaping alone, not anymore. With all they'd been through, there would be fresh pain in her life if they parted ways. Which made what she knew she had to do even more difficult.

"How?" Nasna asked.

"A supply beast arrived earlier this morning. The contents have been stripped, and the Wranglers killed. It's under the control of Con-Ebru, though that is likely to change at any moment. However, I know several Wranglers who would very much like to leave this prison and with their help, you can leave."

She glanced over at him. "Why don't you leave yourself?"

"Oh, I will. Eventually. But I'm curious to see what comes of the prison and there are a few things I would like to do here. Besides, what is there for me out in the great big world?"

There came a groaning from the side and Nasna looked over to see Tsuran awakening. As he sat up, Nasna moved over next to him.

"You're awake. How are you?"

He rubbed his eyes and smiled. "Nas? Are we alive?" His smile then turned into a frown. "Or, does this mean we're dead?"

She shook her head. "No, we're alive. Dalvinder saved us."

Tsuran looked over, noticing Dalvinder. "He did? Well, thanks. What's he want?"

Dalvinder laughed and clapped his hands together. "I'm glad you understand me so well."

"He wants us to bring his spirit vessel somewhere as a memorial for his Partner. Says he knows how we can escape."

Tsuran's eyes widened as Nasna explained. When she finished, Tsuran scratched his chin and glanced at Dalvinder. "It could work. The best option we have, I guess. We'll have to fight our way to the Wranglers though. And then there's likely to be folk guarding the—wait, Nas, your wounds. They're gone." He touched her face and looked down at her arms. She did too. She hadn't cared to notice before he mentioned it, but how hadn't she? Not a single cut on her body, no signs of energy erupting within her, and her legs were whole. In fact, she felt great. Strong.

Both of them looked to Dalvinder who grinned, holding the spirit vessel aloft.

"A simple gift," he said. "The spirit within has healing abilities, which with a coaxing song allowed me to eradicate the damage you had done to yourself. You'd be useless to me dead or injured as you were."

Nasna looked to Tsuran. "What about you?"

"I feel fine, I mean I—" Tsuran froze as one hand reached his side and his face blanched.

"What is it?"

Tsuran pulled his shirt up and Nasna brought a hand to her mouth. Part of his chest and side was no longer flesh. It was red-crystal.

"Unfortunately, the spirit can't do anything about Remnancy growth," Dalvinder said.

Tsuran stared at his chest. The crystal didn't cover a large portion of him, but part of it sat above his heart, starting where his crescent markings ended.

Nasna placed a hand on it. It was cold to touch compared to the warmth of his skin and it held different energy than he did. He had pushed himself too far during the battle with the Colossal. Now, if he were not careful, he would become a Remnant, a soulless husk existing only to sow chaos and destruction.

She tried to meet his eyes, but he stared at his chest, tensed. His jaw tightened and his fists clenched. For a flash of a moment, it looked as though he'd scream or attack either her or Dalvinder. But the moment passed and Tsuran relaxed.

"Thank you for saving her," Tsuran said, though his tone seemed less than pleasant. Dalvinder did not appear to mind or care. He stood and dusted himself off.

"If you agree to the terms, I shall bring the Wranglers to the shaft room on your side of the prison. I hope to see you soon."

His body became one with the shadow and he left.

29

THE PROMISE

The world does not need me, but this child does. I would not put it past Farhata to harm her, to perhaps even hire someone to do his work for him so he does not sully his hands. I understand your words, but as long as she lives, the man you need cannot be me.

Perhaps it is time I surrendered this throne. I never wanted it to begin with, Naresh had always been the better candidate for this. I have already given so much of myself. Perhaps... perhaps this is my chance to choose different than I have. I could find them, rescue them, take them far from his reaches and then... family.

-Yavahush the Forsaken, in the 2967th Lunar Cycle

The two sat and watched the fire while eating the food Dalvinder gave them. Nasna watched Tsuran out of the corner of her eye. He kept the blanket wrapped around him, hiding the growth he would now have to live with for the rest of his life. All because of her.

He glanced up and met her gaze. Her cheeks warmed, and she turned back to the fire. Tatzons were sensitive about any Remnancy growth and it wasn't polite or kind to stare. Though, she'd never cared about anyone enough before to stare. She cared this time.

"How're you doing?" she asked, looking back at him. "All things considered."

He shrugged and smiled at her. "If I had to, I'd do it again."

She looked away but smiled. If he were in the same danger again, she'd not hesitate to draw on twice as much energy as she had.

If only she'd known to draw in the energy first before he'd pushed himself... she shook her head. It was pointless to think about that. There was no going back, there was only forward.

Except, what was forward? Escaping the mountain? Traveling with Tsuran? Living out the rest of this cycle with her one and only friend?

She pulled her blanket closer around her and placed her head on her knees, letting her chest rise and fall with a growing heaviness. Those weren't questions she was free to consider right now. Perhaps never. But perhaps she might at least help Tsuran move forward since Dalvinder had given them a fair proposal. She looked up and let out a breath.

"What do you think of Dalvinder's offer?"

"I'd rather not work with him again," he said. "But we won't be able to use the transport without Wranglers. We might as well go for it."

"I agree. It's our best chance."

"Yeah. Then, I guess we have a plan."

"I guess we do."

Neither stood. The weight of the unspoken kept her seated, and it had to be doing the same to him.

They had limited time and would require every moment to escape. They'd had too many near-deaths already and couldn't afford any others, nor any delays. Yet neither moved. Both stared at the fire. A question hung over them, pinning them here until they addressed it. If only they could ignore it. If only she could do what she had to without asking.

She took out her string. If there was any time she needed it to calm her mind, it was now.

"Tsuran?"

"Yeah?"

She finished forming the first figure and moved on to the second, the familiar movements steadying her hands. "Earlier... earlier you asked me a question." Nasna glanced over at him, but he didn't look up from the fire. "Were you serious?"

The fire crackled and Tsuran placed a piece of wood onto it. "Yeah. I was."

"Why would you want to be my Partner?"

He poked the fire with a smaller stick. Nasna waited for him to speak. She needed to hear all he had to say.

"Why?" He looked out toward the white sky. "Because a tatzon needs a Partner. Needs someone who'll be by their side for all their life. Someone who can pull them up when they fall and who hold them when they're weak. Who can push them to greater heights. They need someone they can depend on in all things." He inhaled deeply. "Someone who will never reject them, regardless of what the rest of the world does."

"But that doesn't answer why me."

He smirked, but it faded. "It's because you're clipped."

"What?"

He sighed and stirred the fire, scooting closer to its warmth.

"My parents and their Partners were leaders in a cult. They called themselves the Seekers of the Lost Gods and they believed that they themselves were avatars of the gods, and once they'd amassed an army of perfect tatzons, then a new age would dawn. For them, a perfect tatzon was one who reached the apex of possession power: the ability to control multiple possessions and then empower them all." He shivered as he spoke despite he proximity to the fire. "A tatzon needs to grow six arms in a single possession in order to do this, but people have a hard time growing more than two. But the cult forced tatzons to push further than they otherwise could."

One of his hands drifted to his armless shoulder, and he opened his mouth as if he were to speak, but the words did not come. Nasna spoke them instead,

"They cut off the priarm."

He nodded. "Once someone grew their first arm in any possession, they removed the priarm. The priarm can access all seven possessions, the only arm that can. They believed that if you severed a tatzon's connection to all seven, that would force them to grow further in one. And the worst part is that it worked. Almost no one inside the cult had any less than three arms."

Nasna gazed at where his priarm had once been. And they'd cut it off from him, all for the sake of power. She looked away. She knew what that was like.

"Once I'd grown my first Guardian arm, my parents' Partners removed my priarm. I was six years old."

"I'm sorry," she said. Such a pathetic statement to such a story. But what else could she say?

"It was in that cult I met Dazh. We became Partners there...and when we were old enough, we were tasked with cutting off priarms. Children's priarms." Tsuran hugged his body and his breathing quickened. "Dozens of kids. So many arms, so many lives. Most didn't survive... I killed them, Nas. I killed over a hundred children... and sometimes, I even enjoyed it. After being hurt for so long, it felt good to inflict it onto someone else.

"And then Dazh and I escaped. At least, I thought we had. We left and came to Rajalend and spent years and years there. But it seemed Dazh never truly left. My parents... they kept trying to make me into one their gods, and it appears Dazh's job was to help me get back on that path."

He turned from the fire and scooted over to her, taking up her hand. Tears pooled behind her eyes, but she dared not let them freeze on her cheeks.

"Why you? Nas, it could only be you. No one else could ever come close to understanding my pain, my anger, my bleeding and tortured heart. No one else could stand by me and get it. And — and it's not just for me. I want to be your Partner, because I want to be that for you."

He spoke with such genuineness, each word seemed so heartfelt. But it couldn't be. With all she had yet to do, this was not a future for her. She took her hand away and shook her head.

"Tsuran, I'm an ordîn. I can't become your Partner. That's not how it works."

He smiled. "And as an ordîn, are you going to teach me, an actual tatzon, about how Partners work?"

"Tsuran, come on. Have you ever heard of a tatzon being Partnered with an ordîn?"

He shrugged. "No. But I don't think it matters."

Nasna threw her hands in the air. "Doesn't matter? Of course, it matters. I don't work like that. The way your mind works, the way your body reacts to a Partner, I don't have that. I don't have the innate desire and need to have a Partner by my side. It wouldn't work."

She grabbed her blankets and pulled them tight around her and stared into the fire. Perhaps if she kept saying this, perhaps if she said it forcefully enough, she'd convince him this was true. But she didn't even convince herself. Because didn't she have that desire? Didn't everyone want someone by their side? A friend who'd never leave them.

"I still want to try," he said. "And even if it means being a Partner in practice without the Formed Connection, then fine. I'm willing to do that."

"Tsuran, my answer is 'no'."

"And I don't believe you."

She looked up from the fire at him but paused upon seeing a stern expression on his face. It didn't look right on him.

"Tell me Nas, is your answer 'no' because you think it's impossible? Because a tatzon and ordîn can't Form a Partnership? Because you don't think you should say 'yes'? Or because you don't want to?"

She opened her mouth. It was because of all those reasons. Of course, she couldn't be his Partner. She was an ordîn, there was no changing that. What was he even thinking? He was a fool. A fool with an idiotic dream that was so detached from reality.

She clenched her fists. If she attacked him, he'd stop this madness. If she struck him, pummeled him, paralyzed him, he'd stop saying these idiotic, impossible, and most wonderful things. Then he'd realize he didn't want to be her Partner. He couldn't want her as one. He shouldn't.

Her Path wanted her to shove him away, even burn him in the nearby fire. He wasn't necessary anymore, and she was delving into a dangerous place with him now. But she didn't say or do anything. Her mouth remained open, ready for her to tell him she never would want to be his Partner.

But that lie refused to form in her mouth.

Down in the depths of her chest, in a place she had been trying to ignore, lived a burning sensation. It grew within her, not a bit painful. This was a spreading and comforting warmth that built with every moment he spoke of being her Partner. It was the warmth that filled her before she'd gone unconscious. Now, it was welling up within her and it wanted to flow out.

"I can't say 'yes'!"

Tears burned in her eyes. Her breathing was hot, and she stared at the fire, not wanting to see his face. All the weakness within her raged like an unending storm, much like her own river of energy. Her Path fought the storm, tried to rein it in, to control it. But Tsuran had touched too deep for this storm to calm. It crashed through the Path's barrier, broke from its chain, and ruptured out of her in a gush of tears and uncontrollable sobs.

"I have to murder a child." The word stabbed into her like a serrated knife.

"What are you talking about?"

It was time. She'd already told him of her past. It was now time to tell him who she was now.

"I was wrong about my target," she said, unable to shake away the image of the girl's face and tears. "I wasn't sent to kill Valerija, but her daughter. I had thought the Strikers had gotten the markings wrong... but maybe I'd just wanted it to be Valerija. My actual target all along has been this little girl."

The last words choked up in her throat and struggled to come out. But the next words were what she dreaded to say most. They were the reason she couldn't say "yes" to Tsuran, why he had to stay away from her, why she'd remain in darkness.

"And I still have to do it. I have to kill her. Because that's who I am... this is who I am. You think I'm so different from Dazh? You're wrong. I'm just like him."

She waited. Waited for him to leave, to shout, to do anything. After what she knew of him and his kids, what would he say to the monster before him?

"Nas, look at me."

She didn't. She would let him say what he needed to, but she did not want to see the outrage in his eyes.

"Nas." He flicked her ear and his voice softened. "Look at me."

She turned toward him and met his eyes. But there was no outrage or anger there. There was no condemnation or disgust. Only a kind smile.

"Now, tell me straight," he said. "Is this because of the Path you talked about before?"

She nodded. "It's the Path I must walk. One of death and destruction and—"

"Do you enjoy it?"

"I... what?"

Tsuran moved onto his knees in front of her, taking her hands into his. "Do you enjoy following this Path of yours? Is this the Path you want to walk?"

She opened her mouth, but he cut her off.

"And don't tell me what you think you're supposed to say. Don't tell me what a good ordîn would say. Tell me the truth."

Words froze in her throat. Tell the truth. That's what he asked. That's what she'd given him already. It was. It had to be. Her Path told her what to say, what she was supposed to say. She was to say that this Path provided her the strength to bring order and balance, that it righted the wrongs done to her and it set Clear Sky free. It would be so easy to say. Wasn't this the truth? It had to be. Her Path said it was.

Except, her weakness said otherwise. Because it was otherwise. She wouldn't say what her Path told her to. She wouldn't lie anymore, not to Tsuran and not to herself. The truth fought against her Path's lies, pulling itself out of the depths of her heart, screaming in Nasna's ears, demanding to be heard, to be voiced.

She collapsed against his chest, head hitting the crystal there but she didn't care. She slammed her fist on the ground and her voice shook.

"No... I don't want this...."

Her Path tried to stifle her, to cut off her words. Enraged, it tore at her with vengeance.

But the door to her heart had opened. This was her weakness and her Path couldn't stop her from sharing it with him,

"I've never wanted to kill, Tsuran. And I've hated myself for every death I've caused. Even when I killed the people who murdered my family, I wept inside and cursed myself. I can't stand it. I can't stand being like this."

Tsuran wrapped his arms around her and pulled her in close without telling her to stop or be quiet. He did nothing but hold her. And she gripped him back, needing his embrace. Needing her friend.

Tears rolled down her cheek and soaked into Tsuran's shirt. "And now I have to do it again. I have to kill a child, one who has done no wrong to me, and be just like those who clipped me. I have no choice. The Path controls me. I can't say no."

He held her tight, and the tears poured from her eyes. Not since her sister's death had she admitted this to anyone. Not since choosing the Path of Death and Destruction had she ever told anyone the truth in her heart. Not since then had she cried like this. And Tsuran didn't balk or move away. He held her in silence until her eyes seemed to run out of water.

"Nas, what would happen if you decided to not follow your Path?"

She sniffed and rubbed her eyes. "That's impossible. I can't decide to not follow it."

"Right, you've said that before. But what if you did?"

She pushed herself up and looked at him. "It's not even a question I can consider. You might as well ask me to stop deciding to breathe. Though, I guess the answer is the same if you did. I'd die. But an ordîn can't choose—"

Tsuran grabbed her shoulders, though not harshly. "Enough of that, Nas. Enough about what an ordîn can or can't do. Because you already can do so much more than a regular ordîn. I mean, just look at that." He pointed to the hole in the mountain, the one she created. "What other ordîn can do that? You said it yourself, you haven't embraced this Path, right? That's because it's not who you are. You say it's a weakness to hate death and pain? Nas, that's not weakness, that's an incredible strength. That's you. That's your soul."

His third hand grabbed her hand and squeezed it. "That's your true self fighting against this stupid Path you cling to. We don't know that choosing a different Path will kill you. But if you keep following this Death stuff, then you, the true you in your soul, will die."

His words sounded so sure, so true. He made it sound like a simple matter for her to just choose a different Path... but perhaps it was.

But her Path wouldn't let her go and it reminded her of this, forcing her to take back her hands and turn away from Tsuran. But her weakness would not let her ignore his words. Not a single one.

"You determine your fate, Nas. No one else."

There sat her first and only friend since Clear Sky's death. Someone who wanted to share his life with her, to offer an everlasting friendship that would never break. There, without judgment or anger, was someone who would walk with her into something new and maybe wonderful. In him, she saw the potential of the dawn's light that would strike away the night.

If you accept his hand, I will have you kill him.

She drew back.

"I can't..." She wiped the tears away from her eyes and pushed herself off the ground and faced the exit of the cavern.

"I ignored Dazh, ignored the signs. Because of that my kids are dead." He stared down at his red-crystal statue. "I will not stop you. I trust you, Nas, to be you, and not someone like Dazh." He rose from the ground and turned toward her, though he did not step closer. "But, I also will not stand for you to be like him. If you... if you choose to go through with this, then the friend I care about will already be dead. I'll ensure it."

Her Path stirred inside her, so she refused to touch him. Yet, she smiled. "Thank you."

30

———◆O◆———

ONWARD, FORWARD

Would you forsake Tifre to become another Oushwala? Will you abandon all to the same death? If we go unprepared for when the Nightmare returns, then that is indeed what shall befall all of us. As one father to another, I understand what this pain is, but we have been chosen to be above simple fatherhood. Leaders do what is necessary for those they lead, even at the expense of themselves. It is a hard burden, which is why we cannot give it to any else. There is too great of an enemy in this world for you to cower from the choices that you must make. Naresh chose you for this reason. Only you can make this sacrifice.

  - Boban, the Sculpted Overseer

Tsuran stepped back from the wind, bringing up his blankets, now a makeshift cloak, to shield him from the cold. The two stood outside the cave, out in the open mountainside. It'd been a long time since he'd been here. A lot had changed since then. A lot was still to change.

He glanced at Nasna who gazed out across the mountaintops. This was the first time either had seen the world beyond the prison since they'd become cell-mates. In one sense, it was the first time they were free.

Tsuran looked away from her to the endless expanse of white and gray. Free? No, that wasn't quite right. Being free should be a joyous moment, one to cry out with triumph. Yet neither spoke, neither smiled.

The snow crunched underneath his feet, the wind whistled, the sun struggled to break through the clouds, and he looked at the path at his feet which led back to the prison. Back to an unknown future.

But he wouldn't turn back or look away. All he could do was move forward. They had spoken everything that needed to be. It was now up to Nasna to figure out who she was.

But if she chose Death... his stomach twisted. What an idiotic thing to promise. He had to be the worst of all tatzons to promise to kill the one he wanted to Partner with. But he would be a worse friend if he let her live on in that torment. After that... well, after that, it would be time for him to be damned to the Abyss.

But until then, he would press forward and hope until the very end.

Tsuran led Nasna down the precarious path from the cave, through old familiar ways back to the mountain prison. It had been such a long time since he used these snow-covered paths and yet they still seemed so familiar he paid little attention to where they were going, his feet moving independent of thought. Snow covered everything, creating even blankets of white, but he strayed away from where the deepest places were and avoided all the hidden drops and covered dangers. The snow gave way to rocky gravel, the rising walls of the mountain blocking the wind.

A loud bleating shot through the air. Both stopped. Tsuran looked over at her, her widening eyes showing she had the same thought.

Transport beast. A three-horned cliff goat from the sound of it.

And it did not sound happy.

They traded stealth for haste and hurried down the rocky path. An unhappy transport could mean many things, none of them good. They turned a corner and the iron door came into view. Tsuran pulled out his statue, possessed and empowered it, and slammed his fist into iron, cutting through the lock. A loud clang echoed from the strike, but Tsuran didn't care for subtlety anymore. He unpossessed the statue, returning it to its smaller size as he did, and pulled open the door.

They crept into the long dark hall, the faintest of light shining around a distant corner, and made their way toward the end. The cliff goat's cries grew louder with every step, the echo being traded for the real thing. But there was something else mixed in with the bleating. Shouting, cracking wood, and screams. Tsuran glanced at Nasna and the two hurried to the end and turned the corner to the loading bay.

Dozens of ordîns, all wielding crystal weaponry, surrounded the beast. Some flew above it, the rest stood in front, facing an onslaught from the prisoners. A flurry of tatzons poured out from the iron gates to the prison. The battle for the prison wasn't over yet.

The transport beast stood inside its holding area, several large metallic bars down around its legs, head, and hindquarters, the large wooden cabin strapped to its back. It shook, roared, bleated, pounded its hooves into the stone. It was out of control. For it to be this wild, that had to mean... Tsuran looked down at the furthest end of the battle and groaned.

Spirits. About a dozen Commons. A group of ordîns and tatzons were fighting with them, and each other, but the spirits looked like they could only see their mortal enemy in front of them.

He glanced back at Nasna. She'd forgone the head wrapping, no point in it anymore, and so nothing hid her creased brow and held breath. He laid a hand on her shoulder and wished he could do more than guess her thoughts.

"I'll take care of the transport," he said. "Go do what you need to do."

She gave him a half-smile, but it didn't last long. Time was wasting, they had to act. He surveyed the room again. It wasn't good. Getting access to the beast would be tough enough, but even before that, they had to get through the throng of ordîns and tatzons. The guards almost had the giant iron doors shut and it wouldn't be easy to open them again.

Nasna tugged on his sleeve. "I have an idea, come with me." She rushed over to the far side of the room and Tsuran followed.

Shattered crates littered the area and a massive chunk of the wall was missing. It looked as if they had added a whole new room. Nasna searched through the debris.

"Found one."

Nasna held up a sliver of a blue-crystal. Tsuran raised a brow but said nothing. She held out her hand, her face constricted and her gaze narrowed on it. She stared out at the horde, wound her arm back, and threw the crystal. It arced through the air and disappeared near the iron doors.

A concussive boom shook through the cavern and the tatzons and ordîns next to the door flew in an explosion of shattered rock and iron. The prisoners and guards stopped, either distracted by the explosive force or thrown by it, but only a moment before they resumed their slaughter. The spirits, however, did not stop even for a moment. They seemed more enraged and drove themselves into the area of the thickest fighting.

"Let's go," Nasna said and ran. She rushed past everyone, her nimble frame weaving between the fray and soon she was down the massive lightstone hallway and out of sight.

Tsuran gripped his statue tighter. The next time he saw her would either be his moment of greatest relief or deepest anguish.

The spirits screeched and the cliff goat stomped and roared. Tsuran slapped his cheek and looked ahead. It wasn't time to worry about her or the future. Find Dalvinder, find the Wranglers. That was all he needed to focus on.

He bounced on his feet and ran head-on into the chaos.

Prisoners ignored him but guards tried to kill him whenever he came too close, but he dodged them or possessed his statue to move between them while maintaining its compact form.

Bodies cut open with crystal and iron fell around him. Tatzons lost arms, and ordîns had wings torn. Tatzons fell with a spear in the chest, and ordîns collapsed with picks in their skulls. The tatzons fought with overwhelming numbers, and the ordîns fought with armor and better weapons.

Tsuran pushed and dodged his way to the iron doors, one of which was missing its entire lower section thanks to Nasna's crystal explosion. The lightstone hallway had less fighting, so he ran through without difficulty. He stopped at the end, his eyes wide. The battle here in the main body was exponentially worse than the one in the loading bay.

Bodies lay everywhere in pools of intermingling blood, shadows ran rampant, and the putrid gore assaulted his nose, forcing him to possess his statue to escape it. Enemies fighting and dying occupied the entire cavernous room. Everything blended into a cacophony of unrecognizable images.

Guards flew, Lightless dropped on top from shadows above. Prisoners moved to shadows behind the ordîns, Exorcists pulled them out and slew them. Skins of blue, orange, yellow, and green mixed with varying colors of gray, all blurring together, almost becoming one. Dark red coated everything.

Several tatzons rushed past him, not seeming to notice his statue. Tsuran watched a moment. They weren't Lightless. Those had come from his section. It looked like all the prisoners were fighting now.

Staying in the statue, Tsuran forced his way through the fighting toward the prison area, running around, and sometimes over, dead bodies. No telling who was winning. The prisoners numbered in the hundreds, but there were far more guards than he'd known were even in this place. They would fight until their last death. It looked like these prisoners just might as well.

He passed the halls leading into the mines, entering an area without fighting. Bodies still layered the ground, results from the first wave of attacks, most likely. Dalvinder stood near a back corner with a small group of tatzons. Tsuran unpossessed his statue and approached them.

"These are the Wranglers I told you about," Dalvinder said. "And a few others who I believe should join you on this little getaway." None of the prisoners greeted Tsuran with any kind of gratitude or friendliness. But most had three arms, so these Wranglers could body-possess the beast, always safer than just mind-possessing.

"Also, here is my little request," Dalvinder said and handed over the black box to Tsuran. Though, didn't it have some symbol on it before? Tsuran couldn't remember. "Instructions are inside."

He acknowledged it but did not take it. "I need to possess my statue to get us out of here. I won't be able to hold on to it." He looked over at the small group. "Can one of you?"

The nearest one to Dalvinder shrugged and took it from him.

"So how are you getting us out of here, Con-None?" one prisoner asked crossing his arms.

"The only way to get to the transport is to make our way through the fighting," Tsuran said. "I figure we stay close to the walls and away from the guards. I doubt the other prisoners will attack us, so we only have the ordîns to worry about. Once we're out of the lightstone hallway, make your way to the beast. It's got its cabin on top already. I'll do my best to keep anyone off you."

"Then let's get going already," the prisoner said, and the others nodded.

Tsuran looked over to Dalvinder. "Thank you again for this."

"There are no thanks in a transaction," Dalvinder said and disappeared, leaving Tsuran with the small group of prisoners.

"Follow me."

Tsuran led them out through the hallway and into the main chamber which had somehow become even more chaotic. Several prisoners had found some statues and were using them well, while many of the guards had created a barrier in front of the lightstone hallway. It also appeared that the ordîns had brought out heavier armor. They were more organized now, and with the lightstone behind them, the Lightless couldn't possess shadow behind the guard to get the upper hand. Prisoners charged the wall, and the guards cut them all down.

A crash sounded from the side. A large group of guards descended the stairs, just as armored as those by the hallway. Just how many ordîns were there in this mountain?

The clash continued. It wouldn't stop until one side subdued the other. But there was a new ferocity in these prisoners. They weren't backing down, none looked dismayed. Tsuran didn't want to wait around to find out what possessed all these people to kill like this. He glanced back at the group of Wranglers.

"I'll make a hole through the ordîns there. As soon as you see an opening go for it." He did not wait for them to acknowledge but charged straight toward the thick barrier of armored guards.

He went along the side, where fewer prisoners were, and jumped over broken tables and severed limbs. No one noticed him yet. A path opened in front of him, a straight shot toward the ordîns. Two guards looked his way. Several spears leveled toward him. He narrowed his eyes, smirked, and threw his statue high into the air.

The guards watched the statue for just a moment before looking back at him, ready to run him through. Tsuran watched the statue. As it descended he possessed it.

He fell amid the wall of ordîns. As his feet touched ground, he empowered the statue, growing to his normal height and spun, arms spread out, smashing into guards. He unempowered the statue, becoming small again, and dashed underneath the legs of another guard before enlarging and attacking from behind.

Hands reached for him. Exorcist hands. That's what he needed to watch for.

Tsuran unempowered the statue, shrinking again, turned, and lunged forward as he empowered only one leg, turning him into a spear launching from the ground into a guard's unprotected throat.

An Exorcist struck him from the side and ripped him from the statue.

He'd expected this. His body materialized next to the statue, and he grabbed it. Since he hadn't unempowered, it remained long and thin, like a spear. He brought it up to block several thrusts and maneuvered away, leveling it toward them.

It was now that he was grateful he'd trained with the human fighters on the *Burning Air*. He didn't know much, but he could defend well enough that many of the guards ignored the wave of prisoners and focused on him. It seemed they recognized the greater threat.

They charged.

He repossessed the statue and empowered it to full size. Six attacked. Four had spears pointed, two had a hand free, which meant four Sensors and two Exorcists.

The Sensors attacked in unison, trying to create an opportunity for the Exorcists to get close. Green-crystal tipped spears sped at him. He blocked and used their momentum to position himself opposite the Exorcists. They were slow in their armor.

One attacked, he sidestepped and grabbed the spear. His red-crystal fist cracked against the guard's cheek.

A sharp pain stabbed into his legs. He stumbled forward and turned in time to dodge to the side, away from an Exorcist's hand. He threw the stolen spear. It made contact but the guard still stood.

Tsuran rushed forward. The second Exorcist flung forward, hand outstretched. Tsuran shrunk, turned, and enlarged, fist driving through another broken skull.

Something grabbed onto him inside the statue, and it ripped his being out and he materialized onto the ground. Three spears sped at him.

He rolled away, grabbing onto the now-dead ordîn at his side and pulling her over him as a shield. The spears sunk into the makeshift shield and he tossed her aside, knocking their spears back. He possessed the statue and turned to the Exorcist, grabbed onto his wing, and yanked hard. It tore, and the ordîn screamed until Tsuran silenced him.

He turned toward the Sensors. They glared, leveled their spears, and took a step away from him.

He smiled. Without an Exorcist, they couldn't beat him. He charged forward, straight for the rest of the ordîns. The Sensors jumped out of the way and he hardened the statue, crashing into the barrier and breaking through them. Guards fell around him, making a gap in the wall.

The Wranglers saw the opportunity and rushed through. Two guards tried to intercept them, but Tsuran jumped between and pushed the guards back. They attacked again, but he broke the spears, and then their shoulders and ribs. Other guards went after the Wranglers, but he sped between, cutting them off and cutting them down.

Few guards still followed, but the Wranglers had made it through and were on their way to the beast. No point in staying here any longer. He unempowered and unpossessed the statue and ran down the hall.

The Wranglers sped as fast as they could and Tsuran pushed back one ordîn that came too close. They neared the iron doors and fled out into the chaos that was the three-way battle of the loading bay. Out here, the prisoners were losing.

Very few had picked up crystal weapons and so either the guards killed them or the spirits had. There was about a score of ordîns and only a handful of prisoners.

But there were so many more spirits than before, and more kept coming. There looked to be almost twice as many Commons as before, and half as many Smalls. The guards focused their efforts on keeping these spirits away from the beast which roared and struggled against its chains, the spirits' presence sending it into a frenzy.

"I got the beast," one Wrangler said.

Tsuran turned to her. "No, don't be—"

Too late. She vanished, and the beast calmed and steadied. A few Wranglers cheered. The idiots.

The beast returned to its stomping and roaring just as suddenly as it had stopped. Tsuran tightened his grip on his statue.

An ordîn had exorcised the Wrangler.

The door of the cabin opened, and the Wrangler flew out, dead. The body rolled off the beast's side and fell into the depths. An ordîn walked out from the cabin into view. He wore armor embedded with red-crystal. Blood dripped from one of the two serrated blades he wielded, both made of red-crystal.

Tsuran gritted his teeth and stared into the expressionless face of the Warden.

31

PATH OF DESTRUCTION

I slept well last night. First time in too long. It brought clarity, clarity I have feared, because you are right. I have pulled myself with two minds, two hearts, and they pull in opposing directions. I have wanted two lives, but at every turn I have seen that I can only have one. And because I have been selfish, my people have suffered. I once believed in the sacrifice of a few for the sake of the many, but it was always another who had to sacrifice. Never myself. Even if my heart must break, sacrifice must start with me.

I walk the Path of Sacrifice. Sacrifice shall I walk.

-Yavahush the Forsaken, Sacrifice

Fighting ordîn and tatzon alike swarmed around Nasna. She moved past, over, and around them. But she did not touch them. Even without doing so, it seemed like their energies cried out to her. The hate, the anger, the absolute blood-lust cried for her.

She sped past them and away from the fighting. Many took notice of her on both sides and tried to attack, but she moved too quickly. She paralyzed those who came too close, though paralysis in this place equated to a death sentence. But she wouldn't think about that. She had to keep moving and find the girl.

She headed toward the Lightless area. The girl would still be there. The surrounding walls, once halls of lightstone, had shattered. Some sections collapsed onto the ground with only a narrow way through. The Lightless had done well in creating shadow. Or at least Con-Ebru had.

She entered the shaft area. They had broken all the grates off and laid them scattered around. They'd also destroyed the pulley systems, nothing but broken wood and strands of rope across bodies of ordîns and tatzons. Most of the lightstone here laid scattered with fading light, but there remained enough to cover the room in shadow without blanketing it in total darkness.

She walked to one shaft and looked into the dimming light. The end of Nasna's journey would be down there. Behind her, the fight echoed into the room, pulsing with rage. Or maybe that rage came from inside her. The rage of her Path.

Nasna climbed down the shaft halfway, checked the ground below, and dropped the rest of the way. She landed in a crouch. It had been some time since she'd fallen like that, and though her legs strained and received a pinch of pain, she was otherwise fine. The bones of an ordîn needed more than a short fall to break.

She surveyed the room. A few ordîns laid on the ground, and the tatzons she had paralyzed earlier. Besides this, the gallery was nothing but shattered lightstone that filtered a dim light around the room.

She hesitated at one lift. This was the moment it would all happen. She clenched her hands. Something in her welled up again. She needed to shove it back down, to ignore it until the very end. What awaited her was inevitable. She descended the shaft.

Nasna gripped the rope of the lift, keeping the tears back. She'd wanted to believe Tsuran, to believe there was a way to be different. In the depths of her, she wished to choose a different Path. But there was no saving her from this darkness, she'd taken too many steps into it and had lived it for too long. There was only one way for her salvation, and she hoped Tsuran would keep his promise to her. He would be her only hope.

"I'm sorry, Tsuran," she whispered, gazing up into the darkened ceiling.

She entered the empty town of the Lightless. It seemed not a single Lightless had stayed here. She glanced over to the grand homes and took gradual steps toward the grandest of them all.

As she came closer, she stopped. It wasn't silent. Someone whimpered. She went to the door and found it open.

Nasna peered inside. What had earlier resembled a home in the prison was now torn apart, everything broken and scattered. This place, once a haven from the rigors of prison life, now existed only as a disordered disaster.

Past the broken chairs and ripped curtains, Valerija's dead body lay amid the clutter, her daughter crying and shaking over her. The girl didn't look up, so Nasna crept forward. No other prisoners had stayed around and there was only the door behind her. So, even if the girl ran, she had nowhere to go.

Like a dark shadow, Nasna came up behind and stood over her. The girl continued to cry into her mother's hands. Valerija still had the same expression she'd had when Nasna killed her. No one had closed her eyes yet, and they stared out into an empty void. And the girl continued to cry.

How long had she been here crying? How long alone? This girl must've been feeling the effects of Solitude. It would be a mercy to kill the girl. She had lost her mother, and she had lost her sanity. This was balance. This was order. This was Nasna's Path.

She reached out. She did not need to debate about what she wanted to do. It did not matter what Tsuran tried to say, what he tried to convince her of. There was nothing he could say. Because she wanted this. Her very body longed for this girl's death. Nasna thirsted for it. She needed this girl to die. Everything wanted her to die.

This was her Path. There was no changing that.

The girl turned wide-eyed and Nasna grabbed her throat. Nasna's strength was enough she did not even need to paralyze the girl's energy. The girl tried to fight against the grip. She was malnourished, small, and only had a priarm. Killing this girl would be easy.

Nasna closed her eyes. *Again, I'm sorry Tsuran. I wish I could have said "yes".*

In one moment it would be over. She would miss Tsuran. She would miss her only friend. But an ordîn's Path was set and unchanging. This would be the moment she fulfilled it. The moment Red Dawn would die forever. She prayed Tsuran would defeat her.

Nasna didn't want to watch, but she would. If this were Red Dawn's last moment, she'd at least watch it until the end.

The girl stood, glaring at Nasna. She did not shiver and shake. The girl didn't flinch and she stopped fighting, her breathing steady and slow. Her eyes burned with total defiance. And the river in her coursed mightier than any Nasna had ever touched.

But this child's energy… it was different. The river coursed faster and wider than any she'd experienced. And in the vortex of her chest, something else joined. Something foreign. Something strong.

This girl was not afraid. Nasna eased her grip on the girl's neck.

If she compared the age of a tatzon to an ordîn, this girl was the same age Nasna had been when the Luminars killed her parents. Half the age of Clear Sky when she had died. And this girl stood facing Nasna with a look of defiant determination she'd only ever seen in one other person.

Only one other person in her life who had been so small and yet so unafraid. Someone who'd lost everything and yet still faced every day as though she held her destiny in her hand.

When Nasna looked down in the small tatzon girl's face, she saw her sister.

Her Path stirred. *Kill her.*

Nasna watched herself following the command. It seemed so natural, so right. So easy.

The Path dictated, but, this time, she resisted.

The strains inside her, made whenever she pushed against her Path, broke.

Intense pain erupted in her mind and body, unlike anything she had experienced before. She grabbed her head. A thousand voices coursed through her mind, a thousand images burned into her eyes.

Her parents screaming and shouting for the Luminous to save them.

The Luminars cutting them open.

Clear Sky grabbing her leg, crying out, *"Big sister, we must go."*

Clear Sky lying dead on the ground.

Tsuran's voice burned in her ears, mixed in with every cry of anguish from the deaths she'd caused. They were all there. All seen, all felt. Every voice ever spoken to her, every painful memory laid open to her, every future of destruction called out to her.

Each voice was thunderous, each image blinding. All bringing agony. But there was one voice that drowned out all the rest and it spoke with a clear image of the girl in front of her.

Kill her. Follow the Path. Kill her.

"Big sister," the voice of Clear Sky cried out.

"That's your true self fighting against this false Path you're on," Tsuran's voice echoed. *"You are the determiner of your fate, Nas. No one else."*

Nasna wanted to scream if the pain allowed her. Her mind and body tore apart, with only a single voice keeping her together.

Kill her. Follow the Path.

Her body moved without her, grabbing the girl by the throat again. The girl was ready and punched Nasna's face. It was unexpected enough that Nasna took a step back. And her mind broke again. She fell onto her knees and screamed.

All the voices pounded in her mind. They were fighting against each other. Tsuran's voice joined with Clear Sky's as they fought against the screams of the killed, all battling for Nasna's acknowledgment. But they were all overcome by the strongest voice, the most alluring voice, that kept crying out,

Kill her... kill her.

This voice overwhelmed all other voices and made them seem so quiet in comparison, so foreign, so frightening. This alluring voice was also terrifying, but it was familiar and so had a comfort about it. It was the voice of her Path. The voice of Death.

She couldn't see in front of her anymore, her vision blurred with pain. She felt the surrounding energy of the girl, of herself, of even the lightstone around them. But all she saw was death. Her village, her parents, her older brother. Her little sister. The dozens of people she had assassinated. Valerija.

Kill her.

Nasna's vision cleared. Her eyes focused. The image of the girl in front of her became the most vivid thing she had ever seen. It was so clear. She had to kill her. This was her Path. A cold fire bit through her veins.

The alluring voice of Death coaxed her forward and Nasna grabbed the girl with both hands and threw her onto the ground. The girl tried to struggle, to fight back, but Nasna was stronger and unfazed by the weak attacks. Nothing would stop her now. Not even her weakness.

Kill her.

Nasna shook her head and reached for the girl's energy in her heart. But she didn't grab any. She'd meant to, though. Again, she reached into the heart, reached to kill this girl.

Again, she grabbed nothing. The girl thrashed against her, and Nasna pushed harder. She would grab the energy... but the energy pushed away from her. The only way she could explain it.

She grabbed for it again, but the river eluded her, changed its course, and redirected itself away from her grasp. Nasna reached outside the heart, then to the mind, then a leg, the priarm. At every point, the river pushed away, refusing her touch. She couldn't grab it. Impossible.

Kill her, Death told her. And so Nasna squeezed. She did not need energy to kill this girl. She would squeeze the life out of her, just like they'd stolen life from Clear Sky. Nasna would take her vengeance and become who she'd always been destined to be. The Touch of Death.

The girl's struggle weakened. It wouldn't be long. The last blood of the betrayers would—

"... big sister...."

Nasna stopped. The girl pushed against her, priarm flailing, but Nasna did not budge. She tried, but her body refused to move.

That voice... it had been so clear. As if... as if it came from inside the room. She darted her gaze from side to side, but no one else was in the room.

"... big sister...."

The voice was small, yet had strength behind it. Nasna glanced back at the little girl who was coughing. She had not said it.

"... big sister, stay here...."

Nasna fell back. The room melted away and her weakness took her back to that fatal night twenty years ago.

She was on the ground, hidden under leaves. One of her legs had been injured and bled, but Clear Sky bandaged it. There were shouts all around them. The ordîns and the tatzon family were looking for them, and they would find them soon.

Nasna tried to shout out a warning to her sister, to tell her to run, but she couldn't move, her body rigid. Clear Sky had paralyzed her energy. Her little sister stood up, smiling down at her.

"Don't worry, big sister, I'll protect you."

No, you're just a kid, don't go. They will kill you. But she wasn't able to speak, her lips wouldn't move. Her little sister turned and walked toward the oncoming voices.

"I'll protect you, Red Dawn. I will always protect you."

Clear Sky, no!

The vision changed and part of her mind ripped back into the mines where the little girl raised a jagged rock and tried smashing it against Nasna's head.

With the part of her still in the present, she reached up and pushed the girl. But the other part of her mind remained trapped in the past.

She recovered from the paralysis and ran to where her sister was. Ran to where her sister lay dead. She cradled the little girl in her arms, while she also tried defending herself from a little girl. She held her sister close and Clear Sky coughed up blood. The child wasn't dead. Not yet.

But life was leaving her small body. Clear Sky placed a hand on Nasna's cheek, while the little tatzon punched the other.

"...Red Dawn...I...told you...I'd protect you...."

Clear Sky died and Nasna's mind returned into the present as the great booming voice of Death shouted in both her ears,

Kill this girl!

Nasna threw the girl backward and stood. Her eyes hurt and she rubbed them. Tears fled from them and covered her cheeks.

A thousand voices still cried in her head, still being drowned out by the voice that told her what she wanted, what she needed, what she had to do. Nasna just wanted to die. The voices were too much. The images were too much. What she had to do was too much.

A thousand voices told her what to do, who to be, and she couldn't hear any of them. There was only the voice of Death that broke through it all. Only that... wait... no... there was one more.

Small, gentle, like a whisper, there came another voice. It was not a timid voice, nor was it weak, but more like one unused to speaking. One more accustomed to listening and sharing what little kindness it had. A voice not used to speaking anything harsh or to speak ill of any. One more comfortable making string figures than standing up to anyone.

And yet, amid the thousand voices, amid all the noise and chaos, this whisper somehow overcame them all, including Death's voice.

It was Nasna's authentic voice. The voice of her weakness, of Red Dawn.

Clear Sky died not for Destruction, but you. To protect her sister.

And all the voices stopped. The images ceased. It was just Nasna and the girl. It was as if all others waited now. Waited to see.

The girl ran forward, shouting. She hit Nasna again and again, pounding as hard as she could. Nasna looked down at the girl. Down at the one so much like Clear Sky. A tatzon born of the family who'd killed Clear Sky. And she was more like Nasna's sister than she was.

No other voice spoke. None told her what to choose. Not Clear Sky, not Tsuran, not Death, not her weakness. But she didn't need to be told anymore. She knew who she was... but she knew who she wanted to be.

Nasna knelt, taking a punch to the face. She reached out, grabbed the girl, and pulled her into a tight embrace. Tears rolled now Nasna's cheeks, and she whispered into the girl's ear,

"I'm sorry. I'm so sorry."

Nasna reached into the energy, now in such turmoil that Nasna could grab ahold of it. And she did. The river was in her control now. And she calmed it, slowing it down and down until the girl became limp in her arms.

Asleep.

"I hope you have a peaceful dream. Your journey doesn't end here."

She spoke with her own voice. It sounded strange and tasted different. But she liked it. Because it was hers. And now, she would take a new Path, the Path of her sister, of her parents. The Path of Protection.

She, right here, fully and truly, rejected the Path of Death.

An intense searing pain struck her mind. So much greater than before that it threw her onto her back and her ears filled with a piercing ring that may have been her screams. Darkness assaulted her body, flaying her soul and ripping her body—her dying body—into pieces. She had gone against Death. She'd rejected it. And now she would face the consequences. Now, Death would take her life.

It convulsed inside her, twisting and breaking her river. Her throat constricted. Pressure built behind her eyes, threatening to shove them out. What she'd gone through with all the energy from the giant crystal was nothing compared to this.

But a fire lit in her now, burning hot and melting the coldness. She wouldn't submit without a fight. Nasna slammed her fist onto the ground and reached into the air, reaching for the energy in the nearby lightstones. She wasn't touching any, but she didn't care. She needed the energy and she would have it.

Her hands sought the crystal, sought the energy within. A scream ripped through her throat and she reached further. But the lightstone remained out of reach, beyond what she could do.

Will you let me help? A voice asked. A familiar voice. The voice of her weakness.

Nasna shut her eyes to prevent them from bursting and nodded. *Yes, help!*

The flames burned hotter inside her, hurting as much as the pain from the Path. But as it blazed inside her, she reached, not with her hand but with her being, out beyond her place on the ground, beyond her fingertips, to all the remaining lightstone near her. And she felt the energy within those crystals. She grabbed hold of the energy there and drew it all into her.

The energy crashed into her and her throat opened and she gasped for air. She used the energy to force the river within her to remain intact. Her mind became blank, her body numb, as though she'd entered oblivion. But she poured energy into herself, gritting her teeth and refusing to yell. Her body cried out, begging for release. Begging for Death.

Nasna pushed further still, grabbing onto more and more energy. But her body wanted to reject life, her river wanted to dry up. But that would not happen. Not now, not ever.

She struggled to her feet, refusing to give in, defying the laws she'd broken. The laws written inside of her very being as an ordîn. With the last of her breath, she shouted,

"I choose a new Path. The Path of Protection. Death... be gone from me!"

She released the energy from her fist and it thundered into the wall and doorway, destroying all in its wake.

Nasna panted, her body ready to fall apart. She stood firm and the fire inside her burned. It ran throughout her and burned away all the pain the Path of Death had caused her. Only the pain caused by the energy remained.

She gasped for breath, hyperventilating as she tried to breathe what air she could. She dropped to her knees and took in deep breaths. Sweat dripped from her face.

She'd done it. Nasna had rejected her Path. And she lived.

Something in her shifted. Something in her chest, really all over her, seemed to move, so she placed a hand to her chest. The river of energy within her no longer coursed in the same direction. It diverged, creating an offshoot river, and more of her energy flowed into this alternate course. She was changing. Nasna wanted to laugh. Instead, she cried.

She wiped her eyes and looked back at the girl, still sleeping amid the noise. Nasna walked over and picked her into her arms, despite the ache that wracked through her body.

"Don't worry, little one. I will protect you."

She hoisted the girl onto her back and sent a surge of energy through the girl's body, causing the girl to wrap her legs and priarm around Nasna. She then paralyzed the energy and locked the girl onto her. Nasna moved around to be sure the girl wouldn't fall off and left the cell.

Everything seemed so strange now, so unknown, so new. She looked toward the shaft and patted the girl's priarm.

"Let's get you out of here."

And she ascended the shaft, leaving behind her old Path and venturing on to a new one. For the first time in so long, she felt like her old self. The self before Death. She smiled. Tsuran had been right. And now he waited for her.

Her future waited for her.

She stepped into the lightstone gallery and headed toward the final shaft.

"This is my lucky day," a voice said from the shadows and Nasna stopped. A tall tatzon walked out of them and stood in front of the shaft. Nasna balled her fists and narrowed her eyes.

"I can kill that brat and the damn ordîn that took my love," Con-Ebru said with a sneer. "All in one go."

32

THE WARDEN AND THE SHADOW

*T*o *Eyes of the Night and the Vole, Masters of the Shadow Strikers,*

You will have your coin, but you must send your most able agent to the Iron Mountain Prison. Time is of crucial essence. They will look for a young female tatzon with markings resembling circles with broad lines striking through them. She will be among the Lightless of the prison and she will stand out because of her light blue eyes.

I ask the death be swift and painless.

-Yavahush the Forsaken, King of Tifre, in the 2967th Lunar Cycle

Voices of cheering tatzons poured from the hallway behind Tsuran, growing with every second. The prisoners were getting the upper hand and it wouldn't be long before they charged down this way again. Once that happened, there was no telling when the Warden would give the order to kill the beast. Killing a beast of this size would take a lot of effort so even if the Warden made the order, Tsuran would have time. Though he wouldn't have a lot of time.

He needed to get his people onto the beast fast. And with the spirits distracting most of the guards, the only ordîn Tsuran had to worry about was the Warden himself.

The Warden didn't leave the beast or fly above it but kept his position on the transport. He was ready for any prisoner that possessed the beast. He was waiting for them to come to him.

There was no way around it. If they wanted to escape, Tsuran had to face him. And he had to win.

Tsuran ran forward. The Wranglers had enough sense not to possess the beast, so he wouldn't have to worry about them dying like idiots. He held the statue in his hand and readied to throw it since it'd be the only way to get around the Warden.

He arched his arm back and threw. It soared through the air, arced over the ordîn, and he possessed it. The Warden kept his eyes on the red-crystal statue and Tsuran returned the gaze. He empowered the statue to full tatzon size and landed onto the top of the cabin, turning as the Warden flew up.

"Well, Con-None, it seems I will witness your legendary Guardian skills. But, is this how you wish for your life to end? Is this how you wish to die?"

Dazh's voice, his haunting words, climbed up into Tsuran's mind. But, for the first time in a long time, he was deaf to those words, because all that filled his mind was Nasna, and she was greater than those words. Today, he did not run. Today he fought.

Tsuran smiled as a strange weightlessness overcame him. "Can't think of any better way to die than annoying you." Tsuran raised his fists and empowered them into sharp blades. The Warden stepped into a stance and readied his crystal blades.

"Then so be it. Judgment has come to you at last."

The two stared off. The cavern echoed with spirits screeching, guards yelling, crystal and rock clanging. Tsuran and the Warden kept their gazes fixed on the other. They watched. Waited.

They attacked.

The Warden lunged forward, striking with both blades. Tsuran met the blow with two arms and sliced with the other two. The Warden jumped back, his wings aiding the jump.

Tsuran rushed forward, striking at the Warden's head, but he ducked. The Warden thrust his blades. Tsuran dodged to the side, trying to dig his arms along the Warden as he moved. However, the Warden was fast and maneuvered out of the way. They clashed again.

Crystal scraped against crystal, spirits sang, the beast growled.

Tsuran circled again. He had to end this fast. The only way to do so was to be faster. He empowered his speed and rushed the Warden. The sudden change in speed gave him just the opening he'd hoped for and the Warden wasn't able to dodge fast enough. He struck across the Warden's side.

The Warden grunted, but his specialized armor took the brunt of the attack. The Warden sheathed one blade and flexed his hand, his face remaining placid. The only reason to do this would be if he planned to exorcise Tsuran.

Tsuran smirked. Let him try.

The Warden dove and Tsuran sped underneath, turning at the last moment and striking. His wings flapped back and smacked into Tsuran, throwing him off balance. The Warden turned and rushed in, hand outstretched. Tsuran shrank his size and ran between the Warden's legs.

Tsuran, needing a moment of surprise, shrank and then enlarged himself, just as he'd done with the guards.

The Warden didn't flinch. He thrust his hand out with unexpected speed into Tsuran's chest. The exorcism ripped him from the statue and threw him backward, landing onto the cabin roof.

Tsuran scrambled to his feet and faced the Warden who grabbed the statue, still in its tatzon size, and shoved it off the side. It rolled off of the cabin and off the beast.

"No!" Tsuran said. The Warden lunged forward, his blade aimed for Tsuran's heart.

The ground in front of Nasna exploded as black tendrils crashed into the stone ground. Sweat built around her brow, it grew more difficult to dodge the attacks with the girl on her back. But if she took the girl off, Con-Ebru would kill her. That would not happen, not while Nasna drew breath. She would protect her.

Con-Ebru laughed. He had to know that she'd be slow with the girl on her back. But she would not give up as if already dead.

He possessed a black shadow a short distance from her, with several tendrils protruding from him. With all the cracks and broken lightstones in the gallery, he had plenty of shadows to use. It'd only be a matter of time before she couldn't outrun him any longer.

She rushed toward a shaft. She didn't need to fight him, she just needed to get out of here. If she got to a shaft, she would escape.

Weaving in and out of columns, she ran to the shaft. Laughter filled the room behind and then silenced. Con-Ebru's shadowy body appeared in front of the shaft and Nasna skidded to a halt.

He was too fast. As long as he saw a shadow, nothing stopped him from moving there as fast as thought. She couldn't run faster than he could possess and so she'd need a more direct approach.

Faint light on the ground in front of her caught her gaze. A small piece of broken lightstone. She took in a breath. There weren't many options left so she'd use whatever was available.

She rushed forward, picked up the lightstone, changed the river's direction, and threw it. It exploded in a bright light near Con-Ebru. He shouted and cursed, but the boom of the lightstone and the cracking and shattering of stone drowned him out. She'd thrown it too close to the shaft and now only a massive hole remained.

She cursed herself. That had eliminated an escape path. That couldn't happen again.

She kept trying to reach out to his energy, trying to take hold of it without touching him as she'd done with the lightstone back in the cell. But it must've been a fluke or a delusion because there was nothing now.

Without touching him, she had no access to his energy. Without touching him she wouldn't be able to defeat him.

Tendrils broke through the ground she just left, following her with great speed. However, the further she ran the slower they became. She glanced back and watched him possess a shadow closer to her before attacking again.

Nasna's eyes narrowed. His tendrils only stretched so far. Based on where he had been possessing before changing shadows, he'd have to change against after she passed two more columns.

Leaning deeper into her run, she rushed past the first column. The second. She looked behind. Con-Ebru's tendrils slowed, and he possessed another shadow.

A column next to her exploded as black shadows burst through it, knocking her off her feet. She forced her body to turn just enough, so she slammed into the wall instead of the girl, the jagged rock cutting up her already injured face.

The far end held a section of lightstone. If she made it there, she'd at least have some advantage against the Lightless. He'd be able to destroy it as he had before, but it'd give her a short time to breathe and think.

Plus, there would be plenty of energy to use.

Nasna turned around a column and three tendrils charged toward her. She didn't have time to dodge, so she brought up her arms and the tendrils slammed and dug into her.

Two struck her shoulders, the third into a leg, and although they didn't pierce all the way through, they drove into her like small daggers. Except the tips wriggled inside her flesh, opening the wounds more. She screamed, twisted her body free, and dove behind the column. The tendrils followed, but she wasn't letting them cut into her again and she dashed between the columns.

Her pace slowed with her injured leg. She grabbed onto one column, one that still had a lightstone inside of it, and drew the energy into her leg. It was not much, but the pain didn't feel as bad anymore.

Nasna pushed herself away toward the area with unbroken lightstone. She turned around one column and Con-Ebru appeared out of the shadow and slammed against her with his whole shadowy body, a greater force than the tendrils. It sent Nasna flying off her feet, but she landed back on them. She turned around and faced the shadow possessor. Her eyes narrowed. He blocked her way to the unbroken lightstone.

———◆◯◆———

The Warden's blade pierced through Tsuran's side, his hand diving toward Tsuran's neck, but Tsuran possessed the statue again.

It was falling, almost off the transport but he reached out to the wooden wall, digging an arm into it. His descent stopped, and he hung over the chasm below.

He pulled himself inside the cabin and empowered the statue again to its full size. Tsuran rushed to the door, but the Warden emerged around it slamming his fist into Tsuran's chest.

Once again, the Warden ripped Tsuran from his statue and tossed him backward. The Warden, pushed the statue aside and brought both fists into Tsuran, the crystal points on the knuckles cutting into him. One fist crushed against Tsuran's head and the other, still holding the blade, drove into his chest.

The Warden landed a solid kick in the chest and Tsuran fell hard onto the ground. Tsuran wheezed. Blood poured from his face. But his chest... Tsuran glanced down and smirked. The Warden's blade hadn't killed him. It had struck against the crystal growth, leaving a chipped crack but nothing more.

The floor beneath them shook and threw them both into the air. Tsuran and the Warden crashed onto the ground, breath escaping Tsuran's lungs. The world spun and Tsuran tried to push himself onto his feet. It seemed the beast no longer wanted to remain still and now fought against its shackles.

With his mind somewhat cleared, Tsuran possessed his statue and stood and faced the Warden. The beast shook its body again and both Tsuran and the Warden flew off the floor. While in the cabin, the ordîn couldn't use the air to his advantage. But Tsuran could.

He shrank the statue, unpossessed it, and threw it as his body fell. It soared through the air and he repossessed, enlarged, and slammed straight into the Warden, two speared fists slicing into his side. Tsuran broke through some armor and cut flesh. The Warden grunted and tried to exorcise Tsuran, but he was already pushing himself out of the way.

The cabin shook again, and the beast roared. Tsuran glanced out of the window. The shackles holding the beast were straining and breaking free from the stone. The spirits' presence had to be getting too much for the beast, and the iron holding it in place wouldn't last long against its all-consuming rage.

Tsuran faced the Warden, who was still getting his bearings from the shaking of the cabin, and readied himself to run. But a familiar feeling crept through his body. Remnancy was growing.

This was the worst timing. Why did it have to happen now? He didn't have time for this.

But he had no choice. He clasped his hands above him, making a point, thinned his body, and unpossessed it. He grabbed the statue, sharpened and elongated much like a sword. Tsuran gripped the statue's legs with two hands and faced the Warden.

The Warden smiled, and a shiver ran down Tsuran's spine.

Con-Ebru appeared in front of Nasna, large shadowy arms thrusting into her chest and sending her flying backward. She didn't turn in time and the girl's body took the impact against the wall.

The world spun for a moment and she closed her eyes. She placed a hand on the girl and checked how hurt she was. Nasna groaned. The girl wasn't leaving that impact unscathed, but she wouldn't die.

Shadows erupted from the darkness toward her. Nasna placed a hand on the wall. There was energy here. It was fleeting, but the river was still present. She drew the remaining energy into her and punched forward, sending the energy out of her. It pushed her into the wall and she watched the force ripple through the dusty air, cutting through the tendrils and into the surrounding columns.

Although it didn't affect the tendrils, it collided with the Lightless and surrounding columns. The force hit him in the chest and he crashed into the exploding rock behind him. It was enough for the tendrils to disappear.

Clutching her side, Nasna ran.

Nasna drew in the energy around her as she ran, pouring it into her legs to aid her speed. Every time her feet were about to meet the ground she released a little energy so her feet never made contact. Instead, the released energy propelled her forward.

As she ran, she placed a hand on the girl, checking her energy. The river within her remained strong, coursing like a storm trying to break a dam. But she remained asleep. She remained alive.

A wall of black shadow appeared in front of Nasna, cutting her off from the unbroken lightstone. Con-Ebru's voice spoke from the shadows,

"I'm done with your tricks. It ends now."

Dozens of tendrils erupted from the shadow-wall, piercing into her legs, arms, chest, and shoulder. Warm blood flowed out of her wounds. The tendrils held her still, bleeding and immobilized. She tried fighting against it but each tendril was like a strong arm digging into her. She struggled against the black spears, but it only aggravated her injuries. Blood poured from all her wounds, taking her strength with it.

Wounded without the strength to fight. Just like she'd been with Clear Sky on that night so long ago.

Nasna ground her jaw. This pain didn't matter. Her breaking body didn't matter. None of it would stop her. She was different this time and she would protect the girl.

She forced her arm up and grabbed one of the black tendrils. Con-Ebru laughed.

"You can't pull them all out. Not before I drive them through you."

"And that... was your mistake." Nasna's eyes burst open. "Because now I feel you!"

All the energy within him blazed in her mind. His energy coursed through all the tendrils in her body, in the spear above her, and his own body, and Nasna had total access to it. It didn't matter if he'd resisted other ordîns. He wouldn't resist her.

She reached into his energy, grabbed a hold of it, and paralyzed it.

The spear above Nasna stopped. The spears in her ceased digging.

Con-Ebru froze.

Nasna blinked. Her heartbeat echoed in her ears and she let out her breath.

It worked.

With his energy paralyzed, Nasna sent a pulsing energy through the tendrils into the Lightless and exorcised him from the shadow. The tendrils disappeared from her body and she dropped to the ground. Blood splattered onto the ground from the various cuts in her body.

She looked up at Con-Ebru. It was strange. She'd expected his energy to be much stronger than what it was. Strong enough to resist an ordîn. But his seemed rather normal. In fact, the girl's energy was stronger than his.

She let out a sigh and placed a hand on the worst cut near her shoulder. Thoughts to consider later. For now, it was time to get back to Tsuran.

The whole side of his face felt wet, as did the several places the Warden had stabbed him. He grabbed onto the wall to stand up, but both became airborne again. Tsuran crashed hard on the floor only for the beast to throw him back into the air.

The beast broke through all of its shackles and thrashed around even more than before. It threw Tsuran and the Warden around the cabin, smashing into all the walls and flooring. Tsuran tried to protect himself by covering his head, but the splintering wood lacerated his body. He couldn't even focus enough to possess.

And then it stopped. The beast stopped thrashing and became still.

Tsuran pulled himself up, grabbing his aching head and looked out of the doorway. The other Wranglers were rushing toward the cabin. He groaned. One of them had possessed the beast, and the rest were coming onto the transport. Just like idiots.

"No!" the Warden said. Tsuran turned to see him raising a fist to slam down into the backside of the beast to exorcise the Wrangler.

Tsuran possessed his statue and jumped at the Warden, crashing into his side. He reached up and grabbed onto the Warden's wings and yanked hard. The Warden let out a loud cry. Tsuran took the opportunity and sliced through one wing and tore it off, blood splattering across the wood and statue. The Warden backed away screaming, grabbing at his back, at where his wing once was.

The other Wranglers rushed into the cabin and before Tsuran shouted out, the Warden charged toward them. Two fell within a blink of an eye. A third died just as the other two were dropping to the ground. There were only a few left, not counting the one possessing the beast.

Tsuran poured all of his power into empowering his speed and dashed in front of the Wranglers in an instant, taking all the blows from the Warden. Tsuran struck back, crying out,

"Get out of here!"

The Wranglers ran past him as he struggled with the Warden. Then the beast moved. The movement threw him and the Warden off balance and they pulled apart. They both looked out at the same time. Tsuran's heart stopped.

The beast was leaving the prison. The Wranglers were not waiting for Nasna.

The Warden yelled and ran at Tsuran. Both of the Warden's fists slammed into the statue and the exorcism wrenched his body out. But if the Warden exorcised him now, he'd be powerless to stop him from killing the other Wranglers. If he exorcised him now, there was no way Nasna would make it.

That wasn't an option.

As the Warden exorcised him, Tsuran repossessed the statue. White flashed across his eyes as the exorcism pulled him out and his possession pushed him back in. It was like being squeezed in two different directions. But he remained in the statue.

The Warden growled and tried to exorcise him again. Tsuran repossessed the statue, again and again, fighting against the Warden's relentless attacks.

The two forces clashed against each other. Exorcism and possession. Tsuran's body seemed to fracture from within the statue. Worse than every stab wound, every broken bone, and even worse than total-control, these two colliding forces tore away at him like two beasts over a meal.

Ringing flooded his ears, drowning out all else. His eyes clouded over, seeing only white. He empowered the crystal, hardened it. He took his arm and sliced up as the ordîn exorcised him from the statue.

Tsuran gasped for air as he fell to the floor, the cold air bringing sudden clarity to his eyes. He coughed blood and looked back at the Warden and his statue, which had broken through all the armor, all the protective crystal, and pierced through the Warden's chest.

Tsuran let out a weak laugh.

But the beast was still moving and was even picking up speed. Tsuran had to do something, had to stop them. But he couldn't move. His body had had enough and refused to obey his commands. He tried to speak but nothing came out.

Nasna wouldn't make it. And he couldn't do anything.

The fighting between the prisoners and guards still raged, the bodies piling in the prisoners' favor. The ordîns would lose soon.

Nasna looked toward the lightstone hallway and rushed forward, making her way past ordîn and tatzon alike. It appeared as though the guards had been trying to prevent prisoners from making their way into the lightstone hallway, to prevent them from going to the transport. But that line of defense had broken. Nasna moved past them into the hallway but the doors on the far end had opened and beyond them was the clear sight of the beast. Of it leaving. Tsuran was leaving without her.

No, Tsuran wouldn't leave without her. Something had happened.

She dared not think of him dead, not yet. She had a more immediate problem. Even if she ran down the hall with all her energy-infused speed, she wouldn't make it before the beast left the mountain exit. She would have no way of getting to it. The mountain would have her and the girl trapped.

She looked at the long hallway made of lightstone. It extended from where she stood down to the iron doors. She closed her eyes and placed a hand on the girl and gave her a gentle squeeze. No matter the risk, she would save her life. Even if Nasna died, this girl would not.

With the lightstone at her feet, she felt the energy coursing beneath her connecting to the lightstone in the walls and ceiling. She had access to the energy of the entire hallway, more than the giant crystal in the pits had. And she drew it all into her.

It was less like drawing in a river and more like flooding herself with a raging ocean of every heaven. Her body cracked and split, and she pressed on, releasing the energy beneath her feet. The energy threw her through the air faster than she had ever gone before. The hallway darkened as all the energy stormed into her, and each step released a force that demolished everything around her. In only two strides, she'd made it halfway down the hall. But the beast began running.

Nasna pressed harder.

The air rushed past her as she passed the iron doors and channeled all the energy into her feet, releasing most of it in a single eruption. The force obliterated the entire cavern around her and sent her shooting like an arrow into the air after the beast.

Spirits screeched, tatzons yelled, the mountain crumbled. A loud wind whistled in her ears, yet she still heard the rumbling and collapsing of the prison behind her.

The beast ran, but Nasna gained on it. She released the last bits of energy in her, pushing her along and guiding her flight. She flew above the cabin, her momentum slowing until she matched the beast's speed and dropped through a broken part of the roof and into the cabin's interior.

Wood fell around her and on top of her, but she couldn't move her broken body. If her ordîn bones had been any weaker, she would have died. But she wasn't a fool. Death was next to her, ready to bring her to the Abyss.

But that was alright.

She listened to the slow breathing of the girl on her back. Nasna closed her eyes.

"You're safe, little one. I promise you'll be safe."

33

---◆◇◆---

THE FORMING

To the Daughter I will never know: I am forever sorry.

If there are gods, I hope they are kind to you.
If there are gods, I hope they punish me eternally.
- Yava, the one who Forsook you

The cabin shook as the Wrangler adjusted to the possession. The other escapees cheered and patted each other on the back, but Tsuran crawled over to Nasna.

Exhaustion filled every part of him, but he forced his arms to pull his bleeding body across the floor. She lay face down with a tatzon girl on her back. He reached out and touched Nasna. Deep gashes ran along her body, blood flowed everywhere. The idiot must have drawn in a huge amount of energy.

Explained why the whole mountainside had just exploded.

"You!" Tsuran said to one Wrangler. "Bring me the box Dalvinder gave you." The tatzon rolled his eyes but then looked at the statue bursting through the dead Warden. He handed the box over.

Tsuran forced himself upright and bent down to peel the girl off of Nasna. His fatigue, coupled with her grip made this more difficult than it should have been, but after a little work, he removed her and lay her beside Nasna. The girl was such a small thing, yet very much alive.

He grabbed hold of Nasna's shoulder and turned her over. He winced. Her clothes, tattered and loose, revealed long gashes and precise cuts. Not a part of her hadn't opened up, blood draining from her.

Tsuran stopped gaping and wrenched the box open. He didn't have time to waste. He pulled out the spirit vessel, ignoring the stares and gasps from the other prisoners. The vessel illuminated the cabin in green light as he placed it onto Nasna's chest and prayed.

Without being a Soulborn he couldn't access the spirit's powers. But he could coax and entreat the spirit.

Tsuran sang. This song, though, differed from the one he sung in the mines. This song did not calm spirits, but beckoned their power. The rhythm faster, the song forceful. He would not lose her here.

As he sang, the vessel pulsed with light, and it grew in intensity with every pulse. He continued the song amid the mumbling and whispering of the prisoners. The light condensed, drawing away from the rest of the cabin and cloaking only the two of them. It was less like light and more like a shining current of water, washing around them. Shimmering green waves swirled around his body and hers, seeping into his cuts, his blood, his voice. Strength ebbed back inside him. The pain diminished but did not disappear.

He raised his voice, and the light intensified even more so he had to shut his eyes. The light lapped against him, moving his body back and forth in its warm glow. He came to the end of the song and finished. But the light stayed bright. Its warmth swirled around him, seeped into him. It didn't stop.

And there was a still a song in the air.

He opened his eyes. From the crystal, some light condensed even more into an arm. A spirit's arm. The spirit sang and sang.

Tsuran tried to drop the vessel, but part of the spirit's arm folded around his hand, holding it there. The arm reached out, and the Wranglers cursed and stumbled over each other. Tsuran couldn't move. The light held him where he was.

But the arm reached over to the little girl and green light shone around her. The song quickened, and the light blared. The girl squirmed underneath it.

Tsuran tried to sing back, to sing his calming song. But his lips stuck together and the spirit's light filled his voice. There was no struggle. He could only watch.

Something like a black mist rose out of the girl, a dark mass amid all that light. The light left the girl and surrounded the mist, pressing it into a tight ball, and the spirit pulled this back into the vessel. The song ended and light flooded the entire cabin again before returning to a gentle glow. And Tsuran breathed.

The vessel was cold to touch again, and he stared at it a moment. He shoved it back into its box and shut the lid tight. The girl lay still again but looked alive. That black mist... had it been....

He rubbed his face and shook himself. The mist could wait. He examined Nasna again. Her wounds had stopped bleeding and had all sealed. They hadn't disappeared as when Dalvinder did it, but she'd live. And he felt great.

He toppled over beside her, clutching the black box to his chest. Sleep took him, and though no dreams greeted him, rest did. When he awoke, a tattered cloak covered him. He must have slept a few hours since the sun had set and darkness had settled around him.

One Wrangler had brought a lightstone with her and his statue gave off its red glow, so the cabin had some light. But the beast kept moving, and it seemed likely the Wranglers wouldn't stop until they'd found a tree to lodge in. Which was fine by him as long as they didn't kill the beast.

Tsuran glanced around in the dim light. His statue stood in the far corner, though it looked like the others had tossed the Warden's dead body out of the cabin. The other Wranglers sat together opposite of him, some asleep, others whispering to each other. The girl still slept next to him. Sitting beside her, awake and smiling, was Nasna.

"You're awake," she said. Tsuran grinned.

"And you're alive. Both good things." He sat up and pulled the cloak tight in the frigid cold. "How are your wounds?"

She showed him her arms but he noticed her clothes, ripped open in several places, her red skin showing through. He threw off his cloak and tossed it to her.

"Nas, take this, you'll die of cold." His gaze darted to the Wranglers on the other side and caught a few who'd been staring.

"I'll be fine, Tsuran," Nasna said. "I've been through worse." Instead of throwing it back at him, she wrapped it around her body, covering what nakedness there had been. "But thank you. And as for my wounds, it looks like they've healed."

Tsuran looked at her closer, but it all looked the same as before. Everything had sealed, but nasty scars, including one big slash across her face, covered her. Besides this, she also looked paler than usual, even in the minimal light. She'd lost a lot of blood. A lot of it still covered her and the floor beneath them.

"The others told me you sang over me," she said with a smile. "Said you summoned a spirit to heal me. Thank you."

"Well, I think it was the elegance of my voice that kept you alive, but the spirit helped."

Nasna rolled her eyes, keeping her smile.

"Of course." She shivered and pulled the cloak tighter around her, her gaze going to his statue. "Tsuran... while you slept, I checked your wounds... your growth has worsened."

He reached inside his clothes and his heart fell. She was right. The crystal had spread so it covered the whole left side of his chest and crept around his ribs to his back.

"Had to fight the Warden," Tsuran said. "It was... I had to push myself—oh, hey. What's wrong?"

Tears streamed down her cheeks, her body shivering in the cold. Tsuran pulled himself to her and held her with two arms.

"Never do that again," she said looking into his eyes. "You can't keep pushing yourself like that. You'll die."

"I know Nas, I know."

"Then stop being an idiot. Don't let the growth spread anymore. Ever."

"You don't have to—"

"Tsuran."

He took in a deep breath. "I won't. I promise this is as close to being a Remnant as I'll ever be. But"—he raised a finger at her—"you also have to promise to never take in energy like that again. Deal?"

She held his gaze for a moment longer and nodded. The two sat in silence together, enduring the bumps and movements of the beast.

The howling winds of the mountain blew cold air through the splintered wood and Tsuran now wished he and the Warden had been more gentle with the cabin. Nasna stirred next to him and she moved closer to the girl and stroked her hair. A small tatzon, weak and malnourished, but alive. He smiled and looked at Nasna. There was a difference in her. Even though she looked close to death, there was a peace about her he hadn't seen before. Her voice even sounded different. Nothing forced, nothing faked.

"You made a different choice."

Nasna nodded. "I did. I'm on a different Path now."

Warmth expanded in his chest. This meant he didn't have to keep his promise to her. If it had come to killing her, he wasn't sure what he would've done. But he wouldn't have to find out now.

"Tsuran?"

"Yeah?"

"Could you lie on the other side of her? I want to drape this cloak over all of us and keep her warm."

Tsuran smiled and moved to the other side, laying beside the little girl. It was warmer with all three of them laying together but neither smiled. Hard to say what her thoughts were, but they couldn't have been too far from his own.

They'd taken this girl's mother away from her. And now they took her away from the only world she ever knew into a much bigger place, full of danger. It was right to take her from prison. But all of this was also so very wrong.

"We need to keep her safe," Nasna said. "Bring her somewhere with a loving family."

"Don't worry, we will. Plenty of tree villages on the borders of Rajalend and I'm sure we can find a family wanting to help her."

Except, if he was right about the black mist, then it wouldn't be that simple.

Nasna nodded, but her lips quivered.

"Hey, what is it?" he asked.

She shook her head. "I just... it's hard to try saving this girl when I'm the reason she needs saving. How... can I help her when I... I...."

Tsuran reached over and grabbed her hand. "I'm here too, Nas. You're not doing this alone. We can carry this together."

Nasna squeezed his hand. They allowed more silence between them as the beast descended and they slid along the floor. Twice the beast had to jump, which shuffled everyone around. The other Wranglers complained, trying to be loud enough for the possessing Wrangler to hear. But Nasna and Tsuran held close to the girl.

He didn't have any right to protect this girl or to keep her safe and warm. He had no right to be this close to her. Another child whose life he had a hand in ripping apart. And he was just an accomplice in her mother's death. Poor Nasna. She was experiencing her own Abyss. Yet for the time being, they would have to take the role of protector. Perhaps one day they would make it up to her. Though, he wasn't sure how they ever could.

There were a few times he worried the girl would awake through the rattling of the cabin, but she did not stir from her sleep. Tsuran continued to look out of the cracks in the walls, although there was nothing to see in the darkness. But it was a strange sensation for him to be here. He guessed he'd been in that prison for close to two years now. Two years since Dazh had ended his life. Now he was free to live again.

"Tsuran?"

"Yeah?"

"If we're carrying this together, wouldn't it make more sense if we were Partners?"

Tsuran blinked. Did he... hear that right? Slowly, he glanced over, and she had a beaming smile that filled him with warmth.

"You mean... are you serious?"

She nodded.

Tsuran's heart leapt, and he sat up. She did too. "You're sure?" he asked. "You've thought it through? Because this is a permanent thing, only undone by death."

"And I figure you'll be the death of me, anyway. So, I will take you as my Partner."

Only once before had anyone said that to him and he and Dazh had no choice, few tatzon ever did. But now, he was doing something he hadn't ever dreamed of. Choosing his Partner. He'd chosen Nasna. She'd chosen him.

Tsuran cleared his throat, trying to push down the lump forming. "Then, place a hand on my heart and your forehead against mine." She did as he said and he also placed a hand onto her heart. They put their foreheads together, letting their breath intertwine, letting their hearts beat synchronously.

"And I take you as my Partner," he said.

A sensation he had only ever experienced once before boiled up within him. It was a sensation unlike anything else he'd ever known. It flooded his whole being like a flurry of bubbles, streaming through his veins, popping and bursting and multiplying.

His heart thudded loud and clear, his blood warmed. At once, he experienced every aspect of himself. Every physical trait and flaw, every emotional tic and mannerism, every secret of his soul bared open before him in every detail. With every beat of his heart, his being pulsed through his body, through his arm, and into Nasna. No pain, no discomfort. Only his bared soul before her, being poured into her. It was the sensation only tatzons would ever enjoy.

The Forming of the Partnership.

And as it continued, a part of him became one with her. The part of his soul that had returned to him at Dazh's death, he now gave to her.

And it was done. It left him and entered her. It was done... but there was a new sensation. Similar to the first but the pulsing did not flow from him to her, but from her to him. At first, he panicked, thinking the Forming was being rejected, but the pulse continued and built. And it was different, not like his or anything like Dazh's had been. This was less like bubbling water and more like a stream of lighting that pulsed into him and filled him with strength and power. It started in his mind and coursed through the rest of his body. It was exhilarating.

This wasn't the Forming being rejected. This was Nasna accepting it.

And at that moment, he saw her. He saw the ordîn in front of him as he'd never seen her before. But it wasn't her body he saw. It was her soul. Nothing hidden, nothing shut away.

However, unlike with Dazh, he didn't see every aspect of her, every minor detail about her. He only saw the culmination of her. Not in images or even sounds, but in the fullness of pure knowledge.

She was more than a clipped ordîn. More than a sacrifice or assassin. Far greater than an avenger or even a protector. He saw beyond the fears and failures, the joys and amusements, beyond even the heart wrenching truths she ignored and did not realize existed. He saw her soul burning with a white fire that blazed across the cosmos, stretching beyond every heavenly body, filling the night sky with dazzling lights.

He saw the truth of her. Tsuran didn't understand what it meant, he only knew that it was.

She was a promise to the damned.

The pulsing stopped from both him and her. They pulled apart, both panting.

"What was that?" Nasna asked. Tsuran looked up.

"Did you feel that?"

"Yeah, I felt that. It was... I can't even explain... what was that?"

Tsuran gazed at her, at a loss for words, still reeling from all that had happened. Though, just like the first time he'd done the Forming, all he'd seen and experienced locked away within him. Away from his conscious thought, away from all memory. Her soul became locked within him, where nothing could touch it.

Letting out a deep breath, he combed his hair back out of his eyes.

"That was the Forming. It's the spiritual contract between Partners. It's what connects us and forms the foundation of the Partnership... it's the sharing of souls."

Nasna breathed out and the biggest smile he'd ever seen broke across her face. The two of them laughed and a few Wranglers told them to be quiet. But the two didn't stop. The Wranglers would not take this moment from them. Though, had they seen what had just happened? Actually, it didn't matter. Tsuran didn't care if they had.

"I didn't expect that," Nasna said.

"Me neither."

"What? Isn't that supposed to happen?"

"Well yeah, but I didn't know if it'd work, you being ordîn and all. That you also felt it is unbelievable." He paused for a moment, the memory of the Forming mostly gone from conscious thought. "There was something different about it, though. I think it felt different from my Forming with Dazh"

Nasna's smile faltered. "What does that mean?"

Tsuran let out a small sigh. There was no way of knowing. Once the Forming had finished, everything about it became empty and void in the person's mind. Forgotten. Even though it was something every single tatzon experienced, no one knew much of what happened during it.

This Forming had differed from Dazh's, but he couldn't tell why. Then again, there was one thing that he knew for sure. He smiled and motioned to her. She leaned. He reached up to her cheek.

And flicked her ear.

"It means that we're Partnered together. From now and always, I am your Partner, Nas, and you are mine."

The corners of her mouth quirked up, and she flicked his ear.

"Then I guess we're in this together, Tsuran."

The two leaned over the girl and hugged each other. This, right here, was what he had been missing. This embrace, this acceptance, this reality of being known fully, of belonging to another.

"Thank you, Nas," he whispered in her ear. A wet warmth came down onto his shoulder and tears filled her voice.

"Red Dawn."

He pulled away. "What?"

She wiped her eyes. "That's my given name. The name only for family... and the closest of friends."

Tsuran smiled. "Red Dawn. It matches you. Tell me, if your skin changes color, will you then be Orange Dawn or Purple Dawn?"

She shoved him away, still keeping her smile, and lay down beside the girl.

"Shut up, that's not how it works. That's just my name."

Tsuran took his place next to the girl, his eyes on his new Partner. "It's a good name. And I will treasure it... Nasna Red Dawn Con-Tsuran."

She reached over and grabbed his hand. "You better, Tsuran Con-Red Dawn. Because like you said, from now and till always, we're Partners."

⬥◯⬥

A Word from the Author

Thank you for journeying with Tsuran and Nasna! Please don't forget to give this book a quick review on Amazon. Even just a two-word, "Liked it" or "Hated it" review helps so much and would mean a lot to me. Positive or negative, I am grateful for all feedback from my readers.

And be sure to sign up for my newsletter receive updates on all new releases. Sign up at tylerjamesbooks.com! Thanks again!

- Tyler

A STUDY OF WORLDS

They call the world
Vicoluntas. Yet, as far
as I can tell, none have
asked what the world
calls itself. Perhaps one
day they will. At the
least, I am curious what
it's Old Name is. For
now, though, it shall be
Vicoluntas.

Tatzon

―――――◄O►―――――

Appearance

T atzons are perhaps the stockiest of the soul-beings, though they have greater variation in body types than, for instance, ordîn. They are tall with variations of gray skin and dull-toned hair. At birth, they only have a single arm, the priarm, which is longer, thicker, and stronger than any other arm they may grow in their lifetime. It also is the only arm that features seven fingers instead of the typical five.

As tatzons grow more arms, the location of their arms follows a typical sequence. Most priarms begin as a right arm, though I have seen a fair percentage of left-sided priarms, and the first arm grown comes from their opposite shoulder. At this point, they resemble the basic template of the soul-beings. Future grown arms come from the side of their torso, which gives them a very spider-like appearance. Their torso grows with each new row of arms in order to accommodate them, though after there are three rows of arms growing from the sides, the next set of arms tends to grow out from the back.

Markings

Tatzons are born with a unique pattern that typically covers the entire body. In some ways, they resemble tattoos. While many of these "markings" can look similar to one another, there are none that are exactly the same. Every set of markings is unique to itself and thus is the best way to identify a tatzon.

Markings tend to be in shades of brown, gray, or black, which appears to be based on bloodlines. They otherwise are truly a varied thing. Markings can be symmetrical or asymmetrical, ordered or chaotic, geometric or amorphous, shapes or animals. And while a child's markings may have some aspects of their parents, there is no way of determining what patterns will arise or even why.

Partnerships

While many soul-beings have a desire for friendship and family, the tatzon's need for companionship is the most enhanced example of this desire. They were not created to be individual beings, but to be two. Thus, without needing to be taught this, every tatzon is driven to a literal sharing of their souls with another tatzon.

In most cultures of Vicoluntas, tatzon children find, or are given, their Partners after the age of ten. They perform a rite called the Forming in which their souls open to one another and merge partially together. In other soul-beings, souls reside only within their own bodies, but tatzons store theirs also with the body of their Partner.

While culture dictates how Partners relate to each other, with some being romantic and others being firmly platonic, there are a few things that all Partnerships share. Whether it is the sharing of the soul or simply the intense amount of time the two spend together in their life, there is no relationship in a tatzon's life that is deeper or more profound than that of the Partnership. Every other relationship is secondary to the Partner. As such, tatzon culture tends to revolve around Partners in some way or another.

A second thing that is a noteworthy tendency across all cultures is the belief that the greatest evil one could commit is to kill someone's Partner but leave them alive. While it amuses me that tatzons would prefer two murders over one, the idea is that the living Partner will have experienced something far, far worse than physical death. And it says something that this belief is ubiquitous among tatzonkind.

Solitude

Partnerships are not the sole example of the tatzon's enhanced need for companionship. The opposing side of the coin is what happens when they are alone. In short, they die.

Dubbed "Solitude", when a tatzon is severed off from others, their body begins to eat away at itself in a rapid manner. It is as though an invisible force is crushing them and pulling them apart at the same time. It is a rather gruesome and, from what I can tell, painful way to die. I believe this is why intentionally abandoning a tatzon to Solitude is often seen as the second greatest evil a person could commit.

Solitude acts quickly. As soon as a tatzon is alone, it strikes them, which is a primary reason you never see tatzons wandering a city by themselves. They will always be with their Partner or some other companion. Depending on the tatzon, Solitude can take anywhere from ten to thirty minutes to kill them.

The only way to combat Solitude is for the tatzon to never be alone. Solitude can even come when a tatzon is asleep.

Ordîn

Appearance

Of all the soul-beings, ordîn have the sharpest features. Their facial structure is far more angular than any other, with most having an almost triangular feel to them. Their eyes, limbs, and even fingernails are angled almost to a point. I believe they were made on the idea of geometric perfection, as all ordîn are perfectly symmetrical beings.

With notable exceptions, ordîn have white hair and gray eyes. Interestingly, only two cultures in Vicoluntas history have had dyed hair as part of their lives. Most ordîn in this world seem to accept the uniformity. Though, a larger number have included tattooing their wings with striking shapes and images. I am beginning to wonder if that is an inevitability for these beings.

Ordîn Life Cycles

Cycle	Cycle Color Identification	Cycle Length	Color Change Intervals	Age in years at start of the Cycle
Infant	Red	7 Years	1 Year	Birth
Child	Orange	49 Years	7 Years	8 Years Old
Adolescent	Yellow	98 Years	14 Years	58 Years Old
Adult	Green	147 Years	21 Years	157 Years Old
Mature Adult	Cyan	196 Years	28 Years	305 Years Old
Elder	Blue	245 Years	35 Years	502 Years Old
Ancient	Violet	294 Years	42 Years	748 Years Old

The above chart shows the life cycle of an ordîn. The most obvious aspect about the ordîn is they have skin tones that shift and change as they age. An ordîn you met a year ago could have an entirely new color tone if you met them today. However, it is neither random nor chaotic. Every ordîn goes through the same sequence, in the same order, and in the same timing.

Should they survive for the entirety, an ordîn goes through seven cycles in their life (as indicated in the Cycle column). Within each cycle, an ordîn's skin will shift through the seven base colors of their kind (which corresponds to the seven accepted colors of the rainbow). However, as noted in both the Cycle Length and Color Change Intervals columns, the time spent in each base color, as well as that cycle itself, grows longer as the ordîn ages. Thus, while they will remain an infant for a mere seven years, it will take their bodies seven years alone to shift from one color to the next when they are a child.

Instead of referring to their age in years, as is common in the other soul-beings, ordîn will simply refer to their current skin color alongside their cycle color. For instance, an ordîn would not say they are an adult of 150 years. They instead would say they were red in green cycle.

Ordîn Paths

It can be said that ordîns have two lives. The first, which is lived for themselves, and the second where they live for another. After their first death, their soul is joined to the body of an ordîn in their late orange or early yellow cycles. While inhabiting their host, the soul becomes a source of wisdom, guidance, and even purpose.

It's interesting to see how different worlds interpret the ordîn's limbonic mission. The inhabitants of Vicoluntas refer to it, and the souls themselves, as Paths. Many cultures even assign virtues and vices to these Paths, such as the Path of Justice or the Path of Greed. While they do not take away the individuals choice, these Paths tend to have great influence on the personality and outlook of the ordîn.

The Standard Categories

Name	Height
Small	5-10 ft
Common	15-25 ft
Large	50-80 ft
Colossal	100-200 ft
Behemoth	500-800 ft

Above is a simplified version of the Standard Categories of Vicoluntan Fauna. The chart indicates the most common heights of the animals and spirits of Vicoluntas as well as their name of these sizes.

While I have several issues with the system, it has been in use across the Meadowlands for over seven hundred years, and thus the language and mentality of it is entrenched in the societal mind.

What I find curious about the fauna of this world is twofold. First, it's notable that insects and birds are not enlarged like the other animals. It appears that while animals of land and sea have been affected like this, birds and insects remain untouched. The second curious thing is that while I have noticed this, few of Vicoluntas' scholars have questioned it.

Beasts

Perhaps as a side effect of using the Standard Categories, most people refer to the large fauna, animals of both land and sea, simply as beasts. As noted, they come in a variety of sizes which does not seem to depend on specie. It is possible to find both a Common and Large wolf as well as a Small walrus and a Colossal field mouse.

All beasts of Vicoluntas have a pair of tusks, regardless of whether the animal is typically a peaceful herbivore or not. These tusks appear to be weapons against spirits, which are incorporeal to other attacks.

On that note, it should be stated that beasts and spirits appear to be mortal enemies. Regardless of what they are doing, a beast will fight a spirit to the death and vice versa.

Spirits

The people of Vicoluntas call them spirits. Another side-effect of the Standard Categories, and perhaps the saddest one.

Spirits are as varied in shape and form as a tatzon's markings. They can be long and slender, short and bulky, amorphous and blob-like. Some may take shapes that look like animals, others could look like a sludge. Some will have dozens of limbs and wings and claws, others will be snake-like. There are three unifying characteristics among them.

First, these creatures can be both incorporeal and corporeal. In general, they can be touched until they choose to phase through physical matter. However, they don't quite have solid bodies. They have a composition more similar to a dense pudding. But they are physical beings, until they choose not to be.

Second, regardless of their bodies shape and form, they appear blue with a soft glow. They are also semi-translucent.

Third, every one of them have a set of glowing white eyes. These eyes have no pupils, they are simply large circles of white. These eyes can travel across their body, and they frequently do. They also don't blink, which unnerved me a few times as I observed them.

The Magic of Vicoluntas

———— ◆◯◆ ————

Tatzon Possession

Tatzon magic is best understood through the Seven by Sevens, a teaching tool used by most possessor teachers. It explains that tatzons are able to possess seven "types", or categories, and within each type there are seven "layers" of power. While the types all differ from each other, the layers are the same for each.

Layers

Mind-Possession: the first kind of possession a tatzon can learn, it entails the possessor to project their soul out of their body and into what they are aiming to possess. This leaves their body inanimate where they left it.

Body-Possession: the possessor now brings their body along with them when they possess. They also bring along any clothing they were wearing as well as other very small things. Larger pieces of clothing, such as a cloak, or other items do not go with the possessor and drop to the ground.

Body-Possession with Empowerment: while body-possessing, the tatzon can now use the three Empowerments: Harden/Strengthen, Speed, and Specialized.

Total-Control: the possessor can fully posses while also remaining in their body. This splits their mind, placing half in the possession and the other half in the body, and thus they become and feel like two people.

Total-Control with Empowerment: while in total-control, the tatzon can now use the three Empowerments.

Multiple Possession: the tatzon can now body-possess or use total-control with more than a single possession.

Types

Statue: commonly known as Guardians in the Meadowlands, these can possess any sculpture of a person or animal. Used predominantly upon naval vessels, Guardians are not the most common sight on land, though you will find them fighting on the front lines of the war between Rajalend and Veirzen.

Harden/Strengthen: This Empowerment doubles the hardness and strength of the material of the sculpture, and usually results in the statue being difficult to maneuver in.

Speed: the Guardian's speed is doubled. (Note: if used in conjunction with Harden, the speed normalizes.)

Specialized: Guardians can alter the shape of their statue in two ways. The first, and easiest, is to only change the shape of the statue without losing or gaining material. The second can only be done with a bonded statue, since it involves changing the shape of the statue by adding or removing material. The most basic example of this second form is when a Guardian enlarges their statue.

Beasts: commonly known as Wranglers in the Meadowlands, these can possess any animal. This is the most common possession type in eastern Meadowland, with the majority residing within Veirzen. While they do make up a sizable portion of the military, Wranglers in all nations are the main sources of transportation through the Meadowlands.

Harden/Strengthen: this increases the beast's toughness and strength, while slowing its movements.

Speed: Wranglers can double their beast's speed and increase their reflexes.

Specialized: this grants the Wranglers access to the beast's inherent reflexes, instincts, senses, and even memories, if applicable. This sharing of senses even occurs with Total-Control.

Plants: commonly known as Builders in the Meadowlands, these can possess any form of plant life. The most common possession type in western Meadowland, especially in Rajalend. Builders make up a large portion of the military and an even larger portion of the working class of possessors.

Harden/Strengthen: this Empowerment doubles the strength and durability of the plant, but slows both movement and growth rate.

Speed: this Empowerment allows the Builder to either increase their movement as the plant or to increase the growth rate of the plant.

Specialized: Builders can alter the shape of the plant in two ways. First, they can change the shape without adding or removing material. This can often be seen with them possessing trees and hollowing out the insides and creating rooms. Second, they can change the shape by adding or removing material. This can be seen as rapid growth, in some cases.

Shadows: commonly known as Lightless in the Meadowlands, these can possess any shadow. Criminals tend toward this possession due to its many applications in theft, blackmail, and even assassination. Because of this tendency, many nations outlaw shadow possession.

Harden/Strengthen: (can only be used in conjunction with Specialized Empowerment) using this Empowerment, a Lightless can triple their natural strength while in an embodied shadow.

Speed: Lightless can use this Empowerment to either double their movement through the shadows or they can triple the speed of their embodied form (this second option can only be used in conjunction with their Specialized Empowerment).

Specialized: this Empowerment gives the shadow they are possessing a physical, embodied form. It may take whatever shape the possessor chooses but the total mass of the form typically cannot exceed that of the possessor's physical body.

Spirits: commonly known as Soulborn in the Meadowlands, these can possess any spirit. Of the accepted types, this is known as the most difficult to master. Due to the need of specialized crystal equipment known as vessels, it is common for only the children of wealth to have access to this type.

Dreams: commonly known as Dreamwalkers in the Meadowlands, these can possess dreams of other soul-beings. Though some in Vicoluntas attempt this possession, there are no records of anyone ever discovering how to move beyond mind-possession and into body-possession. Either the Seven by Sevens is flawed in this way, or dream possession has no further layers.

The Dead: commonly known as Disturbers in the Meadowlands, these can possess the deceased bodies of other soul-beings. Disturbers are strictly outlawed in most nations within the Meadowlands, and even where it is partially allowed one must receive approval from the governing body for any possession.

Ordîn Energy Guiding

In much of the tatzon dominated sections of the world, ordîn magic is seen and taught as a counter to possession. There are two types of manifestations of the magic in these societies: Exorcists and Seekers.

Exorcist: these ordîn are able to remove a possessor from their possession with a single touch.

Seeker: these ordîn can sense a tatzon possessing nearby.

However, in less tatzon focused areas, there are ordîn scholars that have not forgotten the depths of their magic. In truth, ordîn magic is not directly tied to tatzon magic. Instead it is tied to the energy within people.

These scholars have varying theories on what energy exactly is (though none quite hit the mark), but most are willing to agree on these points:

First, energy exists only within people, spirits, and crystals.

Second, energy is only present when a person is alive, though it remains when a spirit is dead or dying.

Third, ordîns can affect the energy inside a person and affect their body, mind, and spirit.

And fourth, ordîns with specialized training can remove energy from a source and unleash it with explosive force in the physical world.

It appears that through many wars between tatzons and ordîn, much of this knowledge is lost to the majority of the ordîn populace. But that is all well and good. There is only one among them that matters in the long term.

About Author

Tyler James was born in Tukwilla and has been reading and writing fantasy since he was a child. He lives and writes in Santa Barbara with his wife and dog. Promises to the Damned is his first novel.